DEFIANT ENCHANTRESS

"The past doesn't matter to me now, *Major.* I have forgotten what happened between us."

"Have you?"

"Yes. I'm going to marry Jeremiah. He is a good man, and will be a good husband."

"I don't doubt that he's a good man. I doubt that he's the right man for you. I doubt that he knows you for what you really are."

"And what am I?"

"A woman of passion. A woman who wants far more from a man than friendship."

"You don't know me, Major. You knew only my weakest self, the daughter of a whore. I am not that person anymore."

Nina spun around and rushed from the room. Damian stood alone, but a smile touched his lips. The ice around her was cracking, the fiery temptress peeking through.

You are mine. When I leave this place, I will have you. Damian looked out the window as the stars kindled their singular fate in the sky. He would have the future as he wanted it. Nothing, no one, would stand in his way.

DANGEROUS GAMES   (0-7860-0270-0, $4.99)
by Amanda Scott

When Nicholas Barrington, eldest son of the Earl of Ul-
combe, first met Melissa Seacort, the desperation he
sensed beneath her well-bred beauty haunted him. He
didn't realize how desperate Melissa really was . . . until
he found her again at a Newmarket gambling club—being auctioned off by her father to the highest bidder. So,
Nick bought himself a wife. With a villain hot on their
heels, and a fortune and their lives at stake, they would
gamble everything on the most dangerous game of all:
love.

A TOUCH OF PARADISE   (0-7860-0271-9, $4.99)
by Alexa Smart

As a confidence man and scam runner in 1880s America,
Malcolm Northrup has amassed a fortune. Now, posing
as the eminent Sir John Abbot—scholar, and possible
discoverer of the lost continent of Atlantis—he's taking
his act on the road with a lecture tour, seeking funds for
a scientific experiment he has no intention of making.
But scholar Halia Davenport is determined to accompany
Malcolm on his "expedition" . . . even if she must kidnap
him!

A Patriot's Heart

Stobie Piel

Pinnacle Books
Kensington Publishing Corp.
http://www.pinnaclebooks.com

PINNACLE BOOKS are published by

Kensington Publishing Corp.
850 Third Avenue
New York, NY 10022

Pinnacle and the P logo Reg. U.S. Pat. & TM Off.

First Printing: January, 1998
10 9 8 7 6 5 4 3 2 1

Printed in the United States of America

To Salli Ritch-Smith. Everyone needs someone who believes in them, and in what they're trying to create. I am so grateful that we have you.

PART ONE
Emmalina

If ponies rode men and if grass ate the cows,
And cats should be chased into holes by the
mouse . . .
If summer were spring and the other way round,
Then all the world would be upside down.

"The World Turned Upside Down"

Old English Marching Song

ONE

"Damnation! It's locked! We need the keys."

Nina banged her fists against the heavy doors of the storeroom and turned back to the waiting children. Sean O'Grady stepped forward and tapped his chin with his dirty finger.

"The bloodybacks have the keys, Miss Nina. I followed their captain from here to his quarters this morning. If we can't break in now, we'll just have to forget it."

She frowned as she considered the situation. Her puppy scratched at her feet and she reached down to touch its long nose. "I know you're hungry, Melly. There's got to be a way . . ."

A tight spiral of hair fell across her forehead. She pushed it away. Her eyes narrowed and she nodded as a new idea formed.

"God's nightgown! If the redcoats have the keys, we'll take them."

Sean shook his head vigorously. "It's too dangerous, Miss. If they catch you . . ."

"They'll never catch me. Now, where did that captain go?"

"Took old Mortimer's house. On Chestnut."

"Mortimer Reed? The old pastor that's with General Washington? Yes, I know it."

Nina hurried across the street, cutting down Black Horse Alley behind the tall, narrow row houses. The children followed her to Chestnut Street, where the group assessed the house occupied by British officers.

The English troops had occupied Philadelphia in September. As the winter reached fullness in February, life grew hard for the rebel families. The group of children huddled together, their thin, worn jackets offered little aid against the frosty night air. Fat snowflakes fell from the black sky.

The children watched Nina walk away, but Sean sighed and called to her. "Wait, Nina. We're coming."

She surveyed her little group. "Who's been watching this house?"

A ten-year-old girl stepped forward. "I have, and Peter."

"Hannah. Good. How many redcoats?"

"There's three of them, all told," said Hannah. "One captain and two officers. There's usually a serving woman and a cook, too, but they'd be done work by now."

Peter nodded. "The servants are all the way upstairs. Above the kitchen. So it's just the captain and two others we have to worry about."

"Perfect. Servants notice what the English miss." Nina thought a moment. She couldn't risk being caught tonight. "We can't all be prancing up to their windows. Sean, come with me. The rest of you wait here. And hide yourselves."

Hannah seized Nina's hand. "Let me come."

"You stay right where you are, Hannah. Those are British officers, after all. God Himself only knows what depravities occupy their time at night."

This appeased the children. It was understood that

the British lived their lives with abandon. The children's parents had no need to give warnings to this fact—every one had seen the drunken soldiers and the working girls they employed.

The children hid themselves in the shadows around the big house. Nina glanced toward the house. Uniformed officers passed to and fro before the windows. "They're so confident."

"And warm," added Sean. "It's cold out here."

"Button your coat, Sean."

"Don't have no buttons, Miss."

Nina sighed. *Maybe I'll steal buttons, too.* The joy of impending, secret battle pleased her. Her shivers eased. The cold affected her less than the others, though she'd never known why. *The Welsh are the most resilient people on the earth,* Iolo Evans told her when he left the city.

Sean clenched his fists. "If only we were armed!"

"There's more than one way to harass our enemy. But tonight, survival is more important."

With practiced stealth, they approached the windows, hidden by the thick branches of shrubbery along the house's edge. They pulled up their hoods to shade their faces.

Nina struggled on tiptoes to reach the window. "It's too high. Here, Sean. Hoist me up, so I can get a good look at them."

Sean knelt and hoisted her up. Two officers sat at a table, working together on a paper. "I see two of them. The officers . . . Where's that captain?" A large, round loaf of bread sat unattended before them, and Nina's stomach churned. "They're writing something. And eating bread."

"Dried?"

"No." Nina sighed. "It's a fat, round loaf. And I believe they have butter."

"Oh."

"Lean me closer, Sean. I can almost make out their words." Nina leaned close to the cold glass. The two men were laughing.

"Is that clear enough?" asked one of the men.

The other read over their words before replying. "Don't know, Phil. They might think you're in the market for a maid."

This comment provoked greater laughter from both. "They seem to be writing an advertisement for help."

"So much for overhearing military secrets," replied Sean as Nina leaned back to the window and listened further.

"How's this? A girl who will 'lay her hand to anything.'"

The other officer laughed and slapped his thigh. "Better. Put that in."

"I would, if I could."

Nina grimaced as she guessed the direction of their conversation. Disgusted, she jumped down from Sean's shoulders. "They're advertising for a charity girl."

"At least they're busy. Did you see the keys?"

"There's no sign of their captain. He'd be the one with the keys. He's probably sleeping. I'll have to go in after them."

"What? You can't be thinking . . ."

"I can, and I will. No doubt he's drunk himself to sleep. He won't wake. This was Mortimer Reed's house, Sean. Do you know it?"

"No, but Hannah does. The Reeds were her grandparents."

"Good. Hannah!" Nina called softly, and the children emerged from the shadows.

"Hannah, do you remember your grandparents' bedrooms?"

"I do. Around the back."

"Which was the biggest, the best?" The English cap-

tain would choose this for his own. They took the best
for themselves, and left the Colonials to starve.

"That was Granny's. It's up the stairs, at the end of
the hall. On the left, I think."

"That should be easy to find. Thank you." Nina
thought a moment, chewing her lip as she considered
the best way to enter the house. "How will I get in without being seen?"

"You can go in through the window of the cellar.
Granny kept potatoes in there."

"Won't it be locked up?" asked Sean.

"It might," agreed Hannah. "But it don't lock tight.
We can open it easy. We used to go in that way to surprise Granny."

"Can I fit through?" asked Nina.

Hannah assessed Nina's size, then nodded. "Think
so. Just hold your breath tight, and squeeze in."

"Very good." Providence was going her way, as always.
In a short while she would emerge with the desired
keys, and enjoy a great feast at the expense of the British.

"Show us where it is, Hannah," said Sean.

They followed Hannah to the cellar door, and Sean
positioned himself in front of Nina, his face set in determination.

"I'll go. It's a man's job."

Nina sighed. He looked so small, yet manly. Less
manly than he believed, perhaps, but his courage
touched her. "You're twelve, Sean. I'm going."

"But you're a girl."

She eyed him doubtfully at the weak suggestion of
feminine frailty. "I'm leader. Until you can best me arm-
wrestling, what I say goes."

Sean's small, dirty face knit in a frown. "I suppose I
can't stop you. But I'll be waiting. You shout if you're
in trouble, and we'll come. You've got my word of

honor. But you ain't that old neither. The bloodybacks have mistresses younger, so have a care."

"Don't worry so, Sean." Nina and Hannah fiddled with the rusty lock. Sean stepped forward to help.

"It's a mistake, going in there. Jeremiah wouldn't like it. He says you're too pretty, and if the English get a look at you cleaned up, you'll be in for trouble."

Nina rolled her eyes. "Jeremiah is wrong." She caught Sean's indignant expression. "Only about me. Your brother is right about everything else."

Sean and Hannah helped Nina dislodge the window, and Nina squeezed into the dark hole. She fought a momentary panic as the hole closed around her hips.

Nina drew a tight breath and exhaled, then forced herself inward. "First, close up this window again, Sean. Then hide yourselves. We don't want them catching sight of you while I'm inside." She paused. "If I don't come back, see that Melly is fed, will you?"

"I will." Sean picked up the puppy. Melody whined as Nina disappeared into the dark hole. Nina slipped into the dark room. She waited while Sean pushed the window back into place.

"We'll be waiting, Nina."

Nina heard Hannah's small, reassuring voice. "There's only three of the redcoats, Sean. Against Nina. They don't have a chance."

Nina's back straightened. *That's true.* She looked around, and found herself in complete darkness. The musty smell of the old cellar stuffed her nose and her eyes watered profusely as she strained to see. *If I knock something over . . .* Her chin firmed. *Providence. I will do no such thing.*

Nina made her way across the room. She held out her hand, guiding her way, feeling with her foot as she moved until she saw faint light coming through a crack in the door.

Perfect. She bent close to the door, peering through the crack, but she saw nothing. *I'll have to risk being seen.* Her heart slammed against her breastbone, but she cautiously wedged open the door.

She heard men speaking, their English accents still disturbing to Nina's ears. She heard it often enough since the English took Philadelphia, but her discomfort at the sound lingered.

I remember her voice. I will never forget the sound.

"What if you get more than one response?" suggested an officer from the next room.

"The more, the better," replied the other.

Nina frowned, shaking her head in disgust. She looked down the hallway, guessing she was in the back pantry. Cans and jars lined the walls, but most were empty. She looked for buttons, but found nothing of value. *So much for minor theft.* She slipped from the room, careful not to make any sound, but the officers' conversation continued unbroken.

"What happens if your Tory sweetheart learns where your energies are spent at night, Phil?"

Nina grimaced. *A particularly English manner. Infidelity is a national trait.* Her heart hardened, and she forced away a memory too painful to touch.

"What Anna doesn't know . . ."

Nina headed further down the narrow hallway toward the staircase. The boards creaked as she stepped on them, she froze. No reaction came from the officers down the hall. The stairs formed a tight spiral upward, and she hurried to disappear from the officers' view.

Nina left the second landing and tiptoed down the hall toward the bedroom Hannah indicated. She peeked in an open door. Red uniforms and other clothing lay strewn about the room, but no one was there. Quick foraging was a poor idea. The storeroom keys were more important.

At the end of the hall, on the left, she found a closed door. No light came from beneath the door, but a long while passed before Nina mustered the courage to touch the knob. She thought of the thin faces of her small friends, she thought of her patient but hungry puppy, and her own stomach churning with hunger.

No choice. Nina caught her breath, holding it tightly in her chest as she slowly turned the doorknob. It made no sound, and swung silently inward when she pushed it open.

Only the faint glow of the shrouded moon illuminated the bedroom, but it was definitely occupied. A tall officer lay atop thick covers, and Nina froze when she saw he was still dressed. She waited a while, breathless and still, but he didn't move. She eased the door closed again, lest the light from the hall awaken him.

She took a step toward the bed. A brass bed-warmer rested against the wall. She moved carefully around it. The officer's chest rose even and slow with sleep, but it was hard to trust a man who didn't snore as did Nina's father.

She glanced around the room, but she saw no keys. The Englishman's coat lay discarded across a chair. It was close to his bed, the most likely place to begin her search.

She drew a deep breath, then stepped forward to examine the coat. Polished buttons. Even in the darkness they glittered perfectly. Nina fiddled with the garment, searching for pockets. Her fingers met a chain and she drew it eagerly forth. A pocket watch. Her heart fell in disappointment.

She glanced nervously toward the sleeping Englishman. She wondered if the keys might be in his breeches. *We'll have to starve.* She touched cold metal, she ran her finger along the jagged edge of a key. Several keys, on a clasp.

At last! She drew forth the keys and clutched them in her shaking hand. They jingled against each other and she froze, but the officer made no motion. She relaxed slightly.

I did it! Now, to get out of here. Slowly, and quietly. Only her toes touched the hardwood floor as she backed away from the sleeping Englishman. She felt the door against her back and turned around. Only now did she realize how frightened she had been. She reached for the door latch . . .

She felt him before she heard him speak.

"I don't think we've been introduced."

Nina froze. Her heart throbbed so wildly she could barely hear his words. She grabbed for the door latch, a futile gesture, a primitive response to fear. His hand caught hers and he turned her to face him.

If he sees that I'm frightened . . . Nina allowed herself to be turned. She looked up and saw a dark giant before her. She couldn't see his face; whether kind or brutal or drunken.

"I believe you have something of mine." His voice was soft, but dangerous. Nina couldn't answer. "My keys."

He waited for a response, but she could give none.

He held her hand in his and led her toward a bureau where he lit an oil lamp. It flickered to life, glowing with bright suddenness that pained Nina's eyes. She squinted as she turned her face away from his gaze.

He held up the lamp and cast the light upon her face. Nina didn't look at him. He said nothing, and Nina got the impression her appearance surprised him.

"What is your name?"

Nina wanted to tell him he had no business asking, but she couldn't speak. The tall man before her was much younger than she imagined, and he was far more handsome. His face was calm and noble, with chiseled, sensual features and a full, angular jaw. His lips curved as he awaited her response. It took all of Nina's will to muster an answer.

"My name is my own concern."

His brow raised at her reply.

Nina hesitated. "Who are you?"

A faint smile curved his lips. "Captain Damian Knox, of His Majesty's Royal Forces, at your service."

"Your offer of service hardly seems likely, Captain Knox. I have no need of you."

"Ah. I see. Only my keys. May I ask what use you intend to make of them?"

Damian Knox spoke idly, but Nina knew he wouldn't allow her to escape until he learned her purpose.

I must tell him something. Nothing came to mind. As he waited, she heard footsteps coming down the hall, and her fear intensified. The captain's brow furrowed and he frowned when someone knocked on the door.

"Brought your dinner, Captain."

Before Damian could answer, the man shoved the door open, and appeared holding a tray. His eyes widened when he saw the young captain with Nina beside him, but then he grinned and nodded.

"But maybe dining is the last thing you have in mind tonight. Sorry to interrupt you."

Nina frowned, but Damian smiled and to her astonishment, slid his arm around her waist. "Thank you." He glanced at her, smiling as if they were close friends. Very close. "But if you'd bring another tray, I'd be grateful."

The servant nodded, then set the tray down on the bed-stand. "I'll get right to it."

The servant left and Nina peered up at Damian Knox in suspicion. "Did he think I was here to . . . ?"

"Yes. Would you prefer he think you were stealing?"

"It's a more honorable reason than what you suggest!" She stopped. It would be easier to reason with one than many, and Damian Knox didn't appear unkind.

"Now, if you would be good enough to tell me your name, and what you're doing here."

Nina hesitated. There could be little harm in doing as he asked. She glanced towards his dinner tray. A better prospect than antagonizing him. "I am called Nina." No, she wouldn't dishonor her father by attaching his name to a thief. "I wanted the keys to your storeroom, that I might steal food."

"Honest enough," said Damian. "But you keep much to yourself, little rebel."

Nina braced. "Such as what?"

"You might be a spy of some sort, though what use you could be to the rebels eludes me. But the rebels often go beyond the conventions of warfare. It's not beyond them to employ children as spies."

Nina's chin firmed into an angry ball. "What we do, we do of our own choice!"

Damian's eyes glittered at her revelation. One brow angled, part teasing, and part knowing. He looked at her face, and his expression changed. "I suppose your methods are better than they might have been."

"What do you mean?"

Damian reached to touch her hair. Nina felt suddenly aware of her grimy skin and unwashed hair. He fingered the faded ribbon that bound her hair behind her head. "You're blond, I believe, though it's hard to tell."

Her chin lifted higher, and she snatched her hair from his touch. "It's dark in here."

"Or are you just dirty?"

"You will not touch me again."

Damian bowed. "You also have lovely eyes. An odd color." He held up the lantern to examine her face. Rather than fear, Nina felt embarrassment. True, she hadn't bathed in a while . . ." Gold and brown and green. Interesting."

He set the lantern down. "You remind me of someone. So much so that you could be his sister." Damian stopped. "But that's impossible . . . Where are your parents? Why aren't you tended by them instead of stealing your meals?"

"My father is a soldier with the Continental Army of His Excellency General George Washington."

"A well-taught little rebel. And so, his daughter steals to survive."

"Honor is a greater purpose than greed. You steal from us, we steal from you in turn. If it's too much for you, then perhaps you should leave."

"Would that were possible! War demands much of us all, little Nina."

The officer returned with another tray. Nina was sufficiently distracted by the presence of hot food to think no further of their discussion. Her stomach churned. She hoped Damian Knox didn't notice.

"Will you join me, little rebel?"

She heard the teasing note in his soft voice. He'd noticed. Curse him! But she couldn't turn aside food. "Thank you. I believe I will."

Damian laughed and drew a chair up to the bedstand. He sat on the edge of the bed and broke off a piece of the warm bread.

"How long has it been since you've eaten?"

She seized a large portion of roast beef and chewed delightedly. She swallowed hard in order to answer him. "I ate this morning," she told him rather thickly. "But it was less than a feast, to be sure. Old roots and dried bread." She reached for another morsel.

It was too good. She stopped and replaced her utensil to the table. "It might be best if I put this in a box or something. So I can eat it later."

Damian smiled and leaned toward her, speaking conspiratorially. "Eat as you wish, Nina. You and I will visit the storeroom later, and I will see you have food for your friends."

Nina stared at him. "How do you know . . ." She bit her lip, silencing herself.

Damian shrugged. "I've seen enough ratty rebel children to guess you're not alone. I take it you are some fashion of leader?"

"You might say that," she agreed with subdued pride.

"How old are you?" he asked as she returned with vigor to her plate.

"I'm seventeen," she told him, her mouth filled with bread. She took a sip of wine to clear her throat. "The oldest."

"It was brave of you to come here. Yet perhaps unwise."

"Why is that?"

"Our soldiers are long away from home. Your unexpected presence in a man's bedroom might be misunderstood."

Nina glanced up at him, then turned her attention back to her meal. "Your officers wouldn't mistake me for a hired girl. Charity girls keep themselves cleaner than this. To attract a man's attention."

"Ah, but few have a face like yours." She eyed him suspiciously, then wiped her face on a dirty sleeve. She wondered why he didn't frighten her. He was blunt, but his words didn't seem suggestive.

"Not all British soldiers are discriminating."

"You can say that again. Especially when they're drunk." Nina studied Damian's face. "I suppose you were sleeping off a bout yourself."

Damian laughed and sat back on his bed, crossing one long leg over the other. "Sleeping off boredom, I'm afraid. Philadelphia doesn't compare to London."

"Maybe you should go back."

"If you rebels would behave, I would do just that."

He was teasing her. Where was the stiff Englishman she expected? "I wouldn't normally invade an Englishman's bedroom, I promise. But we were desperate, you see. It's so cold, and we watched your men loading the storage bins this morning. We waited all day for nightfall, to break in, but we couldn't."

"How many are there?"

"Twelve, thirteen, sometimes more that spend their days with me. Most have homes at night, or patriot families that lend us the use of their barns, but we must forage during the days to feed our families. And to send what we can to our fathers."

"To Valley Forge?"

Nina's mouth dropped. Damian Knox knew too much.

He smiled at her shock. "You needn't worry, little rebel. Englishmen don't fight in the snow."

"Which is why you'll never win."

"Yet every battle we've fought, we have won."

"You've won, Briton. But we have never lost. This is not a war. It is revolution, and you will never defeat us. Not unless you're prepared to set in here, and in every other Yankee city, for a hundred years to come."

He didn't reply. Nina's attention wavered, however, as she finished the last morsels on her plate. Her meal completed, she glanced towards Damian's unfinished dinner. She bit her lip before broaching the subject.

"Aren't you going to eat that?"

"Please, help yourself." He pushed his plate towards her.

Nina took his offer and replaced her dinner with his. She licked her fingers when finished. Damian laughed when she wiped her face with the napkin.

"Satisfied?"

She ignored the teasing note in his voice. She nodded as she rose from the table. "I am, sir. Thank you." She looked back to the table, at the discarded bones from the meat. "Do you think I might take those?"

"The bones?" Damian's voice sounded strange.

"For my puppy."

"Please do."

Nina took the bones from the plate. "Now what?"

He took her arm. "Now I will accompany you to the storage facilities, and see you're given a measure of our fodder."

"That's good of you." Nina gazed intently up into his face. "Why are you doing this, Captain? We are, after all, your enemy."

"You are not my enemy," he replied softly. "You are children."

"No, Captain Knox. You're mistaken. We are more truly your enemy than you could ever know."

Damian led Nina down the stairs, but he held up his hand to silence her before crossing into the rear parlor. "Wait."

He checked the hall. Phil Compton and James Herrod remained engrossed in their search for new entertainment. Damian glanced back at Nina. She waited on the steps, her brow furrowed. Her lips parted in a unique triangle, giving her a surprised appearance.

Her mouth curved to one side as she noticed his hesitation. "Well? Hurry up!"

Rebels are nothing if not brazen. Damian motioned her forward. She stood at his side and peeked into the parlor.

"We should have asked for a bow-legged one. Room for two . . ."

Damian cringed and grabbed Nina's hand. He pulled her down the hall toward the rear door. "Two what?"

He tried to ignore her question. Nina's dark eyes narrowed to slits. "Not two men . . . ?"

"No!" His voice came too high. He cleared his throat. "Two . . . Umm. Never mind."

She seemed content to let the matter slide. Damian breathed a taut sigh of relief. Maybe she wasn't innocent. Maybe she'd seen more than any English whore. Maybe she'd seen the worst life could offer. But she hadn't seen it in him, and she never would.

Damian opened the door to the cold night and held it for her. She glanced at him doubtfully, then passed through before him. The cold bit to his bones, but Nina didn't seem to notice. She looked around, then headed for the hedge behind the house. Damian followed. He heard soft whispers coming from the shadows.

"They've caught her, I know it."

A girl answered. "She'll get free, Sean, even if she has to kill one of the bastards."

Nina aimed for the shadows. "Neither! It's safe, you can come out."

A group of children emerged from the hedge. Like Nina, they all wore tattered clothing, nothing suitable for the frozen winter. Ice wrapped around Damian's heart. He had seen them before, though never Nina. But he never thought about them, nor how they suffered.

The children stopped when they saw him, they huddled together in fear. Nina glanced back at him. "A moment, if you please, Captain." Damian stopped and waited for her to explain his presence to her friends.

"This is Captain Knox. He caught me . . ." A boy interrupted Nina with a groan. "No, Sean. He's kind, truly. For an Englishman. He will take us to the storage room, and promised to . . . loan to us what is needed.

"But Nina, he'll tell the others. They'll be watching for us."

"Perhaps," agreed Nina. "But it's better than starving, isn't it?"

"What if he guesses the rest?"

"Hush!"

Damian's suspicions rose. What "rest?" A grim possibility rose, but he pushed it away. These children were too young to be responsible for the rash of recent weapons thefts. They wouldn't endanger themselves to that level.

"So he's willing to give us food, Nina." Sean didn't bother to lower his voice for Damian's sake. "But do you think he expects nothing in return?"

"What could he want from us? Except maybe softened hearts toward his army."

"Softened hearts toward him. But not ours, Nina. Yours."

Damian sighed and rolled his eyes. "Had that been my purpose, I wouldn't be out here in the cold. Your pretty leader was hardly in a defensible position in my bedroom."

Sean met his gaze defiantly. "Rape isn't your purpose, then. But a longer engagement."

Damian stared at the grubby boy. These words shouldn't come from a child. He didn't know what to say.

Nina straightened indignantly. "You have over-stepped yourself, Sean."

An older boy stepped from the shadows. Nina seemed surprised to see him, and Damian guessed he wasn't part of her usual group. "What's this damned bloody-back here for, Nina? Maybe you're turning us all over to him."

Nina's jaw hardened. "If I am, you're first to go, Simon."

Simon's eyes smoldered. Damian saw both lust and
loathing. No doubt the girl had spurned the boy's advances. Early manhood—a dangerous age. Fat snowflakes emerged in the dark sky, the night turned colder
still.

"What'd you give him, that he'd give us food?"

"Nothing! If you don't like it, then don't come with
us, Simon."

"Don't want no bloodyback's food."

"Good. Then stay here." Nina turned her back to
Simon and Damian resisted the impulse to shackle the
boy.

"If you're satisfied with my presence, we might direct
our attention to the storerooms. I have business early
tomorrow, and I'd rather not spend my night waiting
on your discussion. It seems a trait of rebels to council
overmuch," he added as he considered the Continental
Congress which fled Philadelphia for Baltimore.

"Wise men take time to consider each matter," countered Nina. "Our Congress has many such men, each
with thoughts and purposes of his own. But our country
will be the better for their effort."

Damian stared at her in surprise. No mere street rat
was Nina, but something quite apart. *Who are you?* he
wondered as she came toward him, her wild hair dusted
heavily with snow.

"If you're ready, Captain Knox, we will be pleased to
accompany you to the storage facilities."

Nina waited for his response, but Damian just shook
his head and started for the warehouse down the street.
The other children came out from the shadows to follow. He felt that he was being followed not by children,
but ghosts. Yet ghosts not of the past, but the future.

"This will do nicely." Nina filled her bag with dried
fruit and beef.

The other children eagerly stuffed both their pockets

and their mouths as Damian watched their effort with a mixture of wonder and disgust. His own army disgusted him; each night for the English officers was a party, every meal a banquet.

As he watched the thin children, desperate for food, for survival, his heart quailed. How many nights had he spent in luxury, in excess, while these waiflike figures found their meals in garbage piles? How often did she go hungry when he threw his leavings to the dogs?

"Nina." She turned to him expectantly, her strange eyes shining with pleasure at the happiness of the other children. "May I speak with you a moment?"

She abandoned her task, her delicate face puckered in concern. "Are we taking too much, Captain? Perhaps we should put back . . ."

"No! No, that isn't necessary. Take as much as you wish. Yet my superior officers may feel less willing to share our rations. It may be wise for us to reach an arrangement privately."

He saw her instant suspicion. "I speak only of an agreement between us, Nina. I will provide for you what food I can obtain. You, in turn, must give your word not to steal what isn't offered, and to come to me when you're in need."

He secured this promise for Nina's sake more than his own. Eventually, she would be caught stealing and another man might do exactly what she suspected of him.

"My word is given, Captain Knox." Nina's voice sounded strange to his ears and he couldn't comprehend the weary sorrow that affected its tone. "And I thank you for your kindness and generosity tonight."

Damian bowed, and Nina turned back to the others. But then she looked back at him, her head tilted to one side, her gaze searching his face with a curiosity that was beyond childhood.

"Yet I have heard sweet promises from English lips before, and lived to see an evil purpose beneath. By the fairest faces we are most often betrayed, and I would not have you think I am blind."

He watched the children disappear into the snowy night, but he couldn't guess the reason behind Nina's strange words. He sensed she had been wounded, perhaps deeply, but she seemed too innocent to have been misused by a lover.

No, the sadness in Nina's golden-brown eyes was deeper than that, a part of her. *I will see you again, and change what you think of the English.* That was the British purpose among the misguided Colonials after all: to remind them of what they were, to convince them to return to their own kind. *We have hurt you, maybe. But we are the same.*

"So you took his food, did you?"

Sean glanced up at the older boy, then handed him a portion of salted pork. "Have some, Simon."

Nina ignored Simon's mocking intimations. Sean never cared for Simon much, either. She left Sean to put Simon in his place.

Simon took the meat, but Nina felt his dark gaze. "How long before you lose her to the Englishman's bed, eh?"

He spoke loud enough for her to overhear his comment. Nina pretended she didn't. Sean glared. "You leave Nina be. She'd have nothing to do with you, and now you're mad. So shut your mouth and get out of here."

"You think your brother will want her when that bastard's done with her?"

"Nina found us food," replied Sean. "He didn't ask for nothing."

"Not yet. The Englishman's pretty, Sean. I've seen him before. The Tory wenches follow him all over Philadelphia, just aching to play his whore. It won't take much to convince your sweet Nina into his bed."

Nina clenched her teeth. Damian Knox might be pretty . . . No, "pretty" wasn't an accurate term. He was handsome. But he wouldn't take whores. If that had been his inclination, he would have propositioned her. Nina's brow furrowed. Or maybe he only wanted clean whores.

"Nina hates the English more than the rest of us do combined. If you think she'll end up some Englishman's whore, you're a bigger fool than I thought."

"Ah! Damian, you're headed for the Bunch of Graves, are you?"

Damian turned, smiling at the high, cheerful voice of John André. The young man approached, his pleasant face open and filled with joy.

"Perhaps. And yourself, John? Off to the theater?"

John André's eyes glittered devilishly and he shook his head. "Indeed not, my friend! A fairer destination awaits me tonight, as I am happy to tell you."

André moved closer, lowering his voice in a conspiratorial tone. "It's to the house of Master Shippen that I am bound."

"Yet not the master, but the daughter awaits you," guessed Damian, and John André laughed.

"My dear Peggy is lovely beyond words, is she not? High-spirited, sweet . . ."

"And spoiled. Be careful, John. Such a woman makes a demanding wife."

André sighed. "Such a dear girl would naturally be spoiled. But that is part of her charm, I fear." He paused, and for a moment his bright young face clouded with sadness. "Yet the first flush of love? No, for me that is long past."

André didn't explain further, but Damian knew he referred to his broken love affair with an English girl.

"There are many women, John."

Though André smiled and nodded, the sadness didn't leave his heart when he turned and waved good-bye.

Damian's thoughts darkened. A drink, he thought. The Bunch of Grapes was loud and bawdy, a good place for ale. His heart felt heavy, burdened, though Damian wasn't sure of the reason.

A pretty girl smiled as he walked toward her, he noted she moved nearer the center of his path as he progressed, but he didn't stop to attend her. Damian touched his tricorn hat, smiled, and he knew she sighed heavily when he passed by.

"Damian! You're joining us, yes?" The two officers with whom he lived called from across the street and Damian turned. Philip Compton approached, a voluptuous beauty on his arm, and James Herrod followed dutifully. The woman lifted heavy lids and surveyed Damian's body appreciatively.

Philip saw her interest and laughed. "Allow me to present . . . What is it, again, my sweet?"

"Delilah Hamilton. Hamilton, like the rebel."

"Ah," said Damian.

" 'Course, I'm English."

"That much we detected from your winsome Cockney accent," said Philip, but James rolled his eyes and sighed.

"Another boatload arrived this morning," he explained to Damian, and Damian nodded. He didn't need to ask. More prostitutes in the city were English than native.

"We're headed for the Grapes. Dancers tonight. Join us, Damian!"

Delilah touched the firm muscle of Damian's arm. "Do that, honey. It'll be a night you won't forget."

Philip Compton laughed and slapped the woman's bottom. "Just how many can you take on, my dulcet angel?"

"I could use an ale," said Damian. Delilah's lips parted eagerly. "But that's all."

The night was cold, and Damian stood a while outside the tavern door. Loud, raucous noise, laughter and music, came from inside. The night was cold and windy, muting the noises of the city. He gazed out into the blackness of Philadelphia's snow-covered streets and he wondered where she was. His heart labored heavily and he shook his head.

She's not my responsibility. If she sleeps in a cold bed, if she has no breakfast when she wakes. Yet when he turned and entered the tavern, he remained distracted, his heart's beat unsteady and strange.

The cold wind whistled through the trees and the buildings. Nina's hair flew from its bindings to whip around her face. Her gloves were torn, and her bare fingers touched the frozen brick wall as she peered cautiously around the corner.

"All clear," she whispered hoarsely, striving to be heard over the wind.

Nina looked to Sean. He nodded. "Ready?" she asked.

"No time like now."

Behind the armory were several crates. The cold, dark night prevented the English from storing the entire load within. So they left a few outside, easily taken care of next morning.

They crept along the side of the building; Nina held her skirt tight around her to keep it within the shadow. From across the street came the growing commotion of the Bunch of Grapes Tavern.

"Check the window," she whispered. Sean pulled his cap low over his eyes and looked in.

"Drunk."

"Only one?"

"The others left him with a tankard and no doubt headed off to the tavern."

Nina paused and drew a long breath. It filled her chest, her body, and the fear dissipated. It wasn't much, but every little bit stolen from the English would reach her army, and she would have done her part for her world.

"Let's go."

Bending over, nearly on hands and knees, they made their way to the chests. Neither spoke, Sean slipped a thief's tools from a small bag tied around his waist. With professional ease, he broke open the lock and grinned.

"Lord, if my brother Jeremiah could see me now!"

Jeremiah O'Grady was as fastidious and neat as Sean was unkempt and rough. Serving with Iolo, Jeremiah was the best fighter in the regiment. Nina had known him all her life. Now she was helping him. She was part of the Revolution. That realization exhilarated her as they struggled to open the chest.

Delilah Hamilton sat on Philip Compton's lap, but her gaze was on Damian. Damian drank his ale, took another, but his dark mood didn't alter. He knew without caring that the woman wanted him. He knew Philip wouldn't care if he took her. And Damian wanted respite, he wanted to forget. His gaze met Delilah's, he saw the full red lips part expectantly, he saw the eager rise and fall of her breast.

He recognized a moment when he would feel desire, yet no stirring arose in his groin. It was a lonely, dark night in a room full of people. Something was wrong and he wasn't certain what it was. Tonight, he missed England; its well-tended pastures and green hills. He missed the gentle civilization.

America had no end, it went on forever. The cities were loud and untamed, Indians lived in ancient glory at the borders. And wide-eyed girls ran like savages through the streets.

The dancers took the floor, the men howled. Their skirts lifted, one wore nothing underneath, and Delilah hooted. The music was loud, then louder; deep, bass thumping that beat with Damian's heart.

"Look who's back!" Philip Compton prodded Damian from across the table, and Damian glanced toward the door.

"Damnation, but he takes hold of a room," remarked Compton, but Damian frowned.

"Swaggering little bastard," injected James Herrod.

Banastre Tarleton stood for awhile by the door, allowing the room to absorb his presence, allowing the women to turn his way. Some cast admiring gazes, but more appeared nervous by the Tory officer's presence.

"Just be thankful he's on our side, Jimmy," said Compton.

Damian turned back to his ale. If there was one person he didn't want to see, it was Banastre Tarleton. They had clashed before. Tarleton was a ruthless man, his actions more in line with a barbarian army than the greatest force in the world.

But he won. Every time. And the English generals loved him for it.

"Damian Knox. They've promoted you again, I see. I guess Howe's forgotten that business at Head of Elk."

Head of Elk, where Damian was formally chastised for ambushing the rebel ambushers without permission.

Philip laughed. "He was chastised all right, Tarleton. And promoted a week later. I'd say there was a double meaning to that, wouldn't you?"

Banastre Tarleton's eyes darkened to black. Damian suspected the young Loyalist didn't want any competitors for unconventional-warfare fame. But Damian didn't want fame. He was simply tired of following orders that made no sense. Unlike Banastre Tarleton, he took prisoners.

"So you're off the ambush trail, Tarleton?" asked Damian, resisting the impulse to engage in further verbal warfare. "What brings you here?"

"Supplies. It's been bitterly cold since Christmas," he added with a laugh as he gazed around the filled room. "You might say we're in need of horizontal refreshment."

Tarleton's gaze cast appreciatively over Delilah's buxom form, but she looked away, leaning closer to Philip. *You can even frighten a hard-bitten prostitute. What is in those wolf's eyes that turns blood to ice?*

Tarleton reached to Delilah, catching her chin in his hand and studying her face. "Should I take you off Phil's tender hands tonight, milady?"

"He's done paid full for me."

Damian watched and he felt a tug of sympathy for her profession. Yet by all accounts, Banastre Tarleton was a handsome man. The Tory daughters flocked to him. Young and strong and heroic against the Revolution. More loved and more hated than any man in America.

Tarleton's eyes gave every indication that the lesser

officer's due mattered not at all. But then he dropped his hold on the woman's chin and laughed.

"Unfortunately for us both, my dear, I have more interesting pursuits tonight."

"And what is that, Tarleton?" asked Damian.

"While you fine, English gents have been gracing this establishment, my Loyal Legion rigged a trap for our local renegades."

"Renegades?" A cold flash washed through Damian's heart.

"Aye, Knox. Or hadn't you noticed? Oh, they're little thefts. But anything that gets through to the damnable rebels is more than I'll allow."

"Are you referring to the arms shipment that came in today?" asked Philip, and Tarleton nodded. "Maybe you should speak to the damnable fools who carted the crates in. They didn't bother to finish the job before nightfall."

"Ah, the lackadaisical attitude of the English! And it serves us well tonight that the rebels agree."

"What are you talking about, Tarleton?" The ice grew tighter around Damian's heart. *She wouldn't have anything to do with arms. She gave her word.*

"Those crates, my friends, were left as bait. Rigged to blow the moment they're opened. Soon, very soon, the fish will bite."

Damian closed his eyes. *Nina.*

An explosion shook the room, and the icy fingers dug into his flesh. Everyone in the tavern headed for the door, but Banastre Tarleton was allowed to pass before the others. Damian followed, and he knew . . .

He knew before he saw her standing there, touched by the smoke from a burning crate. Rain began to fall— ice from the sky. Nina's hair hung about her face, her curls tightening in the moisture. She held a pistol ready to shoot. At her feet lay Sean O'Grady, his body sprawled lifeless in the dirt.

She was crying, tears streamed down her face, but she didn't waver. A small, furry puppy sat by her feet, shaking, but faithful at its mistress's side. Banastre Tarleton strode toward her, leaving the stunned crowd. The puppy growled at him and he laughed.

Damian knew she would shoot the Tory officer. He saw it in her eyes. She had nothing left to lose. Tarleton called to his men, they aimed their muskets at the girl.

"Another step, and you die, Tory."

Tarleton frowned, his fists clenched. He walked into a fool's situation, faced a fool's death. Nina's wild hair blew across her face, her torn dress whipped around her legs in a sudden gust.

"Nina." Damian spoke softly, and though she didn't look at him, her brow furrowed and she hesitated.

He stepped toward her, and placed himself in front of the one person he would least enjoy protecting—Tarleton. The puppy growled again. "Nina, don't do this. It won't bring that boy back."

"Do you think I won't kill you? Do you think you, any of you, are worth what he was? What he might have been?"

Damian wasn't reaching her. He wondered if she could be reached at all now. "Would you have your father learn of your death this way?"

She glanced upward into the black rain. It pelted her face, but she didn't seem to notice.

"Your death does this boy no honor. Let your life do that instead. You need not fear, Nina. I will protect you."

Banastre Tarleton wasn't above ordering her shot when she dropped her gun. Damian took a step toward her, then held out his hand.

She didn't move, but turned her gaze to Damian's face. The puppy glanced up at the girl. For a long while, held interminably while the silent crowd waited, Nina stared into Damian's eyes.

He knew she wanted to hate him, as she hated the others. As she hated Tarleton. "I won't hurt you, Nina. I won't let them hurt you."

Her gaze moved from his face to his outstretched hand, then back to his eyes. Damian stepped closer, shielding her from all line of fire. His heart held, the rain stilled and even heaven had no motion while she wavered. Tarleton's men waited, muskets readied for an order few would enjoy obeying.

Nina dropped the gun and fell into Damian's arms. Her side was soaked with blood. Damian lifted her into his arms, and the crowd behind him murmured, some drunkenly, some in relief. Tarleton's men lowered their weapons.

"Put me down," ordered Nina.

"Never a follower, are you?"

"I'm all right."

He didn't want to release her. She was safe, his. But Nina's face was set and determined, so he lowered her gently to the ground.

"That's as far as it goes, Miss." Damian caught her hand firmly in his. "You're going with me, and a surgeon will check you over."

"What then?"

"That, we will discuss later."

The boy lay behind them, the clothes on his still body moving with eerie life in the gusting wind. Nina turned back to the dead child and she swayed. "This is my fault." She fell to her knees, and her voice broke in a harsh sob.

Damian stood beside her, but here was a place he couldn't intervene. "It's not your fault, Nina."

Nina looked up at him, her small face streaked with tears. "He pushed me away when it exploded." Damian helped her to her feet. Again she swayed. He touched her shoulder, steadying her.

Tarleton walked over to them and assessed the dead

boy. "Doesn't look more than thirteen. I must say, Knox, it pays to have a rebel mistress, doesn't it? The little wench was close enough to do serious damage to my waistcoat. Thank you for your timely intervention."

"I didn't do it for you, Tarleton. I know courage when I see it, and this girl is worth a thousand of your kind."

Tarleton studied Nina's face. "She's got a look worth remembering. It might be interesting to learn what has you so captivated. I'll leave you with your little whore . . . for now. But if she crosses me again, you won't be able to protect her."

"I'd think it would take more than a skinny girl to frighten you, Tarleton. But maybe there are a few more cracks in your armor than I realized."

Banastre Tarleton's face hardened, his lips forming a straight line. He lived on the glory of his courage and daring. For a moment, Tarleton faced Damian, a silent challenge of manhood. Damian didn't waver, and Tarleton looked away.

"Watch out, Knox. That one's a hellcat. I wouldn't trust her not to stick a knife in you one night. But maybe the scratches on your back will be worth it, eh?"

Tarleton laughed and walked away, but Nina turned to Damian. "Why should there be scratches?"

Damian's gaze wandered upward and he shrugged. "It's just a figure of speech."

"I suspect there's more to it than that, Captain. But I don't think I want to know."

"That's a sound decision."

From inside the Bunch of Grapes, the music arose again. Someone had a violin, playing an old Irish tune. Nina looked back at Sean, lying lifeless in the dirt.

"We used to sing that song, Sean and Jeremiah and me. In the years before the war. They moved from New York when we did, when we were young children. We came to Philadelphia when our fathers joined the Revolution."

She closed her eyes, but her tears swarmed her lashes and fell to her cheek. Damian touched her arm and she leaned against him.

Tarleton gestured at the boy's lifeless form. "Take the body."

Nina looked wildly to Damian. "What are they doing to Sean?" Damian didn't answer. "Where are they taking him?"

"He'll be buried." When Nina started to speak, he stopped her. "Listen, girl, I've just risked a lot to get you out of here. You can't expect me . . ."

She clutched his arm. "He was a good boy. Please, Captain."

Damian sighed. "Tarleton!"

The Tory turned, his expression mocking. "What are you doing with the boy?"

"Feeding him to the wolves."

Nina's breath caught. "No. Captain, please do something."

"Let me take him. Your men won't be happy about getting rid of him."

"Do what you want with him."

The soldiers dropped the boy's body, and Damian picked him up. "What would you have me do with him?"

"He lived with his grandmother. He should be brought to her."

"Where are his parents?"

"His father was killed last year, but his brother is in the army. His mother died when he was small. Which is why we understood each other so well, perhaps."

Damian didn't ask for Nina's own story. Now was not the time. But they would have time to learn about each other. Banastre Tarleton had seen to that.

Two

Nina left Columbine O'Grady weeping with a priest. She lingered at the front door, uncertain what to do next. She couldn't intrude on Columbine's grief, but she didn't like the alternative, either.

She peeked out the door. Damian Knox sat on the porch with Melody on his lap, just as she'd left him when she went inside. She half-hoped he'd be gone by now. But there he sat, holding her puppy, scratching its ears. Talking to Melly as if she were his pet.

Melody liked Damian, though she growled at every other Englishman. Her little tail wagged and she licked Damian's face. He didn't seem to mind.

He's a good man. Nina couldn't deny that. *It's a shame he's English.* Nina found herself wishing he was a secret spy for General Washington. She subdued her romantic imaginings and opened the door. Damian glanced back and rose to his feet, tipping his tricorn hat to her. As if she were a lady.

He's too polite for a spy. Nina sighed and seated herself beside him. Damian sat down again, too. Melody pushed her nose under Nina's arm, then hopped back to Damian's lap.

"How did the boy's grandmother take the news?"

"Her heart is broken. And now she is certain Jeremiah will die, too. But she doesn't blame me."

"It wasn't your fault, Nina."

She looked up at him. "You know better." She didn't let him respond. "You were very kind to watch Melody for me, Captain. But there was no need. She always waits. And I can find my own way."

Damian hesitated. "Of that, I have no doubt. But I'm afraid your 'way' will be alongside mine. For a while, at least."

"What do you mean?"

"It means you weren't shackled and thrown into prison for one reason, and it wasn't due to your good behavior."

"Why, then?" Nina's suspicion mounted.

"By my actions, they believe you to be my mistress. As such, they trust me to keep you out of trouble."

Her lips parted in offense and shock. So much for *polite*. "You let them think . . . No, you made them think that!"

"I did. Would you prefer prison?"

"No. Still . . ."

"Your honor or your life, Nina. But honor, once lost, can be won again."

"I suppose that's true. After all, I've done nothing. What others think matters little . . . Does that mean I must stay with you?"

"You must."

"What about the children?"

"You may continue to see to their welfare. But you will hold to your promise this time, little rebel. More than that, you have angered Banastre Tarleton. Not the best man to have against you even in good times."

"I shall avoid him."

"I doubt he'll avoid you. As well as angering him, you have interested him. Considering you mine will only make you more desirable to him."

"You don't like him, do you?"

"No. He and I have crossed paths before. Our military philosophies, let us say, do not coincide."

"Attila the Hun wouldn't approve of his 'military philosophies.' "

"Mercy isn't part of his nature. But that makes him an effective fighter."

"He is cruel, but he fights against his own, Captain. He may win today, and tomorrow. But in the end, he will crawl to England, banished by the ones he betrayed."

"You have a way of phrasing things incongruous to the street urchin I first thought. You'll be an interesting companion, Nina."

Damian brought Nina back to his quarters, but she hesitated before leaving the coach. "Am I truly supposed to stay in there with you?"

"Yes."

She winced at his blunt reply. She looked defeated, then suddenly up at him, her dark eyes piercing. "Where will I sleep?"

Damian considered the matter. He had no quick answer. He wanted to be her protector, he wanted to convince this little rebel she was safe in English hands, safe with him. Was he not moved by pity? Was it not this same empathy, his birthright, that caused his young father's death?

Damian suspected that history was shared by the girl at his side. Maybe their futures would be shared, as well.

Nina waited, and still he had no answer. Her loose hair dried in tight curls, long ringlets of earthen gold framed her perfect, little face. A tight spiral fell across her forehead. She pushed it away. It fell back again exactly as it had been, and she ignored it.

Her head tilted slightly to one side as she watched

him. Her lips formed an upright triangle, the perpetual expression of faint surprise that marked her peculiar charm, and Damian's body washed with a sparkling heat.

Desire. He wanted to kiss that mouth, to brush her wild hair from her face and hold her close in his arms.

He forced his gaze from her face and looked at the houses that dotted the snowy city. The Schuylkill was frozen over, and a group of English soldiers had arranged a skating party. They headed west toward the river with Tory belles seated close in jingling sleighs. The air was crisp and cold, but there was no wind.

If she stays with me, I will seduce her. She's vulnerable, and she will yield. Damian looked into her face. She looked back at him, intent and curious. *She does not want to yield.*

"You may spend your nights with your young cohorts. As long as you check in with me daily."

"Why?"

"If you leave, they will doubtless choose another. And over that one, I will have no control."

"Meaning you can control me?"

"Yes." Her face puckered in swift anger. "You can keep them from trouble, Nina. I won't ask you to betray your secrets to me. Only to see the wisdom of my advice."

"Wisdom, indeed! You are tyrannical in the extreme."

Damian waited while she scrutinized his appearance. He wondered if her impression was favorable. Her gaze fixed on his hair.

"Where is your wig?"

"Why do you ask?"

"You don't powder your hair, I see. You look very young."

Damian grinned. "As it happens, I have a violent reaction to powder. And anything else gentlemen put in their hair." He hesitated. "At least, that story worked on my commanders . . . I do have a wig, of course."

"Which you wear only when forced."

A tiny smile curved that beguiling triangle, and a shiver ran along Damian's spine. Beneath the tattered surface, beyond the sylph-like beauty, he gleaned the instincts of a coquette. She could look into a man's heart, then sweetly tease him for what he was, for what he wanted. Like every great seductress, Nina had the ability to see the boy inside the man.

"It would be easier to dislike you, Captain Knox, if you were less kind. You do honor to your faithless people by your generosity."

"We may be from different lands, Nina. But our people are the same. We're both English."

Nina's back straightened and her lips tightened. "I am not English, sir."

"No? What then? German? Or Nordic?"

"I am Welsh."

"Welsh? That would seem unlikely."

"Why?"

"Have you seen the Welsh Fusiliers, Nina? Look at you. You're tall and blond. Forgive me, my dear, but you look as English as any maid ever did."

"There are blond Welshmen. And don't call me 'my dear' again."

He ignored her command. "A few are blond, perhaps. You've never been to Wales, have you?"

"No. But my father was born there. He's dark-haired. And perhaps he's not so very tall."

"You must take after your mother, then." Damian was fishing, delving in dangerous waters. As he suspected, her face darkened into a frown and she looked away.

"That may be."

"She wasn't Welsh?"

Nina didn't like the question, and didn't answer at once. "No."

"Dare I ask?"

She faced him, impatient and annoyed. "She was English. And yes, I resemble her. Or so I'm told. I have no memory of her." She paused, and Damian's suspicion grew towards confirmation. "She died when I was young. Many years ago, during the French and Indian War."

"Then we have something in common, after all. My father died during the Seven Years' War."

"He was in the army?"

"He was. His company was attacked by a war-party from the supposedly neutral Onondaga. When his commander was taken in vengeance for an act he didn't commit, my father falsely admitted his own guilt. He was taken, tortured and murdered for crimes against the Onondaga in which he had no part."

"He gave himself up for his commander?" Nina's voice quavered, but then she shook her head. "I don't understand the loyalty the English bear their vile commanders. He probably went home and got fat with his mistress at his side. And she, no doubt, the wife of another man."

Damian smiled at her impertinence. "I trust you don't refer to our esteemed commander, General Howe."

"Sir William lay a snoring . . . Abed with Mrs. Loring."

The British general had taken the showy blond wife of his prison commissary as his mistress, then paid the man for allowing the affair. General Burgoyne was famous for his sordid mistresses, a fact known to all and well-mocked by the rebels.

Damian laughed. "It is just such disrespect which brought about our present calamity. But this wasn't the case with my father. His commander was a good man, that I know.

"He was younger than my father, the son of a noble family, a natural leader. He was raised for books and poetry, for a tiny elite of England's finest society. But he wanted to feel the rugged splendor of this land. He left at seventeen to fight in America. Within three months, his skill and courage won him command of his own company."

"What happened to him? Did he die, too?"

Damian watched Nina's face closely as he spoke, but she betrayed no more than casual interest. "No, though he was maimed for life during his captivity. His son, Ethan, is a friend of mine. I received a letter saying he has left school and intends to join the army, despite the fact that he's barely fifteen years old. He is much like his father in looks, but he has known nothing beyond England's sweet life."

"That will change here," said Nina. "His father's life was won at a dear price."

"That is so."

"Yet the Indians fight against us now. Have you no bitterness toward them? Or do you blame the French?"

"Toward the Iroquois? No. They have their own honor, and I admire them. In fact, the act for which they demanded vengeance was just, save that they exacted it from the wrong men."

"Were they tricked by the French?"

"It wasn't the French who betrayed my father."

Nina leaned closer to listen. "Who, then?"

"I don't know. There's a reasonable possibility that the commander of the colonial militia was responsible. It was he who ordered them into that territory, but why the Onondaga believed Ian Forbes guilty of heinous crimes against them, I can't guess."

Nina's face went white. Her hands shook.

"Nina, what's wrong?" Her face was so pale, Damian thought she might faint. He reached to her but she pulled away, her eyes wide with something he couldn't comprehend.

"What's the matter?" She had been a baby. She couldn't remember the past.

He watched as she collected herself, as she pulled an unseen, impenetrable veil between them. "Nothing, Captain. Forgive me. I'm still weak from my injury. The shock. I'm sorry."

Nina rose to her feet, but though she appeared unsteady and still shaken, she waved off Damian's offer of assistance.

"If you don't mind, Captain, I would like rest. Sean's grandmother asked me to stay with her. Melody can stay, too." She seized her puppy from Damian. "If that is well with you, I will."

"I will check on you tomorrow."

Nina flinched slightly, but she nodded. She turned and went inside, leaving Damian alone on the steps. He'd found the source of her mystery. His suspicion was confirmed. Nina's resemblance to Ethan Forbes was no coincidence. And the past was nothing but a cruel lie.

"Is he an angel, mama?" The night was black about her. Unseen branches slapped her face. They ran across white fields of snow and ice, but wolves howled behind them. Someone carried her. They had to go faster. They couldn't. Nina's chest was unbearably tight, constricted with terror.

Blinding light split the darkness. In the light, she looked up and saw Ian Forbes. She knew him, she remembered his name. She saw his golden hair, the full curve of his mouth, how gigantically tall he was.

The wolves snapped at her—they would eat her alive . . . The angelic face contorted horribly. And then Ian Forbes threw her toward their snarling jaws . . .

Her wild scream split the night. Nina's breath came in tight gasps. She was shaking. Melody scratched at her, licking her fingers helpfully. Nina patted the puppy's head with trembling hands.

"What is it, Nina? What's the matter?"

Columbine O'Grady rushed to Nina's bedside, bending down over the stricken girl, but Nina couldn't speak. She shook her head, and Columbine sat down beside her, patting her tenderly.

"I know, poor thing. You've been through so much. It's no wonder you'd be having nightmares."

Nina's gaze moved to the old woman, and slowly the wild pounding of her heart stilled. "I'm all right. Just a bad dream."

"I'll get you some water."

"There's no need."

Columbine poured water from a pitcher and handed it to Nina. Nina dutifully drank the water, said goodnight to Columbine, but she lay long awake. She hadn't had that dream in months. It shouldn't surprise her. Damian Knox opened a vile well of memory. Who could have imagined that gentle officer knew Ian Forbes? Not only that, but apparently admired the man and befriended his bastard son.

I must not see him again. She closed her eyes, resisting as sleep stole over her. Damian Knox appeared before her, handsome and strong, his face kind and reassuring. But behind him loomed the specter of Ian Forbes. Farther in the distance she saw a mountain. And the mountain was on fire.

I must reach that burning mountain. Nina's dream left the mountain and wandered to a dark room. Damian's room. He was waiting for her. His white shirt was loose at the neck, his light brown hair was unbound and fell to his shoulders. He held out his hand.

"Are you ready?" he asked, his voice low and husky.

Slowly, very slowly, Nina drifted towards him. Her hand lifted and touched his fingers . . .

Nina woke late and Columbine O'Grady gave her a breakfast of cold porridge. Neither mentioned Sean's bitter death, but in every silence, it was felt by both. Columbine rose from the table, idly glancing out the window.

A well-fitted British carriage came up the street and she snorted in disgust. "Look at that! Redcoats have no shame."

Nina rose to join her. "What is it?"

"Carriage, and one fit for a king by the looks of it. Lord, there's four horses, a coachman, *and* a footman!"

"Probably sent for the general's whore."

"Oh, dear." Columbine wrung her hands. "You young things know too much nowadays. What with the lack of morals displayed in this city, it's no wonder, but still . . ."

Nina's brow furrowed as the carriage drew to a standstill. The footman stepped down, looked towards Columbine's house, then proceeded through the front gate and headed for their door.

"What on earth!" Columbine hurried to the window and looked into the busy-body. She gasped again when she saw the footman's solemn face in the little mirror. "What could they want here?"

The footman rang the bell, and Nina bit her lip. Columbine shuffled down the stairs to answer the door, and Nina followed.

An elegantly attired man met them, bowing low. "Miss Nina . . . Nina."

Nina was tempted to tell him he had the wrong house, then make a run for it.

Columbine gestured to Nina "She's here."

Nina's blood ran chill at the woman's dark guess. "I was in trouble last night. No doubt I'm to answer for it now."

She stepped forward and the footman smiled. She straightened her back, then addressed him. "You've come for me? For what purpose?"

"Captain Knox wishes your attendance this morning, Miss."

"Tell him I'm not well."

The footman hesitated. "Well, Miss, he said you might be feeling that way. I'm to tell you he has arranged that you be properly tended. I'm to insist you accompany me."

The footman sounded nervous. He glanced toward Columbine. "Of course, we'll be glad to wait out here, in the street, until you're ready."

Columbine gasped. "No! A coach such as this cannot remain before my house. The speculation it would garner . . ." She stopped to shudder, and Nina sighed.

"I will go, but I must get my wrap."

She didn't have a wrap. Columbine hurried away and emerged with an old mantle which Nina took. "Can I bring my dog?"

The footman bowed. "Certainly. I was instructed to invite your pet, also."

"Then I'm ready."

Nina hopped up into the coach, followed by Melody, and seated herself within. The seats were covered by soft cushions, the interior walls were decorated and exquisitely carved. She leaned forward and peered out the window.

The coachman directed them down side streets, moving quickly toward the house Damian and the other officers occupied. Nina listened to the jingling of the harnesses, she heard the even plod and crunch of their hooves as they trotted over the packed snow. She sat back lest someone that mattered saw her in this humiliating condition.

They arrived at Damian's house, and she was escorted inside. By the time she saw him, her lips were tightened in fiery anger and her eyes were slits of fury. Melody promptly found a comfortable chair to occupy.

Damian came forward to take her hand from the footman. "Nina, it was good of you to come."

She glared at him. "I had little choice."

Damian smiled as if teased by a petulant lover. "I'll make it up to you, darling."

Before she could respond, he turned to the footman. "That will be all. Thank you."

The man nodded, grinned at Nina, then left. She turned to Damian with barely controlled fury. " 'Darling?' Have you lost your mind?"

"For your own protection, you must be known as my mistress. I can't very well leave you wandering around the streets, can I?"

Damian cast a thoughtful glance over her tattered form. "You could use a bath."

"I bathed last month, and my dog, too!"

He grimaced. "I thought as much. You will bathe today, without your dog. Right now, in fact. There's a tub yonder." He gestured toward a small room. "There's plenty of soap readied, and hot water to rinse your hair. Use it."

She lifted her chin. "I will not!"

"Unaided, or shall I assist you? Forcibly."

She faced him unyielding. He didn't look away and she drew an irritated breath. "Very well. But if you think you're going to parade me around as your concubine, you'd best think again!"

"We'll discuss our itinerary later." Damian eased her toward the bath. "I've located a suitable wardrobe for you, which you will find laid out on the dresser in the room adjoining."

Damian opened the door for her and guided her in. "Now, for your bath . . ."

Nina emerged nearly an hour later, thoroughly scrubbed and attired in her new ivory brocade dress. Melody jumped down from her chair and sniffed Nina to make certain it was truly her mistress. Damian had begun to wonder if she'd slipped out the window when he turned around to see her.

For a long moment, he just stared. The dress, tailored to her slender body, fit perfectly. The sheer cloth of her chemise shadowed the soft swell of her breast, baring a long, graceful throat upon which her lovely head seemed delicately balanced.

Nina's thick mass of hair fell around her face, several shades lighter now that it had been washed. She waited with a frown upon her lips, but Damian struggled to speak.

"You look much better. Quite beautiful, in fact."

Nina's eyes brightened momentarily, and Damian saw that it was only with effort that she forced a smile away. He rose from his chair and held out his hand to her. For a reason he didn't understand, she hopped away as if his gesture threatened her. Her cheeks washed with a hot flush of color. *At least, she's noticed I'm a man.*

"You're almost too perfect for a mistress. But . . . no matter. The dress I chose suits you, Nina." He tried to sound detached, and didn't quite succeed. "Fortunate."

Nina examined her dress. "How did you get this? You couldn't have ordered it made this soon."

"It took quite a bit of persuading, but I convinced a young lady to spare one of her gowns."

"Why would she give it to you? It's beautiful. It could be remade, you know."

"That was her intention. I encouraged her to believe it past its prime."

"She doesn't sound very bright." Nina fingered the buttons of her bodice.

"Her intelligence isn't her main charm, that's true."

"A woman has nothing else that lasts."

"Nothing lasts forever, Nina. Not beauty or intelligence, nor anything else that I know of. Except perhaps love."

"Ha! In fairy tales and songs, maybe. But on earth? I think not."

"There are many kinds of love, Nina. What say, of a mother's for her child?"

Nina's small, square jaw tightened. "About that, I wouldn't know."

"You may, someday. With your own child."

She looked up and met his gaze evenly. "I will never marry."

"Why not? You're young yet. Perhaps when you're older . . ."

"I will never marry. I won't bring into this world a baby I can't protect . . ." She stopped as if surprised by her outburst. Damian let the subject pass.

"Your hair. All is perfect except for that." He directed her in front of the large, golden-framed mirror. He located a soft brush and began to untangle her hair. He settled with softening it into even waves, then proceeded to fashion it together behind her head.

"How did you learn this?"

"The study of women holds long fascination for me."

Nina looked back into the mirror. He smiled. "I suppose you're a typical Englishman."

"There are many Englishman, little rebel. We're not cut from a mold."

She didn't appear convinced. "Are you married?"

"No."

"Why not?"

"There was a time in my youth I considered marriage. While I was at Cambridge, I met the daughter of a local innkeeper and fell in love. My family wasn't pleased, to say the least, but since both my parents had died, there was no one to exact control over my choices."

Nina turned her gaze to her own reflection, away from him. "Why didn't you marry her?"

"I was young then, barely eighteen. When the early flush of first love wore away, I found I hungered for adventure. I told her I wanted to go to America as had my father, and that I would return to marry her. Or send for her, if I desired to stay."

"Didn't she want to come here?"

"She had no desire for adventure. But that wasn't her reason."

"What was?"

"She believed I wouldn't want her after seeing more of the world, that I would forget her. Maybe she was right. I thought of her little once I had gone. Still, it was hard at the time. She married a local boy who doted on her, and I was left to sail for these shores."

He studied Nina's face in the mirror. He'd thought youthful infatuation beyond him, after war, after seeing too much of humanity's dark side. Maybe he was wrong.

"And since?"

He tried to resist his pleasure at her curiosity. "I've been at war since. It's been seven years, and I find no burning desire to marry. I trust you're not inquiring into other matters of the flesh?"

Her face flushed hot and pink. "Of course not!"

"It *would* have been an indelicate question." Damian repressed a grin. "What do you think of your hair?"

Nina studied herself in the mirror. "I look . . . quite different, don't I?"

"You do, indeed."

Damian turned her around and looked down into her face. The hair pulled away accentuated her unique beauty, her golden-brown eyes glittered. *It would be so easy to kiss you.*

He couldn't resist. He bent and gently brushed his mouth across hers. Nina froze. He rested his lips softly on hers, demanding nothing, just feeling her close.

Her breath came swift and shocked. He tasted her lower lip with a light touch of his tongue. Wild shocks of heat surged through his loins, he hardened as his body fought his restraint.

He gently eased her clamped lips apart, moving his lips over hers. She trembled, her fingers tightened around his sleeve. He felt her response, but he knew it was against her will. He broke the kiss and allowed her to pull away from him.

Nina backed away, her breaths swift and shallow. "Don't you ever do that again!"

"Your reaction is extreme, my dear." Damian tried to sound casual. If she knew how much he wanted her, she might flee. "Haven't you ever been kissed before?"

"That's none of your business." She paused. "Once." Nina grimaced and wiped her lips on her sleeve. Damian chuckled. "It's not a pleasant memory. A drunken soldier grabbed me when our army was leaving Philadelphia. It was disgusting. His mouth was hot, and he had a slimy tongue."

He winced at her description. "I trust you're not comparing my kiss to that experience."

She eyed him thoughtfully. "Your tongue wasn't exactly slimy."

"What a relief!"

"But I didn't like it." She seemed anxious to make this clear.

"What did you do when the soldier kissed you?"

"I hit him, of course. He was too drunk to notice, though. I was lucky, because Jeremiah yanked him away and knocked him to the ground."

"Who is Jeremiah?"

"Sean's older brother." Nina's chin lifted in subtle defiance. "He's handsome and he's a patriot."

"But not much of a kisser."

"Why do you say that?"

"You said you'd only been kissed once."

"Jeremiah isn't as disrespectful as you are."

Damian bowed. "Forgive me, my sweet. I was overcome by your newly revealed glory."

Nina rolled her eyes. "You are an Englishman with no restraint."

"Had I no restraint, you would be on the floor."

She didn't understand at first. Damian watched as her mouth dropped. She swallowed quickly and turned away, fiddling with the fat buttons on her bodice.

"What are we doing, now that I'm all dressed up?"

"We need to be seen together. For your protection, of course. Banastre Tarleton has arranged a horse race on the common. I thought we might attend."

"You English and Tory bastards play while our fathers and brothers starve."

"At least you have the language of a mistress," observed Damian as Nina fumed. "But if your rebels want victory, then, yes, they'll have to suffer for it. Shall we go?"

The sun was bright, shining full upon the common as the snow melted and formed tiny rivers along the street. Horses stamped, held by servants as the riders laughed together. The weather turned suddenly warm, tiny blades of grass heralding the distant spring. Nina noted it was the first day she hadn't seen her own breath.

Damian led her through the mingling crowd, garnering glances from all sides, but he ignored them. Melody followed, growling occasionally at horses who came too close.

Surrounded by Loyalists and Englishmen. Nina chewed her lip. "This is awkward. Aren't you afraid they'll think you're a traitor?"

Damian's brow furrowed and he shook his head. "They'll just think I'm led by my groin."

"You are foul."

"Damian!" A high, pleasant voice called across the common. A bright-eyed, cheerful man approached them, and Nina watched him with interest.

"Isn't he the man who's in Ben Franklin's house?" The British and Hessians took Philadelphia's best homes for their officers, a fact much resented by the rebels.

"Captain John André, yes," replied Damian. "You might like him, if you would set aside your prejudices. Even Franklin himself would like John André."

John André joined them, a bright smile on his youthful face. "Damian! So you've come to see Banastre make a fool of yet another opponent, have you?"

"That is generally the result."

"Ah, but you're attended, I see, by the loveliest of companions. And one I've not had the pleasure of meeting."

Damian turned to Nina. "Nina, this is Captain John André of the Seventeenth Dragoons, a fine officer, and my good friend. Miss Nina . . ."

He stopped. Nina hadn't told him her full name.

Nina hesitated. But if he learned her real name, however unlikely it was, he might repeat it one day.

Nina scrambled to think of a plausible Welsh name. She remembered Evan Owens, the Welsh minister in Iolo's regiment. "Nina Owens!"

Damian looked suspicious, but he made no comment on her name.

"Miss Owens," said André. "I am counted most fortunate to make your acquaintance. Damian, who resists the charms of the fairest Tory's daughters, then shows up with the loveliest of all!"

"I am not a Tory's daughter."

Damian sighed.

"No?" André glanced toward Damian.

"No. She's a rebel."

John André looked between them in surprise, but then he laughed. "Ah, where the boundaries of war are drawn fast does love conquer and cross over at will! I like that," he added with self-satisfaction. "I know! I shall write a poem about you."

Despite her reluctance to enjoy the company of an Englishman, Nina found John André likable. His sweet expression could warm the coldest heart. He bent to pat Melody's head, and the puppy licked him.

"A pretty dog," he observed to Nina's great pride. "She looks like a Scot's sheepdog." He beamed at Nina. "Despite your political attachments, certainly the fault of heritage and none of your own, you might enjoy attending our latest production."

"He speaks of the theater," put in Damian.

"Indeed I do! We've taken the South Street establishment. You may have heard of *The Deuce Is in Him*, or perhaps *The Inconstant*. Most entertaining, really. Keeps our mind off the tedium. We are now performing *A Woman Who Kept a Secret*. Afterwards, we entertain at the City Tavern greenroom." John André turned to

Damian. "Come tonight, Damian, and bring your young lady! As my guest. Please!"

The young Englishman's enthusiasm was infectious, and Nina found herself looking up at Damian expectantly. He seemed surprised by her eagerness.

"We will do that, John. Thank you."

"Wonderful!" André caught sight of a pretty girl in the crowd. "Peggy Shippen . . . And she appears lonely."

John André departed with a wink, and Nina watched him greet the young woman. "He is very pleasant. What interest has he in Miss Shippen? She seems dull to me."

"To me, also. There is no vast attachment between them, at least, on John's part. I think it is she who has a greater interest—in any man of prominence and power."

"Captain André deserves a better wife. One who wants him for what he is."

"True. But the woman he loved involved herself with a married man whom she relieved from a bitter wife. John's heart was broken. Oh, he dallies with the likes of Peggy Shippen. Another girl, Peggy Chew, considers herself in love with him. But John can't forget his first life."

"How sad! He deserves better."

"That also is true. Yet in life, it seems, the good do not always get what is deserved, nor do they always live long."

Nina knew Damian was thinking of his own father. The man who died to save Ian Forbes. The good die, and the evil linger. How often that was true! As with Sean, with countless others killed in battle.

"Maybe there's some grace from Heaven we don't understand. I can't say I believe it myself. But at such times, I hope it's true."

"Most young women take great pride in their faith."

"And if they can answer why the good suffer while evil lives to a ripe old age, I might agree with them."

"Life has many mysteries, Nina . . . Owens," said Damian. "And for some things, there are no answers. But you grace the world you live in, my little friend. If you died tomorrow, this land would be brighter for your brief days upon it."

"Thank you, Captain Knox. But I hope I don't die tomorrow."

"As do I, Nina. As do I."

Banastre Tarleton rode toward them. Damian uttered a low groan of misery. "Ah, Damian! Did you see? Yet another fool who couldn't match the stride of my mount."

"I'm afraid I missed the last race, Tarleton."

Tarleton looked at Nina. "This can't be . . . She isn't the same filthy wench you snatched from the gutter?"

"The same."

"Enjoying the pleasures of the enemy. It has its rewards, I'd imagine. I wouldn't have thought you the kind to seduce the enemy, Knox. Weren't you entertaining Colonel Forbes's pretty niece in New York? Ah, but she's far away, isn't she? A man needs something closer. And warmer."

Tarleton laughed and started away, but then he turned back. "One more race, Damian. You've a good horse, they say. Here, I challenge you! Ready the beast, and set him up against mine."

"A half-hour," he called back. "I'll be there."

Nina looked at Damian, then back at Tarleton. "You're going to race him? How silly!"

"I know."

John André hurried up to Damian, followed closely by Philip Compton and James Herrod. "Good for you, Damian!"

"We've sent for your horse," said James.

A shy, attractive girl joined Philip as they awaited Damian's horse, whom he introduced as Anna Fairchild. Like Nina, she was blond, but she seemed far more fragile. Nina remembered her mentioned when Compton advertised for his charity girl. She wished she could blurt out the truth and spare the girl a miserable and faithless marriage.

Her mind wandered to Tarleton's earlier comment. "Forbes's niece?"

"Penelope Forbes is a friend."

Nina huffed. "I wonder if she knows that."

A stable boy brought Damian's horse from the stables, and Nina gazed at the tall animal with admiration. The horse's mahogany coat glistened, the black mane and tail reflected a sheen rendered by careful tending. Even his black hooves appeared polished. A perfect oval star defined his handsome head.

"He's very handsome," said Nina as Damian took the reins from the stable boy. "And well tended. How black are the tips of his ears! Even his nose."

Damian patted his mount's muscled neck. "No one loves his horse like an Englishman."

"I thought the Hessians had better horses."

"Ha!" replied Damian indignantly. "Not so, my lady. Larger, possibly, but not faster. Or smarter."

"Well, he's certainly pretty. What's his name?"

"Gambrinus. For the German god of beer and ale."

Nina shook her head reproachfully. "What possessed you to name him that?"

"I won him gambling at a tavern in Bristol. I'd taken my share of ale, and it seemed to help."

"How loathsome!"

Gambrinus touched his soft nose to Melody's back, and the puppy jumped back. Seeing the giant animal apparently gentle, Melody ventured closer and sniffed the horse.

Banastre Tarleton appeared with his own horse, a restive gray that danced around even while held. "His horse looks fast," said Nina as she glanced back at Gambrinus.

Gambrinus's eyes batted shut and he rested a back leg. Damian bent down and plucked a handful of spring grass which the horse took, chewing thoughtfully.

Nina shook her head. "He'd rather nap than race."

Damian rubbed his horse's ear fondly. "He knows, my dear. What's the point of prancing around? A waste of energy. But perhaps I should warm him up."

He mounted and the horse clearly sighed. Nina laughed. "This isn't promising."

"Wish me well, my lady."

"The best of luck to you, Captain. You'll need it."

Damian leaned down, seized her hand, kissed it dramatically, then started away. James Herrod, Philip Compton and Anna joined Nina. She expected to be despised as a rebel, but no one seemed to care.

"That's a pretty horse," said Anna. Damian guided the horse in a relaxed canter about the common. "It doesn't look particularly fast, though."

"No." Nina sighed. "He doesn't."

"The captain might surprise you ladies," said James. "A good war horse doesn't get excited about everything, you know."

"I might add that Tarleton rides an entirely different steed in battle than that high-strung thing he's using here," added Compton.

"Not without reason. That gray is damnable fast."

Anna and Nina looked at each other. Anna smiled, and Nina realized she liked the Tory girl. Philip Compton wasn't entirely unpleasant, but Nina thought Anna deserved better.

Tarleton mounted and his horse sprang into the common. "Ready, Knox?"

Gambrinus walked toward the starting line, his tail swinging idly, gazing around at the spectators.

"Oh, dear . . ."

John André positioned himself near the starting line, and he waved. She lifted her hand in response, but she felt strange and bewildered. Here she stood among those she once scorned, welcomed and befriended by her enemy. Not only that, but as she looked to where Damian lined up his horse against Tarleton's, her heart fluttered with unmistakable warmth.

What have I become? It is her blood seething in my veins. A shot rang out, startling her, and the horses burst forward. To her unending surprise, Gambrinus kept even with Tarleton's gray, matching the thoroughbred's stride.

"He isn't even trying! Why, he's just floating along."

James Herrod nodded his approval. "He covers ground, doesn't he?"

Anna shrugged. "Who would have thought?"

The gray was a flurry of motion—Tarleton went to the whip to urge it still faster. He pulled ahead. But not for long. As they rounded the turn, Gambrinus's stride extended, his head lowered. Damian was low in the saddle, but he didn't strike his horse.

Nevertheless, Gambrinus gained on the gray, met him, then edged passed. Nina clapped her hands. The spectators shouted, urging the riders to a dramatic conclusion. Her heart raced with excitement, she could barely contain herself.

The horses headed for the finish, neck and neck, but then Gambrinus stretched his stride still further. He seemed to fly, passing Tarleton, then lengthening the lead as they surged across the line. Damian had won.

* * *

He saw her watching him and he shuddered with a feeling he'd forgotten. No, he'd never felt like this. Damian was in a crowd, but Nina's was the only face he saw. She was happy, her face lit in a bright, surprised smile. Escaping strands of wild hair swirled in the breeze as she waved to him.

Banastre Tarleton rode his steaming gray to Damian and doffed his hat. "You've amazed me, Knox."

Damian had expected the worse for his win, but instead the arrogant Loyalist was heartily congratulating him. "Lucky for me you'd raced earlier."

Tarleton eyed Gambrinus. "That's a fine mount. Don't suppose you'd give him up."

"Don't suppose I would."

Tarleton laughed, then rode away. Damian watched him go. *I will never completely understand Americans. Just when you think you know what someone is . . .*

Damian dismounted, leading Gambrinus back to where Nina waited with the others. John André hurried over to congratulate his victory.

"A race that was, Captain! Well done! This, too, is worth a poem, wouldn't you say! You have given me fodder for art today!"

André glanced toward Banastre Tarleton, his face knit in wonder. "Took it well, didn't he?"

"He did."

"They're a strange lot, these Colonials. He has an appealing nature, in a violent sort of way. The ladies seem to like him."

"No more than yourself, John."

"Philadelphia has been kind to us. It will be a shame to leave."

"Why should we leave?" asked Damian. "Have you heard something?"

André shrugged. "No, but if Howe is recalled as he requested in November, it seems likely we'll move on soon after. We should hear from England any time now." He paused, and his face brightened visibly. "Perhaps we should stage a party! Yes, something to send the old fellow off in grand style, to celebrate his command."

"You don't think that would be in bad taste? The Quakers here already disapprove of English merrymaking. An elaborate party . . . I don't know, John. We don't want to make rebels out of Loyalists."

"Good taste is overrated, I fear. Ah, Damian! Who knows what the future holds for any of us? Let us enjoy our fortune while we have it, eh?"

André glanced toward Nina, then smiled and slapped Damian's shoulder. Damian watched him walk away, doffing his cap to the ladies as he passed. A dark premonition surfaced in his mind, but it was uncertain, as if it might be changed. As if it should be changed. A chill passed through him.

He knew things. He'd never known why or how, but since he was a small boy, he'd sensed elements from the future. The day Daniel Knox left London. *I will never see you again.* Clearest, the day the English army rode into Philadelphia. *Here, my life will change forever. Here, I start down the path that led to my father's death.*

Damian's friends came to join him, Nina included, and he forgot his premonition of doom.

"Well done, Captain!" called James Herrod.

"Most impressive," added Compton.

Nina seemed unusually shy, and she looked away from Damian to pat Gambrinus's nose. "He doesn't look tired. Why, he even seems pleased with himself!"

"Naturally. He knows what he's done. Don't you, Gamby?"

Gambrinus rubbed his nose on Damian's red coat. Anna Fairchild chuckled. "He's certainly not excited about it, is he?"

Philip Compton took Anna's arm. "Will we see you at André's play tonight, Captain?"

Damian glanced at Nina. "We'll be there."

Damian took Nina back to his house, but she said very little on the carriage ride from the common. "You're unusually quiet. Is something wrong?"

"No, no." Nina ran her finger across the polished surface of an end table. She seemed distracted.

"Maybe you would like to check on your young friends before our engagement this evening."

"I would like that. They suffer for lack of organization."

Damian smiled. "You mean, when they're not snapped to order under your rule."

She started to nod, then caught herself. "They need guidance. Simon uses them for his own ends."

"Then go. But be back here before evening. We'll have dinner, then go to the theater."

"And after that?"

"Then I will deposit you with Mrs. O'Grady for the night. Does that sit well with you?"

"Very good, Captain." She hesitated. "May I keep the dress?"

"It's yours."

"Thank you." She headed for the door. Nina looked back at him with confusion and wonder upon her face. "It has been an enjoyable morning, Captain. Again, you have been kind beyond my expectations."

Damian said nothing. Nina's courage astounded him—to acknowledge pleasure where she wished to feel none. She left, but he watched her through the window. She walked with purpose, followed by Melody, marching along with a sturdiness that belied her graceful form. He had no idea where she was going.

Nina found the barn where the children congregated. She heard their voices, high laughter as they played within. Here is where I belong, she thought, and she pulled open the barn door. Silence fell instantly, and the faces that turned to her were written with doubt.

"It's just me." Nina tugged at her bound hair and it fell about her shoulders. She waited expectantly, but the children looked away as if annoyed.

"What's the matter?"

"That's not your dress," said one.

"No. But I'm wearing it."

"Did you steal it?" asked a small boy hopefully.

Simon swaggered to the group's center. "Or was it payment?"

"No, Simon, it was given to me."

"I thought so," said Simon.

"What of it?"

Simon looked up at her, but even Hannah refused to look her way. *"He* gave it to you, didn't he?"

"If you mean Captain Knox, yes, he did. After he kept Tarleton from shooting me."

"He's all kindness, isn't he?" mocked Simon.

"He has been kind. And nothing else."

"So he's dolled you up and now you're parading around as his whore."

Nina advanced on the boy, intending to strike him. "You watch your tongue, you little varmint! I am no such thing. It was necessary for the English to think that, or they'd throw me in prison. That's all."

Hannah rose to her feet and studied Nina's new dress. "You're not his mistress, Nina?"

"No! Of course not." True, Damian Knox had kissed her. But not a demanding kiss. It meant nothing, save only that she tingled to her toes.

Hannah considered this. "It's a pretty dress. But Sean is dead."

"I know," said Nina. "Captain Knox took his body from the Loyal Legion and brought it to Columbine."

Simon sneered. "He's a real saint. Maybe you'll be marrying him next, if he'll have you."

Nina whirled. "I will not! Don't ever say that!"

The boy sat back, surprised by the intensity of Nina's response. "Didn't mean nothing by it."

"It's forgotten. Now, to business. I came to see that you have food." The children nodded. "Blankets?"

"Plenty. It's warmer now, anyway," said Hannah.

"I'll see you continue to get food. And I'll check on you as often as I can."

"You staying with him?" asked Simon.

"No, I am not. I will be staying with Columbine O'Grady for the time being." Nina checked her pocket watch. "I must go."

"Why?" asked Hannah.

"Never mind."

Simon sneered. "You're going off with your bloody-back, ain't you?"

"I just have to go, that's all." Nina turned away to hide the sudden start of tears.

"You will come back, won't you?" called Hannah as Nina headed for the door.

"Of course I will. I haven't changed, Hannah. I'm doing what I have to do."

She opened the door, but she heard Simon's chuckle and muffled words. "I'll bet. Just like Mrs. Loring."

The other children laughed, but Nina didn't look back. She went out into the street. She wanted to run, but where would she go? Her tears spilled hot on her cheek, she sniffed and brushed them away. She looked up and down the streets, across the closely packed buildings.

All around, the snow was melting, even as the afternoon waned. Spring was here, but the winter never felt so cold.

Damian stood impatiently by the window. The sun was setting gold and red over the distant hills, glancing off the sides of the row houses across the street. He opened the front door and looked in all directions, but there was no sign of Nina.

He stepped outside, intending to call for his horse, but from around the house, he heard a muffled sob. He went in its direction, and found Nina sitting on the back stairs, her puppy at her side.

"Nina! What happened?" Damian sat down beside her. "Are you hurt?"

She buried her face in her arms and she shook her head. Damian laid his hand on her shoulder, resisting the temptation to draw her into his arms.

"Come, tell me what's wrong. What are you doing out here? I was waiting inside for you. You haven't forgotten the play, have you?"

She burst into a deep sob. "No, no! I can't go with you. Go without me."

"That doesn't sound enjoyable. What's wrong, love? You wanted to go earlier. Much to my surprise, in fact."

She looked up at him, her small face streaked with tears. "I can't. I can't, Captain. I did want to, yes. But the children, they think I'm a traitor now."

"I see. Because of our friendship?"

She nodded, sniffing. "They called me your whore."

"Those children spend more time on the street than they should." Damian put his arm around her shoulders. "You know it's not true, Nina. Maybe our friendship is bad enough in their eyes, but is that fair? Shouldn't we judge each other for what we are, and not for what side of a war we find ourselves?"

"I don't know, Captain. You've been good to me—that, I will not deny. And it's true that nothing here has changed my loyalties. I shouldn't have to hate you to know you're wrong."

"That's my little rebel. Now, shall we go inside? There's a nice dress for the theater . . ."

"No. Please understand, Captain. I can't go with you. Not now."

"I understand. But it would be unwise for me to go without you. Let them think we chose to spend the evening alone."

"I'm too tired to care what the English think. Can I return to Columbine's house now?"

"I'll send for the coach."

Nina was relieved that Damian didn't accompany her. The coach left her in front of Columbine O'Grady's house just as the last light of evening faded. She went to the door and pulled the bell, but no one answered.

She knocked, but still there was no response. She waited a moment, confused. Columbine would never go out at night. It didn't make sense. She glanced up into the busybody mirror, then knocked again, louder. Finally, she heard footsteps and the door opened a crack.

"What do you want?" Columbine's voice sounded harsh and unfamiliar and Nina hesitated.

"It's me, Columbine. Nina. I've come back for the night."

"You can't sleep here." The old woman started to close the door. Nina caught it and held it open.

"Why not?" Her chest felt tight, constricted, and her heart beat unsteadily.

"I'll have no Englishman's whore in my house, be she Iolo Evans' daughter, or not! Bad blood. Why he kept you, I'll never know. And now you've disgraced him, just like that slut who birthed you!" She shoved the door, and Nina let it close.

For a long while, Nina stood motionless, arms hanging limp at her side, staring at the closed door. The night turned cold around her. She turned away and walked aimlessly down the street. She knew Damian would take her in.

If I go there, I will become what they've accused me of being. No, I know this town. I know its hiding places. I will find a place. Let him think I'm with Columbine. Damian Knox needn't know where I spend my nights.

THREE

"Did you sleep well, Nina? You look tired."

Damian scrutinized Nina's disheveled appearance as he let her in the door, surprised she arrived so early in the morning. He noticed that Melody also apparently suffered a hard night. The puppy was sound asleep in its favorite chair.

"Oh, yes . . . I just didn't want to wake Columbine, you see." Nina paused. "You needn't bother with a carriage again, Captain. Columbine isn't entirely happy with its presence. And I prefer walking."

"I see." Something about the way Nina's bronze-lit eyes fixed on his made Damian doubt her, but he thought it best to leave the matter unquestioned.

"As you wish, Nina. The walk isn't far, after all."

"What are we doing today?"

"Unfortunately, I must attend my company this morning. It seems they indulged overmuch at the Indian Queen last night, and I've been ordered to drill them severely as punishment."

"You're not going to have them flogged?" The British weren't mocked as bloodybacks for nothing.

"Fortunately, I have say over their punishment. Having myself overindulged in the past, flogging seems too high a toll."

"I suppose they are very fond of you."

Damian shrugged. "They follow my orders in a pinch. But treated with respect, they respond likewise. That, I learned from Colonel Forbes."

He watched closely for her response. She didn't meet his eyes. "Colonel Forbes? The man your father saved?"

"Yes. My mother died a year after my father was killed. Ian Forbes became as a second father to me, though I was left with my mother's family."

"So he's still in the army?"

"He is. Though inactive in the field due to his injury, his familiarity with this land was considered valuable. He knew New York well; he gives pertinent advice on our strategies there. Though I believe it was hard to convince them to return here."

"I should imagine so." Nina's eyes narrowed. " *Them?* "

"Yes, he brought his wife, Cora."

Nina stared. She didn't move. "His wife?" Her voice was toneless. Damian waited for a confession, for her to spill her long-broken heart. Then he would hold her and heal her, and make her life the way it should have been all along.

"Ian married a Colonial woman, Cora Talmadge. After his injury in the Seven Years' War, they went back to England, where Ethan was born."

"They're in New York?"

"In the city, yes," replied Damian. "Ethan is bound and determined to join the war effort despite his youth. I expect him here in June. You'd like Ethan. He's a cheerful boy." He paused. "He looks a lot like you."

She turned away. He heard a light, contrived laugh. "Do you mean to say, Captain Knox, that I resemble a boy?"

"Not at all." Damian adjusted his coat and placed his saber on his belt. "One of those times." He sighed, then went into his bedroom while Nina waited.

He emerged coifed in a wig, and she laughed. "Well,

you look very distinguished, Captain. Though twenty years older."

"It's worse in summer. And how will you spend your morning, Miss Owens?"

"I thought I might bathe."

"Very well. Enjoy yourself." He went to the door, then turned back. "I don't imagine you're interested, but the officers have arranged a ball at the Smith City's Tavern. If you'd like to go . . ."

"I don't know how to dance. Not really. Only Welsh folk-dancing, and Irish."

"I could teach you. Unlike the events at the Cockpit, these balls are quite respectable, I assure you."

Nina hesitated. "Thank you, Captain Knox. I will accompany you."

Damian bowed. "I'll return to escort you, my lady. You'll find a proper dress in the room next to mine. Phil Compton has taken a room elsewhere, and won't be around for a while."

"So he can have his whore? What about Anna?"

"It's to protect her from the sordidness of men that he spends his nights elsewhere."

"Greater protection would be the truth, I think. So she could choose a man worth attending her."

"She hasn't agreed to marry him. A girl's first love isn't always her last. But you're right about the truth, my dear. Sometimes, it is the only protection we have."

Nina spent the day resting. Only a cook and a housekeeper were in the house, and neither took much notice of her. She bathed after a long nap, then tried on her new gown. It was ivory with dark blue embroidery, and as far as she could tell, it had never been worn before.

Like the other dress, this one fit perfectly, and she

admired her reflection in the looking glass. Neat slippers had been provided, with stockings, a new set of undergarments, petticoats, a delicate corset and a fine lace camisole.

Damian returned at sunset. Warm rays of red and gold flooded the hallway when the door opened, bathing his tall form in nostalgic light.

"Are you ready?" He held out his hand, and Nina shuddered. He reminded her of his dream, almost as if he knew.

"I am." She refused to meet his eyes.

"Your carriage awaits, my lady."

Nina took his hand, and his strong fingers closed around hers. It felt too intimate. Too good. He led her to the coach where Philip Compton and Anna were waiting.

Anna reached for her hand and squeezed it tightly. "I'm so pleased you came, Nina. We missed you at the theater."

Nina didn't know what to say. She harbored nothing but contempt for the spoiled daughters of wealthy Tories, but Anna Fairchild treated her with genuine kindness.

She must know what I am. No doubt there had been gossip about Damian Knox's strange relationship. Yet Anna seemed to have no qualms about befriending a questionable rebel girl now the supposed mistress of a British officer.

Smith City's hall was filled with people, young and old, congregating amidst the strains of a very capable orchestra. Dancers swirled about the floor. It seemed no expense had been spared, and Nina drew a deep breath.

Damian sighed and shook his head. "Lavish, isn't it?"

Nina frowned. "Yet the prisoners at Sixth and Walnut depend on the kindness of Quakers to survive."

"If war was easy, we would never be without it," replied Damian. "But it would be a sweeter night if we forgot our differences."

"We forget too much, I think." Yet the music filled the air, and Nina peered enviously at the graceful Tory ladies who took the floor.

"Shall we?"

Again he held out his hand to her, and Nina bit her lip. "Must you do that?"

Damian didn't lower his hand.

"I told you, Captain. I can't dance."

"Ah, but I can."

Damian seized her hand and drew her out onto the floor. He began with simple steps, but Nina followed with ease. Soon they were twirling around, her hand upon his shoulder, guided elegantly across the floor.

Nina was lost. Damian's gaze fixed on hers, she couldn't look away. Her body moved in perfect accord with his, as if bound together by an invisible cord. When the music stilled, the cord remained, and she felt as if he drew her into another world. A world turning upside down.

Damian and Philip Compton stepped away to greet their colonel, leaving Nina alone with Anna. "Are you enjoying the evening, Nina?" Anna sounded wistful, and Nina glanced at her questioningly.

"Yes," she admitted, but then she paused. "Are you?"

"Oh, yes . . ." replied Anna, but she didn't sound convincing.

"Is something wrong, Anna?" Nina didn't want to care. But Anna's fragility appealed to Nina's protective instincts.

"No . . . Oh, it's nothing, truly. It's a lovely evening. And Philip is entertaining. Handsome, everything a girl could want."

Nina wanted to disagree, but she wouldn't hurt this frail Tory girl. "Then what's troubling you, Anna?"

"Philip has asked for my hand." Anna sounded neither breathlessly happy nor particularly in love.

"What did you say?"

"I've given him no answer as yet."

"There's no hurry. Marriage is nothing to be rushed into."

"True," sighed Anna. Something was wrong. There was an element in Anna's manner that Nina didn't understand.

"But it might be best." Anna's voice faded, and Nina detected tears in her eyes. "I must forget . . ."

Nina touched Anna's arm. "Is there someone else?"

Anna didn't answer. "Love is so strong, Nina. For it, we cross rivers and oceans and mountains. Look at you and Damian. Opposite sides in a war couldn't keep you apart."

"Anna! Do you love a rebel?"

"If only it were that easy!"

"Who, then?"

"I can never be with him. Should I reach for the moon, it would be more attainable."

"I don't understand . . . Is this man married?"

"Not that I know of, no." Anna took Nina's hand. "I can't speak of it, Nina. It's not that I don't trust you. But it's too painful. No, I must forget. I should marry Philip, go to England. America is too wild, too filled with temptation. I was raised to gentility, to quiet sitting rooms, to be a gracious hostess. Why should I long for a world its opposite?"

"You're a lovely dancing partner, Nina."

They sat in the coach together, alone. Nina looked up at Damian as if he could provide the answers to the long-running questions of her life. "Do you ever feel all the world is confused? That nothing makes sense?"

"At times. What makes you feel this way tonight?"

"I'm with you. I'm worried about a Tory girl. The ones who matter to me think I'm a whore. My father is starving with our tattered army, and I'm dressed in satin, dancing with an Englishman."

Damian took her hand and lifted it to his lips. "You are strong, Nina. But it's an unfortunate fact that one's enemies aren't always evil. More often, they're simply misunderstood. Or two rivers forced to part. A lot of water swirls around before deciding which way to go."

"But to the same ocean."

"Sometimes."

They looked into each other's eyes for a long moment. *I will protect you.* As if she heard his silent promise, Nina smiled. A curling wisp of hair fell across her forehead and Damian brushed it gently away. At his touch, her eyes closed, but when his finger ran along her cheek, she looked at him again. His finger found her mouth, tracing the unusual shape with infinite tenderness and fascination.

She trembled as his head lowered to hers, but she didn't resist his kiss. Damian cupped her head in his hand, deepening the kiss. Her lips parted against his sensual play, but he fought his desire.

She pushed away, then scrambled to the far side of the coach.

"It's just a kiss, Nina."

Nina trembled, her breath shallow and swift. She cast an accusatory glance his way. "What have you done to me?"

"Or have you done it to me?"

"I told you not to kiss me."

"Ah, but you looked so delightfully kissable just now. How could I resist?"

Her chin lifted as she regained her composure. "In the future, you will restrain yourself."

Damian nodded. "And live on the sweet memory for the rest of my days."

A tiny smile played on her lips. "I suppose it's not so bad. After all, no one saw. No one need know." She paused, looking at him intently. "You won't tell anyone, will you?"

"Of course not."

She nodded, reassured. "Kissing isn't so bad. It doesn't mean anything."

Damian grinned and reached for her hand. "I hope you remember that. Because if we do it again, sometime in the distant future . . . well, that won't mean anything, either."

Her smile widened and he eased her back beside him. "The distant future, Captain?"

"Maybe sooner." He didn't wait for acquiescence as he bent to kiss her again.

The coach turned down Columbine's street, and Nina sat upright, chewing her lip in agitation as her mind worked. "Captain . . . Do you think your coachman might let me off a bit down the street? Columbine isn't entirely pleased with my association with you."

"Very well." Damian called to the coachman, who brought his horses to a halt well before Columbine's house. Nina hopped down from the coach before the footman could attend her. "I don't like leaving you this way."

She stuck her head in the door. "I've been left in worse places."

"But not by me."

"Don't wait." Nina glanced down the street to Columbine's darkened house. It wouldn't do at all for Damian to guess her exile.

"I'd think she'd wait up for you."

"She's old. I told her to go to bed early."

"She could leave a lamp on."

"I don't need light. Good night, Captain Knox."

Winter gave its full way to spring, and by mid-May, Philadelphia was once again a city of beauty. Damian entertained Nina every day, and every week, they danced together at Smith's City Tavern. He gave her new dresses and hats, took her to horse races and parties on the English ships. As he promised, Damian saw that the rebel children had food and clothes.

Nina grew increasingly comfortable in Damian's company. Simon took over her rebel group, but since he accepted Damian's offerings, she had little to do with them anymore. It hurt her to see her small friends following the smug boy who insulted her, but she was helpless to intervene.

The rebel families of Philadelphia universally despised her, so Nina was left to the comfort of her English and Tory friends. She and Anna became close, though neither mentioned Anna's secret love again.

"I've decided to accept Philip's proposal," Anna told Nina one afternoon as they sat together on benches in the common.

Nina's face fell, but she forced herself to congratulate her friend. "I'm sure you'll be happy, Anna." Her tone was faintly conciliatory. "Lieutenant Compton is very lucky to have you."

"His family is old and prosperous in Kent," said Anna. "We'll return to England when his commission is over. I can't stay here, of course. Whoever wins."

"That seems wise."

"What about you, Nina? Will you soon be marrying the handsome Damian Knox? You've no idea how many girls are green with envy over his attachment to you."

Nina blushed. "He's merely kind to me." She remembered the fire of his kisses, and her blush deepened. She hadn't considered the possibility of marriage, nor did she think Damian had.

"You do love him, don't you?"

Nina didn't answer. Her breath stopped, then came swift, and her heart beat unsteadily. Her mind raced in furious denial. *No, I can't love him! He's just companionable. And terribly handsome.*

"I'm a rebel," she replied in a small voice. "That hasn't changed."

"Don't let that come between you, Nina. Enough destroys love without political intervention. Marry him, Nina."

"I doubt he wants to marry me." Nina felt shaky and uneasy. Love terrified her. *I love him so, Emma. Can you understand that? I would die for him.*

"Damian!"

Damian had just finished drill and turned to see John André riding towards him.

"You're coming to the Meschianza, yes?"

"What's that?"

"A mock tournament in honor of Sir William Howe's departure. There are great pavilions by the jousting square. Soldiers have already donned knight's costumes for the next day's grand affair. Tell me, Damian. Do you prefer to join the Knights of the Blended Rose or the Burning Mountain? Or will you ask your lady which she prefers to defend her?"

"I think I'll enjoy your spectacle from the pavilions, John."

"Enjoy yourself, Damian. We don't have much time."

"No? Why? What's going on?"

André's voice lowered and he glanced around for

anyone who might overhear them. "Just heard this morning. Our new commander, the esteemed Sir Henry Clinton, intends to remove our forces by early June."

Damian considered this as he stared out over the spires of Philadelphia. "Sooner than I expected."

"A formidable French fleet is on its way, I'm told."

"Are we moving north or south?"

"Don't know," replied André. "Just moving. But it seems the war at last returns."

The sky darkened early. Distant thunder heralded a storm's approach. Flashes of light ripped at the sky as Damian rode Gambrinus down the streets of Philadelphia. His drill ran late, and he hadn't seen Nina since the previous afternoon. Soon her city would be returned to rebel hands, and the English would be gone.

A light pattering of rain began to fall, darkening Gambrinus's coat as Damian rode to Columbine O'Grady's house. The thunder boomed louder, but the horse didn't notice. Damian dismounted, tying Gambrinus to the post, then went to the door.

Nina wouldn't like his unexpected arrival, but Damian had to see her. He couldn't tell her they were leaving. Such information would be invaluable to the rebels, but he had to see her.

He knocked, and the door opened. A gnarled old woman greeted him with suspicious eyes. Damian doffed his tricorn hat respectfully.

"Forgive me, Mrs. O'Grady. I've come to call on Nina, if she's available."

Columbine O'Grady snorted. "How should I know? You'd know better than I the whereabouts of your whore."

"You're mistaken, Mrs. O'Grady."

"I doubt that. But I warn you, boy, any man fool enough to get involved with Emmalina Evans deserves what he gets! I just thank the Lord Almighty my Jeremiah is spared her as a wife."

"Emmalina Evans? You misunderstand, madam. I am looking for Nina Owens."

"Owens? Is that what she told you? Well, at least she had the decency to protect the name of Iolo Evans."

"Iolo Evans?" It was the proof he needed. His suspicion had been right, and more. Nina knew exactly who she was, and she'd kept the truth from him deliberately. No wonder she'd lied! No wonder the name of Ian Forbes shocked her. Iolo Evans's daughter . . .

Damian's mind whirled, but confronting Nina about her disguise might prove costly. Heaven only knew what the old Welshman told her.

"Do you know where I might find her?" Damian asked with forced calm.

"Don't know. Don't care."

Columbine slammed the door and Damian returned to his horse. He thought a moment, then rode to his commander's quarters.

"I need to get a letter through to New York City as soon as possible."

"Urgent, sir?" asked the lieutenant.

"It is." Damian wrote the necessary information hurriedly, then posted it to New York. "This must get through before June."

"Should be fine, sir."

"Where is she?"

The smug-faced boy sat back, grinning as he glanced at the children behind. "How should we know? Leave it to an Englishman to misplace his whore!"

"Good one, Simon," piped in a younger boy.

The other children laughed, but Damian stepped toward Simon with murderous intent. How long had she suffered this way! How much worse had he made her life!

Damian towered over Simon. "Tell me, rodent, or you'll find yourself rotting in prison."

"What charge?"

"Does it matter?"

"What'll you give for it?" Simon's bravado soared as he guessed the leverage of Nina's whereabouts.

Damian sighed. "Fifty gold. Or prison. Which is it?"

"Take the gold, Sim," shouted a boy.

Simon nodded. "Good enough, squire. Hand it over."

Damian withdrew the gold pieces and placed them in the grubby boy's hands.

"You'll find your little tart in Beecher's old barn, the one down Walnut, behind the prison."

Damian had seen the run-down old barn before. It was a dirty, dangerous section of the city, avoided by the officers, frequented by thieves and beggars. The prison stank from blocks away, drunks ambled along, and Damian's heart quailed as he passed by.

The rain fell in torrents as Damian rode up the crumbling barn. Lightning burst across the sky, closely followed by thunder as the storm descended over Philadelphia. He dismounted and led Gambrinus around to the entrance of the barn. The doors were broken in and falling apart.

She can't be in there. The little rebel bastard lied. Damian pushed the door inward and led Gambrinus into the dubious shelter. The horse picked his way across fallen boards, but Damian saw no sign of Nina.

"Don't move!"

She spoke from the darkness behind him. He knew instinctively she held a gun. "Nina."

A long pause followed. "Damian?"

Damian turned and saw her standing in the shadows, a pistol held in her firm grip. "Not much of a welcome." Melody scurried across the rotten floor to greet him.

Nina's face went white. "I was on my way home! And the storm started. I just thought I'd find shelter here until it was over."

"Nina, I've spoken with Columbine."

"What made you do that?"

Damian pulled the saddle and bridle off Gambrinus, who went in search of hay across the barn. "I had my reasons."

He looked around the barn as Nina waited with her head bowed. Rain dripped through open holes, and he shuddered to think how she existed since winter in this place. "You've been here all along?"

"Yes."

"Where do you sleep?"

Nina pointed to a dry patch under the eves. Damian saw torn blankets, but his heart expanded with misery and remorse when he saw the dresses he had given her lined up and neatly hung across a feeding bin.

"It's not so bad," said Nina.

They stood facing each other in the graying light, and all the pretense of gaiety between them fell away.

"Why didn't you tell me? You've gone on with this charade for months. You've been living here, where anything might have happened to you! Why didn't you tell me?"

"I don't need you. I've got this." Nina held up her pistol. "I know how to use it."

"You knew I'd take you in."

"I couldn't do that. It's bad enough what they think of me now . . ."

"Damn their treacherous hides! Look what they've done to you."

She looked at her feet. "I betrayed them."

"You've done nothing, save arrange for a goodly supply of food for their children." Damian went to her, she turned away. He caught her by the shoulders and forced her to face him. "Have I dishonored you, Nina? Have I?"

She wouldn't meet his gaze, but she shook her head.

"Do you think I would do anything to cause you pain? Yet you're here because of me. If I'd only known . . ."

Damian pulled her close and took her in his arms. Nina leaned against him as the tears broke from her eyes. "I will arrange your placement. You will stay with Anna."

He took her face in his hands, brushing the wayward hair from her brow. "I won't let you live this way. You must know that."

"Why not?" Tears streamed across her cheeks. "Why do you care?"

"Don't you know?"

"You seem a good man." Nina sniffed and wiped her eyes dry. "I imagine you feel sorry for me."

Damian touched her lips. "Can it be you know so little of me, after all the time we've spent together? Nina . . . When we met, I pitied you. I pitied you when you gobbled up your dinner, then turned with ravenous eyes to mine."

Nina's mouth twisted to one side in embarrassment. "You weren't eating it."

"But within that first hour, I knew . . ."

"Knew what?"

"That you were the strongest, bravest, most beautiful woman I'd ever met."

Her tears started again, but she didn't look away.

"I love you, Nina."

She started to shake her head, but Damian stopped her. "I love you. I've loved you since I first saw you."

She looked away, but Damian gently turned her face back to his. "Can you say you don't love me, too?"

A small gasp escaped her lips, a gasp of shock. "I love you. What did you think?" Her voice was so tiny, he barely heard her. It sounded like a pronouncement of death.

She went weak and fell against him. Damian caught her and lifted her into his arms, carrying her to her ragged pallet beneath the eves. The rain beat hard on the roof as he lowered her gently to her bed.

"I do love you, Captain." She sounded stronger now and she held out her arms to him. "How could I not?"

Damian pulled off his coat and tossed it aside. She sat up to be closer to him. Her golden-brown eyes glimmered in the fading light, and she reached to touch his mouth. "I do love you, after all . . ." She leaned to him and softly kissed his face. She pulled the binding from his hair and let it fall to his shoulders. "You look like you did in my dream."

"Your dream?"

"I dreamt you were waiting for me in your room. Your hair was down and you were holding out your hand for me. You asked if I was ready, and I gave you my hand."

"Is that the end? I'd hoped it went on a bit more."

"It might have. I got the impression there was more to come."

"There is, my love." Damian took her hands, drawing them to his lips, and he kissed her fingertips. "Marry me, Nina."

She didn't answer, her lips parted in astonishment. "Marry you?"

"I want you to be my wife."

"But what about . . ."

"Did you think I wanted you only for a mistress?"

Nina hesitated, then nodded. "Yes."

Damian's lips quirked to one side. "Well, you were wrong, weren't you?"

"It appears so."

She didn't like to admit she was wrong. Damian grinned. "You love me, Nina. That is what matters."

"I want to be with you, Damian." She gazed into his eyes. She touched his hair, then kissed his mouth.

He trembled as she ran her hand along the expanse of his shoulder. "Nina . . ."

She kissed his face, then his neck, stopping his words as he fought with his desire. "I love you."

Her fingers found the buttons of his shirt and she unfastened them. She touched his chest, then pressed her soft lips against his flesh. She tasted his skin with a small lick. Damian groaned.

"I only have so much restraint . . ."

"I don't want your restraint, Damian Knox."

Damian caught her hair in his fingers and took her mouth in a passionate kiss. "Is this what you want, little rebel?" He didn't let her answer as he kissed her again.

Nina drew back to look at him. "You're especially beautiful when you want me, Captain."

"I would say the same of you."

She touched his face, his mouth, then kissed his lips. Damian trembled and she slid her tongue between his lips. They clung to each other, kissing as she stripped away his shirt. She kissed his shoulder, his back, then moved around him to cover all his body with her love.

He let her explore his body while she delighted in his response. He felt himself balanced perfectly between his English restraint and the untamed forces within him, those same that now inspired the English descendants to war against their sovereign.

She moved away from him, watching him as if possessed by the muses of lust. Her earthen-gold eyes holding his, Nina undid the tiny, pearl buttons of her bodice.

She slipped out of her dress and stood before Damian as she removed her petticoats, her camisole and corset.

Her gaze never left his. Clad only in a gauze-light chemise, she knelt in front of him.

"You are beautiful, little rebel."

"Like you, Captain."

She was a woman, this night. A woman's desires burned in her eyes, the need to please, to seek pleasure. Her skin, pale gold and cream, glistened in the glow of the lightning. The barn trembled with the force of thunder. The air was heavy, charged with fire. It throbbed within Damian as he drew her into his arms.

Her firm breasts brushed against his chest. He kissed her hair and untied it from its ribbon to let it fall around her shoulders. He ran his hands along her shoulders, down her arms, across her back.

She pressed against him, kissing his neck, desperately seeking fulfillment of the storm within her. Damian kissed her face, he tipped back her head to graze her neck with his lips. He felt the swift-flowing pulse of her throat, heard her soft gasp as his lips trailed lower.

"Damian," she murmured. "I want you tonight."

"I would deny you nothing, love." He slid his hand up her side and brushed across her breast. The taut peaks hardened still more at his touch.

He slid her chemise from her shoulders and kissed her soft skin. The thin gown slithered to her waist and exposed her breasts to his sight. His touch adored her sensitive flesh, as he traced spiraling lines from her collarbone to the rosy peaks.

He ran his tongue over the nipple and she arched beneath him. Damian returned his kiss to her mouth and lowered her to the bedding. He pulled away what remained of his clothing. Nina's eyes widened when she saw the size of his arousal as it stood swollen and erect from his body.

Nina sat up. "Is that . . . normal?"

He glanced down at his condition. "It is when the daughter of Venus lies before you, yes. Come, love, this is nothing to fear."

He took her hand and placed it against his staff. "It's hard."

He caught his breath as her fingers closed around his thick shaft. "It is now."

She looked up at him, again comfortable as a temptress. She moved her hand, watching for his reaction. Damian's eyes closed as the heat of his erection soared.

He seized her hand and drew it away. "Is that wrong?"

"Too right, love."

Nina lay back, waiting for him. He bent to her and kissed her tenderly. He lay beside her and ran his hand along her stomach, lower, until he met the soft triangle between her thighs.

His fingers grazed the light curls, delving inward as Nina waited astonished by their intimacy. He found the welcoming moisture, then the tiny peak above. His touch centered there as Nina experienced the sweet currents of need.

The storm was above the barn, the thunder and lightning approached unison outside as the rain beat upon the eves. Nina's body surrendered to his command, twisting with ever-increasing abandon as he teased her.

"Are you ready?"

She looked up at him and touched his long hair. "I want you, Damian Knox. I want to know."

He rose above her and positioned himself between her legs. He felt the dewy warmth urging him inward. Pleasure consumed him as her satin walls closed tight around the blunt tip of his shaft. He moved in and out of the shallow depths, torturing himself with exquisite delight.

He felt her maidenhead resisting his full entry. Nina

whimpered in soft breaths of encouragement. He could wait no more. He entered her slowly, careful not to shock her with pain. Nina's body resisted, then opened to him, allowing him into her innermost self.

She arched slightly, and Damian responded to her primitive invitation. He sank into her moist flesh. Her honeyed sheath tightened around him. When a shocked gasp of pleasure escaped her lips, he drove himself inside her.

"Damian," she moaned, her voice throaty, delirious with pleasure. "I am . . . you."

They moved as one. He cupped her slender hips in his hands, moving inward as she rose to meet him. He withdrew to enter again with greater force. Nina's breaths quickened until each was a gasp. Her heart throbbed close to his.

She was made for him, as if designed by the gods to receive his passion. Her body grew moister with every thrust. Damian drove deeply inside her, harder and faster as the storm outside raged. Thunder and lightning came as one. As if the storm itself was within them, their bodies mirrored its force.

Her body twisted beneath him. Her wild pleasure seized him and sent him splintering into ecstasy, as if its light soared into the heavens to travel endlessly across time.

As the storm broke away and the rain stilled, Damian guided her into his arms. "Was that a yes?" He sifted her thick hair. He was happy. He had never known such perfection.

"You may take it as such." She paused. "I would have my father's permission first. He won't take kindly to an Englishman at first, but once he meets you, he will understand."

Nina sighed with innocent bliss, but Damian was silent. Iolo Evans wasn't likely to approve the marriage of his daughter to the son of Daniel Knox. The old Welshman would remember the man he condemned to death.

"It might be wiser to introduce me as your husband."

She hesitated. "My father isn't entirely fond of the English, Damian. I'll need time to convince him that you're different."

Damian didn't want to pressure her. But if he had to wait on Iolo Evans's approval, she would never be his wife. And there was still the matter of the British departure from Philadelphia. Such a meeting as Nina desired wouldn't be easy to arrange.

"After what we've just done here, my love, you might well bear my child. The wait for our marriage mustn't be long."

He touched her stomach, but Nina closed her eyes. "A baby. I hadn't thought of that."

"I love you, and you love me. Our child needs us both."

"I need time . . ."

Damian kissed her forehead and drew her closer into his arms. "We have a while." A little while. But when he left Philadelphia, Nina would be with him. Then he would return her where she was meant to be. And Iolo Evans could rot in hell.

"I've come to beg your attention on this most delicate occasion." Damian bowed low before Lavinia Fairchild, but Anna's brow arched in surprise. "As perhaps Anna has told you, my heart is given to a rebel girl."

Lavinia clucked her tongue. "Anna has mentioned it, Captain. Do you think that's entirely wise?"

"Miss Evans is young, the daughter of a rebel by no fault, certainly, of her own," said Damian. "I found her living in rags, alone on the street, eating from our garbage."

Lavinia grimaced in sympathy. "The rebels care nothing for their children. Poor little things."

"Indeed. I saw to it that she was fed, and believed her safely placed with an elderly woman."

"That sounds fitting."

"As I also believed. Though my attachment was based on sympathy, it has grown to an emotion more tender. I've found a refined lady beneath the tattered surface, as perhaps Anna will attest."

Damian glanced at Anna. "Captain Knox is accurate, Mother. Nina is as dear a girl as one could imagine. She and I have become friendly, almost like sisters."

He folded his hands and bowed his head. "Then you can imagine my shock to learn her true situation."

"What is that?" asked Lavinia with deep concern upon her face.

He gazed at the ceiling. "She has been living in a barn, Mrs. Fairchild. A barn near the prison, with holes in the roof, rats scurrying across the floor."

He hadn't seen any rats. But rats there must be.

Lavinia Fairchild was horrified. "Rats! Dear heaven! What of this old woman where the poor child was placed?"

"A fair question, and one I posed myself. It seems for her innocent association with me, Nina has been branded an enemy by the rebels in Philadelphia. They have spurned her, berated her, accused her of the vilest acts."

He needed to say no more. Lavinia murmured in sympathy.

"She said nothing?" asked Anna quietly.

"Not a word. She knew I would come to her aid, naturally. But her pride and sense of decency was too great.

So she has suffered alone, in that horrible place, for months."

"Oh, Captain! What shall we do?"

Lavinia was beside herself, wringing her hands, but Damian looked upward, considering the matter thoughtfully. As if it just occurred to him. Anna smiled.

"I have asked Nina to be my wife, and she has sweetly consented." Lavinia beamed. "Yet a time must elapse before our wedding. I'm afraid she insists on staying where she is."

"That is out of the question, Captain! She will stay with us."

Damian's eyes widened in surprise. "Truly? No, I couldn't place such a burden on you or your daughter, Mrs. Fairchild. No, I'll find a place for her. Perhaps you might suggest an inn . . ."

"The girl will stay with us. We'll care for her. Won't we, Anna?"

Anna smiled. "Of course."

"Gather her things immediately, Captain. She won't spend another night in that hellhole. I will tend her here, and perhaps instruct her in the manners of a true lady."

This could prove problematic. Damian hesitated, then bowed low. "You have been gracious beyond my wildest imaginings. Thank you. I will bring Nina this afternoon, if it pleases you. She also has a puppy, very well-behaved."

"I adore dogs. Bring them right away, Captain. We will have tea ready."

Damian said his farewells to the ladies and went to find Nina. He heard Lavinia's voice as he left the front hall. "A wonderful young man, isn't he? So tender-hearted. To think, he was nearly forced to place his sweetheart in an inn!"

* * *

"Why can't I stay with you?"

Nina's unexpected response took Damian off guard. She was seated in his coach, gloved hands folded neatly on her lap. Her brow furrowed as she awaited his reply.

"I can't say the idea doesn't appeal to me. But I want you as my wife, Nina. I won't have you ridiculed as a mistress."

"I've had enough of that, true." But the golden flecks sparkled amidst green and brown as her gaze searched Damian's face. "Anna has little freedom, I believe. How will we be alone together, you and I?"

Damian's pulse quickened when he saw the look in her eyes. He took her hand and drew it to his lips. "If you would agree to marry me now rather than later, we'd be 'alone' every night."

Nina's unique mouth curved with pleasure at the thought. "Even so, days or even weeks must pass. Now that I've spent a night in your company, I would never spend another alone."

Damian's eyes closed as he held her hand against his face. "Nor would I. But I'm afraid we must exercise restraint, for the time being. Mrs. Fairchild will have me for luncheons and tea, we will go for walks and carriage rides. Delight in each other's company."

"But not . . . ?"

"The mere pleasure of my company isn't enough for you?"

"It's very pleasing, Damian. But not entirely satisfying."

He repressed a groan. His loins tightened with a familiar ache and he shook his head at his own willingness to surrender judgment for passion. *I could take you now, here, where all the world surrounds us.* A violent surge of lust took hold of him.

The coach rounded a turn, then drew up to Lavinia

Fairchild's elegant, Chestnut Street manor. "Saved, it seems, by our timely arrival."

Nina's eyes twinkled. "For now."

He helped her from the coach, but she glanced up at him, her gaze dancing across his face, centering on his mouth. "For now."

Damian's face drained of blood as it raced downward in readiness for a passion he couldn't resist. *You enjoy tormenting me.* But Nina looked up at the Tory's elegant home and she sighed.

"One does what one must."

Life with Anna and Lavinia Fairchild was easier than Nina expected. She reminded herself they were Tories, but Lavinia doted on her. Lavinia was a pretty woman, slightly scattered, but friendly and kindhearted. Anna proved a true friend, and Nina enjoyed her company like the sister she'd never had.

As he promised, Damian visited daily, but Nina's desire for privacy with him grew more and more powerful. It was afternoon late in May. A light breeze blew through open windows, lifting Lavinia's lace curtains in a lively dance. The ladies' skirts rippled in the soft wind, and Nina's hair loosed curling tendrils to tickle her face.

Damian sat opposite her, making polite conversation with Lavinia, but his gaze remained fixed on Nina. She said little as Lavinia rattled on. She preferred to study his face across the room.

He had a beautiful face, both strong and gentle. He would age well, and be handsome even as an old man. When the sun flooded through the window, it illuminated the gold in his light brown hair and lightened his blue eyes to the color of the sky.

"So, naturally, we refused Priscilla's invitation. It was

the only proper thing, under the circumstances. Don't you agree, Captain?"

"Without question," replied Damian.

Lavinia nodded. "I knew an Englishman would understand. The serving of scones at luncheon would be quite unthinkable."

Damian eyed her doubtfully. Nina repressed a grin. "Captain Knox is an expert on the matter of scones."

Anna paid little attention to their conversation. She patted Melody's head and gazed out the window. Anna had grown increasingly distracted since she accepted Philip Compton's proposal. Her only interest seemed to be in news of war, especially on the western frontier, but if not for the sake of a rebel soldier, Nina had no idea why.

Lavinia's housekeeper escorted Philip Compton into the sitting room, then poured him a cup of tea.

"You appear overwrought, Lieutenant," observed Lavinia as he splashed tea from his cup. "What has happened?"

"We almost had Washington's frog! Our generals, Grant and Grey, had him cut him off clean between Valley Forge and Barren Hill. We were that close! He was surrounded. Sneaked out of it, though. Lafayette is a crafty little devil."

"It was fiendish of the rebels to engage the French," agreed Lavinia.

Damian appeared weary at the prospect. "Are we being sent out in pursuit?"

"Not a chance," said Compton with a sigh. "Everyone's preparing for André's Meschianza."

Nina eyed him doubtfully. "The mock tournament? The British choose a strange time for gaiety and festivities."

"There's costumes for a crowning, and food enough

for seven armies. I trust you and your lady will attend, Damian?"

"I hope you're not going, Lieutenant!" interrupted Lavinia in disgust. "Anna will not take part in such a garish display of poor taste!"

"Of course not, Mrs. Fairchild. John André is fond of Captain Knox. I thought he might have pursued the matter."

Damian sighed. "He did. Though the idea has its drawbacks, John André is the master of fine parties."

"We shouldn't disappoint him." Nina was fond of the excitable little Englishman, but beyond that, the idea of a mock tournament, with knights and splendid ladies, sounded enjoyable. She could picture Damian as a knight. And the idea of irritating the restrained Loyalists appealed to her.

Lavinia took a sip of tea and shook her head woefully. "Then I suppose you must go, since you're so fond of this young man."

Nina turned her attention back to Damian. She delighted in teasing him with meaningful looks, with carefully chosen words. She bit her lip and allowed a flash of erotic memory to enter her thoughts. She moved her gaze to his lap, and allowed the tiny tip of her tongue to dampen her lips as her gaze returned to his.

Damian drew a long, deep breath and forced his attention to Lavinia Fairchild. Nina chuckled.

Lavinia fiddled with her shawl. "I can't think of a world run by rebels. They have no sense of history, of true importance."

"We are all Englishmen, after all," said Philip Compton.

Nina turned on him, releasing her hold over Damian. "We are not Englishmen, Lieutenant. We are Irish, German, Welsh . . . We are everything mixed together, nor do we care for the purity of our blood. How many on the frontier are part Indian? We want a world for all, and not for those born to a life for the few."

Lavinia's mouth opened, then closed, and Philip Compton drew back in surprise.

"This is a big country," added Anna. "What of the red man? And what of those we now hold as slaves? What shall become of them?"

"A world free for all," repeated Nina.

Damian met her gaze across the room. "But do your leaders speak for the Indian or those brought against their will from Africa?"

Nina faltered. "They should. They *will.* One day. But all things have a beginning."

"More tea?" asked Lavinia. Her hands shook.

The conversation returned to less explosive matters, and Nina's attention returned to Damian. He could climb the tree outside her window and sneak into her room. He would tear away her shift, thrust into her body, and hold their silence with a kiss. Silence. No, that was impossible. Nina frowned.

Damian's expression changed, as if he read every thought. Nina smiled, and he closed his eyes. She waited until he looked back at her, then purposefully wet her lips. He adjusted his position in his chair.

When he finally stood to leave, Nina felt certain that his knees were weak from her provocation. Her own felt suspiciously quavery.

"Shall I order a seamstress to begin a lovely dress for Nina?" asked Lavinia as she escorted the two officers to the door.

Damian took Nina's hand and drew it to his lips. A wild current of desire swept through her at his touch. "Nina wishes to wait for her father's permission to marry. That may be a long while yet."

Lavinia turned to Nina. "Will your rebel father approve the match, I wonder, my dear? It might be better to offer the situation as complete when next you see the man. Fathers can be difficult."

"As I have told her," agreed Damian.

Nina didn't answer. He still held her hand, her body trembled at the proximity to his. His hair was tied behind his head, but she remembered it loose about his face as he bent to kiss her.

"Perhaps I might walk you to your carriage, Captain."

"Do that," said Lavinia. "You need time alone. Naturally."

Philip was still talking to Anna, and Nina hurried out for a moment alone with Damian. "We do indeed. I hardly see you at all."

"You've seen me every day for three weeks, my love."

"That isn't what I mean, and you know it." Nina looked up at him. "I think of it so often, Damian. Every night, when I can't sleep imagining you with me. Every day, when I pace the rooms awaiting your arrival. I have seen you, yes, for an hour or so. There are so many hours to pass each day without you!"

"Your subtle teasing does little to alleviate the tension between us, love."

"I don't mean to alleviate tension, my friend. I mean to lend it fire until it consumes you, so that you will come to me."

"Then we'll tease each other, my love. There won't be enough nights to sate ourselves after this torment between us."

"Then we'll make good use of the days."

Fire kindled in Damian's eyes. "I could take you in the grass, when the sun shines like gold on your sweet face and that perfect little body . . ."

Nina bit her lip and Damian tilted his head back, drawing a hoarse breath. He glanced toward the house and saw Lavinia waving to them through the window. Forcing a smile, Damian waved back.

"We can elope, Nina. Let that be your choice."

She watched him leave, then sighed heavily. Another long afternoon slowly passing into a long night of dreams. Dreams that blazed with memory, yet held no true fulfillment.

Nina went to her room for a nap and lay on her back imagining a night alone with Damian. Where reality failed, imagination was the best course left.

Anna peeked in the door. "Are you sleeping?" She didn't wait for Nina's answer. "Not anymore!"

Nina smiled. "Please, come in."

Anna seated herself on the edge of the bed. "Well? Did you convince him? Will he meet you tonight?"

A shrewd, and unexpected, guess. "If only I could! Damian can be stubborn. He feels if your mother found out . . ."

"Mother needn't know. You can persuade him in privacy. It's not far to the officers' house. You've done far more dangerous things. Go to him!"

Anna leaned forward and seized Nina's hand. "Go to him, Nina. I will see that Mother learns nothing. She's rather obtuse about such matters."

"Have you and Philip . . . ?" Nina stopped. If Compton had taken advantage of Anna while enjoying the pleasures of Delilah Hamilton . . . Well, Nina knew how to use a gun, and use it she might.

"No, not with Philip."

"There was someone, wasn't there? I know it! Who was he?"

"I can't say. There are some things too painful to speak of."

"I won't ask, then." *I might pry into the matter on my own, however.* Someone touched Anna's heart. It occurred to Nina that Lavinia might offer an inadvertent suggestion.

"Now, for tonight," said Anna. "When shall you go?"

"I'm not sure. Lieutenant Herrod is ill, I believe, and is at the infirmary. But what about Philip?"

"Philip will be with his whore. Damian will be alone except for the servants."

Nina stared at Anna in blank horror. "You know?"

"I'm not a fool, Nina."

"You aren't upset?" Had Damian a mistress, she was certain she would attack without question, then die of a broken heart.

"We are doing what we must, Philip and I. That is life's duty, isn't it?"

"Why?"

"I don't know."

Nina had no idea what to say. Anna saw her expression and patted Nina's knee gently. "Fortunately, you and Captain Knox are free to love without obstacles to your happiness."

Nina thought of Ian Forbes, a man Damian loved like a father. Her chest tightened, her breath caught, but she forced the image away.

"It's easy enough to slip from your window unseen, Nina. I'll keep Melody with me, so she doesn't cry. The old oak is within reach, though you must take care to use the branches on the left side. Those on the right creak most dreadfully."

"Anna! You've done it before!"

"I have, once. And nearly broke my neck. Be careful."

"I will." Nina couldn't imagine the fragile Anna creeping from her window and swinging out onto the branches. She shook her head, but Anna was smiling, reliving a memory Nina couldn't guess.

"You've lived such an admirable life," said Nina as she sat sewing with Lavinia. She had foregone her nap in favor of questioning Anna's mother, but so far received few pertinent responses. "Anna is a wonderful girl. I hope Lieutenant Compton is good enough for her."

"His family in England is most respectable."

"Still . . ." Nina considered what might appeal to Lavinia. The answer was obvious. "He's not titled. I would think Anna deserves a regal life." Nina paused, trying to bring up the subject in a casual manner. "She must have had many suitors."

"Until Lieutenant Compton, Anna has been most reluctant to entertain the attention of gentlemen."

"Truly?" Nina's brow furrowed as she considered this. She was getting nowhere in her interrogation.

"Her father's death upset her dreadfully, of course. It happened only two years ago, when Anna was sixteen. I was ill at the time. Dr. Hart was convinced I had consumption."

Obviously, he was wrong. "Oh, dear." Nina waited, wondering what Lavinia's imagined illness had to do with Anna.

"Because of my delicate condition, Mr. Fairchild was forced to take Anna with him . . ." Lavinia paused as if broaching a sensitive issue. "Into the New York frontier. Where he had dealings with, of all people, the Iroquois Indians."

"The Iroquois?"

"Charles was a Loyalist officer. Having served during the French and Indian War in New York, it was his duty to enlist various tribes. He went to the central tribe, the Onondaga. How he ever endured their vulgar . . ."

"He took Anna with him to meet the Indians?"

Lavinia sighed. "He did. I was against it, naturally. And it nearly proved disastrous."

"What happened?"

"Their party was attacked by a Tuscarora war party enlisted by the rebels. Charles was injured, and save for their Indian scout, the rest of the party killed."

"How dreadful! It's strange Anna never mentioned this. What an adventure!"

"Charles's wound festered and he died on the way home. It was deeply shocking to Anna, as you can imagine. If not for the scout, she would have perished in that dreadful land."

"The scout? Who was he?"

"He was just an Indian. I'm not sure which tribe he was from—an Onondaga? He spoke very inadequate English, I'm afraid."

"But he brought her home?"

"He did, yes. I paid him handsomely for his efforts, and he went back wherever he came from."

"What was he like?"

Lavinia's brow angled doubtfully. "An Indian. Long black hair, paint marks on his chest and arms." She paused to shudder. "Why do you ask?"

"Oh, just curious . . . How old was he?"

"I have no idea." Lavinia redid a stitch. "Who can tell with their kind? I suppose he was young."

"What was his name?"

"Black Eagle? Or some kind of bird, as I recall. Black Hawk, maybe. Or was it Gray Eagle?"

Nina considered the matter as Lavinia hummed to herself. It was odd that Anna hadn't spoken of her adventure. The Iroquois scout might have mistreated her. Yet though Lavinia obviously had little respect for the Indian who saved her daughter, neither had she animosity.

Anna might feel shamed had she been raped, and told no one. But if the scout was the kind of man to rape a woman, surely he would have taken her to his tribe rather than return her to Philadelphia.

I'll fish it out of her somehow. Anna deserves better than that faithless Philip Compton.

FOUR

Ragged bark scratched Nina's legs as she slid down the bole of the old oak. She caught a branch, then swung to the earth below. She brushed herself off, then nodded with self-satisfaction. She glanced furtively left and right, then headed in the direction of Damian's house.

No one saw her as Nina crept from shadow to shadow. Her simple, dark blue dress reflected no light. The lamps of Damian's house were dimmed to near blackness. She didn't go to the front door. She'd considered knocking, but the seductress she discovered in her heart demanded a more interesting meeting.

No, Damian Knox, you will not refuse me tonight. Were I to come knocking at your door, you might find the will to escort me home. Tonight, I will not be denied.

Nina fumbled with the window to the cellar. It opened, and she lowered herself into the darkness below. Once inside, she stopped, her heart racing. *In this way, I first met you.* It had been cold that first night, but now it was hot and musty. Nina sneezed.

She made her way up the short stairs, then down the darkened passageways. She stopped to listen for the servants, but they occupied the rooms on the far side of the house. Pleased with herself, she walked quietly to Damian's room.

Nina hesitated outside his door. Her heart was pounding so loudly she was sure he would wake. *I want you so.*
But into her pleasure shot a dark, cold fear. *I will lose
you. Maybe I will never see you again.*

Her premonition was so strong that Nina began to
shake. As if the end was near, a ending so bitter she
couldn't begin to face it. An ending that was unavoid-
able, when all the forces surrounding them collided
and destroyed all light.

I can't lose him. Love must be stronger! She touched the
door, but though the premonition faded, its effect remained. *If I'm to be without you, I will make you part of me
for all time. Then nothing can truly part us, no matter what
the fates decree.*

Nina opened the door, slipped inside, and closed it
soundlessly behind her. Only the dim light of the moon
entered the room, but she saw Damian lying on his bed.
She heard his deep, even breaths as he slept, and her
heart expanded with love.

This time, I will make no noise to wake you. She tiptoed
to his bedside, but she wasn't certain what to do next.
She imagined slipping into bed beside him, naked, but
now that seemed inadequate.

As Nina considered the matter, the moon came full
from behind a cloud, illuminating Damian's body. Her
gaze traveled appreciatively down his lean form, but widened when she saw the hardened bulge beneath his
sheets. She recognized his male organ in a state of
arousal, and fiery shocks of pleasure surged through her.

Damian moved in his sleep, his head turned to one
side. He murmured softly. Nina shuddered when she
heard her name. Her eyes closed and she bit her lip,
but when she looked at him again, she knew how to
wake Damian Knox.

She undressed and left only her light chemise cover-
ing her body as she knelt beside his bed. She peeled

away his covers. Her breath caught at the moonlit sight of his full glory, and her hand trembled as she reached to touch him. Her fingers tingled as her touch ran the length of his shaft.

A moan escaped Damian's lips and his eyes popped open. Nina tightened her grip and caressed him with a firm, greedy stroke. He didn't move, but his gaze turned downwards in complete astonishment.

"Consider me, please, a dream."

"Nina." His voice caught when her hand moved along his length.

"Shall I stop? Will you send me away now, Damian Knox?"

"Not if heaven itself demanded it." He leaned back into his pillows.

Nina released him, then slid above him to gaze down into his beautiful face. "Will you deny me tonight, my love? Or will you take me, and love me again as I have dreamt night after night?"

Damian grabbed her shoulders and pulled her higher above him. Her body settled on top of his, but he guided her hips down upon his shaft, then entered her with a low groan of pleasure.

"I will take you," he growled as he moved upward, deeper into her moist cavern. "I will take you, and fill you, then take you again."

Damian thrust deeply inside her. Their hips rocked together in ecstatic abandon, taking them higher and higher, far beyond restraint. Nina kissed his face with wild passion. She twisted above him, and joined him as they rode the crests of their love-making.

She stilled, and he cradled her head against his shoulder. She moved to lie beside him and snuggled close. "I've missed you, Damian. I thought nothing could touch the sweetness of our first night, but maybe that was only a beginning."

"It was."

Nina studied his face. His breath came shallow and rapid. A faint sheen of perspiration covered his skin. "Are you well? You sound hoarse."

"I am near death."

Nina shot up in bed. "Oh, no!"

Damian laughed and pulled her back. "I've never known, nor dreamt, nor imagined a woman like you, little rebel."

"You dreamt of something, it seemed."

"Ah. I was dreaming that you were standing in a stream."

"A stream? That doesn't sound particularly exciting."

"You were rather wet."

"Was I?" Nina's brow furrowed. "So what?"

"Well, it's hard to explain, love. I was watching you, though you didn't notice me at first. When you did, my little temptress, you just smiled. Looked at me that way you do. Which is when reality intruded so sweetly into dream."

"That sounds innocent. My dreams are less . . . subtle."

"Really? I'd like to hear them some time. But for now, my love, I think I'll fulfill my promise and take you again."

He eased her onto her back as Nina watched with bright anticipation. He rose above her, then took her mouth in a lingering kiss as he entered her once more. They moved slowly together, languorously building to a new crescendo of love.

The moon set outside, darkening the room to black. Not until the sun's first rising did they notice the time, but in that hour, nothing intruded on their happiness.

* * *

Nina moved stealthily through the morning's shadows to Lavinia's house. Anna was waiting for her at the front door. She waved frantically. "Hurry!"

Nina scurried up the stairs. "Your mother?"

"She woke early. She's washing . . . Thank God you're here!"

From inside, Lavinia issued orders to the servants. "I hear the girls outside. Start the porridge now, if you will, Constance."

Anna rolled her eyes. "Porridge again. Bloody hell!"

Lavinia appeared at the door. "You girls woke early. Why, the sun's barely risen!" She looked at Nina more closely. "Isn't that the dress you wore last night?"

Nina froze, but Anna laughed. "It is, Mother. Nina fell asleep completely dressed. I've been teasing her about it since we bumped into each other upstairs."

Lavinia issued a series of *tsk* noises. "That's what happens when you miss your nap, my dear." She went back inside and Anna shook her head.

"You see, Nina? Thick as a plank."

"Anna!"

"Oh, Mother is kindhearted, to those she considers her equal, anyway. Her world is small. Though I love her, I do wish she could see things more broadly."

Anna said no more, and Nina followed her into the house. She'd never known anyone like Anna, who understood so much and asked no questions. Anna protected her from yet another humiliating confrontation. Nina vowed silently to do the same, one day, for her.

"What's this?"

Damian deposited an elaborate costume before Nina. "John André requests you replace Peggy Shippen in his pageant."

"Why isn't she doing it?" asked Nina.

"Apparently her father has decided his daughter will have no part in the Meschianza, after all."

"How sensible!" said Lavinia.

"Perhaps. The girl, however, is crushed."

Nina's brow rose. "I'd almost think that pleases you, Captain."

Damian grinned. "Miss Shippen is spoiled. And I don't want her with John."

There was more to it than that, he realized with a sick chill. More than irritation with a pretty girl's vanity, Damian sensed that Peggy Shippen was dangerous to the young Englishman. Ian Forbes had told him that Daniel Knox had the gift of foresight. If so, it passed on to his son.

Damian didn't want to see the future. No harm would come to the gentle André. The future was waves on an endless sea. And by God, Damian would find a way to alter its course.

Nina fingered her dress. "I'm to wear this silly contraption?"

"It is ridiculous," agreed Damian. "Be that as it may, the good Captain André pleads with you to take Miss Shippen's place. You, my dear, will represent a beautiful heathen whose heart is won by a crusading knight. That would be me. A fitting scenario, isn't it?"

Nina picked up the dress and glanced doubtfully at Damian. "What do I do?"

"Watch our knights make fools of themselves. Myself included, unfortunately."

"What will you wear?"

Damian sighed. "As a Knight of the Burning Mountain, I'm to don the most foolish black and orange costume any man has ever worn."

"I expect you'll be very handsome."

"Only for John André would I do this. It's bound to

infuriate the Loyalists of Philadelphia as well as the rebels."

"It is a shameful display of vulgarity," agreed Lavinia.

Nina went to change into her costume while Damian
and the ladies waited. "I would think General Howe
would have better sense than to engage in such an activity," said Lavinia.

"Good sense? No. But good sense didn't get him returned to England."

Nina returned, dressed in bright swathes of cloth
complete with a gauze turban edged in gold. She
looked beautiful, erotic, and Damian's blood heated.
Lavinia gasped.

"It's a pretty dress," observed Anna, but Lavinia
frowned.

"Why, it barely covers . . . There's not enough cloth
for decency."

"Bright colors," replied Anna. "I like it."

"Oh, dear," moaned Lavinia. "I hope none of my
friends know Nina is attending dressed like that!"

Anna eyed her mother doubtfully. "Most of your
friends are sending their daughters."

"Ha! Wanting to catch some fine Englishman for
their daughters, no doubt. I know Priscilla is sending
Phoebe."

"What about your costume?" asked Nina as Damian
studied her appearance.

"Mine awaits me at the pavilions, I fear. Complete
with lances, swords, and gauntlets. But Gambrinus will
make a fine warhorse."

The Meschianza was to take place at the Wharton
Mansion, a grand home confiscated from the rebels.
John André greeted Nina and Damian as they got out
of their carriage. His face had high color, his eyes spar-

kled with happiness. He was already costumed, his
shield depicting two gamecocks fighting with the motto,
"No rival."

"Damian! You're late, but no matter. We've taken the
liberty of readying your steed, and your wardrobe is yonder."

André waved his hand toward an already crowded pavilion. "I designed your shield myself. *Many arrows aim
at the heart, but it's pierced by only one.*"

A black slave clad ornately with a gold collar appeared
leading Gambrinus. The slave looked at Damian and
shook his head. "Yours, Cap'n?"

Damian nodded.

Nina cringed on Damian's behalf. "Even your horse
looks embarrassed."

The slave's brow rose, but he restrained his opinion.
Gambrinus was caparisoned in silk, hooded and decorated elaborately.

Damian patted Gambrinus's neck. "He may never forgive me."

John André beamed. "Magnificent, isn't he?"

Nina and the slave looked away. Damian went in
search of his costume, and Nina was directed to her
place in the ladies' pavilion.

"You're Damian Knox's fiancée?" asked a girl she recognized as Priscilla's daughter, Phoebe. She didn't
sound particularly friendly.

"I am, yes," replied Nina.

Phoebe studied Nina's appearance. "They say you're
a rebel."

Nina fixed her gaze on Phoebe's face. "Aren't I fortunate Damian has seen fit to overlook that fact?"

Phoebe looked away and Nina settled herself in her
seat. The other girls had rehearsed lines for the pageant. Nina wondered why she had accepted the part.
"What do I say?"

"Just wave and smile. When the winner asks, say not to kill the loser."

"What? What do you mean, *'kill?'* "

Phoebe rolled her eyes. "It's for show." She turned to a friend. "No one ever accused a rebel of being overly bright."

Nina's fists clenched, but she retained her composure. "True, but when we say *'kill,'* we mean it."

The Knights of the Blended Rose appeared, taking their places in front of the ladies. They were attired in red and white silk, followed by pages with lances. Their herald stepped forward amidst the blaring of trumpets.

"Mark the challenge, gentlemen! Whosoever doubteth the perfection of our Ladies, let him ride forth!"

The Knights of the Burning Mountain galloped forward to meet the challenge. The gauntlet was thrown in and picked up, the battle began. Nina recognized Gambrinus before Damian.

A valet handed him a spear, but Nina was surprised at the easy way he readied it. He turned toward her, and for a moment they faced each other. A strange foreboding swept through her.

We have been here before. He might die, and it's my fault.

Phoebe prodded Nina's arm. "What's the matter with you? You're supposed to stand and wave with the rest of us.

Nina rose hurriedly to her feet and adjusted her turban. Damian met his opponent, then readied Gambrinus for the charge. As if he fought this way all his life, he drove Gambrinus toward his floundering enemy, then knocked the stricken Knight of the Blended Rose from his horse.

With surprising intensity, Damian leapt down to engage in a mock swordfight. "What's he doing?" gasped Phoebe. "Captain Pickney's supposed to win!"

Damian parried a forceful blow and knocked Roger

Pickney to the ground. For a frightening moment, Nina thought he might really kill the other officer.

"Damian, no . . ."

"They're not really fighting," Phoebe informed her coldly. "And Captain Knox is supposed to lose."

With that, Damian fell to the ground, and Roger Pickney leapt up, standing over him in doubtful triumph. Nina sat back and allowed air to fill her lungs again.

"To the death?" cried the Knight Pickney.

Phoebe fanned herself with delicate grace. "Please, press the matter no further."

Nina clenched her fist and waved it at Pickney. "Don't you dare!"

Damian laughed from his death pose, then stood up. Other jousters followed, though none with the dramatic realism given by Damian and Roger Pickney. Nina learned to wave at the proper times, but by the end, she was distinctly bored.

"Now what?" she asked as the last jouster was unhorsed.

Phoebe gestured at theatrical arches, designed to honor the departing General Howe. "Now we join the procession beneath those arches."

Nina followed the other girls, hoping Damian would find her soon. They entered Wharton mansion. The walls were painted in fresco, in marble-swirls of pink with flowers and silk of green. Candles burned with medieval glory, and when Nina finally saw Damian, her heart nearly burst with joy.

He was waiting for her, still dressed as a knight. *Why do I feel this way?* As if the whole thing really mattered. Damian saw her. Through the mingling crowd of knights and their ladies, Damian and Nina tried to reach each other.

A strange desperation took hold of her as she pushed her way through the crowd. *Don't take him away from me!*

She shoved an officer too hard, and he turned to her in surprise.

"I'm sorry!"

The officer looked at her doubtfully, then stood back to let her pass.

She couldn't reach Damian. The music started. She fought dancers and spectators to find him. From across the hall, she saw that he did the same.

As the music surged into triumphant glory, the pages blew out the candles at once, and the room fell into darkness. Nina panicked. She ran blind, she bumped into people. An explosion shook the room. She tried to scream, but no sound came.

A huge, sparkling light split the night, and the crowd pressed outside. Nina was pushed along with them, dark figures guided her into the night.

Outside, the cooler air did nothing to calm Nina's terror. Another explosion burst forth into the sky, a thousand lights shattered the blackness. Nina shook with terror, but no one noticed. People laughed and cheered, unmoved by the thunderous roars.

"Nina." Damian touched her shoulder and she whirled around. In the light of the rockets, she saw his face, and the world calmed again. He pulled her gently into his arms and kissed her forehead.

"It's just fireworks, love. Performed by our chief engineer. There's no need for fear."

Nina's heart slammed against her breast as she held tightly to Damian. In his arms, she felt safe again. There was something about that blinding light, being lost . . . She should have known what was happening. The fear came from her nightmares.

None of this is real, she thought as the sky filled with colors. She had seen Damian die and rise again laughing. She had seen him dressed from another time, and felt she knew him more completely then.

She opened her eyes and looked up at the sky. Like giant flowers, the rockets burst in wondrous colors. Nina's fear was gone, almost as if it had never been. Even the loud explosions didn't frighten her.

"It's pretty," she said to Damian. Her terror faded, forgotten as she grasped his hand excitedly. Nina's lips formed a small circle. "Boom," she murmured. "Boom!"

"We mock war," said Damian quietly. "No one is torn asunder by the shells. I fear for us tonight . . ."

Nina turned to him in surprise. The glow of the rocket's glare shone upon his regal face, he stood beside her like a young prince from a time far apart.

"What's wrong, Damian? Don't you like the party?"

"It is extravagant, nothing spared. Where will it lead, I wonder?"

Damian paused, and his gaze went to where John André stood applauding. Nina followed his gaze, she felt his sorrow. John André headed blindly into the future, expecting only joy and pleasure along the way. In the midst of war, it seemed odd.

A huge arch was lit with a sudden explosion of balloons and rockets. Flaming Latin letters appeared. "What does it say?"

Damian sighed. *"Your laurels are immortal."*

"Whose?" asked Nina doubtfully. "Not Howe's?"

"John André's work, I'm afraid. He can be very dramatic."

"Immortal, indeed. Howe is a fool."

"He was a good leader in the field, my dear. He can be lazy, he spends too much time with his mistress, perhaps. But he bested your Washington every time."

"But Howe is leaving, and Washington remains. It is our general whose laurels will be immortal."

* * *

The fireworks ended at midnight amid speeches and a poem read by John André himself. Candles blazed as the company seated itself for a feast. Nina seized a portion of bread and stuffed it into her mouth without preamble. Damian laughed as she closed her eyes and sighed.

"You certainly learned to appreciate food as a result of your urchin-days."

"I did. We learn what we must, I suppose. Which reminds me, how on earth did you learn to joust? You were very impressive."

"I'm not sure. I didn't expect to know anything. It came naturally, surprisingly."

"For Gambrinus as well."

"There was something about looking up and seeing you watching me. I felt as if it happened before, that I had to defend you at any cost. Poor Roger Pickney got knocked off his horse, I'm afraid, in my unexplained fervor."

"I felt that, too! As if you might lose your life, and it would be my fault. As if I had to do something to save you, though I wasn't sure what, exactly. Of course, then you laughed and got up, and I forgot about it."

Damian took Nina's hand and kissed it. He held it awhile, studying at her fingers as a smile formed on his lips.

"What's the matter? Why are you looking at my fingers that way? Are they dirty?"

"No. Quite clean and perfect." Damian kissed her fingertips. "But this one in particular is missing something."

Damian drew a silver ring from his pocket, and Nina's eyes widened. "For me?"

"Those rockets, my love, weren't for Howe's departure. Remember them, because they blazed across the sky for you and me."

Damian slipped the ring on her finger and Nina looked at it closely. "It's beautiful. What is the stone?"

"It's an amethyst. It was my mother's ring. She made me promise I'd find a woman worthy to wear it, as it was a gift from my father."

Nina sniffed as warm tears flooded her eyes. "And you've carried it with you all this time? That's very romantic of you, Damian."

Damian didn't tell her that Cora Forbes had kept the ring for him. It arrived by courier that morning. But now wasn't the time to share this information with Nina.

A ship filled with British reinforcements arrived bound for Philadelphia in June. Damian brought Nina to his house and ordered the servants away. Something troubled him, but Nina was almost afraid to find out what it was.

"Is something wrong, Damian?"

Damian closed the door and locked it. He turned to her, his bright eyes fire. "We're leaving."

"We are? You and I, do you mean?"

"The British are evacuating Philadelphia."

The blood drained from Nina's face. "I've heard rumors . . . Why have you said nothing?"

"You're a rebel, and might be tempted to repeat my knowledge."

Nina couldn't disagree, but her eyes welled with tears. "When?"

"Within two weeks, maybe sooner."

"So soon?"

"We have no time. Clinton could order us out tonight. Make your choice, my love. Will you stay here and await your father's consent? Or will you come with me, as my wife?"

Iolo Evans would be destroyed if she ran away with

an Englishman. *Understand, Papa. I love Damian so. Can you understand? I have to be with him.*

"I will go with you, Damian. Wherever you go."

Damian smiled and held out his hand. Nina took it and kissed his palm. "Tonight, we marry. I've asked John André to stand for me, and Anna will take your side."

Nina nodded, but she couldn't speak. A deep fear crept across her heart, as if they were racing against some unknown evil. An evil that was nearly upon them.

She kissed his neck, then pulled his head down to hers as she sought his mouth. "Don't let them stop us."

"Nothing can stop us."

He returned her kiss, then swept her into his arms. Without words, he carried her into his bedroom, lowering her atop his covers. They stripped away their clothing without preamble, then lay together as if only here were they truly safe.

"I don't want to wait. Not anymore."

He met her plea and rose above her to find her moist and ready for him. Distant thunder raged in her mind as he drove deeply into her welcoming body. Nina clasped her arms tight around his shoulders as her fingers dug into his back.

Damian covered her face with kisses. Her hips rose to meet his, her legs wrapped around his as she held him close against her. She felt the wild passion surge through him, into her, then into blazing light around them as their bodies shook in violent ecstasy.

"Damian, I love you so."

"Nothing can stop us."

Nina rested against him, sated by his love, and she closed her eyes. He was a part of her. Nothing could come between them when their love and trust was certain. She would marry him that very night, then run away with him as he fought a war against her people.

She would be at Damian's side, and that was all she wanted.

Nina fell asleep beside Damian, but a loud rapping at his front door woke them both. He rose, bleary-eyed, and pulled his uniform on, leaving his shirt unbuttoned, while Nina donned her more cumbersome attire.

She heard him go to the door, and she recognized the shock in his voice when he greeted the caller. She pulled on her dress, wrapped her hair into a knot, then went into the hallway to meet Damian's guest.

"Damian! Where is she? Is she here?"

Nina came into the sitting room and saw a very tall, slender boy standing with Damian. He had blond hair that fell recklessly about his forehead despite its tie. His face was almost angelic, with an innocent, eager expression of wonder.

The boy saw Nina enter and his face lit. He glanced at Damian and Damian nodded. The sweet-faced boy stepped toward her as Nina watched him doubtfully.

"Emma . . ."

Nina's heart stopped, then beat in a creeping madness. "That is not my name." Her gaze shifted to Damian in disbelief. *It can't be . . .*

The boy looked to Damian, and Damian went to Nina's side. "Nina, I'd like you to meet Ethan Forbes." He paused. "Your brother."

Nina didn't move. Her world went black, she was blind in the shock of what he had done to her. She had no control over anything as her blood ran cold.

"I have no brother."

"You do, Nina." Damian took her hand. "Cora Forbes is . . ."

Nina jerked her hand from his. "You knew!" Her

voice shook, wrought with a flood of emotion. "You've known all along!"

"Columbine O'Grady told me your real name," said Damian. "Nina, you needn't fear. Iolo Evans can do nothing to you now. You're safe. I've written to your mother and Ian. They're waiting for you now in New York."

"Better than that," chimed in Ethan. "They're on their way here, Emma. They couldn't wait to see you."

It was worse than death, worse than war. Nina swayed, her entire being shaken to the core by his betrayal. She felt sick, sure she would vomit, but her rage prevented it. All the darkness surrounding her seeped inward and became part of her.

Nina shook violently, and Damian reached to comfort her. "This must be a shock . . ." She yanked away from him.

"They will not come here! They will not find me. Oh, what have I done?" Nina clutched her stomach. "Curse you! What have you made me do?"

Damian stood before her in regal perfection, more handsome and gentler than any man had ever been. He wrapped her in desire, to betray her when she trusted him. Nina backed away from him. She turned to Ethan.

"I don't know who you are, but you're not my brother, sir." Seeing his stricken face, Nina's heart softened despite her anguish. "This is not your fault, I know. But I am not your sister."

"Nina." Damian tried to go to her, but she backed toward the door. She tugged violently at his ring. "Nina, no . . ."

She threw it at him. It clattered at his feet and rolled towards his bedroom door. Frightened by the noise, Melody jumped from her chair and followed the ring into the bedroom.

"I will not be your wife! I'll not follow you when you lead me to that woman. She is not my mother. My mother is dead."

"Cora Talmadge is your mother. Nina, she believed you were dead. They searched for you for years."

Nina's abrupt laugh cut his words short. "Is that what she told you? Or what you'd have me believe? You had no right, Captain. You would seize me by the bonds of marriage to return me to her, but I will not go. You spoke too soon. I will never be caught by you now."

"Nina, please listen . . ."

She gripped the door, opening it as he moved toward her. "In a thousand years, you will not find me. Go with your army, tell her I *am* dead! You yourself have killed me."

Nina whirled and raced through the door. Damian leapt after her, Ethan close behind him. Ethan's horse stood tied by the walk, and Nina seized the reins, scrambling onto its back before Damian reached her.

"Nina, wait!"

She kicked the horse's sides, and it shot away, galloping heedless down the street. She saw nothing through her tears.

Ethan's horse was found grazing loose on the common. A week passed, and still Damian found no sign of Nina. Beecher's barn was empty, untouched. It was raining, hard, and Damian sat atop Gambrinus, his head bowed as Ethan mounted and rode up beside him.

"Where could she be?" he asked, but Damian just shook his head. "Those children, do you think they knew and just wouldn't tell us?" Ethan glanced irritably back to the group of tattered youths, glaring at the smug-faced leader.

"I doubt it," replied Damian. "We offered them enough money to make them forget any loyalty."

"True. What now?"

"I will find her." But Damian's voice lacked the conviction it held earlier. Nina knew Philadelphia too well. And if she didn't want to be found . . .

"Damian, we're leaving tonight. We're nearly out of time."

"We'll find her."

Damian urged Gambrinus onward despite the driving rain. His horse tucked his head down, shielding vulnerable eyes from the downpour.

"What happened?"

"Be damned if I know. Iolo Evans can't be much of a father, but he certainly filled her head with horror stories about Ian."

"What about Mother? Damian, this will kill her. To learn Emma . . . Nina is alive, then lose her again."

"We haven't lost her."

Nina would come to her senses. She loved him, she couldn't forget that. When she calmed, she would return to him. The cord that bound them was too strong to be severed this way.

Blackness. Nina was running, this time. No one was carrying her now. She was alone. A thick blanket of smoke blocked her way, filled her lungs with molten agony, but she kept running. A huge shape emerged before her, giant and strong.

It was a mountain, the mountain for which she was bound. But as she neared, she saw the summit cloaked in red and orange: the mountain was on fire.

PART TWO
Iolo

FIVE

Tappan, September, 1780

"Arnold's turned traitor!"

Jeremiah O'Grady startled and rose to his feet as his commander charged into the room. For his size, Colonel Iolo Evans made an astonishing racket.

"Surely not!"

Iolo Evans slammed his gloves onto the thick wooden table and threw his hat across the room. "He has, Major," groaned the little Welshman. "All set, he was, to turn West Point over to the bastards."

Iolo never referred to the English by name. He called them "the bastards," even when speaking to higher-ranking officers. Even when speaking to George Washington himself. Only the past military successes of the gritty Welshman excused him from chastisement over languaging.

Perhaps, thought Jeremiah, it was the eccentric Welsh accent that saved him. "How? Why?"

Iolo sat down, his head in his hands. "Followed him north through Maine into Canada, I did, in the glory years. He could fight, could Arnold. We trusted him like damned-fool children!"

Jeremiah positioned himself by the colonel's chair. "Why would Benedict Arnold betray us?"

"Money, of course," replied Iolo. "Had to keep his young Tory wife in style, didn't he?"

"So that's why he wanted command of West Point. I wondered why he'd left Philadelphia."

"Ha! Bastard turned down a field commission. Washington was surprised at that, I remember. But he trusted Arnold. We all did."

"So he's been caught?"

"Hell's bells, no! Caught some bastard calling himself John Anderson. An officer, as it turns out. Pretending to be one of our spies, they tell me. All done up in civilian clothes, caught trying to get up to White Plains, he was."

"In civilian clothes?"

"Aye, we'll hang the bastard for that error, we will."

Jeremiah felt less pleasure at the grim prospect. "Strange that an English officer wouldn't have the sense to keep his uniform about. Had he left Arnold wearing his coat, or with a flag of truce, he'd be back in England free and clear."

"Tom fools, they are, O'Grady. But they say Arnold insisted the boy leave his uniform behind."

Jeremiah grimaced. "He betrays all, on both sides."

"Gives me some satisfaction, that." Iolo seated himself at his desk, still muttering.

Jeremiah felt pity for the unfortunate Englishman, whatever side he aided. Benedict Arnold meant little to Jeremiah. He was a pompous leader, ambitious, and now revealed as a ruthless traitor. Let him hang. But justice wouldn't be served by destroying his pawn.

"What am I supposed to do with 'em?"

Iolo Evans was irate. Again. Jeremiah O'Grady seemed unaffected by his wrath. "I don't know, Colonel. The British requested this major speak for the spy.

They've got a ship out in the Hudson, waiting on news. Washington asks, since we're the closest command, that he be housed with us. Here."

"Damnation! Don't want a bastard here, not with my Nina about."

Nina stared out the window. "I don't mind, Papa. He's coming to defend the spy. We won't see him often."

"Hell's bells, we won't!" Iolo reread his order. "We're to feed him, treat him well." No doubt the specificity of the order came from Washington's understanding of Iolo Evans's hostile politics.

Jeremiah cleared his throat. "I've taken the liberty of arranging the back area for our guests."

"Damnation! No bastard officer is staying in this house," shouted Iolo. "You put him in that hovel out back."

Nina straightened the folds of her skirt as she sat, then took a sip of tea as Iolo fumed.

"That's hardly fit for habitation," Jeremiah reminded Iolo, but the Welshman smiled with devious pleasure. "I'll fix it up."

"Don't understand it," muttered Iolo. "Why should we give a ha'penny about respecting the likes of them?"

"It doesn't matter, Papa."

Iolo glared. "What about guards?"

"No guards, I'm afraid, sir. That was deemed disrespectful and inflammatory."

"Curse it all to bloody hell! Well, see to it, Major. See to it."

Jeremiah nodded, then seized the opportunity to vacate his commander's room. He returned accompanied by a wide-eyed courier. "The identity of the English spy has been discovered."

The messenger nodded eagerly. "Have indeed, Colonel! And wait 'til you hear!"

"Wait?" boomed Iolo in an explosive voice. "I don't have to wait, Master Zebulon!"

Zebulon jumped, and Jeremiah O'Grady grinned. "Speak."

"Well, Colonel . . . It seems this spy is none other than Clinton's aide de camp, the adjutant general, John André."

Nina turned to the messenger. "John André?"

"Yes, Miss. Posing as John Anderson, he was."

Nina's gaze went to her lap. Iolo Evans chuckled to himself, but Jeremiah's attention was on Nina. "Did you know him, Nina?"

Nina lifted her chin. "I met him during the British occupation in Philadelphia. He was not . . . unkind."

"So I've heard," said Jeremiah. "In fact, even his guards are developing attachments to the young fellow. He sits, writing poetry, drawing . . . Endearing himself to all."

"Have you seen him?" asked Nina.

Jeremiah nodded. "I have. Seems a good sort. It's a shame to hang him."

"Christ Almighty, Major!" Iolo Evans stood up and marched back and forth across the floor. "I don't care about that bastard's thin neck!"

"Papa, John André was a gentle person. I liked him."

"Hell's bells! What are you meaning, girl? 'Liked him,' indeed."

Zebulon peeked in from the front hall. "They're here, Colonel."

"Who?" growled Iolo.

"The English, sir," replied the aide. "The one speaking for the spy."

"Damnation. You go, O'Grady," Iolo ordered. "Send the bastard in here."

Nina watched Jeremiah go to the front door to greet their guests. She hesitated, then followed him outside.

It was her place to greet her father's guests, to soften the effect of his temper.

An American coach stopped in the road, but the riding horse tied to the back was British. Nina stood on the porch, shading her eyes against the sun. The horse's tail swished idly back and forth as he strained to reach grass. Her pulse took an erratic leap.

A man stepped from the coach, but it was no Englishman. An Indian clothed for wilderness life greeted Jeremiah. Nina's pulse slowed, she relaxed. The Indian waited for someone else. A tall man in full dress uniform stepped down from the coach.

"Major Knox, we are pleased to welcome you."

Nina's breath caught in her throat. *Damian.* He removed his cap. He wore no wig, but his brown hair was tied at his neck. She could run. She could run, and never stop.

It was too late. Damian turned her way. He revealed no surprise to see her. He knew. He held her gaze for a moment, then followed Jeremiah to the house. Nina couldn't move.

Jeremiah saw Nina waiting and turned to Damian. "Major, allow me to present . . ."

"Miss Evans and I have met before."

"I remember you, Major Knox." She felt frozen, buried in ice. "Allow me to introduce Major Jeremiah O'Grady." Nina paused. "My husband."

Damian's face revealed no emotion, but she saw the shock in his blue eyes. "No . . ."

Jeremiah looked at Nina in surprise. "Well, almost. Fiancé, actually. As a matter of fact, this business set our wedding back a bit."

Damian's expression softened, his eyes glinted. A mistake. She shouldn't have lied. "Unfortunate." She heard the teasing note in his voice. "I believe I have something of yours, Miss Evans."

"You have nothing of mine."

Damian turned back to the coach. He whistled, and from within the coach came a dog. A brown and white dog with a full coat and a long nose. Nina stared in disbelief. The dog went to Damian's side, then moved slowly to Nina.

It sniffed, then wagged its tail excitedly. Nina reached to touch its head, then went to her knees. Her eyes clouded with tears as she hugged the dog close. "Melly."

She buried her face in Melody's fur for a moment, but when she looked back at Damian, her expression was cold. "You stole my dog."

Damian's brow rose, but Jeremiah seized his arm and pulled him in the front door. The Indian nodded to Nina as he passed, smiling slightly at her tight frown. He was a beautiful man. Like Damian, he owned an innate nobility, blackened by his knowing expression.

Considering this, Nina determined at once that the Indian wasn't to be trusted, either. Nina watched him follow Damian into the house, but she couldn't move.

Why, oh, why hadn't she married earlier? *I'm practically married. That will have to do.* Three years had gone by, after all. Her dark side was buried deep. She would never surrender to it as her mother had.

I can't let him think I'm affected by his arrival. Nina rose to her feet, and followed by Melody, entered the house to hear her father greet Damian Knox.

"Knox, is it?" Iolo was seated at his desk with Jeremiah. Damian and the Indian stood before him. "Well, what are you doing here?"

"I have come to persuade General Washington to spare Major André."

Iolo snorted. "Mighty fine chance, that! Caught fair, he was. But you give us Arnold, and André goes free."

"I am advised this request is impossible," replied

Damian. "But there must be other arrangements, short of hanging an officer all consider worthy."

Nina listened from the doorway. She couldn't help but agree. Killing John André would serve no purpose.

"Who's the Indian?" asked Iolo.

"My aide, Black Hawk," replied Damian. Black Hawk said nothing. Nina peeked in the door.

Iolo studied Black Hawk intently. "You are Onondaga?"

"I am," replied Black Hawk.

Black Hawk. Nina's memory returned against her will to Philadelphia.

It couldn't be the same. Anna and her mother fled Philadelphia for New York when the British evacuated. She was probably married to Philip Compton and living in England by now.

"So you think you can convince Washington to let this André get off Scot free, do you? Fancy that."

"There must be possibilities," said Damian. "But first, I must see him. Where is he kept?"

"Major André is at Mable's Tavern, under guard," said Jeremiah. "He's to be interrogated by the board under Nathanael Greene at the Tappan church soon. The question remains whether he knew he was within American lines, and why he was in disguise."

"I understand those circumstances, yes."

Iolo Evans rose from his seat. "Do what you must, Knox. Don't hold out much hope, though. It's wasted." Iolo turned to Jeremiah. "You take him, Major. See he doesn't stay too long."

Nina moved away from the door and hurried to her room. She didn't want to see Damian again. She heard him outside with Jeremiah, and despite herself, she positioned herself at a window to overhear their conversation.

"Do I remember correctly that Sean O'Grady was your brother?" asked Damian.

"He was, yes," replied Jeremiah.

"I'm sorry for your loss."

"There's no need, Major Knox. Sean was a brave lad. But war takes a high toll, doesn't it? We fight on opposite sides, but let us not be enemies. Sean deserved life. But your John André deserves to live, as well. Enough die in our battles. The cold, deliberate hanging of a good man should be prevented."

Jeremiah O'Grady made it difficult to dislike him. Unfortunately, the same could be said of Damian Knox.

"Have you seen her, Damian?" John André leaned forward in his seat.

"What are you talking about, John?"

André sighed in exasperation. "For God's sake, Damian, why do you think I requested you here? Your Nina."

Damian hesitated. She was more beautiful now than he remembered. Her girlishness had faded into a woman's lush, intoxicating allure. And she belonged to another man . . .

"John, I'm here to save your neck. Not for anything personal."

"I met her fiancé," continued André. "Nice enough chap, I thought."

Damian frowned. Jeremiah O'Grady was friendly. Neither boastful nor weak, not ingratiating nor abrasive. The kind of man a woman might appreciate. "Could we return to the subject of your life?"

"There's no point. I meet with their board in a day or so. I either convince them, or I don't. Clinton won't turn over Arnold, and that's what they're after."

"Maybe not. But surely we can persuade Washington to take something less than your life."

"Have you ever thought about it, Damian? Death?"

"We're in a war, John. Of course, I've thought about it."

"Naturally. You've been on the fighting end of things, haven't you? It was exciting though, getting through to Arnold. Good thing I endeared myself to his wife."

"His wife?"

"Peggy Shippen. You remember, Damian."

"I remember she fancied you."

"She did, at that. She still carries a lock of my hair," he added with pride. "The lovely Mrs. Arnold wrote to me when her husband decided to realign with his Sovereign."

"You mean when his wife convinced him money was to be had for turning traitor."

"Cynical, Damian, but probably true. Peggy thought little of the rebels. Though her new husband had a high ranking, he didn't seem elegant, I suppose."

"Where is she now?"

"General Washington has treated her with the utmost respect and tenderness."

Damian rolled his eyes. "The rebels can't be stupid enough to believe her innocent."

"She's a pretty young woman. With a new baby. They don't want to doubt her, Damian. I believe she's safe with her father in Philadelphia."

"And Arnold is protected in New York. While you face death here. Arnold's wife is as guilty as he is."

"It doesn't matter, Damian. I told you, didn't I, to seize the pleasure of the day? For me, that is no longer a likelihood. But for you . . . Damian, when I heard your little rebel was near, I had to do something. Win her back, Damian."

"She intends to marry another man, John. To all appearances, she has forgotten me."

"Ha! I doubt that. She's a strange girl. You know that. Learn the reason for her strangeness, Damian. Then you'll know how to take her back."

John André's cheerful face darkened and his voice lowered. "Love is fleeting, for most. For three years, I've watched you hunt for that girl. You've never looked at another. Please, Damian, don't let her get away this time. If I'm to die, let it be knowing that love, at least, survives."

Nina sat in the library of her father's appropriated house. It was small, but quaint, with overhanging eves reminiscent of the Old World. It had been seized from a Tory family who had fled to England when the Americans took Stony Point from the British.

Nina held a book, but she found it impossible to concentrate on the words. Damian would be back soon. From the kitchen, she smelled the dinner being prepared. Roast pig, with yams and apples. Nina was hungry.

She heard the coach outside. She pulled the curtain back, and saw Damian, Jeremiah, and Black Hawk approach the house. With his light, Irish complexion and reddish-blond hair, Jeremiah seemed a marked contrast to Damian.

Both were handsome, but there was nothing in Jeremiah O'Grady that drove her from her senses. Damian held some mysterious power in his core, a power that blinded women in clouds of heated desire. *No. I will never feel that way again.*

"Back, are they?" Iolo came up behind the sofa and looked out the window. Nina looked back to her book.

"It appears so," she replied.

"Can't believe Washington forced that bastard and his ally on me!"

"They'll be gone soon, Papa." Nina heard the young men enter the house. To her annoyance, they were laughing.

"Thought you'd get us then for sure," Jeremiah said cheerfully. "Escaped by the skin of our teeth that time!"

"It was well done," admitted Damian. "Just when I think we've won, you rise again somewhere else."

"Just in time for supper," added Jeremiah.

Nina and Iolo met them in the dining room. Had it not been for Jeremiah, the meal would have been very strained indeed. A natural diplomat, Jeremiah O'Grady seemed to know when the conversation was becoming strained and artfully directed it elsewhere. Nina silently thanked him for his kindness.

Iolo noticed Melody sitting by Damian's chair. "Where'd you get that dog?"

"He stole her from me," said Nina before thinking better of her declaration. Damian's blue eyes glittered, and the others at the table looked at her awaiting explanation.

"Stole her?" repeated Jeremiah. "Why, that's not the same mongrel pup you had in Philadelphia, is it?"

Nina nodded. Iolo Evans watched her closely. Damian smiled. Even Black Hawk had a particularly knowing look on his stoic face.

"She is, yes," admitted Nina.

Iolo eyed Damian. "How is it that you made off with my daughter's dog?"

"Actually, as I remember it, the puppy was left in my care. I did try to locate your daughter before we abandoned Philadelphia. But after much searching, I was unable to find her. I considered the dog her parting gift."

Nina glared at Damian. *Parting gift, indeed.*

"You've met this man before?" asked Iolo suspiciously.

She drew a deep, calming breath. "I attempted to steal from him, Papa. He caught me. There's nothing more to it."

Damian's brow rose, but he said nothing. Jeremiah watched Nina as she jabbed at a yam. His presence comforted her, as always.

"Stealing, were you, girl?" Iolo didn't seem perturbed. "A theft for a theft. We'll forget about it then, shall we?"

"A good idea." Nina refused to meet Damian's gaze, but she knew he was smiling.

"The *theft*, on both counts, is forgotten."

"Major Knox."

Damian stood alone in the library. His heart quickened when he heard Nina's voice. He turned, but a wave of disappointment flooded him when he saw her aloof expression.

"Miss Evans."

"May I speak with you a moment? Privately."

"Of course."

Nina checked the hallway, then closed the door behind her. Damian noticed that her hair was brushed nearly straight and tied in a tight knot behind her head.

"What is it, Nina?"

"The matter of our past relationship needs to be discussed."

"If you wish."

"I do." Nina hesitated. "It would be a great comfort to me if I could be assured the matter would remain, well . . ."

"Secret?"

Nina nodded. "Yes."

"You have my word."

"You'll say nothing to Jeremiah or my father?"

"Of course not." Damian frowned. This wasn't what he planned between them.

"I must also ask you to keep the matter of Cora Forbes from my father. He mustn't know she was in New York."

"She still is."

"Have I your word?"

"You do."

"Thank you." Nina turned to leave.

Damian fought his need to grab her, to pull her close and remind her of the passion that once enthralled them. "Nina."

She didn't look back. "There's nothing more to say."

"Not for you, maybe. But there is something I must know."

"What?"

Damian moved closer, standing behind her. He didn't touch her. "Do you love him?"

She glanced back, but she didn't look at him. "Jeremiah?"

"Yes, of course, Jeremiah. Who else?"

Nina turned around, and her eyes gleamed with a bitter light. "He is my friend. I trust him. But love? Love destroys everything, Major. It boils up from within, blackening every decent impulse. I will never love again."

"So that's where your passion has gone. It has transformed into denial."

Her chin firmed. "It crumbled before reality."

"You have a twisted sense of the sweetest emotion."

"At least I didn't use 'the sweetest emotion' to trick you!"

"I didn't trick you, woman."

Her brow angled. "Why didn't you tell me you knew about me? Did it slip your mind, Captain?"

Damian resisted growing irritation. " 'Major.' And no, it didn't slip my mind. At first, I couldn't believe it was true, then, later . . ."

Nina rolled her eyes. "You probably hunted me down. I trust she paid you well for the information."

His teeth ground together. She was not only more beautiful, but more infuriating. "No one knew you were alive, Nina. I was told about you when I was a child. I remember hearing Cora . . ."

Nina's anger flamed and she stepped toward him, her fist clenched. "Never speak of her in my presence again."

"Why does it bother you?"

"That's none of your business!"

"Very well. So you'll cut away part of yourself, you'll cut out your heart if you have to. For what? For Iolo Evans?"

"Don't you dare . . . Don't you dare say a word about my father."

"Why do you protect him? He's not worth it, Nina."

"I won't have my father hurt again."

"Nina, he has destroyed everything in his path. He sent Ian Forbes to the Onondaga who killed my father."

"It was Ian Forbes who seduced my cheap mother and she who disgraced my father. If your father died for him, then he died for nothing!"

"There are two sides to everything, Nina. You've heard one. I doubt very much it would agree with reality."

Nina turned away again and went to the door. "You have no questions, no need to hear of those who once shared your life?"

"There's nothing I need to know."

"No? You care nothing for me. John André faces death by your violent leaders, and that doesn't trouble you."

Nina said nothing.

"What about Anna Fairchild?"

"Anna? I assume she married Lieutenant Compton."

"Philip Compton was killed at the Battle of Monmouth shortly after we left Philadelphia."

Nina glanced back at him. "What happened to Anna?"

"She and her mother are in New York City."

"What about that boy, the one you called my brother?"

"Ethan has joined my company in New York."

She hesitated. "He seemed very young."

"He was fifteen. He is eighteen now. Yes, he is young. But he has no fear."

"He should go home."

Damian smiled. "Like his sister."

"I am not his sister." Nina's chin lifted. "The past doesn't matter to me now, *Major.* I have forgotten that year."

"Have you?"

"Yes. I'm to marry Jeremiah. He is a good man, and will be a good husband."

"I don't doubt he's a good man. I doubt that he's the right man for you. I doubt that he knows you for what you really are."

"And what am I?"

"A woman of passion. A woman who wants far more from a man than friendship."

"You don't know me, Major. You knew only my weakest self, the daughter of a whore. I am not that person anymore. You will never see that again."

Nina spun around and rushed from the room. Damian stood alone, but a smile touched his lips. The ice around her was cracking, the fiery temptress within peeked through to assail him.

You are mine. When I leave this place, John André will have his life, and I will have you. Damian looked out the window as the stars kindled their singular fate in the sky. He would make the future as he wanted it. Nothing, no one, would stand in his way now.

Damian and Black Hawk were given guest quarters near the house. Damian looked out of the shack's dirty window, up at the bedroom windows in Iolo's house. Nina passed by the first window. She peeked out, saw him, and snapped the curtains together. She blew out her candle, and disappeared to his sight.

Damian stared up at Nina's darkened window, then sighed heavily. "Am I wrong?"

"Do you expect an answer? Would it matter?"

"It might."

"You may be wrong. You listen to the voice of passion."

Damian frowned. "O'Grady seems a good man. She might be better off with him."

"She might. She sits beside him in comfort."

Damian said nothing.

"If you convince her, it is with passion. You take her where she doesn't want to go."

"She doesn't know what she wants. She's wrong to deny her own mother."

"Perhaps. We know little of those years."

"I know Ian Forbes isn't the monster Nina believes."

"What forces do you stir in motion if you take her? Those from the past mix with the future. The ending is not peaceful."

"If I leave her with Jeremiah, there will be no conflict."

"In yourself only."

Damian shook his head. "I can't do it. I can't walk away from her now."

"Because you claim her. She owns your heart."

"It's not that I can't stand to think of her with another man. Not a good man, anyway. Nina doesn't love Jeremiah O'Grady."

"What cost is passion if it threatens the woman you love?"

Damian fell silent and Black Hawk prepared a bed for himself on the floor. "What's wrong with the bed?" asked Damian. "Ah. You prefer sleeping close to the earth."

Black Hawk's brow arched and he shook his dark head. "Bugs." He pointed to the sloping ceiling above the bed. Damian laughed when he saw a small spider dangling from a web.

Damian turned his attention back to the main house. "He isn't what I expected, this Iolo Evans."

Black Hawk lay down on his pallet, hands folded behind his head. "No? Why is that?"

"He's volatile, I saw that. But I saw nothing particularly cruel or evil in him." Damian paused. "I believed he would know my name, remember my father. But there was nothing save dislike for my uniform."

"You expect evil snapping in his eyes?"

"Nothing that obvious. But surely his actions have left some mark on his character."

"You expect madness. Or madness in disguise. The Welshman blusters and curses, he is nothing dangerous. You miss the truth."

"What truth is that?"

"The most dangerous truth of all—Iolo Evans believes he's right."

"What of it? Don't we all?

"Do you doubt, Damian? You wonder if you are wrong to win back your woman. Do you think the Welshman questions?"

"Are you calling staunchness of will evil?"

"The only evil, my friend. Such a man never calls himself wrong. He kills, destroys. He does not see the blood on his hands. I see that in your people. You march in without thinking of what is destroyed."

"Are you saying we shouldn't have come to this land? Exploration is human nature."

"I say nothing. Only that if they questioned the rightness of their actions along the way, our common history might be less violent."

Damian shook out his sheets while Black Hawk watched the floor suspiciously for spiders. "He who is one with the earth is less so with the insect realm."

"Their realm walks alongside mine. Not across."

Damian lay down on his bed, staring at the cracked beams on the ceiling. "She is devoted to him. I was sure Iolo Evans had been a cruel father. He abandoned her in Philadelphia, after all. But to all appearances, he is good to her."

Black Hawk arched his brow. "She has never crossed him."

John André sat despondently in his room. Drawings were scattered across his desk—of himself, mainly. Damian picked up one of the pictures.

"You look wistful in this one. Are the Americans treating you well?"

André sighed. "They are most kind in their attentions, yes. I've been questioned daily. One moment, I think the future is bright, the next . . . There is no future."

"I've spoken with Alexander Hamilton and Major Tallmadge," said Damian. "They feel your death would serve no purpose. From what I've gathered, few desire an execution."

"Arnold has written a letter accepting all blame," said André. "Easy enough, safe with Clinton."

"Well he should. To save his own cursed hide, he forced you into the role of spy. Why did you listen, John?"

John André shrugged. "I had little choice. Benedict Arnold is a man of strong will. He insisted I remove all sign of commission."

"I see little chance that Clinton will trade Arnold for you, however much he wants to."

"No."

"Our only hope is that you'll be accepted as a prisoner of war rather than a spy. I've arranged meetings with members of their board; in particular, their General Knox with whom I apparently share a common ancestry. Nathanael Greene may listen, and I had some success in a brief introduction with Lafayette."

"The Frenchman seems a good soul," said André. "My own Gallic ancestry aside."

Damian leaned closer to André, his voice lowered. "There is some question as to whether you arrived to Arnold beneath a flag of truce. Were that so . . ."

"It isn't."

"Arnold insists it is, supported by Clinton."

John André shook his head. "I'm afraid they've issued an untruth. I intended to appear as a British officer, as Clinton ordered. That was thwarted by Arnold."

"It may be an untruth, John. But it could save your life."

John André's eyes widened. "That wouldn't make it right."

Damian sat in Iolo Evans library, seething in frustration, as Black Hawk waited. "They won't listen. Oh, they sit attentively, professing every concern for Major André's welfare. Then, just when I think there's a ray of hope, they insist upon Arnold's exchange."

"Washington," said Black Hawk.

"Apparently Arnold's betrayal has set him in an evil mood. If he can't have Arnold's blood, he'll take André's."

"He believes he is right," said Black Hawk. "He is betrayed by one he trusted. He is made a fool. He will not let André go free."

"I'm not asking that he be freed. Just kept alive. Let him be kept in prison 'til the war's end. His death serves no purpose."

"His death blackens Benedict Arnold. If the English win or lose, they do not forgive Arnold for the noble André. George Washington knows this."

Damian's heart labored. The forces against him were strong. He spent the day fighting unyielding opposition. Night approached, and no ground was gained.

"Clinton doesn't know. He believes they'll spare John."

"He is mistaken."

"I fear you're right, my friend. Clinton thinks the Americans will find a way to save face and keep André alive."

Black Hawk shook his head. Damian rose from his chair. "He must be warned, convinced. If I leave here now, I'll miss any opportunity that might arise to persuade the Americans."

"I'll go," said Black Hawk. "I may not reach Clinton before they kill your friend."

"Take this letter. Use whatever influence you've got. Make him understand, they will kill John André. Take my horse, Black Hawk."

"There's no need. By the paths I will take, no horse is swifter." Black Hawk studied Damian for a moment. "You need his speed."

"Why? I have a coach. I'm here under a flag of truce."

"Ah, but you leave with something unexpected."
Black Hawk paused. "Where do I meet you, if you fail?"

"I'll go to New York."

"You won't go the way we came. You never reach ship.
Head west. I am there."

"West?"

"I'll find you."

Damian said little during dinner, but Nina felt his gaze
on her constantly. Jeremiah didn't seem to notice, nor
did Iolo.

"How fares Major André?" asked Jeremiah.

"Well enough," replied Damian.

Nina glanced up at him. "Have you found a way to
save him?"

Iolo Evans snorted. "Save him? Sounds to me as if
André walked into a death trap. Where's the Onondaga?"

"Black Hawk is delivering a message for me."

"Better be a good one." Iolo rose from the table.
"Von Steuben has called a meeting in Tappan for tonight. Major O'Grady, if you'll see to things here."

Jeremiah rose in salute and Iolo left. Nina felt uncomfortable alone with Jeremiah and Damian. The servants cleared the table, and Nina followed Jeremiah
into the sitting room.

"You'll stay for tea, won't you?"

Jeremiah took her hand and kissed it. "I wish I could,
Nina. I am expected with my company tonight."

Nina bit her lip. Damian stood by the fireplace, his
arm braced on the mantel. She glanced toward him as
Jeremiah put on his hat.

"I'll walk you to your coach."

Nina felt hot and unsteady as she left Damian alone.

She went out onto the porch with Jeremiah, and waited with him as his coach was brought around.

"Will we really execute Major André?"

"I can see no way around it, Nina. It's a sad fact that while few desire it, such a man may still be hanged. We deny vengeance, but it colors the decisions made today."

Jeremiah looked toward the house behind him. "Major Knox has been persuasive. Despite pretenses, our leaders listen to the word of an English nobleman. But it's not enough. As soon as he leaves, their hearts waver. And Washington is adamant. Without Arnold's return, André dies."

"His temper will cool."

"If there was more time, maybe," said Jeremiah. "But André may be dead ere we see other possibilities."

The coach was brought to the front of the house, and Nina followed Jeremiah to the door. She felt Damian watching them.

Jeremiah started to get into his coach. "Jeremiah . . ." He turned back.

"What is it, Nina?"

"I thought . . . I mean, I wondered . . . Would you kiss me good-night?" It was a strange request between them, one she never made before. Jeremiah had kissed her cheek, her hand, but even after he proposed to her, he never kissed her mouth.

Jeremiah's gaze cast to the house where Damian Knox waited. "If you wish." An enigmatic smile crossed his face, but he bent and gently touched his mouth to hers.

Nina touched his shoulder in hopes the kiss would appear common. Jeremiah took her hand.

"Good night, Nina. Sleep well."

Jeremiah left her, and Nina drew herself together to face Damian. As she suspected, he was waiting near the door when she entered. She passed by him without looking.

"Not much of a kiss."

Nina whirled and faced him in astonished fury. "You were spying on me! Eavesdropping!"

"Nothing of the kind, my dear. I merely happened by the window at an appropriate moment."

Nina's eyes narrowed into slits of fury. "For your information, Major Knox, it's none of your concern what I do with my future husband." She paused as her blood seethed in anger. "And it was a very good kiss."

She brushed by him, but Damian caught her arm and pulled her back to him. "No, Nina. That wasn't a kiss." Damian drew her close, his strong hand firm on her arm as she resisted. "This is a kiss."

Nina tried to pull away, but Damian held her tight. His mouth descended upon hers, demanding her response as his arms surrounded her. Nina struggled, but his lips played against hers, first insistent, then gentle.

Damian's body molded to hers, and despite herself, Nina pressed closer. She felt his tongue against her lips, teasing her into accepting him, she felt the power of his manhood against her body.

She gripped his shirt and her knees went weak as Damian deepened the kiss. His tongue slid over hers, tasting her sweetly, teasing her with the passion they once shared. The world seemed to spin around them. The world had been righted, everything had been in order. Until Damian . . .

With a final effort, Nina pushed away from him. Damian was smiling. The final indignity. Nina lifted her hand to slap him, but Damian caught her arm.

"I've had enough rebuttals from your side today. Though none as pleasurable as this."

Nina fumed. "Don't you dare do that again!"

He bowed low. "We'll forget it ever happened. You will forget that my desire surges like fire across dried fields. And I will forget how your perfect breasts . . ."

Nina gasped. "Stop that!"

"Forgive me, my sweet. Feeling the flash of your ardor has sent me beyond decency."

Nina's eyes narrowed and a frown tightened her face. "I felt nothing."

"I see. It was my imagination then." His knowing gaze centered on her breasts.

Her traitorous body had assumed a state of arousal. Her nipples were taut and firm, pressed eagerly against her bodice. Nina blushed furiously.

"That is what a real kiss is supposed to do," said Damian.

Nina wanted to strike him. He wouldn't let her. She wished she had a gun.

"Fortunately for me, you're unarmed this time." He laughed, then went to the door. "Good night, my darling."

Nina watched him leave. She wanted to say something to cut him to the quick. She stared at the door, but no parting words came. Her heart slammed against her rib cage. She felt the hot blood in her cheeks, filling her body with shame.

I have to avoid him. Nina trudged up the stairs to her room. *I will avoid him.* She peeked out her window and saw the light in Damian's shack. She saw the silhouette of his tall, lean body. Bad enough to have shameful dreams of him, now her waking self betrayed the curse of her desire.

They met at breakfast. Nina was ready. Her chin was high, she was cold and distant. She met his gaze when he walked in, addressed him politely. It made no difference. Damian's mouth curved knowingly.

She remembered every dream that tormented her through the long night. She remembered the feel of him inside her, she remembered his eyes dark with desire, his face as ecstasy seized him. She remembered his deep, penetrating thrusts.

"Did you sleep well, girl?" asked Iolo Evans as he scrutinized her strained face.

"Perfectly, yes, Papa."

Damian grinned at her deceit.

Iolo eyed her uneaten plate. "Eating, are you? Too skinny, you are."

"I recall no lack of appetite in your daughter," put in Damian.

Nina glared at him. "I stole food."

"Didn't Columbine feed you? I told the old crow to look after you."

"She did, naturally." She felt Damian watching her, but she didn't look at him. "But during the winter, food was hard to acquire."

"You came through it right enough." Iolo reached to pat Nina's hand. "That's my girl. Takes more than one army to hold her down."

Damian met her quick gaze. "That much is certain."

Iolo Evans went to oversee his regiment, leaving Nina once again alone with Damian. He followed her into the library. "Don't you have somewhere to go?"

"Nothing occupies my time at the moment. Clinton has sent a commission to meet with Washington. I will join them later today to present a different interpretation of André's involvement with Benedict Arnold."

Nina seized a book and pretended to scan the index. "Shouldn't you be preparing?"

"Should I?"

She jabbed the book back into its slot and took another. "It would seem wise."

"Our two armies are fencing, my dear. We all know

what happened. Are they willing to find a punishment short of hanging to save a good man's life? That is up to Washington."

Nina replaced the book. "He wants Benedict Arnold. Why don't you give him back?"

"I might. But I don't have the weight of England's hopes on my shoulders."

"You have John André's life." Damian's face darkened and Nina felt a surge of pity. "Washington has delayed the execution once already. Maybe he will again."

Damian moved closer and touched her cheek. He touched her hair and freed a wayward curl. Nina shoved the curl back into its binding and Damian sighed. "I seem to have less power than I imagined to bring about desired endings."

Nina looked away to hide her emotion, and Damian seated himself in a high-backed chair. "Where is Black Hawk? Why did you send him away?"

"I felt it necessary to convince Clinton that action must be taken swiftly if André is to be spared. Black Hawk will reach someone who has influence with the general."

"Who?"

Damian looked up at her. "Ian Forbes."

Nina turned her back to Damian, refusing to hear further of the man who destroyed her life. "Who is Black Hawk, anyway? How do you know him?"

"He's an Iroquois, son of the Onondaga chief. He was taken prisoner by the Sauk as a boy and called Black Hawk. His Onondaga name is thoroughly unpronounceable. He was scouting for us, and happened to be in New York at the height of my degradation."

"Degradation? What were you doing?"

"I was a hair's breadth from being beaten to a bloody pulp. Drunk and engaging in insults with a Hessian company, I fear to admit. They were large, angry, and as drunk as I."

"How disgusting," offered Nina, but Damian laughed.

"I'm afraid after I left you in Philadelphia, I entered a particularly disgusting period of my life. Fortunately, I remember little of it. Swimming in drink has a way of clouding one's memory."

"You drank too much? How foul! What happened?"

"I joined the Hessian group for a fine evening at the Harbor Lights Tavern, a seedy establishment closed down weekly for the brawls engaged in by its patrons."

"It sounds awful. Why do people go?"

"The women are friendly. And cheap."

"Do you mean they're ladies of the night?"

" 'Ladies' may not be the best choice of words."

Nina couldn't speak. Picturing Damian with a prostitute made her sick. She thought she might cry. *I have to get out of here. If I should cry in front of him* . . .

"I'm afraid I humiliated myself beyond my usual capacity that night. I engaged the attentions of a young . . . *lady,* shall we say, both amazingly voluptuous and surprisingly eager for attention."

Nina felt sick, but Damian wouldn't stop. Vomiting would be worse than crying. "You're telling me more than I want to know."

"I believe you asked how I know Black Hawk."

"I didn't expect the story to involve a brothel."

"As I was saying, in the company of . . . Marie, I believe, I thought to ease the burdens of life's peculiar misery. Unfortunately for us both, I found myself completely unable to . . ." Nina's face paled and Damian stopped. "Well, let us say Marie was disappointed."

"I don't want to know."

"You already know. Yes, my dear, I'm afraid you were responsible. Drink didn't help, but it was your refined and beautiful image dancing across my brain. Not drink nor Marie nor anything could blot that out."

"How does this involve Black Hawk?"

"I knew, even drunk, that your hold on me wasn't slacking. And it made me angry. So angry I went and started a fight with a Hessian soldier twice my size and accompanied by several others just like him."

"Did they hurt you?" She moved a little closer to him, but Damian just laughed.

"Fortunately, drink has a numbing effect. I have a vague memory of being thrown through a window. It goes rather blank after that, until I opened the eye that wasn't swollen shut and saw a stone-faced Indian looking down at me."

"Black Hawk saved you?"

"He did, though I don't remember it. Six drunken Hessians were no match for him. Especially sober. But it was unnerving to see him at first. I thought I was about to repeat my father's death."

"It was good of him to rescue you, especially since you were in such a loathsome condition. Is that why he's with you now?"

"Mainly."

"This was in New York? Has he seen Anna?"

"Anna Fairchild? No, I don't think so. Why?"

"I think they met once. Maybe not."

"He's never mentioned it, though he's been a scout for several years. They might have met, I suppose. Her father had dealings with the Onondaga, as I recall."

Nina fell silent, and her mind went reluctantly back to the prostitute. "What were you doing in a brothel?"

"What do you think?"

"Never mind, I don't want to know." Nina stopped and went to look out the window. Why had she asked?

Damian rose from his chair and stood behind her. She felt his hands on her shoulders. Nina swallowed hard, fighting tears. She felt the heat of his body and longing filled her heart.

"I was trying to forget you." Nina swallowed again, but her eyes misted with burning tears. "Unsuccessfully, I might add. I found myself babbling to a very confused harlot about the woman I lost. The very picture of a driveling idiot."

Nina's chest rose and fell in quick breaths as she fought a sob. "It doesn't matter. What women you've been with, I mean."

Damian caught her chin in his strong hand and turned her face to his. "There have been no women, Nina. I hunted for you like a man possessed. I sent spies to look for you. After that, I was too drunk. When Black Hawk found me, I realized I was running from something I could never escape. You were inside me."

He waited until her gaze met his. She tried not to look at him. He would see too much. She peeked at him and saw tears in his eyes, too. Her heart ached. "God help me, you still are."

He eased her into his powerful arms. Nina knew he would kiss her and she closed her eyes. She felt his mouth on hers, tender and sweet. Her lips parted beneath his.

"Nina! Where are you?"

Jeremiah O'Grady called from the front hall and Nina lurched away from Damian. Jeremiah entered the room, but he said nothing. Nina couldn't speak as Damian pulled on his jacket and donned his tricorn hat.

"If you'll excuse me, I've got one more chance to convince your superiors that John André is a man worth saving."

Jeremiah sighed. "We know his worth, Major. I wish you well."

Jeremiah touched Nina's shoulder as Damian left. His

eyes were kind and sympathetic. "I'm sorry, Nina. I didn't intend to interrupt you."

Nina swallowed hard. "I'm glad you did." Her voice broke, and Jeremiah drew her gently into his arms. He cradled her head on his shoulder, stroking her hair. "It's not easy, Nina. I know. I know."

SIX

"Perhaps it's better, Damian, to die a brave man than live as a traitor."

"You need do neither, John."

"I've written to Clinton, assuring him my treatment here has been kind and that His Excellency General Washington has offered the most gracious hospitality."

Damian frowned. Seeing his expression, André smiled. "I will be remembered as a good man. Think of my life! How I loved the theater, how my poems touched hearts! Here, Damian, take this portrait."

John André pushed a small drawing into Damian's hands. "Do you recognize her?"

The lips were triangular, peaked at the summit with childlike determination. Tight curls with varying direction swirled about the exquisite face.

Damian took the picture. "It's a good likeness."

"When you leave here, my dear friend, leave with both the likeness and the girl." André paused. "Maybe you should leave now."

"I can't leave. Not until I'm certain your life is spared."

"I've a bad feeling about your departure. If my execution goes forward, Damian, restrain your anger."

Damian hesitated. He hadn't considered himself a

man of quick temper, nor had anger a strong hold over him. "I learned long ago to exercise control."

"Mark my words, you'll have need of restraint. You're behind enemy lines, too, Damian Knox. Should you cross the Americans, especially that little Welshman, your own life might be in danger as well."

"What do you know of Evans?"

"Actually, it was Jeremiah O'Grady who spoke of him. Even his aide doesn't seem to trust the man. Your lovely Nina needs to be removed from his care."

"O'Grady said that?"

"Not in so many words, no. But if you take the girl, I suspect you'll have more to bear from the father than the fiancé. Funny thing, that."

"Evans is all bluster. I have little to fear from him."

"His path is the only one that matters to him," replied John André. "It reminds me of Benedict Arnold. Take care, my friend, for such men care little for those in their wake."

Every effort George Washington made to exchange John André for the treacherous Arnold had been met with icy disdain from the British commanders. Washington's own commanders had grown fond of the young Englishman, and even his guards couldn't speak of his death.

All this seemed certain to spare André's life, yet as Damian sat alone in his run-down quarters, the execution remained set. He rose from a broken Chippendale chair and looked through the window. Nina was brushing her hair, preparing for dinner.

Damian heard Iolo Evans shouting at a servant, and he shook his head. A door slammed, and he heard Jeremiah O'Grady's soft voice in consolation to the chastised slave. It wasn't easy to dislike a man with gentle manner, as the Americans were learning about John André.

Nina was seated at the dining room table when Damian entered. She didn't look up, but she fidgeted nervously. Jeremiah was beside her. He, too, glanced at his agitated fiancée. Damian saw a faint smile touch Jeremiah's lips, though it was quickly removed.

He knows you. Damian wondered if Jeremiah had heard rumors of Nina's involvement with a British officer. If so, Jeremiah O'Grady clearly harbored no ill will.

"Major Knox," said Jeremiah. "I'm afraid I've had to excuse myself from dinner tonight. Please take my seat."

Both Nina and Damian looked at Jeremiah in surprise. Jeremiah gave no sign of understanding their reaction. He turned to Iolo. "After dinner, Colonel, I might entreat you to go over our orders."

Iolo slammed his spoon on the table. "Orders? What orders?"

Jeremiah glanced purposefully at Damian. "Well, sir . . ."

"Can't talk in front of him," agreed Iolo. "Bring it to my study."

"Unfortunately, Colonel, it will be necessary for you to accompany me to the camp."

"Now? That will take all night!" Iolo banged his fist on the table. The silverware clattered against the plates.

"Your tent is readied, for your convenience."

"Hell's bells! What about a coach? I'm not riding out there in the middle of the night."

"It awaits you."

"I can finish dinner, can't I, O'Grady?"

Jeremiah hesitated. "Naturally."

"Then sit down, and let me eat."

Damian sat in the seat beside Nina, and Jeremiah sat

down across from them. The tension between them seemed obvious, but Jeremiah took no notice. Thanks to Jeremiah, however, dinner passed easily.

Jeremiah left with Iolo, and Damian wondered how blind a man could be. He followed Nina into the sitting room. "Your future husband has a fairly careless attitude about the company you keep."

"He trusts me."

Damian's brow rose. "Indeed? But then, kissing doesn't seem to have much appeal for him, does it?"

"As I said before, that is none of your concern."

"True. It would concern me more if kissing was paramount in his brain."

"I'm very tired, Major. If you'll excuse me, I will retire to my room now."

Damian watched her make for the stairs. He waited until she was on the first landing to call her back. "I, too, will retire to my glorious quarters."

Nina nodded and took another step upstairs.

"And there I will await you."

She stopped, frozen in her tracks, then slowly turned around. "You'll *what?*"

"Await you. Our windows face each other, fortunately. I'll leave my lantern on as a reminder."

"You'll do no such thing." Nina stomped down the stairs, and stood in front of Damian with her hands on her hips.

Damian donned his tricorn hat. "I want you, little rebel. I've waited three years to feel you wrapped around me, to bury myself in you and forget all the time apart."

Her pretty mouth gaped, a wider triangle than usual. "You expect me to come to your room?"

"You'll come."

"I will not!"

Damian went to the door. "But I will wait. Good night . . . For now."

Damian left Nina standing in mute astonishment. She shook her head, trying to rid herself of the madness he instilled in her. His room, indeed! Damian was teasing her, that was it. He didn't really expect her.

"Is there anything you'd like before bed, Miss?"

Nina jumped, startled by the servant's soft voice. "No! Thank you. You may retire."

She was shaking. She hurried to her room, but her heart was racing. How dare he suggest such a thing! He had no respect for her moral structure. Naturally. He knew her mother.

She would marry another man. A man with the good sense not to arouse her this way.

Nina began to undress. She ripped her bodice open and buttons flew across the floor. "Hell's bells!" She took off her stays and her petticoats. She cut her finger on the buckle of her shoes.

"Damn you for this," she mumbled as she sucked her finger.

Nina peeked out the window. A lantern glowed in Damian's quarters. She snapped the curtains closed. She turned from the window, pulling her shift over her head. She lay on the bed. She tossed and fidgeted, then got up to look out her window again.

The lantern was still burning. *Reading is a good distraction.* Nina picked up a book of poetry. *Shakespeare. Another Englishman!* She hurled the book across her room. It banged against the wall.

Damian was still waiting. Perhaps he really did expect her. She'd been less than resolute in her resistance to his advances. Nina considered this. She had given him the wrong impression. Naturally, he expected her to succumb.

I must convince him I've forgotten him. Nina dressed again. She put on slippers instead of buckled shoes, and left her corset and petticoats behind. It would only take a minute.

Nina knocked, very softly, but the door opened immediately. Damian seemed taller than usual. Melody came out wagging her tail and Nina patted her head. Damian held the door for her without speaking, but Nina shook her head.

"I'm not staying."

Damian's brow rose, but he glanced up at the house. "Do your servants know that?"

Nina looked back at the house. "It might be misconstrued." She walked past Damian into his room.

"You're not staying? I'd hoped for a longer interlude, but if that's what you want . . ."

Damian began unbuttoning his shirt. Nina gasped. "No! Stop that!"

"No? Then why have you come?"

Nina straightened her back and looked him directly in the eye. "I've come to tell you I'm not coming."

Damian's gaze wandered to the side in confusion. "I see. And now that you're not here?"

He was grinning, and Nina's temper rose. She forced it away. "I felt I should explain. I had feelings for you, once." Damian was so close, she could feel the warmth of his body. "Which might understandably lead you to believe I would be here tonight. Which is quite impossible."

Damian waited. Nina checked his expression, but his handsome face remained impassive.

"However, in three years I have quite forgotten you, Major Knox. I'm almost the wife of someone else."

"Who would be, overjoyed to find you here."

"Jeremiah understands. I told him, you see."

"Told him?"

"When he asked for my hand, I felt I had to. Because Jeremiah is a good man, he deserves an untarnished wife. I felt he should know I'm not pure."

"Pure? So I *tarnished* you?"

"You know what I mean, Damian. I will never be a virgin wife."

"Except to me."

Nina ignored him, but her heart throbbed. He was achingly beautiful standing before her. His shoulders were strong, his body lean and hard.

"So Jeremiah knows about our relationship?"

"He knows I was the mistress of an English officer. And yes, he knows that officer was you."

"You were not my mistress. You were my fiancée. We were lovers, my dear."

Her words hurt him. Nina didn't want to care. "I will leave now." She hurried to the door, half expecting Damian to stop her. He didn't move.

"Do you love me?"

Say no! Nina couldn't speak. Her hands trembled so violently she couldn't close her fingers around the door-knob.

"Do you love me?" This time, he stood close behind her. His lips grazed her neck, then her shoulder. A wild, surging hunger shook Nina's body. He kissed the sensitive lobe of her ear, he took it between his lips, his tongue touched lightly.

Damian lifted her loose hair, kissing the nape of her neck. Nina couldn't move, couldn't begin to order him to stop. His hands ran along her shoulders, down her arms, drawing her back against him.

She felt his stiffened manhood against her bottom. He rubbed against her as his hands cupped her breasts. Nina's insides turned to fiery liquid, her knees went weak and she leaned against him.

"Tell me you don't want me tonight, Nina," he whispered hoarsely in her ear. "Tell me to stop."

Nina couldn't answer. Damian made circles around her breasts with his palms. He teased the rising peaks with his thumbs, brushing back and forth until her breath came in swift gasps.

He deliberately attempted to seduce her. And it was working. He buried his face in her mass of soft, thick hair, finding her neck, kissing her as his body fitted against hers. Her bottom pressed against his throbbing erection.

His hips ground against her, his hands caressed her breasts. Damian unbuttoned her bodice with shaking hands, freeing her full breasts to his touch.

"Do you know how beautiful you are?"

Nina shook her head, but she couldn't speak. Damian didn't let her, anyway. He pulled up her skirt, feeling the satin skin of her thighs, the velvet curls between her legs. His fingers met her moist flesh and Damian groaned. He searched for the tiny peak that would shatter what remained of her resistance.

He knew what he was doing. He did it on purpose, because he knew her body so well. Nina's breath caught when Damian's touch centered on the small, sensitive spot. All the passion contained within him was focused there.

"I can't . . ." Nina's words trailed. She turned her face to his and he kissed her mouth, his tongue sweetly mimicking what would come between them.

Nina's hips twisted against him as he teased her far beyond control. "Are you mine?" he murmured, his voice heavy and thick with passion.

Nina couldn't feel the floor beneath her feet. "Damian . . ."

Damian didn't wait. He sank to his knees before her, drawing her with him. He tore away his clothes, but he couldn't wait for her to remove her dress. He pushed open her bodice, and freed her breasts to his sight.

Nina's head tipped back as his lips grazed across her nipple, first one, then the other. His tongue circled an aching peak, he took it gently between his teeth and teased her until she cried out in wanton pleasure.

Damian eased Nina back on the floor. She clutched at his back, her fingers wound in his brown hair. Damian's kiss lowered across her taut stomach, awakening every nerve as his lips descended across the soft skin. Nina was mindless to anything save pleasure, a willing vessel to all he might do.

Damian pushed her skirt above her waist and tore away her dampened underwear. She felt him kiss her thighs, but when his tongue grazed the spot his fingers adored, she cried out.

"Are you mine?" His tongue laved the tiny bud, circling, teasing.

Her body spasmed as he suckled gently. "Yes," she moaned. "Damian . . ." Nina's voice trailed as he drove her beyond words. She was writhing and squirming beneath his mastery, pleading with him in gasps and moans to end her torment.

Damian needed no encouragement. He pulled her onto his lap. A harsh groan escaped his lips as her moist opening met the tip of his staff. Nina bit her lip as pleasure coursed through her. The weight of her body pressed down on him, she felt him hard and stiff within her.

Damian was encased in her tight flesh, caressed by her heated moisture as he drove deeper inside her. He drew her legs around him, they rocked against each other as she kissed his face and neck with wild hunger.

He was hard and thick, filling her completely. She had been empty since he left, but now she was whole. He was shaking as his climax neared. Nina twisted to

increase the friction between them, crying out in muted
tones of pleasure when she succeeded.

Damian took her mouth, kissing her with unrestrained passion as their bodies surged together. She
wouldn't let him slow, she wouldn't let him hold back
his climax.

Nina writhed against him as her senses reeled and
spiraled outward. Her hunger sated itself greedily as
Damian spilled himself deep inside her. They lingered
together, hearts pounding a furious pace.

"I will never lose you again, little rebel. Never."

Nina couldn't think, she could only feel him still
within her, filling her. She didn't want him to move
away.

"Don't go," she whispered.

Damian buried his head in her neck. "Dare I move?
Where would it lead us?"

Nina didn't want to talk. She couldn't face what had
happened between them. Damian was hard, deeply
molded to her hidden flesh. Once was not enough.
Nina wiggled against him, pressing her hips closer, then
circled his length with abandon. Later, she would think
of what she had done this night. She might even dare
mourn her amazing lack of restraint.

But not now. Now Damian Knox filled her with desire,
answering the hunger that had tortured her for three
years. Damian eased her on to her back, cradling her
in his arms to protect her from the bare floor. Nina
would have loved him on stone. Nothing could ease the
fire between them save its full burning.

"Is this how you deny me, love?" Damian kissed her
forehead, but Nina's eyes remained closed.

"Please," she whispered, her voice a tiny plea. "I can't
talk now. I must go."

Damian didn't want to release her from his arms. He held stubbornly to her slender body, his jaw set hard. The moisture from her tears touched his neck, and he knew she was crying.

"Nina, you know you love me. How can I let you go to another man?"

"I don't know." He could barely hear her. But he understood. She fought her passion and it exploded between them. She needed time . . .

Damian sighed heavily and let her go. Nina scrambled to her feet, averting her eyes as she buttoned her bodice and straightened her dress. Damian stood, too, watching her with a painful mixture of frustration and tenderness.

"You came because you love me."

"I came because I can't resist you." She looked weary and defeated. She was fighting to maintain balance on a raging sea, to remain upright when her world was spinning out of control.

Damian watched her go to the door. He didn't stop her, though his heart ached when she turned away. His body was fired by their love-making, already he longed to take her again. With passion, Damian would make right all that had gone so horribly wrong between them.

Nina opened the door, but then she stopped and looked back at him. "Damian."

"Nothing else matters."

"How can you say that?" She fell silent, her head bowed, still holding the door. At last she looked at him again, her golden-brown eyes pleading for something he couldn't give.

"Everything is so confused. Nothing is as I thought it was."

Damian heard her, but he was reminded of his army's marching song, of sweet England far away. *"Then all the world would be upside down."*

Nina looked toward her father's house. "Upside down."

Damian watched her trudge up the slope to the house, her head bowed, her shoulders slumped. But as the song ran through his head, Damian Knox knew there was a different meaning, one far apart from the meaning Nina took.

"Your world is turning, my love," he murmured into the night. "It has been backwards all your life. This time, it is turning to the right."

Nina slipped back to her room and lay staring at her canopy. Her thoughts were scrambled, denying she had weakened, longing to repeat her weakness again. *I don't know what's right. I want to be good as Papa would have me, I want to be honorable. But one touch of his hand, one kiss, and I'm lost. I love him, I can't help it.*

I've honored General Washington, yet the kindest Englishman I ever met may be hanged without purpose. I've hated the English, but only Damian Knox could make me feel love this way. Nina's mind attempted a bridge to the past. Damian cared for Ian Forbes. Ian Forbes had stolen her mother, destroyed her life.

Her mother, whom she loved more than anything, deserted her for love. For desire. Loving Damian, she would again hurt her father. But this was different. She promised herself to Damian before Jeremiah. She loved him. And she wasn't already married, either.

Nina sat up in bed. Jeremiah would understand. She was strangely certain of that. Perhaps Iolo would, too. If she approached the subject just so. *I love him, Papa,* she thought as she lay back on her pillows. *Please understand.*

* * *

"He'll be hanged like a worthless criminal."

"His Excellency has rejected delay. He has rejected reason. Does the manner of Major André's death need to include humiliation?"

Nina stood outside the door, but her heart quailed. As she feared, both her father and Damian spoke in anger.

"I must speak with Washington." Damian was forcing calm to his voice, but Nina heard the emotion behind his words.

"Listen, you . . ." Iolo couldn't think of words insulting enough for an English nobleman. "His Excellency has better things to do with his time than banter words with the likes of you, boy."

"Then the risk to your own prisoners matters nothing? Arnold's letter to your leadership spoke of the dangers to prisoners we hold, those guilty of breaking parole. Their execution, also, may be spared for the safe return of Major André."

This was a mistake. Nina cringed. Never threaten Iolo Evans.

"Don't push me, boy. I'll not get you through to Washington. O'Grady, Hamilton . . . All of them have gone soft on that baby-faced bastard, but don't think you'll save his miserable hide."

Iolo's voice grew louder and louder. Nina felt on the verge of tears. "Damn you, you pounce in here thinking we'll do your bidding! I've known enough blue-blooded bastards to recognize you, Knox."

"Do you, I wonder?" Even as Iolo's volume indicated his fury, the coldly lowered tone in which Damian spoke indicated the same. "Then you would recall my father, Daniel Knox, whom you ordered without reason into an Onondaga massacre. In this war, also, death is arbitrary and determined by fools."

A long pause told Nina that Iolo was shocked by

Damian's revelation. Was he responsible for the death of Daniel Knox? Nina wouldn't believe it, except that Daniel Knox died for Ian Forbes.

"I know no Daniel Knox," replied Iolo.

"No? Yet you were the commander of Ian Forbes's company, were you not?"

Oh, no! Damian was accusing her father of Daniel Knox's death. He mentioned Ian Forbes to confront her father. Nina's stomach tightened in a wave of misery. *How could you?* She swayed as she stood. Just when she trusted him . . .

"Boy, you leave my office." Iolo Evans was restraining himself. That wasn't like her father at all. He wanted to say more.

Nina backed away from the door, but a gentle hand on her shoulder stopped her. She jumped and spun around, but Jeremiah put his finger to his lips, hushing her.

"Come," he whispered, and she followed him from the house. He led her toward the garden, filled with the drying leaves of harvest.

"It was bound to happen, Nina. Your father has no liking for the English. Certainly not a nobleman."

Jeremiah touched her shoulder and hot tears flooded Nina's eyes. He took her in his arms, comforting her gently. "Your father isn't flexible. It may be, one day, that your wishes and his conflict. Should that happen, it might be wiser to avoid him rather than confront whatever issue it might be."

Nina looked up at Jeremiah. His face was gentle and kind, revealing an inner strength she admired. *I wish I loved you. It would be so much easier.*

Damian stormed from the house. He stopped when he saw Nina and Jeremiah together. Nina felt his shock and his pain. He said nothing. He turned away, took Gambrinus, and galloped away.

Iolo called from his window. He sounded both impatient and agitated. Jeremiah walked her to the door, but Iolo waved him away. "I'll speak to my girl alone, O'Grady."

Jeremiah nodded, but he glanced at Nina with silent words of comfort.

"What is it, Papa?"

"That Englishman, Knox . . . What do you know of him?"

Nina bit her lip. "Know? I don't understand, Papa. I know very little. He treated me kindly in Philadelphia."

"Did he, now?" Iolo's lip curved scornfully. "Did he know who you were?"

"What?"

"Whose daughter!"

"I'm not sure. Not at first."

"He knew, all right. You stay away from him, girl."

"Why?" Nina's heart throbbed.

"Ian Forbes."

Nina trembled. Blackness descended around her. The dark fears of her past rose up to engulf her.

Iolo laid his hand on her shoulder. "Don't you be worrying, girl. You're all set to marry O'Grady. Do it, girl. And don't let anyone be stopping you."

Nina went to her room and remained there all day. She sent word to her father that she was ill, and had her supper in bed. She saw Damian's light, but she closed her eyes and tried to sleep. She knew the dream would come that night. She tried to face the terror this time, to see what frightened her so.

Nina woke screaming.

"What is it? Nina . . ."

Iolo Evans was sitting by her bed. She gripped his

arm. "It was the dream." She needed to say nothing more.

Nina heard footsteps, someone running up the stairs. Her door swung open, and there stood Damian Knox.

Damian moved menacingly toward Iolo. "What have you done?"

"Damian! It was a dream!"

He looked between them, but Iolo's black eyes gleamed. "What in the Name of God are you doing here, bursting into my girl's room? Boy, you get yourself out of here, or your André's going to have company."

Damian tried to see Nina's face, but she looked away from him. "If you're all right . . ."

Iolo rose up between them.

"I'm fine," Nina whispered. She couldn't let herself look at him.

Damian started to leave. "I'm not far."

Iolo's face flushed angrily, and Nina burst into muffled sobs when he left. They hated each other. There would be no peace.

"There's no point, Damian. My request to be shot has been denied. I die as a spy." John André was calm, his large eyes held no tears. But Damian had no words.

He left, found Gambrinus, and galloped headlong to the quarters of the commanding general of the American army.

"You may not enter."

Several aides said the same, but Damian was undaunted. "A man's life is worth something. I will shout through the windows if I have to, but he will hear me."

Damian towered over the smaller man. The door behind him opened. George Washington ducked as he came through the low threshold.

"An invasion?" he asked with a faint smile.

The aide turned nervously to his supreme commander. "Your Excellency, forgive me. This Englishman, Major Knox, has repeatedly been told . . ."

"John André," guessed Washington wearily.

"I would speak with you on that matter, Your Excellency."

Washington sighed. "Come." He turned and led Damian into the privacy of his study. His aide started to follow, but the general waved him back. "Leave us."

Alone, he turned to Damian and studied him intently. Few matched Washington's height, but Damian met him eye to eye. "You've come to convince me to save the life of a good man. That is in my power."

"That is so. I understand the depth of the crime committed. I understand the conventions of war. Yet surely held as a prisoner of war until this war's end . . ."

"Will that deter other spies? Will it deter those who might follow Benedict Arnold?" Washington's modulated voice hardened at the traitor's name. "Make no mistake, Major Knox. I see that John André is a good man. Alexander Hamilton is moved to tears on his behalf. But I can't do what you ask. Not without a fair exchange for the man responsible."

Damian saw the resoluteness in the American general—a formidable opponent. "But a man's life must have some meaning . . ."

"This is war, Major," said Washington. "You Englishmen fight war as if it was one of many campaigns. We are fighting it as the only one. Do you understand? Should I succumb to sentiment, free your André because he is a good man, then I change the standards by which this war must be fought. It must be fought to win, whether we win one battle or a hundred. We will win the one that matters."

"Could the sentence be passed at the war's end? Then muted when the situation is resolved?"

"Was he fairly condemned? The board, most highly favorable to the man himself, said unanimously André was guilty of spying behind American lines, without any marks of office. He doesn't deny this. His own honorable word attests this when Arnold accepts all blame."

Damian had tried everything. "Damn Arnold."

"Indeed," agreed Washington. "Indeed. Now, Major Knox, I have an army to guide. I have consorted with the enemy long enough."

The general's words were amiable, but they were also final. Damian had pressed his luck heavily in barging into the office. He had ridden hard, with determination, but he had failed. Only some new word from Clinton, some gesture of greatness from Benedict Arnold could save John André now.

Damian returned to Iolo's house and found himself amidst a crowd of busy servants. "What's this?"

A seamstress sewed lace on white cloth, another woman fiddled with what looked like a veil. Damian picked his way across the floor to Nina. She stared blank-faced out the window. Iolo and Jeremiah O'Grady were conferring in the corner with a minister.

"I want it tomorrow," insisted Iolo, but though the minister apparently had no wish to disappoint the Colonel, he shook his head.

"That's impossible, Colonel. They're to hang the English spy tomorrow. I can't do a wedding the same day as an execution."

"Wedding?" Damian's voice startled all but Nina. She didn't look at him.

"My daughter and Jeremiah insisted on marrying, despite the commotion," said Iolo. Jeremiah glanced at him doubtfully.

Damian couldn't speak. His gaze went to Nina, but she just stared out at nothing. *What has he done to you?*

"You are a fortunate man, Major O'Grady." He heard himself say the words, he saw the sympathetic and confused look on Jeremiah's face.

Damian turned and left the dining room. He found himself in the library, and he drew the door shut behind him. The shutters were closed to keep out the heat of Indian summer, and the room was bathed in warm darkness. Everything was ripped from him. It was an ancient feeling, one he'd known before.

"Your father has died." No words remembered afterwards. *"Your mother has died."* He couldn't stop them. He tried, but he made no difference. Damian's heart beat with angry force. He heard soft footsteps beyond the door. She was trying to slip upstairs . . . unseen, unheard.

Damian opened the door and saw her. Without a word, he grabbed her arm and pulled her inside. He pushed the door closed and pressed her back against the heavy wood. Nina was pale, her face still empty and defeated.

"What do you think you're doing? Have you lost your mind?"

Nina tried to look away, but Damian seized her chin and forced her to meet his gaze.

"I'm going to marry Jeremiah. You knew that."

"The hell I did! Last night you spent with me, tomorrow you have your wedding night with him, is that it?"

Nina didn't answer, and she didn't meet his gaze.

"Answer me!" Damian pressed her harder against the door.

"I can't."

"No, you probably can't. Will you tell him this, Nina? Will you tell him how I took you? Will you call it rape, or will you say you wanted me?"

His mouth came down hard on hers. Damian was lost in anger, in frustration. His kiss seared her mouth, tears fell to her cheeks, but Damian didn't stop. He pulled up her skirt, her petticoat, he ripped away her undergarments and threw them to the floor.

Damian tore open his breeches, freeing himself to enter her. Nina clung to his back, he drove high into her, lifting her from her feet. She braced herself as he thrust inside her, but she didn't resist. She didn't fight. He knew when primitive pleasure took the place of anything else in her mind and in her body.

Damian cupped her bottom in his hands and he lifted her off her feet, driving into her with primal force. Nina's leg wound around him, her breath came in hot gasps as he drove her to climax. He spent himself in a violent eruption deep within her, then lowered her to her feet.

Nina leaned against the door. Damian watched her, his senses on fire. Anger destroyed his judgment, passion ruled where reason once reigned supreme.

"Will you tell him this, Nina?" Damian seized her shoulders, but she wouldn't look at him. "Will you bear my child and call it his? Will you?"

Nina had no response. Her skirt fell back around her legs, and she picked up her tattered underwear. She stuffed what remained beneath her skirt and darted from the room. Damian stood alone, he buttoned his breeches, redid the tie in the back of his waistband.

Damian's heart beat in defiance of all that surrounded him. He liked Jeremiah O'Grady. But he would kill the man that tried to take Nina this time.

Neither Damian nor Nina attended dinner. Iolo was unmoved by their absence, nor did he seem to notice anything amiss in his daughter. Jeremiah O'Grady had no wish to trouble the world. It had always seemed wisest not to interfere. He'd spent the night debating the future, but when word came of André's imminent execution the next morning, Jeremiah returned to Iolo's house with the intention of doing just that.

Nina sat alone on the edge of an old well. The tides of her life battered her, and she had no more strength to fight. Jeremiah walked toward her, and she sighed. "Nina."

"Have you heard Major André's fate, Jeremiah?"

He sat down beside her and took her hand gently in his. "He'll be executed before noon today."

Nina closed her eyes. Damian had left early in a last effort to prevent what now seemed inevitable. "No." Hopeless tears fell across her face.

"There's nothing to be done for John André now. He will be surrounded by those who like and admire him, yet are his worst enemies. A man who cares for him insists upon his death. Nothing is real, Nina."

Nina glanced up at him. "You are real," she offered, but Jeremiah laughed.

"I, least of all." Jeremiah fell silent, then sighed. "Do you remember when I asked you to marry me? Do you recall what you said?"

"Not exactly."

"You told me you were tarnished. You told me you had discovered a sordid place in yourself and that you wished to be free of it, for it brought only pain and betrayal."

"I remember."

"The man you loved in Philadelphia was Damian Knox."

Nina swallowed hard. "Yes."

"You love him still."

"I can't."

"But you do, despite everything. Though your father insists you marry me."

Nina covered her face with her hands and wept, but Jeremiah patted her shoulder. "When you said you wanted to be free of your dark side, I understood."

"How could you understand?"

"Because I am the same."

Nina glanced up at him doubtfully. "Have you a mistress?"

Jeremiah hesitated. "Not exactly."

"Then what darkness have you, Jeremiah?"

"Oh, Nina, in the blackness of mine, yours is the sun. I have loved where a man should never love."

Nina's gaze wandered to the side. She knew one soldier who loved a woman of color, but it was Jeremiah who defended the man, and encouraged their marriage. And Jeremiah had proudly told her that his uncle married an Iroquois woman.

"Where should a man never love?"

Jeremiah smiled. "It depends on who you ask that question, I suppose." He stopped and sighed. "I admire your Englishman, Nina. He is all a man should be—strong and brave, handsome and kind."

"Those things are true of you also. The men follow you, Jeremiah, not Papa. I've seen that myself. You are a born leader."

"I am, perhaps. I feel little fear in battle, it's true. And I fight better than most. But I'm not like other men."

"Why not?"

"I've known something was different for most of my life." He spoke as if the words caused him pain. Nina recognized that feeling—to confront one's darkest self. She touched his arm gently. "Sean and I weren't the same. I didn't know why, not really, until I was seventeen. A man, older, explained it to me, shall we say."

"Explained what?"

Jeremiah hesitated. "What was different. I thought until that time that I couldn't love. He proved differently."

"How?"

"By showing me love of another kind. You have no idea, do you, that men might . . . love each other?"

Nina stared at him. She sensed he spoke of more than brotherly love. "What do you mean?"

"I mean men might make love to each other."

Nina chuckled. "That's not possible. Men wouldn't . . . fit."

Jeremiah laughed. "It's probably wisest not to explain this too graphically. Suffice to say it's possible. And I discovered my nature was thus suited."

Nina's gaze went to the side as she considered this. Jeremiah waited. He looked tense, as if he expected revulsion or condemnation. Nina studied his face. Nothing had changed between them. He was the same as ever before.

"This other man, what happened to him? Do you love him?"

"That was years ago. I was horrified to learn what I really was. I spent years denying it, I spent years bedding women for whom I cared nothing. Until I met a man my own age. I fell in love with him. Not just . . . well, in a sordid way, as you said. But love. We befriended each other, we never spoke of what we both knew. We fought together. I watched him risk his life to save a slave from a burning fort. And I loved him."

"He sounds very honorable."

"More than that, he is amusing. In the darkest hours of battle, with death all around, he finds something cheerful to say. He'll sit among the wounded men, and within ten minutes, they're all laughing. I'm never quite sure if his humor is intentional or not." Jeremiah paused. "That, perhaps, is the humorous element."

"Where is he? He wasn't killed, was he?"

"He remains in my company. We gave in to the passion between us, we reveled in it. Secretly, of course. God help us if anyone knew. But we believed we couldn't live that way. We both wanted normal lives. We decided to subdue our impulses, marry, and maintain our friendship throughout our lives."

"Is that why you wanted to marry me?"

Jeremiah took her hand. "I've always loved you, Nina. You were bright and brave and lovely. I could picture us married. When I came back to Philadelphia three years ago, I knew you'd been hurt." Jeremiah paused. "Actually, Columbine squealed like a stuck pig."

Jeremiah laughed at this, and Nina laughed, too. "I should have known. I spent three months living in a barn because of her."

"When you told me about your lover, I believed we'd both seen sides of ourselves best forgotten. I thought we might forget together. And for a while, that seemed true. Until your Damian Knox crossed enemy lines with every intention of freeing a gentle man and winning a heartbroken girl."

"He has a way of confusing matters."

"I saw him look at you, I saw you tremble when he was near. And then I knew love couldn't be denied. Maybe it isn't meant to be easy. Maybe it's meant to set us apart. But I want you to have the one you love. God help me, I intend to find a way myself."

"What do we do?"

"I'll return to my company. My friend and I will find some way to live our lives as we desire. Maybe run a farm somewhere, out of the way. We both like farming. After the war, naturally. But you, my dear, will go with your Englishman. Your father won't like it, Nina. I suggest you write to him once you're gone."

Nina sighed, but she wasn't hopeful. "I'll see that the manner of our broken contract doesn't reflect poorly on you."

Damian stood among enemy soldiers on a green field overlooking Tappan. He hadn't been allowed to see John André, nor to walk with him to the execution. Guards stood on either side of Damian, but none seemed concerned with watching him.

All eyes focused on the procession that came up the country road toward the field. Spectators massed in waiting, fife and drums played the death march. John André walked toward his death, his arms linked with his two guards. He walked in time with the music.

The young Englishman's composure stunned the crowd into silence. No minister attended him, much to the chagrin of the Quakers in Tappan. John André was a freethinker; his soul would be counted likewise.

André faced the American officers who ordered his death, bowing in turn to each one. They nodded back, and he proceeded to the gallows. A cart was ready, horses harnessed to pull it from beneath the spy.

John André looked to Damian. He heard the silent words, *"It's not your fault, remember me . . ."* He wanted to fight, he wanted to destroy the mob, the rebel soldiers. But he could do nothing.

John André smiled and nodded, then went up to the cart. He hesitated briefly, then climbed to his death. The death sentence was read again. "Have you anything to say?"

"I have nothing more to say, gentlemen, but this: you all bear me witness that I meet my fate as a brave man."

The spectators moaned and wept, but Damian stood

frozen. The hangman tried to put the noose around
André's neck, but André seized it and fitted it himself.
He tied a cloth over his eyes, his hands were bound . . .
The hangman fixed the rope above André's head, then
jumped down. He cracked a whip at the horses' backs
and the wagon jerked away . . .

Damian stared in silence while the crowd wailed and
sobbed, their shrieks as if the dying man was one of
their own. Damian felt André's soul when it departed,
as if the wind itself bore John André on its wings. The
body hung lifeless, and Damian turned away.

It was over. The crowd convulsed with sorrow and the
drama of a good man's death. Damian turned from his
grieving guards and walked back down the country road
toward Tappan. His thoughts were blank, his body
numb. The world was ripped beneath his feet. He had
lost André, he was losing Nina. And there was nothing
he could do to stem the tide of disaster.

"John André was hanged by the neck until dead."

Nina stared at her father. He showed no emotion as
he returned to the papers before him. Tears flooded
her eyes and she clutched her waist.

"Are you sure, Papa?"

Iolo looked up. "Of course, I'm sure. I was there."

"You watched him die?"

"I had business with Major Tallmadge. He insisted
on accompanying the little fool to the gallows. As did
a ridiculous crowd. Knows how to play to an audience,
he did. Begged us to remember he met his death a
brave man."

"Oh!" A sob broke from Nina, but Iolo scoffed.

"He was an actor, for God's sake."

Nina sniffed. "Actors feel things very deeply. He was
a fine man, Papa."

Iolo rolled his eyes, then went back to his paperwork. "Was Major Knox there?"

"How should I know? There was a crowd, I told you. But he'll be gone today, too."

Nina stood outside Damian's door. His horse stood ready. "Gambrinus." The big horse touched her with his black nose, pushing her gently. Melody lay on her back, stretched out in the autumn sun.

Nina knocked, but she heard no answer. She pushed open the door and saw Damian seated in the broken Chippendale, his head bowed, holding a small portrait in his hands. He was in full-dress uniform, a bag already packed sat by the door.

He looked up at her, and Nina's heart quailed. His blue eyes seemed drained of light, of purpose.

Nina knelt before him, she kissed his hands and drew them to her wet cheek. "You're leaving?"

"I am."

"Then take me with you."

His gaze met hers, and she saw a flicker of surprise and hope in his eyes. "Yes."

"I must tell Papa."

"He won't let you go."

"She left that way, without saying. I must tell him."

"I'll go with you, then."

Remembering how Damian and Iolo fought, Nina frowned. "That's probably unwise. Let me go. You wait here, and when I'm ready, I'll meet you."

"He won't let you go, Nina. Come with me. I've packed your bag."

Nina glanced at the small bag beside his chair. "How did you know?"

Damian smiled. "I didn't. I hadn't planned on giving you a choice."

"You were going to haul me along with you?"

"I was."

Nina rose to her feet and kissed him. "I should have known. But I have to tell Papa, Damian. I owe him that."

"I won't be far."

"I know."

Nina left Damian in the shack and went back to her father. Iolo was still at his desk. He didn't look up when she entered.

"Papa."

"What is it, girl? Can't you see I'm working here?"

"Yes, I'm sorry, Papa . . ." Nina felt nervous. But Iolo loved her. She had nothing to fear.

"There's something I have to tell you. I'm afraid it can't wait."

Iolo put down his quill and waited, a small frown of impatience on his lips. "Women think their little doings should stop the whole bloody war. Well? Go ahead, girl! I'm waiting."

Nina cleared her throat. "Jeremiah and I have decided not to marry."

He sat back in his chair. "What do you mean, 'not marry'? Damned sure you'll be marrying tomorrow."

Nina shook her head. She was trembling. "No, Papa. Jeremiah has left."

"We'll call him back." Iolo's voice was controlled. He rose from his seat and approached Nina.

"Papa, I don't want to marry him, and he doesn't want to marry me, either."

"Be damned, he doesn't! You've been set to marry since you were children."

Nina looked at him doubtfully. Neither she nor Jeremiah had known that.

"I don't love him. He doesn't really love me, either."

Iolo didn't speak. His mouth was a tight line of anger, but Nina knew she had to go on.

"We didn't realize it at first." Her voice quavered.

"What made you realize it now?"

Nina's shoulders slumped. There was no easy way. "I'm in love with someone else." It was said. She couldn't turn back, nor hide from the truth now.

"Who?" Iolo Evans stepped toward her. His black eyes glinted with anger. The temper Nina avoided all her life now flashed to the surface.

She drew a tight breath and exhaled slowly. "Major Knox."

"No."

"Papa, I love him. He's not like the others, Papa. I love him . . ."

His broad hand cracked across her face and she stumbled back, stunned. Iolo took another step toward her, his hand raised again. "Papa, don't!" Nina scrambled away from him. This wasn't her father. Her father wouldn't hurt her.

"You little whore. How often did you lie with that bastard while we starved at Valley Forge? Aye, is that how you got your meals?"

"No, you don't understand. He wants to marry me . . ." Iolo lunged toward her and grabbed her by the throat. She couldn't breathe, but she heard his words.

"You're like her, aye. But you won't disgrace me again."

He had lost his mind. In his eyes, Nina repeated her mother's betrayal. Iolo loosed his grip on her throat and Nina dropped to the ground, gasping for air. He towered over her, bending down as if to strike her again.

"Get away from her, old man, or I'll kill you now." Damian stood in the doorway, his pistol readied, his eyes blazing with hatred and disgust. "Nina, come here."

Nina struggled to her feet and went to Damian's side. Her lip bled, the side of her face felt swollen and raw. Damian caught her arm, then aimed at Iolo's head.

"No! Damian, don't. Please."

"You'll never have peace if you take her, boy. I'll hunt you down, I'll slaughter you like a pig."

Nina swayed, leaning against Damian. "You'll do nothing. She is going where she belongs." He glanced at Nina. "We'll bind him. If we're lucky, no one will learn we've gone until we're behind English lines."

Nina bit her lip, but she nodded. "That is fair."

Damian looked back at Iolo. "I won't kill you, for her sake. One word could change my mind." He gestured at Iolo's chair. "Have a seat."

There was something strange about Iolo's reaction. The way he walked toward the desk without hesitation. Terror swelled in Nina as Damian moved to bind her father. "Damian . . ."

His name barely passed her lips when Iolo Evans lifted a gun himself and pointed it at Damian's head. Damian leapt toward him as the gun fired. The shot ripped into Damian's arm. Nina screamed, but Damian knocked Iolo to the floor. Iolo's gun clattered out of reach. For his age and small size, Iolo fought like a madman.

Nina watched in horror as the two men fought. Her mind blackened, as if she was seeing her past and future in this one horrible moment. Iolo struck viciously at Damian's wounded arm, reached for his gun. It met his fingers.

"Damian!"

Nina grabbed a weight from her father's desk, then slammed it against his skull. Iolo crumpled. Damian rose to his feet, taking her into his arms.

"Did I kill him?"

Damian let her go and checked Iolo's body for life. "He lives." Nina breathed a sigh of relief. "He'll be awake in minutes. We've got to get out of here, Nina . . . Now."

Nina knelt by her father, tears streaming down her face. "I'm sorry, Papa. Please forgive me." Damian grabbed her arm and dragged her toward the door. "I can't leave him this way."

"Nina, that man nearly killed you, would have killed you had I not known enough of his character to follow you in here."

"He lost his mind. I wasn't careful enough. If I could've explained better . . ."

"You defied him, Nina. Have you ever done that before?" When Nina didn't answer, Damian nodded. He glanced out the door. "Where are the servants?"

Nina couldn't think. Her mind whirled, savage fears and shattered dreams dove down upon her like vultures. "I don't know."

"His aide? What about O'Grady?"

"Jeremiah has left. The rest . . . I don't know."

"Come, love, we must go." Damian took her hand and kissed it. Behind them, Iolo Evans groaned and stirred.

A wild chill of fear swept through Nina. "Yes."

They slipped from the house unseen, but as he lifted her onto Gambrinus's back, Iolo's aide arrived. Seeing Nina behind Damian, the aide's eyes widened.

"What do you think you're doing there?"

Nina searched for an easy explanation, but nothing came. The bag Damian had prepared for her dangled at the horse's side, Melody waited beside them. Damian had no answer, either. They both just stared at the man.

"Hold on!" shouted the aide as Damian eased Gambrinus down the path away from the house. "Does the colonel know where you're off to?"

Nina gulped. "Yes . . . Everything's fine."

"We'll just see about that! Can't be thinking Colonel Evans will care much for his girl heading off with no bloodyback!"

"Wonderful," muttered Damian. "We might have handled that better."

"Neither of us would be particularly effective spies."

A shout rang out from within the house. The aide had found Iolo. "Hell's goddamn bells, Zebulon! Get after him, that's what!" Iolo Evans lived, and he wouldn't let his daughter go without a fight.

Damian took a deep breath. "Hold on." Without a sound, Gambrinus sprang into a gallop, Melody racing furiously behind him. Nina clung to Damian's back.

"Do you know where we're going?" she shouted into the wind.

"West," Damian shouted back.

"That's very comforting."

They rode for hours, but Nina was certain they'd gotten nowhere. The sky darkened, purple and orange streaked across the western sky. Damian headed for the horizon without thought to roads or pastures. They slowed to a walk as Gambrinus picked his way through a wooded area beyond a farm.

"West?" asked Nina, finally relaxed enough to question Damian's navigation. "Don't you know where we are?"

"I have no idea."

"That's not entirely reassuring, Damian. Do you think they'll try to find us?"

"They will."

"Won't they expect us to take a road? Is that why we're going this way? Off into nothing, I mean."

"I don't know what they expect. I imagine they assume we'll head for English lines. And they have the positions northward to stop us."

"So we're going west? What's west?"

"Black Hawk."

Nina closed her eyes. Damian, the strongest, bravest, most intelligent man she knew, had cracked. She felt a surge of pity.

"I know you're under a terrible strain, Damian." Nina paused. "But, *Black Hawk'*?" Her voice grew a little shrill. "You head west and think in all these miles, all these woods, across every field, you're going to find one black-haired Indian in the middle of the night?"

"That's my plan."

"Saints preserve us."

PART THREE
Cora

4 BESTSELLING HISTORICAL ROMANCES BY YOUR FAVORITE AUTHORS CAN BE YOURS, FREE!

Kensington Choice brings you historical romances by your favorite bestselling authors including Janelle Taylor, Shannon Drake, Rosanne Bittner, Jo Beverley, and Georgina Gentry, just to name a few! Each book is filled with passion, adventure and the excitement of bygone times!

To introduce you to this great club which is part of Zebra Home Subscription Service, we'd like to send you your first 4 bestselling historical romances, absolutely free! And once you get these 4 free books to savor at home, we'll rush you the next 4 brand-new books at the lowest prices available, as soon as they are published.

The way the club works is that after your initial FREE shipment, you will get our 4 newest bestselling historical romances delivered to your doorstep each month at the preferred subscriber's rate of only $4.20 per book, a savings of up to $8.16 per month (since these titles sell in bookstores for $4.99-$6.99)! All books are sent on a 10-day free examination basis and there is no minimum number of books to buy. (And no charge for shipping.) Plus as a regular subscriber, you'll receive our FREE monthly newsletter, *Zebra/Pinnacle Romance News*, which features author profiles, subscriber benefits, book previews and more!

 So start today by returning the FREE BOOK CERTIFICATE provided. We'll send you 4 FREE BOOKS with no further obligation: A FREE gift offering you hours of reading pleasure with no obligation...how can you lose?

We have 4 FREE BOOKS for you
as your introduction to
KENSINGTON CHOICE!
To get your FREE BOOKS, worth
up to $24.96, mail the card below.

FREE BOOK CERTIFICATE

Yes! Please send me 4 Kensington Choice (the best of Zebra and Pinnacle Books) Historical Romances without cost or obligation (worth up to $24.96). As a Kensington Choice subscriber, I will then receive 4 brand-new romances to preview each month for 10 days FREE. I can return any books I decide not to keep and owe nothing. The publisher's prices for Kensington Choice romances range from $4.99-$6.99, but as a preferred subscriber I will get these books for only $4.20 per book or $16.80 for all four titles. There is no minimum number of books to buy and I may cancel my subscription at any time, plus there is no additional charge for postage and handling. No matter what I decide to do, my first 4 books are mine to keep, absolutely FREE!

Name _____

Address _____ Apt. _____

City _____ State _____ Zip _____

Telephone ( ) _____

Signature _____

(If under 18, parent or guardian must sign)

Subscription subject to acceptance. Terms and prices subject to change.

KF0198

SEVEN

Rather than heading northward along the Hudson, Damian rode westward, though the safety of English lines lay to the north. They skirted the town of Newton.

"Are we near the Delaware?"

"I hope so," replied Damian. Nina sighed.

They rode on into the night, following the sparkling light of moon and stars. Nina leaned against Damian's back. He loved her and they were together. For the moment, what loomed ahead meant nothing.

Nina was asleep when Damian brought Gambrinus to a halt. Missing the accustomed motion, Nina woke and tapped Damian's shoulder. "Why do we stop?"

"There's a river nearby. Hush." Damian stared into the darkness ahead. "Off." He dismounted, bringing Nina with him.

"What are we doing?"

"You're staying here. I'll go ahead . . ."

"No, you won't!"

She grabbed his arm, but Damian took her hand and kissed it. "You hold Gambrinus here for me. If I don't come back, if you hear shots, then get on and ride back to your father . . ."

"I will not!"

"Tell him I abducted you, tell him you killed me and stole the horse."

"Damian Knox, don't you dare . . . don't you dare go without me."

"I love you." In the darkness, his blue eyes glittered. He could say these three words, and she crumbled.

"Take care."

"Naturally." He handed her the reins and headed off into the night. Melody sat beside her, staring intently after Damian. Nina patted the dog's head.

Gambrinus accepted his master's departure, finding grass an easy distraction. Nina pulled his head up and led him a few paces after Damian. She stopped and let him return to grazing, but beyond his slow chewing and the stream's rushing noises, she heard nothing.

In the silhouettes of night, she saw the outline of a building close to the stream's edge. His enemies might lie in wait, ready with Colonial genius to ambush a hated redcoat. Once Nina took pride in her army's skill. Now her heart beat in wild terror for its toll.

No shots split the night. Moments dragged until Gambrinus lifted his head and gazed with night eyes at his returning master. Nina felt Damian long before she saw him, though he made no sound.

"What's there?"

Damian approached from the shadows. "There's an old mill. It's caved in, but it should be a good place to spend the night."

"Isn't it rather obvious? They'll expect us to find an old, abandoned place, won't they?"

"Probably. But it will take a while to find the right one."

This wasn't entirely comforting, but Damian helped her back onto the horse. They rode down the bank, and Damian tied Gambrinus near the water. The horse drank, then rolled in the tall reeds.

They picked their way across the rotting floorboards to a comfortable, relatively sheltered spot in the old mill. Melody curled between the door and her two masters. They didn't undress, but Damian drew Nina into his arms and held her close against him. She rested against his shoulder, listening to his strong heartbeat until it lulled her to sleep.

Nina's hand brushed across his aroused manhood and she woke. Her body filled with liquid fire, but she didn't open her eyes. She felt Damian's restraint even as she heard the demanding thump of his heart. Her fingers explored the bulge beneath his breeches, feeling it grow harder still.

This is why I came with you. My love lives within this desire. My desire flowers here, where I am joined to you. Nina kissed his shoulder softly and turned her face upward to kiss his neck.

"Yes, little angel," Damian murmured as she tasted the corner of his lips. He pulled her against him and returned her seeking kiss with sweet passion.

The night around them turned cold, but it didn't matter. Damian pulled up her skirt and petticoats. He ran his hand along the soft skin of her thigh.

"We're one thing, Damian. No one can hurt you now." Gambrinus moved restlessly outside and Nina hesitated. "What's the matter?"

Damian touched her hair and kissed her forehead. "They're coming."

"Who?"

"Your father, I assume, and whatever soldiers he's gathered. They were close behind us."

"You saw them?"

"I took a roundabout route, and we lost them in the woods. I thought if we followed this stream that leads nowhere, they'd think we'd taken the straighter route, or cut north. But it seems 1 was overly optimistic."

"How do you know?"

"I saw them on the far side when I walked down here.
I thought they'd pass by."

"Why didn't you tell me?"

"There's no point."

Nina looked wildly around the broken-down mill
room. She heard Gambrinus's snort and whinny outside. "What do we do?"

Damian didn't answer.

"Damian . . . What do we do?"

He rose to his feet and readied his pistol. "If we try
to escape, they'll hunt us down, they'll shoot wildly. The
shots fired might hit you."

"What do we do?"

"I'll see you safely returned. Find O'Grady, Nina. He
will protect you."

Damian sounded resigned, certain. Nina struggled to
her feet beside him, but her knees were nearly too weak
to hold her. "You won't die. And I won't go back."

He moved to the caved-in wall and looked out. Nina
peeked over his shoulder. Shadows moved from tree to
tree. The first light of morning was still an hour or more
away. She couldn't guess how many were advancing
upon the mill, but they were out-numbered in any case.

Gambrinus snorted and reared, seized by enemy
hands, pulled away as plunder from the small engagement. Melody growled. "Quiet," Damian ordered, and
Melody dropped obediently in wait. "Get down, Nina."

She drew a small pistol from her dress. "I can shoot."

"I doubt they'll get close enough for that."

"Major Knox!" An American voice pierced the night,
loud and assured. Nina swayed, but she, too, readied
her small gun.

"Send out the girl!"

"The woman is mine, just payment for John André's
life, payment for my father's." Damian's voice sounded
harsh, unfamiliar. Nina eyed him doubtfully.

"You'll never leave this hovel, Knox!" Iolo Evans's voice rang out with furious emotion.

"What assurance have I that the girl's release guarantees my safety?"

Nina glanced up at Damian. Reality and illusion were one. This was the Englishman Iolo expected, not the gentle man who loved her. She backed away from him, her eyes wide with confusion and fear.

"I won't go." Her voice quaked. "Not you, nor my father, nor anyone will decide my fate again."

Damian's jaw hardened as he turned to her. "You've been my whore. My revenge is satisfied. Go."

Ignoring the soldiers outside, she walked to him, her gaze never leaving his. She stood close before him, searching his face without words. "You don't love me?"

"No. I could never love the daughter of my father's killer."

Nina's eyes glimmered with tears. But she didn't look away. She half believed him. It was possible. The night around them fragmented reality, filling it with illusion. Nina lifted her hand, with one finger she touched his mouth. Her head tilted to one side, a tight ringlet of hair fell across her forehead.

"Send her out, Knox!" Iolo's voice boomed, ringing of impatience and anger.

"Damn you, go!"

Nina just stared at him, her finger still resting on the curve of his perfect mouth. "You're a poor liar, Damian Knox. You and I . . . We are one thing. I won't leave you."

His eyes clouded with tears. She touched his face, then his long hair. Nina rose on tiptoes to kiss him.

"I can't save you unless you go."

"I haven't asked to be saved." Her lips brushed his. "Only to be with you."

For a fleeting moment, the soldiers outside were forgotten. Nina drew away, then went to the broken wall.

"I'm not coming out, Papa. You can let us go, you can kill us, but I am staying with the man I love."

Nina heard her own voice like an echo from the past. Somewhere, in the far reaches of her memory, in the depths of her nightmares, she had heard those words before.

"Open fire!"

Nina heard the harsh command in disbelief. Even after her defiant vow, she hadn't believed her father would order her death. She stood immobile by the wall, but Damian grabbed her and shoved her to the floor beneath him.

The soldiers didn't fire at once. They seemed confused by Nina's defense of Damian.

"Damn your eyes, and all to hell! I said, 'open fire'!"

The muskets roared. Shots slammed into the mill's rotting sides, shattering already cracked bricks into splinters. One round was fired, then another. Damian held Nina beneath him as the walls collapsed. His gun was ready, but he didn't fire, not yet.

"Fix bayonets! Move in!"

"Stay down." Damian rose to his feet and found a place from which to shoot.

Nina crept up behind him and aimed her pistol into the darkness. She felt Melody's nose touch her leg.

"Fire!" Iolo's voice echoed through the enclosure of the mill. Her father was ordering her death. It was a nightmare.

Shots flew around them while they hid behind the shelter of the brick wall. The round completed, Damian answered their fire, and Nina shot, too. Two shots came from farther away. Then two more.

"What's that?" asked Nina. "Echoes?"

"That's musket fire."

"It's not shooting at us."

The surprised Americans fired back at their unexpected attackers. Damian fired, too, sending the Colonial soldiers into dire confusion.

"Come about!" Iolo shouted commands, but his soldiers had no idea how many were attacking. Again, four shots in close succession rang out.

"There's four!" exclaimed Nina.

"Three muskets in our defense, at least," said Damian. "And one pistol."

Damian shot again, but shouts split the night. The attackers charged down upon the Americans. The first light of the morning sun illuminated the skirmish ground, revealing the enemy before them.

"Indians! By the Name of God!"

Wild cries, fearful and savage, echoed in the breaking darkness. War cries, sure to turn both English and Colonial blood to ice.

"Damn you fools! Turn and fire!"

Iolo shouted commands, but his men were in wild disarray. His men fell back and scrambled toward the river, but Iolo held his horse in check.

"You've made it today, Knox," he yelled toward the mill. "By the skin of your teeth. But I will find you. And by God, you will envy your father's death!"

Nina heard Iolo's words, and her heart quailed. Iolo left with his men, but the fear of his vow lingered. Her father wasn't given to idle threats. Damian would never be safe.

"Damian . . ."

Damian ignored Iolo Evans, intent on the battle outside the mill. It became a rout. The attackers crashed loudly toward the fleeing Americans. The Indians' terrifying war cries followed the retreat.

Nina peeked out through the ravaged wall. "What on earth is going on out there?"

"I'm not certain." Damian stepped out through the rubble. "Stay here."

Nina followed him, despite his order. Melody waited within the destroyed mill, pacing to and fro, then came cautiously out behind Nina.

Two men came toward them from the direction the Americans fled. Two Indians, with long black hair loose around their shoulders, approached Damian. Black Hawk had come at last.

"You come none too soon, my friend," said Damian.

Nina breathed a vast sigh of relief, then joined him, though she looked suspiciously at the other man.

"I owe my life, and Nina's, to your timely arrival."

"We wait upriver," said Black Hawk. "You ride without speed."

"I ride blind," countered Damian. "But west."

Black Hawk laughed and shouldered his musket. "We follow your Welsh friend here."

Damian glanced at the other Indian. "I am indebted to you also."

The young man laughed, a distinctly English ring in his voice. He tugged at his black hair. Nina gasped when it came off, revealing bright blond hair in the morning light.

"Ethan!" Damian laughed and clasped the boy's hand in his.

The young man wore buckskin, with a long strand of beads and feathers tied to his loose hair. Nina wondered why hair covered in a black wig needed decoration, but Ethan Forbes looked proud. A bright smile lit his face, his eyes gleamed with the thrill of battle.

"The war cry was his idea," injected Black Hawk. "Where I come from is not as bloody."

"Set the fear of God, or the Great Spirit, rather, into them, didn't it?" said Ethan. "Crashed through the trees like twenty, we did. We'd readied three muskets, and I had my pistol."

"Brilliantly done," said Damian. Ethan beamed.

Ethan turned to Nina. He looked shy. "Are you well?"

"I'm fine." She lifted her small gun. "I can shoot, too."

Ethan stepped toward her, the curiosity and wonder of a small boy written across his face. "Em . . ." Ethan caught himself and paled. Nina smiled as he cleared his throat, then coughed. *"Nina . . .* It gives me the greatest pleasure imaginable to find you safe from harm."

The sun peeked from the horizon, and Nina gazed into her brother's face. He was young, no more than eighteen. He was handsome, with a refined, beautiful face, and full, expressive lips. He was tall, as she was. Nina couldn't deny their likeness.

Do you look like our mother. I remember nothing of her face. Why do I not remember her in you?

"They'll be back. They took my horse," said Damian. "Damn them."

"No, they didn't," piped in Ethan. "We did. Black Hawk and I found him, thinking we'd draw them off. Didn't work. But he's back about a quarter mile away, with ours."

"That's better news than I'd hoped. I've no idea how to get out of here without speed." He turned to Black Hawk. "Which way now?"

Black Hawk smiled. "North."

Days of travel through secret paths only known to Black Hawk followed. They crossed rivers, became entangled in thick woods, skirted miles north of West Point, then finally crossed the Hudson north of New Windsor. From there, Black Hawk directed them south again. When at last they reached the first British picket lines, Nina was numb with weariness.

"Where are we going now?" asked Nina. They were safe in an occupied farmhouse outside New York City, and she sated her painful hunger on a hearty supper of roast pig and potatoes.

Damian glanced at Ethan. "I'm taking you into the city, where you'll be safe."

"Have you a house there?"

"There's a house where I'm welcome, yes."

"Where?"

Damian sighed. "With your mother and Ian Forbes."

"No." Nina didn't want to hurt Ethan. She had grown fond of the boy, and she knew he watched her intently for her response. "I can't do that, Damian. You don't understand."

"Nina, you'll be safe there. You haven't seen your mother since you were a tiny child. Isn't it possible your impression of her might be misguided? You've seen Iolo Evans isn't exactly reasonable."

Nina didn't reply at once. That her father had proven himself unbalanced seemed certain. But her mother betrayed her as well, abandoning her for a cold and dangerous lover.

"She's desperate to see you, Nina." Ethan's voice was soft and poignant. "Whatever happened when you were born, please believe it wasn't what she wanted."

"She left me." Nina looked at her brother and her voice quavered.

"She thought you were dead."

This wasn't true. Nina knew this, but she couldn't tell her young brother. Damian touched her hand. "Give her a chance to explain. Her story may vary greatly from your father's."

Ethan touched her hand. "Please."

Nina didn't want to go. More than loyalty or childhood prejudice, she realized she was afraid. Not of her mother, but of Ian Forbes. But looking at her brother, she nodded.

"I will go."

New York was bustling, an occupied city that bore little resentment towards the British army now firmly ensconced amidst the large Tory population. Carriages with elegant officers and beautiful ladies passed to and fro as Nina looked around.

They had spent the night in an inn on the outskirts of town, where Nina washed and mended her tattered dress. Gambrinus was stabled, and Ethan arranged for a carriage to take them to his parents' house. Melody sat on the seat beside Nina, looking out the door, barking at dogs on the street.

When the carriage stopped in front of a grand home, Nina's resolve faltered. Within those high walls, the mother she hadn't seen in twenty years awaited her.

"What will I say?" she asked Damian.

Damian took her hand. "Say nothing, if nothing moves you. But listen."

Ethan led them to the door. Nina held up her worn skirt as she climbed the steep stairs that led to the arched doorway. Ethan pulled the bell cord, and the door opened. Nina's heart stopped, but it was an elderly black servant who greeted them.

"Caesar!" Ethan slapped the old man's shoulder and the man embraced him. Melody greeted the servant warmly, but Nina felt betrayed that her dog long ago befriended her mother's household.

"Young master Ethan, it's good to have you back in one piece!" Caesar turned to Damian, greeting him with similar enthusiasm, though he ignored Black Hawk. "Now, then, milord, you've come a long ways, haven't you? Thought the Yanks might string you up alongside poor Major André, we did."

"No, Caesar, though a few did try."

Nina looked up at Damian doubtfully. " 'Milord?' " To her surprise, faint color touched his face.

"An unnecessary title."

Ethan stooped in an exaggerated bow. "But a given one, my Lord Knox."

"You're some sort of royalty?" asked Nina in amazement.

"A baron," said Ethan.

Damian glared at Ethan. "A title bestowed on my family which reflects nothing of my own life."

"So my Englishman disowns his title. I wonder, *Lord Damian*, if you aren't more American than you know."

Caesar studied Nina. "Can this be Miss Emmalina?"

"I am called Nina."

Caesar glanced at Damian. "You sure you got the right one?"

"Yes. Why do you ask?"

"Isn't what I figured." Caesar shook his head and escorted them into a large, open hall.

"What's wrong with me?" asked Nina. "Is it because I'm a mess?"

Damian shrugged. "I have no idea."

The walls of the hallway were wallpapered, the ceilings were high and molded with exquisite detail. A large but delicate chandelier hung by the staircase. Nina had never seen such a grand home. Her eyes widened with wonder as Caesar held open the door to a sitting room.

Damian held her hand, and with Black Hawk, they followed Ethan into the room. It was small, but furnished with golden upholstered settees and comfortable chairs. Muted rose damask images drew Nina's gaze to the wallpaper, with scenes of family life and small children fishing.

"Would you care to sit, Nina?" asked Ethan. Nina shook her head, then examined the books in narrow cases, running her fingers along the gleaming cherry wood. Unlike the books in Lavinia Fairchild's elegant library, every one appeared well-read and interesting.

"What a lovely room!"

"Mother designed it."

Nina's hand dropped. "Doesn't this house belong to someone else? You have made a habit of appropriating American homes for your officers."

"Not this one. Father bought it from a Loyalist who was fleeing back to England. Mother wanted to make it like home."

"Oh," said Nina. Home, in England. Home with Ian Forbes.

Caesar left them, presumably to alert Cora Talmadge to their presence. Nina's breath came swift and shallow, her fingers felt numb with nervousness. Damian put his arm around her waist.

Nina felt his strength, his comfort, but still her mind tortured her with doubt and fear. All her life, she hated her mother. Her dreams were filled with betrayal, with abandonment. Yet she wondered desperately if her mother would be disappointed to see the woman Nina had become. She was acutely aware of her unkempt hair, her travel-worn dress.

"Nina." Damian spoke her name, and Nina turned.

A woman stood in the doorway. She was tiny and dark-haired, and very beautiful, but she couldn't be Cora Talmadge. The men in the room waited expectantly, but no recognition surfaced in Nina's brain.

Nina's brow furrowed as she studied the woman. Her hair formed tight curls like Nina's, but it was very dark. She was small-boned, delicate, and much younger than Nina's mother should be. Her eyes and mouth seemed young, yet there was a maturity about the way she stood.

She's shaking. Her hands are clasped. She's shaking. Her eyes opened wide with emotion, the tiny face was frozen with shock. Nina's head tilted to one side, she felt Damian's hand on her waist.

Ethan moved to the woman's side and placed his hand on her shoulder. The woman wanted to move. Nina knew that. She wanted to step forward, to greet them. But she couldn't. Nina felt herself moving to the woman at Ethan's side. She looked closer, down into the woman's face. The woman's golden-brown eyes glittered with tears, her bowed lips trembled.

You can't be my mother. My mother looks like me. Papa said so. My mother was tall and blond, a perfect Englishwoman.

"Emma."

Her voice was a whisper, her chest rose with tiny, jerking breaths. But Nina knew her now. *Emma, I love him so. Please understand . . .*

"Mama." That word had never passed her lips in twenty years. She felt as if a child spoke through her woman's body.

Cora swayed, Ethan supported her, but she reached out a shaking hand to touch her daughter's face. "You're alive," she murmured, her voice shaking and weak. "Damian found you, after all . . ."

"She's fine," said Damian.

"And very brave," added Ethan. "Evans nearly had them, Mother." He sounded cheerful, and missed the sudden paling of his mother's face entirely. "He was no match for me. And Black Hawk, of course. We routed the whole lot of them! Don't know why it's taking so long for us to win, when the rebels run like that."

Cora glanced at her son. "Buckskin? Where did you get buckskin?"

Ethan adjusted his Indian tunic. "I nabbed it off a scout. Handsome, isn't it? Perhaps you notice my resemblance to a barbarian warrior?"

Cora shook her head and sighed. "Why me?" She took Nina's hand and squeezed it tightly.

"You're safe now, Emma. I have a room ready for you upstairs." Cora glanced at Damian. "Are you married yet?"

Ethan rolled his eyes. "Mother, we were running from the rebels. There weren't many chapels along the way."

"Oh, of course. It doesn't matter. You will be married, I expect. Damian can have the room next to yours. There's a door between, actually."

Nina's brow rose in surprise. Iolo told her that Cora Talmadge had no moral structure whatsoever, but somehow, the offer seemed more practical than sordid.

"Damian, the colonel wishes to see you and Ethan," said Cora. "I'll take Emma upstairs and see that she's comfortable. Black Hawk, your room is beside Ethan's. Upstairs to the right and down the hall. Ethan, if you weary of your barbarian warrior costume, you'll find a new uniform and cravat upstairs."

Ethan fingered his tunic. "No wig?"

"It's boxed."

"Good."

Nina's studied her mother's face. *She's so beautiful. More beautiful than I imagined. She must be forty years old, but she remains ageless.*

"Are you all right, if I go?" asked Damian.

"You'll come back?"

Damian kissed her hand and smiled. "I'll always come back. Don't you know that by now?"

Cora took Nina upstairs, down brightly lit hallways, and into a spacious bedroom. It was decorated with dried, autumn flowers, and to Nina's wonder, the wardrobe chest was filled with dresses. A bed was prepared for Melody beside Nina's, and the dog immediately made herself comfortable.

"They should fit," ventured Cora as Nina fingered the elegant dresses. "There's something suitable for every occasion; for balls, for walking, even for riding."

"For me?" asked Nina, and Cora took her hand.

"Of course, my dear."

"How did you know that I was coming?"

Cora smiled. "They've been here for three years, Emma. Since I first heard from Damian that he'd found you, that you were coming home to me. When he returned from Philadelphia without you, I had the gowns made anyway, in hopes he would find you again."

Nina looked away from her mother, gazing out the window to the busy street beyond. "It's Park Place. Quite the most elegant spot in New York. You can watch every array of carriages going by."

British officers hurried to and fro accompanied by well-dressed Loyalist belles. Cora looked out the window, too. "It's a lively city. Quite unlike Philadelphia. But it can be enjoyable, if one doesn't think about it too much."

Nina glanced at her mother. "Think about what?"

"The war. About what will happen to those young men who think so little of their fate."

Nina looked back out the window. "They should return to England."

"Most will, naturally. But it's the ones who will remain forever, that I was thinking of."

"Such as Damian's father?" Nina paused, fearful to tread far back into the past. "Did you know him?

"I knew him, yes. He was a fine man, like Damian. He was handsome and brave. He loved his son very much."

"Then why did he . . . ?" Nina bit her lip to silence herself.

Cora studied Nina's face intently, and for a while, she said nothing. "Daniel Knox was a man of honor. It was easier, perhaps, to suffer death, however horrible, than to see it inflicted on another."

Cora didn't mention Ian Forbes's name. Nina wanted to question her, she wanted to confront the issue that shattered her own life. She couldn't. Cora's beautiful face was composed, but Nina saw the grief that was written into her being. Somehow, despite everything, Nina couldn't bring it to the surface now.

So much was unsaid between them. The matter of Nina's supposed death, her childhood with Iolo. But the connection between mother and daughter was so fragile, neither dared risk it in conversation.

"You must be tired, Emma. It can't have been restful on your journey here."

"I am a little sleepy." Nina eyed the bed. It was large with a thick, downy mattress and soft quilts. The pillows were round and puffy, and Nina longed to merge herself in their midst.

Cora drew out a soft, filmy chemise from the wardrobe. "Put on your shift. I'll brush out your hair, shall I? And then you can sleep until dinner."

Nina sat in front of the vanity mirror and her mother began to brush out the tangled curls. "You have lovely hair, my dear."

Nina glanced up into the mirror at her mother. "My grandparents must have been light-haired. Papa is so dark."

Cora hesitated. "Yes . . . My mother was blond."

"Do I look like her, then?"

"You do, a bit. Your mouth, in particular, is shaped like hers. And she had greenish-brown eyes just as we do."

Under Cora's skill, Nina's hair fell into a soft blanket of shimmering waves, then Cora helped Nina out of her dress. Nina crawled beneath the covers of her new bed. She sank down into the soft mattress and closed her eyes. She felt safe, peaceful, like a small child.

Cora sat beside her, gently patting her head. "Forgive me, my dear Emma, for treating you as a child. I can't seem to help myself."

"I don't mind, Mama," replied Nina sleepily. To her own surprise, she took Cora's hand and squeezed it. "It makes me feel safe."

Cora smiled, but tears flooded her eyes. "You are safe, my dear. Nothing will ever hurt you again."

Damian sat on the edge of Nina's bed, watching her sleep. She looked content. Melody was sleeping on her back, legs pointed at the ceiling. Snoring. Nina opened her eyes and smiled.

"She likes her new room," observed Damian.

"As do I." Nina yawned and stretched, then smiled up at Damian.

Outside the windows it was darkening to night, but Damian lit a candle and the room glowed warm.

"How long have you been here?"

"An hour or so." Damian bent down to kiss her. Nina's lips parted. She started to pull him down next to her, then shoved him away.

"Damian! You can't be in my room!" Nina sat upright in her bed and peered guiltily around.

"Why not?"

"My mother might discover us, in . . . well, in an indecent position."

"It was your mother who suggested I wake you."

"Was it?" Nina paused, considering the matter. "Still . . ."

"I'm pleased her opinion holds value to you. But she

considers us practically married. I doubt she would object."

"Possibly not. It is a bit surprising that I care. I didn't expect to care. But then, she's not quite what I expected, either."

"No, I saw that. Why not?"

"She doesn't look the way I thought she would. I thought she looked like me."

"I remember you mentioned that once," said Damian. "But then, a child's memory is often distorted. I remember my own father as a giant."

"What do we do now?" Nina roused herself from the bed, and Damian smiled.

"Since you object to the obvious, I suppose you must dress for dinner."

"What should I wear?"

Damian rose reluctantly from the bed and perused Nina's new wardrobe. He drew out a muted blue gown and held it up in front of her. "This might suit."

Nina fingered the material. "It's lovely. Silk."

"It has a low neckline," Damian observed with pleasure.

"I'll keep my chemise tied high."

Damian sighed.

Nina donned the required undergarments and three petticoats. Damian assisted with her corset. He tied her hair in a thick, silk bow, and Nina examined her reflection in the looking glass.

"Am I ready, do you think?"

"You are perfection, my love."

Nina's eyes glowed. How easily she turned from the street urchin to a lady! She was beautiful, yet beneath the refined exterior, Damian sensed the same untamed quality he first loved. Nina hadn't changed.

As he led her to the door and down the stairs, a faint premonition surfaced in Damian's mind. It was all proceeding too easily. So much was concealed deep in Nina's mind, the same rage and fear that ripped them apart in Philadelphia. He'd seen nothing of it. Why? What would it take to unveil that madness again?

Damian brought Nina into the parlor where guests waited for the announcement of dinner. Nina felt happy, she wanted to please her mother. Yet there was something she hadn't considered. Hadn't let herself consider.

Cora was waiting for her in the parlor. "Emma, how perfectly lovely you are!"

Nina followed her into the room. Everything seemed to have slowed as her gaze moved to the guests. Even their facial expressions, the way they rose from their seats, seemed slow. As if it happened in a dream.

Ethan rose, smiling. Black Hawk stood in a corner. He nodded slightly when she glanced at him. Nina saw Caesar bearing a tray of crystal glasses around the room. And then, slower and slower, her gaze went to the tall man who stood at the far end of the parlor.

Is he an angel, Mama? The devil himself stood before her. His face, the face of a god, appeared frozen. The blue eyes glinted like a storm raging over an eternal sea. Golden hair crowned his menacingly angelic head. His full, expressive lips were parted.

Nina's breath came in tiny, forced gasps. Her blood turned to ice, her fingers and hands were numb. She swayed as dizziness descended over her. Damian caught her arm, supporting her.

Nina shook her head wildly, backing toward the door. "No." She pulled away from Damian. "What is he doing here?" Her voice was shrill, shaking with terror and hatred.

"Emma . . . This is my husband, Ian Forbes."

Nina whirled to her mother. "I know who he is! Why is he here?"

"This is his house. He lives here, darling."

The dark past loomed before Nina, blotting out all reason, all joy. "Then I will not! I will not live in the same house with him!"

"I will leave." Ian's soft, English voice reached her ears, but at the sound, Nina screamed, pushed Damian aside, and fled upstairs.

Cora started after her, tears upon her cheeks, but Damian stopped her. "I'll go."

Nina lay awake in her bed. She insisted that Damian leave her. She said a brief good-night to her mother, but refused to let anyone question her outburst. The room was dark, the noises from the street beyond lulling and peaceful. Nina lay in terror.

She dreaded the dream. She knew it would come. Dear God, he looked just the same. In twenty years, he hadn't changed. She remembered him so vividly. The terror was so acute she couldn't begin to examine it. Nina got up and looked out the window. *I can't let myself sleep. Not tonight.*

She had seen Ian Forbes leave the house. She saw him hug Cora, she saw Damian standing with him beside the coach. She saw Ethan and Black Hawk bid him farewell. Even Melody wagged her tail in his presence. They all admired him, loved him. Nina closed her eyes in dark despair.

Nina couldn't sit still. She got up and paced restlessly around the room. She looked back out the window. Several redcoat guards rode by. A coach passed, then another, but the street grew quieter.

Damian knocked on their connecting door and Nina jumped. She went to the door. "What do you want?"

"I want to talk to you."

"I'm sleeping."

"For someone asleep, you're making a lot of noise."
Damian opened the door to find Nina standing on the
other side.

"I was about to sleep. You are interrupting me."

"I see."

"What do you want?"

Damian took her arm and directed her to the bed.
"Sit."

Nina obeyed. She folded her hands on her lap and
sat rigidly beside him.

"I want to talk to you about Ian Forbes."

"No."

"Nina, you've been fair to your mother. Can you not
give the same consideration to her husband?"

"No."

"What is it that bothers you so? Ian Forbes is a good
man."

"He is a monster. I know it, Damian. You trust him,
I see. You all trust him. But that is the most dangerous
thing about him. That people trust him."

Damian shook his head. "You're not making sense,
Nina. You know nothing of the man. If you saw him at
all, you weren't even two years old."

Nina's eyes narrowed. "I remember him as if it was
yesterday."

"When he took your mother? Nina, you don't know
what happened. They tried to take you. Somehow, your
father prevented it."

"They abandoned me. They threw me away. No, *he*
threw me away!"

"Threw you away? Nina, you're remembering a
dream . . ."

"No! My dream is memory. It is a *warning*. My mother
tried to keep me, but he threw me away, into the dark-

ness, to the creatures that were trying to get me, to those black wolves."

"Wolves?"

"Yes!" Her memory was coming back. "They were chasing me, and he threw me at them. Ask him!"

"This is absurd, Nina. Ian Forbes has been through enough grief in his life without you accusing him of nightmare crimes."

"He left, didn't he? He left because he knows it's true. He wanted my mother. He didn't want me. He wanted to kill me. Papa saved me. He hid me, so that Ian Forbes wouldn't get me."

"You sound like a child, Nina, and a very young one at that. Surely you see this is just some wild story Evans concocted?"

Nina's mouth tightened. "I remember, Damian."

"You couldn't remember."

Anger flared in both and they glared at each other. "You take his part over mine."

"I take the part of reason."

Nina fumed. "You can go back to your room now," she said coldly, though her throat tightened with misery. She needed him to hold her, to silence her fears. Instead, Damian Knox defended her enemy. Again.

"I will leave, yes." Damian rose from her bed. "Maybe you need time alone. You have suffered. You were raised by that hotheaded Welshman. But Ian and Cora suffered more, Nina. Because of Iolo Evans."

"You know nothing of my father!"

"I know he tried to kill us both."

"Because I betrayed him. Just as Ian Forbes made my mother do."

"I will leave until you can see reason." Damian went to the door between them, but then he looked back. His gaze cast along the length of her body.

Nina saw the flash of his desire and her body responded. *I will not give in to you.* She got into her bed and pulled the covers defiantly high. Damian understood her unspoken denial.

"Very well. When you are ready to see reason, we will discuss this matter again."

"If you expect me to change my mind, then we will never speak of it."

"Then it lies between us."

Nina looked away, hiding the tears that fell across her face and soaked into her shift. "It has been between us all along."

Neither Cora nor Ethan mentioned the disastrous meeting with Ian Forbes, but Damian was cold and silent during breakfast. Nina didn't look at him, but his betrayal hurt.

Cora seemed to notice the tension between them, but she said nothing. She directed the conversation toward Ethan instead. "Are you free for the day, darling?"

Ethan swallowed a large portion of bread, then shook his head. "Afraid not, Mother," he replied thickly. He swallowed again. "Damian and I are required at a muster of the Light Dragoons. A new division is being added."

Nina looked at Damian, but she couldn't speak. Fortunately, Cora voiced her concerns anyway. "The Dragoons? But they'll be sent South, won't they?"

"So it appears," answered Ethan cheerfully as he reached across the table for more bread.

"You're leaving?" Nina couldn't help herself. It hadn't occurred to her that Damian would return to the war. "I thought you served here."

"So I have done, for nearly three years. After evacuating Philadelphia, after the battle at Monmouth, I was transferred to Colonel Forbes's command." He paused and glanced at Cora, who looked off into space with a faintly guilty expression on her small face.

"As was I," put in Ethan. "Haven't seen much in the way of fighting."

"Which is for the best," said Cora. "There is intellectual work to be done in New York. That is what you are best suited to accomplish."

Ethan frowned. "Not so, Mother! I'm a good shot. You know I studied fencing at school. Just let me at those rebels, and I'll put them in their place."

"Which is why I'm accompanying him to the Dragoons," added Damian.

Nina understood. Ethan was young and hotheaded. Without restraint, he would risk his life. Damian would join him as his protector. A cool chill washed through Nina as she watched the two young men. Was this not also Daniel Knox's reasoning when he gave his life for Ian Forbes?

Nina glanced at her mother. Something in her expression told Nina her mother was thinking the same thing. "You'd both be wisest to stay here." Both she and Nina knew this would never happen.

"South to Virginia, Mother!" declared Ethan. "Black Hawk is coming along, as Damian's aide. With three such fine specimens of manhood, we'll be invincible! If only soldiers were permitted to wear buckskin . . ."

Cora uttered a small whimper. "Oh, dear."

"When are you going?" asked Nina. Damian was leaving her. He had deposited her with her mother, and now his duty was complete. She fought an impulse to cry.

Ethan didn't seem to notice their distress. "We move south in a week." He rose from the table and dropped his napkin. "Come, Damian, or we'll be late. Black Hawk is waiting at the stables."

Nina watched them leave the dining room with a

heavy heart. She and Cora sat quietly, sipping tea, until the servants came to clear the table.

"Don't worry, Nina. I've planned a pleasant outing for us this morning. I believe you were acquainted with Lavinia Fairchild and her daughter in Philadelphia."

"I was."

"We'll take lunch at their home, if you like. Anna is anxious to see you. I believe she's quite fond of you."

"As I was of her." Nina thought of Black Hawk. "Perhaps we might entertain them here. Anna traveled amongst the Iroquois. She might like Black Hawk."

"It would be a rare young woman who didn't," said Cora.

"Mother!"

"Well, he's quite handsome, isn't he?"

"Yes, I suppose he is."

Accompanied by Melody, Cora took Nina all around occupied Manhattan. British soldiers and Loyalists consumed the city, but it was lively though rather dirty. Pigs scurried down back alleys in search of garbage.

"They need a better way of cleaning the streets," observed Cora in disgust.

"Pigs are nice," replied Nina wistfully. Melody darted after one of the smaller pigs. "No, Melly!"

Melody stopped and regretfully abandoned the chase. "Good girl."

A large coach whirled around a corner, nearly knocking both Nina and her mother off their feet. Nina grabbed Cora's arm and pulled her out of danger, lest the reckless coachman bowl them both over. Nina shook her fist at the driver, and Melody barked.

"They should be reported!"

"True enough," agreed Cora as she brushed herself

off and patted her hair into place. "But not bloody likely."

Nina looked at her mother in surprise. "Why not?"

"That was Benedict Arnold and his wife. On their way to General Clinton, no doubt."

"Arnold! So he's here, is he? The bastard!"

"Language, dear."

"His wife is with him? Peggy Shippen?"

"Yes. Did you know her in Philadelphia?" Cora's coach stopped for them and the footman helped them inside. Nina seated herself beside her mother.

"I remember the girl," replied Nina as the coach started off. "But I remember she was taken with John André before marrying our villainous Arnold. I expect he did it for her. The Shippens were Loyalists, terribly conservative."

"How dull. But don't underestimate the young lady, my dear. She's quite as guilty as he, mark my words. It was she who lured John André into communication with her husband, or so I've heard. She's pretty, innocent . . ." Cora made a noise that resembled gagging. "The worst kind. They say she threw a terrible fit of hysterics before General Washington himself. That took nerve. And here she is, parading around New York like a queen."

"Now that Arnold has defected, perhaps many will follow." Despite her father's madness, Nina's loyalties remained firmly American. She couldn't believe America would endure tyranny ever again.

"You echo the vain hope of our commanders. But they know nothing of us, of Americans."

Nina stopped and stared at her mother. *"Us?"*

"I came here with my parents as a small child, though my brother claimed an estate in northern Wales and refused to join us. His son, your cousin, Enoch, lives in

Boston. I understand he's made quite a name for himself."

"As a loyalist or rebel?"

"Rebel, of course. I saw how we were treated as inferiors during the French and Indian war. No, Iolo wasn't wrong to resent the way the Colonials were treated during that war. And then to have England raise our taxes in payment . . ."

Cora hadn't mentioned Iolo Evans until now. Nina was astounded. "Papa says the same was true in Wales."

"I remember that. He was sold . . . 'indentured,' by the English, and sent to America. It left him very bitter. And his sense of outrage was indiscriminate."

Nina couldn't argue that point. "Why did you marry him?" She was nearing dangerous waters, but Cora was unperturbed.

"Our marriage was arranged by my parents. Iolo paid off his masters and went to live in western New York. He did very well there, commanding the Colonial militia and trading with the nearby Indian tribes.

"My parents' farm was in Onondaga territory. It was burned by an Iroquois war party, and they were unable to pay their debt to Iolo. Rather than humiliate them with debt, he requested my hand."

Why did you betray him with Ian Forbes? Nina wanted to ask, but she couldn't. Romantic notions surfaced in her mind. Perhaps Forbes threatened her father's life, and Cora had been forced to go with him.

Another elegant coach passed by them, at a more reasonable pace than Arnold's, but Cora shook her head disgustedly anyway. Nina glimpsed a hawk-faced man in uniform with a much younger woman at his side.

"Who was that?" asked Nina.

"Our esteemed General Clinton. And his pretty Irish whore."

"Mother!"

Cora shrugged. "Clinton bribed her husband. But the girl wouldn't relent until she caught her husband in bed with a strumpet. So she trotted off to Clinton's bed in revenge."

"How tawdry!"

"It's revolting. You have no idea, my dear child, how many men spend their nights in brothels. How many with wives in England take mistresses here, and those more often than not, wives of other men. I find it depressing."

Nina's brow rose at her mother's strong sentiment. Hadn't she left her husband for her golden-haired lover?

"Love is sacred, Emma," declared Cora. "We shouldn't fiddle around with it. For love, a man may perform the most heroic deeds. As you've seen with Damian."

"He saved me," remembered Nina. "When I was caught stealing arms from the Loyal Legion. Banastre Tarleton wanted to shoot me, and Damian stepped between us. I almost shot him, I was so afraid. But I couldn't. Did he tell you that?"

"He didn't mention it, no. He spared me the more frightening details of your life. He told me he had met you, that he loved you and intended to bring you to New York as his wife. He asked for his mother's ring, which he left in my care."

Nina sighed. "My ring. I'm afraid I threw it at him. I suppose it's lost."

Cora said nothing about Damian's ring. "You're older now, Emma. Perhaps it's for the best. Seventeen is young to marry, though it's common. Maturity makes a happier wife."

"How old were you?"

"I was sixteen when I was betrothed to Iolo. But twenty-two when I married Ian."

Nina's mouth hardened, but Cora didn't go on with the subject. "We were unusual, perhaps. Ian was only eighteen."

"He's younger than you?" Nina was surprised enough to ask, though she didn't want to hear about Ian Forbes.

"He is, yes. Just the same age as Ethan is now, though I don't remember he was as youthful as your brother. Ethan's life has been too easy, too pleasant, I think."

"Ethan is very likable. Innocent, somehow."

"He is, yes. I question the description 'innocent,' though. Women fawn too easily over him."

"Do they? He seems young for romantic attachments."

"I'm not certain his encounters can be termed 'romantic.'" Cora sighed wearily. "Women, of surprisingly varied ages, adore him. Perhaps I should say, lust after him."

"Mother!"

Cora shrugged. "It's that sweet, innocent face of his."

"And the twinkling eyes. My brother is on his way to becoming a rake."

"Well on his way. After the trouble at Eton, I hoped he would calm down. But no."

"What trouble?"

"Don't ask. Let it suffice to say it involved a pretty barmaid of easy virtue. Easy, at least for Ethan. Naturally, he charmed his way back into school . . ."

"Naturally." Nina repressed a smile. "Did he love her? Damian almost married an innkeeper's daughter, after all."

"Damian's Elaine was different," said Cora. Nina frowned. How dare her mother approve of Damian's first love!

"You knew her?"

Cora patted Nina's arm. "Damian brought her to our home, though his mother's family disapproved intensely. Yes, I had sympathy for their situation. Ian's father disapproved of me, too."

"Did he?" asked Nina indignantly. "Why?"

"For no good reason. Sir Percy was, and is, the most cantankerous old coot I've ever encountered."

"Sir?"

"A baronet." Cora didn't sound impressed by the title, but Nina's frown deepened. Ian Forbes was the son of a nobleman. A cantankerous nobleman.

"Elaine was a pleasant girl. Beautiful, naturally. Chestnut hair, blue eyes." Nina's eyes narrowed combatively, and Cora laughed.

"She didn't compare to you, my dear. Not so much sparkle."

Nina was not assuaged. She issued a *humph* noise.

Cora smiled. "And her eyes *were* a trifle close together."

This satisfied Nina, and her mouth curved into a slight smile.

"I thought they might be happy together, but Ian said Damian would tire of her. It was Ian who suggested adventure in America, actually."

Cora watched Nina's expression. Nina bit her lip. She didn't want to attribute one speck of her happiness to Ian Forbes. Her chin rose. "Does he interfere in Ethan's life likewise?"

"Occasionally. Less than I do, perhaps," Cora added with a guilty smile. "That boy is too charming for his own good."

"You love him very much."

"I do. After losing you, Ethan was someone I could protect. But he can be reckless. He yearns for excitement. Adventure. But more than that, I think he's always wanted to prove his worth." Cora sighed. "Ethan is a good boy. He knew he had a sister. I think it bothered him that you suffered while his life was so sweet."

Nina endured a wave of emotion on her brother's behalf. "I didn't suffer, Mother. Whatever you think of Papa, he was good to me."

"I can see that. But it was hard to imagine, then . . . We tried to keep your loss from obscuring the joy of Ethan's life. But he knew. He thinks he must prove his worth in battle, as young men often do. More's the pity. It is fortunate for Ethan that he's so endearing. I take great comfort knowing men with cooler wits, Damian and Black Hawk, have seen fit to watch him."

"Damian is very fond of him."

"Damian has a kind heart," said Cora. "It is part of his appeal to women, I suppose. Though it's the suggestion of, well . . . prowess that enthralls them."

"Prowess?"

"Yes, my dear. A sense that along with that magnificent, lean physique goes a fair idea what to do with it."

"Mother! You can't mean . . ." Nina stopped, a hot blush flooding her cheeks.

"Surely you know? I would have thought, considering everything, you two would know each other fairly well, shall we say." Cora looked out the window and called to the footman. "Next street on the right, Garrison." She turned back to Nina. "I would imagine Damian would be quite accomplished at the romantic arts."

Nina's mouth dropped. True, her mother was accurate, but to hear the subject of her intimacy with Damian discussed so casually was embarrassing.

"Do you know, it shocked me to learn I could feel that way, want something so much," continued Cora pleasantly while Nina's face paled. "But love-making is the true bond between men and women. Though misused, its true flowering is through love. Don't you agree, dear?"

"I suppose so. It doesn't seem decent to talk about it this way."

"Well, I wouldn't talk about it with Lavinia Fairchild. But we're alike, you and I. And we might as well be honest."

Nina gazed out the window. "I can't seem to escape that portion of my nature."

"Why should you wish to escape, Emma? How fortunate we are to feel this way! Pity the poor woman who gives herself without love, but more, the woman who won't give herself at all."

Cora directed Nina's attention to a tall, narrow brick town house. "Here, this is where Lavinia stays now."

Anna welcomed them at the door and led them to the parlor. "We've expected you for years! We feared something dreadful happened to you."

"I'm perfectly fine," said Nina. "And you?"

"We are happy here," said Anna, but Lavinia sighed heavily.

"Oh, but it's not Philadelphia, my dear. How I miss my old city, the quiet streets, the dignity! Curse the rebels for stealing it back."

Anna rolled her eyes. "Come, Nina, let me show you my room. It has a lovely view of the park."

Nina sensed Anna wanted to talk to her alone, and she followed her up the stairs eagerly. Anna's room was unremarkable, and the barges in the river seemed less than scenic. As soon as they entered, Anna seized Nina's hand, her eyes gleaming with excitement.

"Tell me, quickly, Nina . . . How is it with Damian Knox? Have you married? I heard some wild story that you were engaged to someone else, but I knew it couldn't be true."

They sat on Anna's bed as Nina confided the details of her reunion with Damian. "I was engaged, actually."

"But you didn't love him."

"No. He didn't love me either. At the time, that seemed the best arrangement."

"I know. I felt the same about Philip. It was easier not to love. I wish my life had gone as yours. But it pleases me vicariously to know you have your love again."

Nina didn't want to discuss her recent troubles with Damian. "How do you know the same isn't true for you?"

"Oh, Nina, it's been years. The man I once mentioned has no doubt forgotten me. He probably has many children by now."

"Perhaps." Nina decided not to mention Black Hawk yet. "It's unfortunate my brother is so young. You might like him. But if you come for dinner tonight, as my mother has asked, you will meet him."

"That sounds pleasant."

Nina watched her delicate friend as she fingered the lace of her bedspread. *She expects no adventure, but she longs for it anyway.* If Nina had her way, Anna would meet not only Ethan Forbes, but Black Hawk as well.

EIGHT

Cora and Nina returned home to find a young woman seated in the parlor. "Aunt Cora!" The girl rose and hugged Nina's mother. Nina's brow furrowed.

"Emma, my dear, this is my niece, Penelope Forbes. She will be staying with us since her mother is returning to London."

Penelope inspected Nina with a cool appraisal that left Nina feeling inadequate. Like Nina, she was tall and blond, but there the similarity ended. Penelope was thoroughly well-tended, not a hair out of place. Her gown was lavish, her motions studied and careful, her manners those of an accomplished lady.

"Emmalina, I've heard so much about you." Penelope's manner was both gracious and condescending. "From Damian, naturally. But didn't he call you by another name?"

"I am Nina."

"Really? How . . . unusual. Who named you that?"

"I named myself."

Cora smiled. "So you did. You were quite adamant about it, even before you were two. Of course, you couldn't pronounce your *L's*. I think you were too proud to admit it."

"How wonderful that Damian brought you back to

Aunt Cora." It didn't sound heartfelt. Penelope looked purposefully around the room. "Where is Damian?"

Cora poured tea, serving Nina first. "He and Ethan will be back soon. Mrs. Fairchild and her daughter will also be joining us at dinner."

"Anna? That dry little thing? How tiresome!"

Nina glared at Penelope. "Actually, Anna has led an exceedingly adventurous life. She was even lost among the Iroquois."

Cora looked at Nina in surprise, but Penelope grimaced as Nina bit her loose tongue. "How dreadful! It's amazing she survived."

"She is an amazing girl."

"How lucky you are to be with your mother." Penelope's gaze traveled disdainfully down Nina's thin figure. "I can't imagine growing up without a mother's careful schooling. You have so much to learn. Why, Aunt Cora and Uncle Ian have been like second parents to me."

Cora set her teacup aside. "Penelope, perhaps you'd like to check on your room?"

Penelope left and Cora spoke in a low voice to Nina. "If I'd been her 'second parent,' she'd know a thing or two more about tact."

"She's very polished, isn't she?" Nina hesitated. "I suppose she's the sort of wife Damian expected to have."

"Ha! She's too polished, if you ask me," replied Cora with a huff. "But she insisted on staying here when her mother fell sick. Ian and I were obligated to take her in." Cora leaned in, speaking confidentially in Nina's ear. "She wants Damian, of course. You can expect more rot from her, but don't you listen. You go take a nap, my dear, and I'll see Penelope is kept too busy to bother you."

* * *

Nina took her mother's advice. She lay on her bed reflecting on her peculiar circumstance. Cora Forbes was nothing like she'd expected. She'd expected an older Penelope. The day in Cora's company revealed to Nina the hidden similarities between mother and daughter. *Love is sacred, Emma. We shouldn't fiddle around with it.*

Soft voices reached her ears from the street below. Nina got up and peered out the window, but the speakers were out of her sight.

"She is well, I promise you, Ian."

Cora spoke to Ian Forbes. Nina couldn't hear her stepfather's reply. She thought a moment, then opened the door to Damian's room. She moved furtively to his window. As she hoped, it proved a better vantage point from which to eavesdrop.

A momentary pang of guilt passed, and Nina listened to her mother's conversation. "If you came back, if she could see you as I do . . ."

"No." Ian Forbes sounded bitter. "That isn't possible, Cora, and you know it. It's best for me to stay away."

"The nights are too long without you." Cora's voice lowered and Nina frowned. She looked out the window and saw Ian Forbes kiss her mother. Cora's arms were around his neck. Nina sat back. It was like watching herself with Damian.

Ian Forbes was handsome, she had to acknowledge that. She could imagine he would be attractive to women. He looked young and somehow innocent. It was that angelic appearance that was so deceptive.

"What does she know?"

"Nothing," replied Cora. "It's too early to explain, Ian. She's been through so much. We must be patient. Let us leave the matter until she's stronger."

"It will make no difference."

Nina watched Ian Forbes ride away and she went back

to her own room, trying to decipher what she'd heard. He was probably bitter because she was in his house. Perhaps he feared Nina would destroy his marriage as he destroyed her life.

Nina fell asleep pondering the issue. But Ian Forbes didn't intrude on her dreams. Damian filled every image, she explored his body with wanton delight. She was consumed with a love and desire that would never abate. When Nina woke, her body felt warm and restless inside.

The erotic imagery of her dreams returned in force. A tide of desire coursed through her. Nina wanted Damian. She wanted to hold him, to love him. They didn't have to agree on every little matter.

She heard him arriving outside with Ethan and Black Hawk, and her pulse quickened. *Tonight I will love you. I will go to you and make you forget our differences.* She dressed hurriedly and pulled her chemise low above the bodice of her dress so that the swell of her breasts would be visible.

Nina met Penelope on the stairs. Alone, there was little need to pretend affection between them, but for her mother's sake, Nina forced herself to be polite. She didn't want to waste time with Penelope Forbes tonight.

"Is your room pleasant, Penelope?" she asked as Penelope moved to the stairs.

"You have *my room*," replied Penelope. "But that won't last long."

Though Nina guessed Penelope disliked her, the girl's venomous attitude surprised her all the same. "Why? My mother gave it to me. She never mentioned it was yours."

"Your mother? That seems unlikely, *Emma.* Tell me, how were you able to convince Damian that you were Cora Forbes's daughter? I find it hard to believe Damian would care for a strumpet like you."

Nina's mouth dropped. "I am her daughter!"

"You don't look a thing alike."

Despite the truth of her statement, Nina was hurt. "We're alike inside."

"Ha! Cora Forbes is as much a lady as you are a street rat."

"I look like my grandmother. Mother told me so."

"Apparently Uncle Ian doesn't agree. He won't come near the house while you're here."

Penelope whirled away and headed down the stairs, but Nina stood still as stone. *So that's why he left! Just as I suspected he's angry with Mama for bringing me here.* Nina's heart filled with hatred for Ian Forbes.

Ian Forbes may have convinced Penelope she wasn't Cora's real daughter, but he'd never convince Cora. *She may have to choose between us. But this time, you'll be the one who falls into darkness.*

"Damian!" Penelope greeted Damian and Nina's anger grew. Penelope's voice was so sweet, but it was also flirtatious. Nina listened for the tone of Damian's response.

"Penelope, you're prettier each time I see you."

Nina rolled her eyes. She went down the stairs to greet them also, but it was Ethan who came to hug her. "My beautiful sister!" He spoke loudly, with the obvious intent of irritating Penelope. "How was your day? Did you enjoy New York?"

"It was a good day," said Nina, careful to keep her chin high lest Penelope see her annoyance. "We visited friends from Philadelphia. We even saw Benedict Arnold and his wife."

Ethan chuckled. "Imagine they're lonely."

"Why would they be lonely? Isn't he a hero here?"

"No, indeed! He'd get a better welcome in Philadelphia. This was John André's city. The English don't think much of the trade."

Penelope wound her arm through Damian's. He didn't cast her off. "That much is certain."

"Damian, is it true you've joined the Dragoons?" asked Penelope breathlessly. "But you can't be thinking of leaving us so soon?"

"We leave tomorrow," said Ethan.

"So soon?" Nina's face paled and Damian looked disapprovingly toward Ethan.

"There's a push toward Virginia. I'm afraid we're moving out earlier than expected."

Penelope hovered at Damian's side as they awaited Lavinia and Anna in the parlor. "Where's Black Hawk?" asked Nina.

Ethan gestured toward the door. "He's coming. Buckskin takes longer to assemble than a uniform." He cleared his throat. "When it's done right."

Cora sighed. "You would know."

Lavinia and Anna arrived, and Caesar led them into the parlor. Nina was beginning to think she should have warned Anna, but at that moment Black Hawk entered the room. Had Nina any doubts about their past relationship, it vanished as soon as they saw each other.

Anna froze, her face whitened. Black Hawk stood still as stone, but he saw no one in the room except Anna Fairchild. Voices surrounded them, introductions were made, but Nina knew that neither heard anything that was said.

Damian turned to Black Hawk. "My aide, Black Hawk of the Onondaga."

"Black Hawk and I have met before." Anna's voice was clear, though a little shaky, and her blue eyes were aglow with feeling.

"What?" Lavinia turned to inspect the Indian. "You've met him? Where?"

"Black Hawk was the scout who saved me, Mother."

"Oh. I didn't recognize him. It's good to see you well, Black . . . Hawk."

"You are well, it is good, Mrs. Fairchild," said Black Hawk, but his gaze was on Anna.

Lavinia glanced apologetically at Cora. "His English could stand perfecting."

"Ah, but his French is flawless," put in Damian with a grin.

Black Hawk wasn't listening. He noticed Anna's mourning dress, and his eyes narrowed. "You wear black."

"Anna is in mourning," explained Lavinia. "Her fiancé was killed in battle."

"I bleed for your loss," said Black Hawk.

"My loss came long before I knew Philip Compton."

Lavinia's brow furrowed at Anna's words. Cora coughed and waved toward the dining room. "Shall we dine?"

Penelope seated herself at Damian's side. Nina sat between Ethan and Black Hawk, whose placement at the far end of the table couldn't keep his attention from Anna. Lavinia chattered on oblivious to the currents between her daughter and the Indian, and Penelope maintained a running conversation with Cora and Ethan.

Nina's gaze rested on the curve of Damian's lips, her own mouth curved into a smile. *I will have you tonight, my love. Nothing will stand between us now.*

The evening passed in pleasantries, but when Lavinia and Anna finally made ready to leave, Anna took Black Hawk's hand. "I thought our parting was 'til the world's end. Wishes have power, after all."

Black Hawk said nothing, but Nina detected a rise of color in his face. Damian's brow rose, but Anna smiled sweetly as she said good-night to the others. Cora's cheeks looked flushed, as if in anticipation of adventure. Nina eyed her suspiciously, but Cora retired to her room.

Penelope made Nina's own exit more difficult. "The night is so young."

"Young for those who haven't drilled all day," replied Ethan. "I, for one, am in need of bed tonight. Black Hawk, where are you going?"

Black Hawk was standing by the door, staring at the wall, lost in indecision. "Walk." He opened the door and left.

Nina eyed Damian, a teasing smile upon her lips. "Restless, isn't he?"

"He has much on his mind tonight, it seems," replied Damian.

"As have we all."

Ethan seized Penelope's arm. "I'll see you to your room, cousin."

"That's not necessary."

"I'd hate for you to get lost."

Ethan led her forcibly from the parlor, leaving Damian alone with Nina. Nina headed for the stairs. She stopped on the fifth step and looked back.

"I, also, am going to bed. And there I will await you."

Nina's room was dark, but the curtains were drawn back letting in the lamplight of the city. Damian opened the door to find her waiting for him. She wore only her chemise. The outline of her body was revealed as the city light streamed in through the open window. Her hair hung loose about her shoulders, tossed gently in an evening breeze.

"I have come."

"I feared you might not."

"You knew, my love. A sailor could resist the Lorelei better than I could deny you."

Nina moved toward him, her steps so light that she seemed to float across the floor. She placed her hand on his chest. Her fingers played at the clasp of his shirt.

"If you must leave, I would make you a part of me for all time." Nina unbuttoned his shirt and slid her hand against his bare chest, then kissed his mouth. His lips played against hers.

Damian felt the eagerness of her kiss, and the last vestiges of his anger with her disappeared. She could be unreasonable, she could be annoyingly willful and defiant. She was surely the most stubborn woman he'd ever known.

Nina's kiss left his mouth and traveled to the strong cord of his neck, down to his shoulder as she pushed his shirt away. Her tongue touched his skin; licks of fire shot from nerve to nerve. Her hand ran the length of his muscular arm to his hand, her fingers entwined with his.

Nina looked up into his face and smiled. "I love you so." She reached to untie the binding of his hair. "You are beautiful, Damian Knox. When I dream of you, you look like this."

Damian shuddered with anticipation when Nina sank to her knees before him. She tugged at his breeches, sliding them down over his hips, down his thighs. His erection sprang free, proclaiming his rampant desire beyond doubt.

Nina took his length in her hand, lovingly caressed him while Damian stood spellbound before her. She looked up at him, and a tiny smile formed on the triangle of her lips. Agonizingly slow, she kissed him. With torturous leisure, she brushed her lips back and forth across the blunt tip.

Damian's knees went weak, a harsh groan escaped his lips as she took his staff in her mouth His fingers clasped in her hair when she ran her tongue along the slick surface. He might find such pleasure in a harem, but Nina seemed born with the instinct to please him.

He was in her power, his pulse raced as she teased him. She urged then slowed until his every breath was a moan. He was wild with lust, shaken to his core with need. He seized Nina's shoulders, then pulled her up against him.

Nina laughed when he swept her into his arms. She wrapped her arms around his neck and pulled his head to hers. He kissed her passionately, delving with his tongue in sweet premonition of what would come next.

Damian stripped away her shift, then set her beneath him on the soft bed. Nina sank back into the pillows, the look of an enchantress upon her face. She reached out and touched his throbbing length, wrapping her fingers snugly around his shaft.

"You torment me, little rebel." Damian grabbed her hands, and pinned them above her head. "I can take no more of your witches' art without spilling myself."

Nina squirmed beneath him, but Damian prolonged her raging desire. He moved his length against her, sliding back and forth against her sex. Her hips rose to meet him, an invitation Damian couldn't refuse. He plunged deep within her and Nina cried out in delirious pleasure.

He filled her completely, then withdrew to thrust inward again. His lips molded to hers, her fingers entwined with his as their bodies fused together. Damian's body surged with primal force.

Nina's legs wrapped around his as her slender hips ground against his. His name came with every breath as the spiral within reached its pinnacle, snapping and unwinding with blinding intensity. The rapturous contractions enveloped him, urging him beyond endurance as he, too, exploded within her perfect warmth.

They collapsed against each other, breath intermingling in shuddering gasps. Damian lifted his weight away from her and she sighed. He kissed her, then withdrew from her body. They lay face to face, their hands clasped as they looked into each other's eyes.

"I wish this night would never end," Nina murmured. "I fear to sleep, for the morning will come and you'll be gone."

Damian drew her hand to his mouth and kissed her fingers. "We'll marry before I go, my love. I must leave, but I'll come back. Don't worry."

"How can we marry, if you leave tomorrow?"

"It's time enough."

"My mother might be disappointed if we elope. She's mentioned our wedding several times. But I don't want to wait."

Damian considered the matter. "We're headed west, I understand, before south. I'll return here, to New York, when we board the ship to Virginia. That will be two or three months. We could marry then."

"It seems a long while. But it will give my mother time to prepare."

Damian moved away and fumbled with his discarded breeches.

"What are you doing?"

"I have something of yours." Damian lay back beside Nina, taking her hand in his.

"What is it?"

Damian just smiled, then slipped an amethyst ring on her finger.

"My ring! You didn't lose it?"

"Of course not, though it was hard enough to locate. I've carried it, waiting until I was sure you were ready to keep it."

Nina kissed the ring, then Damian. "I can wait until you come back. It will give Mother time to prepare. She'll like that."

"So you wish to please her, after all."

"I love her, Damian. I think none of it was her fault. I remember how I loved her before, and now I know why. She's so direct, so honest."

Damian kissed her forehead. He didn't dare broach the subject of Ian Forbes. But if Cora had such sway already with her daughter, surely she would find a way to unite them.

Morning brought a cold, gray drizzle, and Nina stood despondently on the front stairs with Damian. Ethan and Black Hawk had gone for the horses, and Cora left them alone to say their farewells.

The soft rain fell into her face, blending with her tears. They stood hand in hand, but neither found words for goodbye. "You'll come back?"

Damian drew her into his arms. "Of course, love. We won't see much fighting, if any. The real war is in the south now."

"Must you go?"

"It is not my desire. But your brother will go with or without me. As you've seen, Ethan can be unrestrained." A smile crossed Damian's face. "Not unlike his sister, I might add."

"You're going to keep him out of trouble?" Nina couldn't argue with Damian's assessment of her little brother. "Ethan is a bit sure of himself, isn't he? What about Black Hawk?"

"He seems restless. He'll go where I go."

"Why? You've never explained why he was looking for you in the first place."

"He had something of mine."

"What?"

"A letter from my father."

"Your father? How did he get that?"

Damian's face clouded. "My father gave it to Black Hawk before he died."

"Black Hawk was there?"

"He was. He befriended my father, and believed in his innocence. He was a small child—no one listened. But he believes the Onondaga chief, his own father, killed an innocent man, and that it is his duty to clear the victim's name."

"How?"

"By finding the one who was responsible. Someone destroyed that village, and it wasn't Daniel Knox."

"After all these years? That seems impossible."

"Not to Black Hawk."

Black Hawk and Ethan rode up leading Gambrinus, and Damian kissed Nina softly. "I must go, love."

"I will miss you, Damian."

"You'll have more letters than you can read. Though they take awhile to arrive. And I'll expect the same from you."

Nina's face was wet with tears. "I love you."

"It will be a short while apart, and then we'll marry. Nothing will separate us again."

Damian kissed her again, then without looking back, he walked to the horses. Cora came out onto the stairs and put her arm around Nina's shoulder while the three men rode away.

"The days will pass swiftly, Emma. We will spend every hour preparing for your wedding. When Damian Knox returns, you'll have the most beautiful ceremony any girl ever had!"

Nina sniffed and nodded, but her pulse moved slow and heavy. Despite Cora's words, a voice within told her much would befall them before she saw Damian's face again.

* * *

"You look pale," observed Penelope as the women sat reading and sewing in the parlor.

Nina flipped a page in her book and gritted her teeth. "I'm perfectly fine."

"Well, you certainly sleep enough. You missed breakfast again."

"I was awake late . . . reading." Another lie. She wasn't fine, and she was sleeping a lot. But she couldn't help it. She had even been too tired to finish her latest letter to Damian.

"I suppose now that Damian is gone, you have no need to keep yourself looking well," said Penelope.

Cora frowned. "Emma has been through a great deal. It is natural she would need time to recuperate."

Nina puffed an impatient breath. "I'm not recuperating. I was just sleepy. In fact, I think I'll go for a walk this afternoon."

"Shall I come with you, my dear?"

"I'm just going a little way, Mother." Nina was afraid Penelope might join them. She felt testier than normal, and she didn't want to snap at Penelope in front of Cora. Maybe alone, but not in front of Cora.

"Be careful, Emma. It's easy to get lost in New York."

Nina drew her shawl around her shoulders. "I won't go far."

Despite Cora's warning, Nina found herself wandering farther than she'd intended. On an unfamiliar street, she realized she was lost. A group of redcoats passed by, and she decided to follow them. They passed by an unobtrusive building, but Nina was too tired to go any farther. A small courtyard was nestled behind the brick house, and she slipped inside to rest.

Voices came from just inside the greenroom, and Nina froze. She recognized that soft, low English accent, but the woman to whom Ian Forbes spoke was not her mother. Nina's pulse quickened in anger and she crept

nearer the door with the purpose of once again eavesdropping on her treacherous stepfather.

"Ian, my darling." The woman's voice was low and
decidedly seductive. Nina felt sick. The bastard had a
mistress. "She's so unfair, darling. Even if that girl is
her daughter, which I doubt, your wife has no right to
treat you this way."

"You know nothing, Sarah." Ian Forbes's voice was
surprisingly hard speaking to his cloying mistress.

Nina dared peek in the window. Ian Forbes sat behind
a large desk. A young, red-haired woman stood close
beside him, her hand fondling his shoulder. Nina
fumed.

However wrong, Cora loved her husband. How dare
he betray her beautiful mother for this tart? She wasn't
English, but many British commanders took American
mistresses. The girl was pretty, but she couldn't compare to Cora.

"Ian, you know I love you . . ."

Nina felt sick. Aided by a cane, Ian Forbes stood up
from his desk and went to the woman's side. "You don't
know what you're saying."

"I do. Ian, you are magnificent. You fill me with a
hunger I can't resist. I ache for you . . ."

Sarah ran her hand across his chest, the gesture both
intimate and greedy. "The god Apollo would pale in
your shadow."

Ian shook his head, then limped toward the window.
Nina ducked, then scurried out of the yard. Her heart
was pounding. What strange fate led her below Ian
Forbes's window just as his mistress declared her love!

I should kill him. Fury bubbled in her veins. She found
her direction, then stomped back to Cora's house with
the intention of telling her mother everything she'd
seen. Nina stopped outside the front door.

I can't tell her. She loves him, it would kill her. She might not believe me, anyway. But Ian Forbes won't get away with this.

Nina kept Ian Forbes's secret, but her hatred for him intensified as the weeks passed by. Christmas came with wind and snow, but Nina overheard Caesar letting Ian Forbes in the front door, anyway. She stood at the top of the stairs listening as Cora greeted her treacherous husband.

"It's brutal out there," Ian told Cora. *Why didn't you stay away, then?* Nina heard him stomp his feet, ridding his boots of the sticky snow.

"Uncle Ian! You naughty thing, you're getting snow everywhere." Penelope's voice rankled Nina's ears and she bit her lip hard.

"It's getting worse, and that's a fact," added Caesar. "You ain't going make it back tonight, sir."

Nina's heart fell. She looked forward to Christmas with her mother. She'd worked secretly on a lovely shawl to present Cora, but Ian Forbes's presence would ruin everything. Nina left the landing and returned to her room.

Cora knew Nina listened upstairs, she knew when Nina left. "Where is she?" Ian looked around for Nina, then back at Cora.

"She was dressing, I believe. Emma will be down shortly."

"I've brought her a gift." The spark of hopefulness in his blue eyes pierced Cora's heart. He held up a small package. Cora knew what it held and tears started in her eyes.

"That is sweet of you." He looked so young. He wasn't yet forty, but Cora remembered the seventeen-year-old boy she first saw riding towards her on the New York frontier. A boy with supreme confidence, with laughing eyes and the sweetest smile she'd ever seen.

Cora remembered how she fought those first wild surges of her heart, how she trembled when their eyes met. Iolo never suspected, but her mother warned her. *You're betrothed to Iolo Evans, Cora. That English boy will use you, make you his whore, and leave you with nothing. Don't make an enemy of our benefactor.*

Cora remembered standing alone behind the woodshed, hiding. Hiding, lest Ian see how much she adored him, lest she succumb and betray her family and her fiancé. But Cora felt his hand on her shoulder, she saw his beautiful face, his blue eyes black with desire.

You are mine, Cora Talmadge. I will never let you go. And then they fell to the ground in primal celebration of love's fire . . . He had never failed of his vow.

Ian turned to Penelope and kissed his niece dutifully. No, he wasn't young anymore. The laughter had long ago left his eyes, he had seen his power ripped away, he'd seen the ones he loved most destroyed.

Ian sighed. "Perhaps she'll take my gift as a peace offering."

"Emma should be giving you a peace offering," put in Penelope.

Ian ignored Penelope and set his gifts aside. "I hope my presence won't ruin the day for her."

"It's the perfect time for Nina to get to know you," decided Cora, but inwardly she worried over her daughter's reaction. She glanced up the stairs. "I'll check on what's keeping her."

Nina sat on the edge of her bed, fighting anger. Cora entered the room, and Nina steeled herself against confrontation. "What's the matter, dear? I thought you were coming down."

"It might be wiser if I stayed here."

"Dinner is almost ready. Please, Emma. Ian is my husband." She paused, considering the best way to convince her stubborn daughter to attend. "It would mean the world to me if you'd join us. Give him the opportunity to change your impression of him."

"That won't happen, Mother. I don't want to disappoint you, but my feelings about Ian Forbes won't change because it's Christmas."

Cora's face fell and Nina endured a wave of guilt. "But I will come down. I'll try to be civil."

That wouldn't be easy. She could picture Ian Forbes with his red-haired mistress. No doubt he came from her bed to his wife's dinner.

"Thank you, Emma." Cora took Nina's hand and squeezed it. "He means so much to me," she added softly, but her voice was rich with emotion. "Whatever you believe of our past, know Ian Forbes has been a good husband to me, and a fine father to Ethan. I can't bear to think my daughter will see no good in the man I love."

Nina didn't respond. Had Cora seen her beloved husband in another woman's arms . . . Nina fought the temptation to blurt out the entire story. She went downstairs with her mother, but her gaze was cold and hard when she greeted her step-father.

He wore full-dress uniform, but Nina noticed that, like Damian, Ian Forbes wore no wig. His golden hair was tied behind his head. Without joy, Nina realized how little age showed on his face. Only his eyes revealed the strain of the years. Had the sadness in those blue depths been found in any other man, Nina's heart might have been moved to pity.

"Happy Christmas, Emma." Ian Forbes was nervous. "You look lovely."

He's probably a notorious womanizer. His mistress didn't look much older than herself.

"Colonel Forbes. It's good of you to come." *And to take time away from your harlot's bed.*

Cora seized Ian's hand, then Nina's. "Shall we dine?"

Nina sat at the far end of the table from Ian Forbes, issuing only the most perfunctory responses to his attempts at conversation.

"Have you enjoyed New York, Emma?" He was fumbling for anything. "Though enduring occupation, the city can be interesting."

"It is little different from Philadelphia," replied Nina. "English officers parade in garish coaches with their whores, the Loyalists preen and sell their wives at bargain prices. All the while, the Americans step closer to victory."

Nina spoke defiantly, her gaze burning into Ian's, but to her surprise, he merely smiled. She was referring to him, but he didn't seem to make the connection.

"Ah, but fortunately for New York, the war is far to the south today. The South consumes General Cornwallis while Clinton fumes. He fears Cornwallis wants his job."

This seemed to please Ian Forbes, and Nina eyed him doubtfully. "You will not win," she vowed, hoping he caught the double meaning to her assertion.

"No," agreed Ian without anger. "We will lose."

Cora smiled faintly, but Nina's eyes widened in surprise. "What?"

Penelope gasped. "Uncle Ian! You can't mean it!"

"I would guess we have a year, maybe less, before our will runs out, before your esteemed General Washington destroys the last vestiges of our resolve."

"You think we'll win?" asked Nina in amazement.

"Has there been any doubt?"

"Then why are you here?"

Ian didn't answer at once. He glanced at Cora. "Because my heart is here."

Nina looked away. No wonder her mother was so blind. Ian Forbes spoke with the sweetest honey on the tongue of a liar. Nina fell silent through the remainder of dinner, and the conversation deteriorated into strained comments on the weather. When they rose from the table, all but Penelope seemed dismal and ill at ease.

Cora touched Ian's arm. "I have something for you." She found a small package and thrust it into his hands. He opened it and drew out a little book. He opened the pages and read.

"Did you write these poems, love?"

Cora's cheeks turned pink, but she nodded.

"They're wonderful, angel." He kissed her cheek, but Nina looked away. Cora spent her hours writing love sonnets while Ian Forbes entertained his buxom mistress.

Ian brought forth his own gifts, handing first Cora's to her. She opened it eagerly, her eyes misting when she saw a lovely, gold ring.

"It's an emerald. To match the green in your eyes."

Cora flung her arms around his neck and kissed him.

"Won't you open yours, darling?" suggested Cora. Nina's gaze met Ian's with what she hoped was a knowing look.

"I want nothing from him." She turned to her mother. "I will be in my room. Good night, Colonel Forbes."

Nina left, and Ian Forbes stared after her. Cora touched his arm. "Give her time."

"Two months have passed already. I can do nothing right in her eyes." He took Nina's package and headed for the door.

"You can't leave. Not tonight!"

Ian shook his head. "My presence brings only distress. Forgive me, love, but I must go."

It was cold in February, and another discouraging letter came from Damian. His men were held up in the snow, and he didn't expect to reach New York until late March. Nina's appetite failed, and often she fought painful bouts with nausea.

Her distress grew when she realized Cora left almost nightly, no doubt to visit her husband. Nina knew this, because Cora rose late in the morning and seemed especially happy on those days. Nina was consumed with finding a way to remove Ian Forbes from her mother's life.

She couldn't tell Cora about Ian's mistress, and she didn't want her mother to suffer. But as another snowfall whitened the trees and rooftops, Nina began formulating a plan to prove Ian's true nature. She had missed supper and lay in her bed in acute distress, which served to heighten her resentment.

Cora knocked, calling softly through the door. "Emma, can I come in?"

"Yes, Mother."

Cora entered the room and placed her hand on Nina's forehead. "Are you ill, my dear? You look very pale. And you haven't eaten in days."

"I'm not hungry, Mama."

"You're not warm." She studied Nina's face intently. "Have you been sick?"

"Yes, but it doesn't last. I feel better, and then . . ."

"When was the last time you bled?"

"What?"

"Your monthly experience, lady trouble."

"I have no idea. A while ago, I suppose." Another wave of nausea crept through Nina and she buried her face in her pillow.

"I see. Let me see your stomach, dear."

"My stomach?" Nina was mystified, but Cora pulled up her shift and proceeded to examine her daughter's abdomen.

"When is Damian coming home?"

"His letter says they were delayed again. Why?"

"He'd best return soon, I think. Damn! You should have married before he left. If only I hadn't wanted an extravagant wedding! This is all my fault."

"Mama, what are you taking about?"

"You're going to have a baby, Emma. By the looks of your stomach, I'd guess you've been pregnant since October."

Nina stared at Cora blankly. "I can't be."

"No?"

"Wouldn't I know?"

"With your first baby? Not necessarily. We must inform Damian at once."

Anna came to visit daily, which cheered Nina's dismal spirits. They sat alone in Nina's room, both silent and depressed. Lavinia was taking tea downstairs with Penelope and Cora, but Anna stayed with Nina.

"I'm going to have a baby," Nina confided with that strange mixture of joy and doubt that consumed her since Damian left.

"I know," replied Anna. "How I envy you!"

"Damian doesn't know."

"He'll be pleased. Oh, Nina, you're so very lucky!"

"Am I?"

"You bear his child. Do you know what I would give . . ."

Anna stopped and looked out the window.

"To bear Black Hawk's child?"

Anna's eyes widened in astonishment. "How did you know? Was it so obvious?"

"Not to everyone, perhaps. But I saw your face when you saw him, and I saw his. It's not hard to imagine that you would fall for the man who saved your life, especially when that man is Black Hawk. He's quite exceptional."

"I was terrified of him at first, though I admired him as well." Anna stopped and cleared her throat. "He's very strong. My father warned me about the Iroquois. When my father died, I was left alone with Black Hawk. My father was wrong. Black Hawk didn't touch me, we barely spoke. But he protected me.

"By the time we reached Philadelphia, I knew I loved him. I told him so. The world stood between us, but I knew he cared for me. That first night, safe again with my mother, was when I slipped away, out of my window."

"Did you . . . ?"

"We did. We had one night together, one night in perfect bliss. And then, he was gone."

"Why?"

"There was no other way." Anna paused, her eyes misted, but she didn't cry. "I've never forgotten him, Nina. To see him again, after so long . . . I never stopped loving him."

Nina took Anna's hand. "From the look on his face, I'd guess he's never forgotten you, either. He'll come back, Anna. And when he does, nothing on earth will keep him from you."

Another month passed and Nina's belly grew larger. The snow melted in two weeks of steady rain, and when it was over, Nina saw flowers out her window, tiny leaves on the trees. Her appetite returned in force. A letter arrived from Damian, but it gave no indication he'd heard of her plight.

He wrote sweetly of his love, promising to return as soon as he could to New York. But all indications were that he would continue to move farther south. General Cornwallis was making a determined effort to wrest the South from the rebels once and for all.

Even more disturbing, the Dragoons had seen tougher battles than Damian expected. Ethan proved himself courageous and bold, and Damian promised Cora that the boy revealed surprisingly good sense despite his bravery.

Ethan's subsequent letter revealed the same, though in more glowing terms. He mentioned Damian's brilliantly unorthodox command, and Black Hawk's achievements. Ethan seemed to be enjoying the countryside, issuing detailed descriptions of every village and farmland they traveled through.

Nina finished the fifteenth page of Ethan's letter and set it aside. Her young brother's cheer lifted her downcast spirits. "I feel like I've been there."

"He does run on a bit, doesn't he?" Cora picked up Ethan's letter and smiled.

"From these descriptions, I'd think we could trace their position in days."

"The trouble is, our couriers haven't been able to find him. Ian has sent three already, but when they arrive at their destination, Damian's Dragoons have already left. That's a problem with the horsemen, I'm afraid. They're too mobile."

Nina didn't answer. Cora left the matter in Ian Forbes's hands. This could explain much. "I think I'll go for a short walk this morning, Mother."

It was time to confront her stepfather once and for

all. She couldn't tell Cora about Ian's mistress, but she could threaten Ian with her knowledge.

Nina returned to the house where she'd found Ian Forbes several months before. She hid herself in a large juniper bush, hoping it would conceal her face from her stepfather, then leaned close to the open window. As she suspected, a woman's voice was heard within. Nina peeked through the window and saw Ian Forbes with his red-haired mistress.

"Ian, you're so young, so handsome. You must desire a woman whose lust isn't abated by the years. Cora spends all her time with her daughter. She has none left for you. I can make you forget her, Ian."

Nina gritted her teeth. She leaned closer, watching her stepfather intently. He put his hand on the woman's shoulder. The woman waited breathlessly. Nina grimaced in disgust. *If he kisses her, I'll burst through the window and attack them.*

Ian Forbes sighed heavily and shook his head. "You're an attractive woman, Sarah. I suppose you know how to make a man forget his troubles."

Nina cringed.

"I've had a lot of practice, Ian. If you hadn't turned me down, you'd know."

He turned her down? Nina's brow furrowed as she pressed her ear to the wall.

"I've made love with only one woman in my life, Sarah. And though Cora's experience can't match yours, she has a vivid imagination when it comes to . . ." Ian paused. "Certain things."

"You inspire imagination, Ian. If you've only had Cora, you don't know what you're missing. We're both married, Ian, but you know I don't love Josiah. We could find such pleasure together."

"Any woman with reasonable experience can please

a desperate man. But have you the skill to match love's touch?"

"I love you, Ian."

"You're bored, Sarah. You're married to an old man. You think a lover will make your wealth more bearable. Then choose one who would find joy in such a union. I am not that man."

"But, Ian. I want you. I ache for you. Ian, when I'm near you, my body quivers, I become damp . . ."

Ian cleared his throat, then coughed. He seemed embarrassed. "You envy my wife."

"I'm much younger than she! No doubt she was beautiful once . . ."

Ian laughed. "Once? Cora may be older than you, but there's not a man over sixteen whose head doesn't turn when she walks by. Do you know what love is, Sarah? I know. I know when she walks in a room she's entered a thousand times, and my breath stops."

Tears burned Nina's eyes. She hadn't expected such beautiful words of sentiment from this man she hated.

"Emma! What on earth are you doing?"

Nina jumped at her mother's voice, then bit her lip hard as she struggled for an explanation.

"Come out of there!"

Nina extracted herself from the juniper bush, a guilty expression tightening her face as she stood before her mother.

"Mother, I can explain. He's . . . Well, look." She pointed to the window. "He's in there with some trollop."

"Sarah? She desires my husband? Do you find this surprising, Emma? Ian Forbes is a handsome man."

"She's his mistress! Why else would she be in there with him?"

"This house is owned by Sarah's husband. He's a Loy-

alist officer under Ian's command. Although no doubt
her intentions are as you say."

Nina's temper flared. "He's mad at you for keeping
me. That's why he's here."

"He left our house to spare you pain. To make our
reunion easier."

"Penelope says he thinks I'm an impostor."

"Penelope is wrong. Ian knows better than anyone
who you are."

"You can believe no wrong of him, Mother. Why?"
Nina's voice rose with emotion, and she no longer cared
if Ian heard her. "He took you away from me, he destroyed your marriage. Mama, Ian Forbes is a devil!"

Nina spun away and started down the lane, but Cora
didn't move. "Ian Forbes is your father."

Nina turned, her senses reeling, her body unwilling
to respond. "No."

"He is. Look at him, Emma. Do you not see your face
in his? You knew you didn't look like me. You certainly
bear no resemblance to Iolo Evans."

Nina couldn't speak. She shook her head. It couldn't
be. *My father.* Her old fear doubled. She had no idea
why.

"Iolo Evans is my father."

"No, Emma."

"How do you know whether your husband or your
lover fathered your child?"

"I never married Iolo. We were betrothed, as I told
you. But when Ian came with his company to our
farm . . . I loved him from the first moment I saw him,
and no other. You can accuse me of this: I lay with Ian
though I was promised to Iolo."

Nina trembled. This, she had done with Damian.
She'd been fortunate that Jeremiah O'Grady had felt
empathy rather than anger. Save for that difference,
she repeated her mother's sin.

"He was seventeen when we met. He was so beautiful, like an angel. I adored him, Emma. I thought Iolo would understand."

"That can't be." Nina backed away toward the street beyond. "You ran away with Forbes a year after I was born."

"That is so. I told Iolo that I had fallen in love with Ian Forbes. I told him I carried Ian's child. I begged his forgiveness. And he gave it, Emma.

"He promised to release me from our engagement so I could marry Ian. And then he sent Ian to council with the Onondaga. The Iroquois were divided in the war—the Mohawk fought for the English, others divided as they saw fit.

"Ian's company was massacred—Ian was taken as a prisoner. But the Onondagas didn't return him as is done with officers. No, they believed him responsible for the senseless massacre of an Onondaga village. Their women had been raped, murdered, their children killed. And they were told Ian Forbes was responsible, had himself perpetrated the worst of the crimes."

Nina swayed. "Papa didn't tell them that."

"He must have, Emma. Iolo had close ties with the Onondaga. For those supposed crimes, Ian was tortured. Do you know what the Iroquois do to those they deem guilty? Do you know why he walks with a cane?"

"No." Nina didn't want to hear. She couldn't bear to hear. *My father.*

"They tore the tendons from his leg, while . . . no, I can't say." Cora's voice choked and she bit her lip hard. "Daniel Knox survived the massacre and hunted for Ian. He found him barely alive. And he confessed to the crimes himself. He was convincing. The Onondagas freed Ian and tortured Damian's father to his death."

Nina shook her head, blotting out the horror of her mother's words. Cora saw her daughter sway and she stopped. Tears streamed down her face. "Emma, I loved him so. Iolo led me to believe Ian was killed in battle. He told me we would pretend to marry, and promised to care for my child."

"Why didn't you marry him?" Nina tried to force her mind from Ian Forbes.

"I don't know," replied Cora. "Maybe I sensed something wasn't right about Iolo. But I couldn't bear the thought of laying as his wife. So I told him I married Ian in secret.

"Iolo honored my mourning. I've never understood why. He left me alone, he treated me well, in fact. We moved to Pennsylvania, but I was brokenhearted without Ian.

"Ian found me in Pennsylvania nearly two years after you were born. He told me that Iolo sent him into Onondaga territory, but I couldn't believe it. Iolo had been good to me, he was good to you. But I saw what the Onondaga did to Ian.

"Emma, he was seventeen years old. You have no idea how he suffered. Worse than his own affliction was watching his closest friend die in his place. For this reason, he treated Daniel's son as his own."

Hot tears streamed down Nina's cheeks as she began to comprehend the depth of her error. Darkness descended all around her. Memories deep beyond words surfaced in her mind, shattering images of chaos, of terror.

Is he an angel, Mama?

"I made a fool's mistake. I thought Iolo would understand. I couldn't believe he was responsible for the massacre. And I went to him . . ."

Nina squeezed her eyes shut. As she had done.

"I tried to explain. He knocked me down when I told him I was going with Ian. Ian stopped him from killing me, and we fled, the three of us. But he vowed to kill the thing dearest to us both. You.

"For over a year, he pursued us. I lived in terror. He sent the militia after us, men who would do his bidding without question."

Nina's dream came real before her eyes. Blackness, running through snow, the mindless, brutal slap of branches in her face.

A sudden clatter of hoofbeats coincided with her memory, and Nina whirled around to see a cloaked horseman gallop toward her. With one swoop, he seized her and pulled her onto the saddle in front of him.

Cora screamed. "Ian, he's taken Emma! Help!"

Nina saw Ian burst from his office, she heard him shout. *My father.* Something cracked over her head, and Nina drifted into blackness.

NINE

"She's gone." Ian Forbes sat in the study of his home, his head bowed, his broad shoulders slumped despondently. "For the second time, I have failed my daughter."

Cora fought her tears and wrapped her arm around her husband's shoulders. "Iolo didn't kill her before."

"He had sympathy for a baby. What of a woman who has defied him and carries an Englishman's child? Daniel's grandchild, and mine."

"If he wanted her dead, he would have engaged an assassin. Emma isn't a fool, my love. She will find a way to appease Iolo Evans." She paused. "How will we find Damian?"

"I've sent couriers. He will return when he learns she carries his child. We will have to tell him that child is now in the hands of the enemy, an enemy far worse than the rebels."

"We can't lose her now. She's everything I dreamed she would be, Ian. She's so like you."

"I doubt that would please her—to learn her father is a man she despises."

"She doesn't know you. Apparently Penelope convinced her you believed her an impostor."

"It may be time for Penelope to return to London."

"Emma saw you with Sarah," added Cora. "She was certain you had a mistress."

"I can see where she'd get that impression. Sarah was quite insistent. She described—in amazingly vivid detail—the strangest alternatives to intercourse I've ever heard."

"Indeed? You'll have to tell me about them."

Ian grinned. "I thought I might show you. Some of them, anyway—the ones that wouldn't hurt." He kissed her cheek. "Do you know, I woke three times to find her in my bed? I had to forcibly remove her."

Ian sounded mystified by Sarah's pursuit of him, but Cora touched his golden hair and bent to kiss him. "Her husband probably encouraged her. The Loyalists seem to attach a favorable stigma to loaning out their wives to noblemen."

"My bed is complete with you." Ian drew her onto his lap and kissed her soft mouth. "We will find our daughter, Cora. Fate brought her back to us. I cannot believe it will take her away now."

The merchant ship rocked in Chesapeake Bay, rolled on the waves of a savage storm. Nina was bounced from wall to wall of the tiny cabin. She seized the bedpost and held herself in place. Seasickness combined with the queasiness of pregnancy left her too miserable to worry about her fate.

How long had she been in that horrible trunk? It was a dark nightmare, but fortunately she'd slept through those first hours. She didn't know who had taken her. Her abductor gave no name. He hadn't boarded the ship which now battled the storm.

She guessed Iolo Evans was responsible, but none of the ship's crew told her anything. They seemed an unsavory lot, from what she'd seen. Their connection to the Continental Army was doubtful, though the French fleet had granted them passage.

A crewman banged loudly on Nina's door. She hesitated before calling out. Though they respected her enough to knock before entering, she felt decidedly uncomfortable beneath their leering eyes.

She had told them that she bore a child. She exaggerated her duration and moaned loudly about the less attractive female complaints. This seemed to work, but apparently they had strict orders to leave her untouched.

"Come in." She heard the door unlocked, and a grubby sailor entered her cabin.

"Brought ye vittles, missy." He handed her a rusted tray of dried meat and stale bread. "Them's the best we's got."

"Thank you. I'm afraid I vomited my last meal right back up."

The man grimaced and Nina felt pleasure with herself for disgusting such a filthy man. "Storm's a'passing. There's a boat waiting to take ye to shore."

"Where am I going?" asked Nina, careful to chew her meat with her mouth wide open.

The sailor grinned. "Can't be saying. Shame to see ye go, ain't it? Yer a pretty little thing."

"I wish I could get rid of the lice, though. And all these itches."

That was enough for the sailor. He left her and Nina returned to her meal. She forced herself to eat everything given to her. Her baby needed nourishment, and she was determined to protect the little person at any cost.

Nina finished her meal and her thoughts wandered to Damian. She rested her mind on memories of his love. It saved her through the long days, but her longing for him was painful. *Where are you? Do you know about our baby? Do you know that I'm gone?*

Nina thought of her mother. Cora must be miserable. More reluctantly, Nina's mind turned to Ian Forbes. Was he, too, trying to find her? Her father. No wonder she looked so much like Ethan. Every time she thought of Ian, her stomach clenched in fear. Something about him terrified her, but she didn't know why. Was it the past she remembered, or the future she sensed?

Nina fell into an uneasy sleep, woken again when she heard loud voices outside her room. "Get her out here!" shouted the sailor who passed for a captain.

Nina wrapped a blanket around her shoulders, then waited at the door. The sailor who brought her meals came to fetch her.

"You've done been sent fer. There's a boat waiting to take ye. Best get moving."

Nina followed him onto the deck. From there, she was assisted into a rowboat. It was still dark from the rain, and night appeared near. But the crewmen made good speed, and she found herself at last on firm ground.

A carriage stood ready, but Nina didn't recognize any of the soldiers who waited for her. Like the sailors, they told her nothing.

"Get in, Miss. You've got a long ride ahead of you."

Damian rode to Ian Forbes's house, followed by Black Hawk and Ethan. Gambrinus stumbled on the cobblestones, his mahogany coat dark with sweat. Damian leapt from his back and raced up the stairs.

Caesar opened the door, but Damian hurried in without the customary pleasantries. "Where is she? Have you found her?"

Damian had been on his way home when Ian's last

courier found him. Nina had been kidnapped, and she was pregnant with his child. They rode through the night, stopping only to allow the horses water. But the grim set on Caesar's face told Damian he was too late. "Let me fetch the colonel for you."

Ethan and Black Hawk joined Damian in the hall, but when Ian entered, their worst fears were verified. Ian looked thin and gaunt, and dark circles shadowed his eyes.

"What's happened?" asked Damian. "Where is Nina?"

"She's been taken, Damian. By Evans, we assume. A man grabbed her and carried her off. I was unable to stop him, or to find him afterwards."

Ian's voice was soaked with pain, but Damian fought his fear. "You have no idea if she's still here?"

"She's not in New York. I've searched every nook. The most likely explanation is that she was smuggled on board a merchant ship."

Damian sat heavily in a chair. "She could be anywhere."

Cora entered the room. "Iolo has taken her. I'm sure of that."

Ethan looked between them. "Then we'll take her back! He'll kill her."

"He goes to much trouble for killing," said Black Hawk. "To kill is easy. The Welshman wants control."

Cora looked up at the tall Iroquois. "I think that's true. If so, Nina will be safe. For now, at least."

"The baby?"

"The baby should come in July."

"Then I have time." Damian stood up, his face set and determined.

"What are we doing?" asked Ethan eagerly.

"The Continental Army fights Cornwallis in the South," said Damian.

"Cornwallis will, in victory, move toward Virginia," offered Ian. "Evans will be there."

"We'll find him, then go in after Nina."

"Go in? How?" asked Ethan. "With an army or under a flag of truce?"

"Neither. I go alone, and in disguise."

"Disguise?" asked Cora doubtfully. "That was Major André's mistake."

Ian met Damian's gaze. "If they catch you, they'll name you a spy. You will be hanged."

"They won't catch me."

"I should be able to locate Evans. I can send couriers, then send them on to you." Ian frowned. "Or perhaps go with you myself."

"You're needed here," said Damian. "All army intelligence comes back to New York."

"She's my sister," said Ethan. "Let me go with you."

"One can do what two cannot," said Black Hawk. "You and I will find another way."

The coach drove onward relentlessly. Stops were made to change horses and for short nights, but Nina was kept under guard like a prisoner. Like the sailors who abducted her, these men were fringe elements of the Continental Army. Nina guessed they answered to the power of bribes rather than honor.

Directly answerable to the one who wanted Nina, they treated her more carefully and she no longer suffered under unsavory gazes. She was fed and treated decently, but she was able to extract no information from them.

She had no idea where she was, though it was warmer than New York and the trees were full with leaves. The voices she heard were slower, more southern. Nina guessed she was very far from New York, probably in Virginia.

Bored and fearful, Nina took to examining what she could see of the landscape. The ground over which the coach covered grew less sandy and rolling hills slowed their progress. They were moving inland, and Nina strained her memory for what she learned of geography.

They crossed a large river, though Nina wasn't certain which one it was. "Where are we?" she asked when they stopped for the night.

The driver was removing the harness from his horses. Since he was the most accommodating of her guards, Nina decided to pursue her whereabouts with him.

"Now, miss, I don't know as I should be telling you that."

Nina drew a breath of sheer frustration. "Name of God! Why not? I've been dragged by land and sea. Who do you think I'll tell, anyway?"

The driver's eyes widened at her unladylike language. "You sound just like the colonel!"

Nina's face knit suspiciously. "Do I? You mean my father, of course. Iolo Evans."

The man bit his lip and looked away, but Nina rolled her eyes. "It had occurred to me already. I ran away, it's true. He's gone to a lot of trouble to get me back."

"Your papa wants what's best for his girl, miss. Don't want you caught up with no Englishman. Said you might not cotton to us taking you. But don't you worry none. Why, any pa'd be proud to have a girl like yourself."

Nina didn't answer. She prayed Iolo Evans would demand only obedience and not punishment. When he learned she was carrying Damian's child . . . Nina thought of her last conversation with Cora.

He treated them well, as long as they didn't cross him. He threatened her life, but he didn't kill her. And he had been a kind father. But Nina was determined to find Damian again. She would cross Iolo Evans, just as her mother had done. He didn't have to know that, however.

Nina turned her attention back to the driver. "You sound Southern. What's your name?"

"Going by Zachariah. But folks call me Zack."

"Zack. Are we near my father now? I have disobeyed him, true. But I'll feel safer in his care." If her father learned she had been an agreeable prisoner, his temper might soften.

"We've got a bit to go," replied Zack as he hitched up the horses for the night. "Heading for them hills."

"Hills? Do you mean the mountains in the distance?"

"Yes, Ma'am. Them's the Alleghenys."

"What was that river we crossed?"

"That back yonder was the old Rappahannock. We're heading a bit north, and there we'll find your pa."

"So we're in Virginia. What's he doing in the mountains? I thought the bulk of the army was with Greene in the South."

"General Wayne and his Pennsylvania line are awaiting on Washington's orders, ma'am."

Nina considered this. Iolo served beneath General Wayne, who commanded the same Pennsylvanians who mutinied earlier in the war. But if Iolo Evans was secluded in the mountains, how would Damian ever find her?

Nina's bed was prepared and she lay down for the night. She knew Damian was searching for her. She felt his restless heart, his troubled thoughts as if they could touch her from afar. She felt his desperation. It occurred to her that in fear of her life, Damian might do something rash.

I will be with you again. But I can wait. Please, don't risk your life.

Nina remembered with painful clarity what Iolo had done to her young father. He was merciless in anger.

She couldn't let that happen to Damian. Somehow she knew the danger was greater to Damian than it was to herself.

"Bring her in."

Nina stood outside the tent, waiting. She shivered violently, though the evening was warm. Iolo sounded restrained, controlled, but that was more frightening than his bluster.

"Go on, missy." Zachariah held out his hand, directing her through the tent's opened flap.

A strange, chill feeling wrapped itself around Nina's heart as she tried to screw up her courage. *I have felt this way before.* The feeling was primitive, the reaction of a child. *If I'm very good, he won't hurt me. If I don't make him mad* . . .

Once, long ago, Nina stood outside Iolo Evan's door. A huge woman had clutched her hand, an unfriendly scowl on her face. In her mind's eye, Nina saw Columbine O'Grady. But Nina towered over Columbine in Philadelphia. She was remembering her childhood.

If I'm very good . . . Nina swallowed hard and walked in.

Iolo was seated behind a rough-hewn table. He didn't look up when she entered, just went on examining the papers before him. Jeremiah O'Grady stood beside him, and Nina felt a rush of relief. Jeremiah wouldn't let anything happen to her.

"Papa . . ." Nina's voice shook. She stopped when he looked up at her.

His gaze assessed her, but she couldn't tell if he noticed her child. Perhaps the guards told him, for she kept her pregnancy no secret.

"Did they treat you passable, girl?"

Nina nodded. "I am well." She waited for him to

continue, but he said no more. "What are you going to do with me?"

"I'm seeing to it that you're on the right path. Don't want you stepping off it again."

It was a warning, and Nina dared not argue. Her position was too tenuous. She glanced at Jeremiah, but he wouldn't meet her eyes.

"Your tent is beside the colonel's," said Jeremiah. Nina was astonished by the harshness of his voice. "And I assure you, it will be well-guarded."

"Jeremiah?" Nina was stunned. He wouldn't turn on her, she'd been certain of his friendship.

"You made a fool of me. But not this time, woman. We marry tomorrow."

"What?" Nina stepped back in horror. "I can't marry you!" She turned to Iolo, her eyes wide with fear and misery. "Papa, you don't understand. I bear a child, Damian's child."

"Did he marry you, girl?"

From his mocking tone, Nina guessed that Iolo already knew the answer. "He didn't have time."

Jeremiah issued a derisive snort, but Iolo's face hardened. "The child will belong to your rightful husband. Now go. O'Grady, take her to the tent."

Jeremiah seized Nina's arm and dragged her from her father's tent. "Jeremiah, you can't mean . . ."

"Silence, woman! I don't want to hear a word."

" *'Woman?'* You have lost your mind."

Iolo was watching them from his quarters, and the men of his unit laughed when Jeremiah shoved her into her small tent. "Don't even think of escaping." He paused, looking triumphant. "Woman."

Tears streamed down Nina's cheeks and she refused to look at him. How could he betray her this way! He encouraged her to go with Damian, vowed friendship, they shared their deepest confidences. Nina stumbled back into the tent and fell sobbing upon the little cot.

"What in the name of God is he doing out there?" Damian balled up the letter, then threw it on the ground.

Ethan sighed. "Heaven knows. Washington expects Cornwallis in Virginia. That seems plain. Lafayette is in Richmond waiting. Our army is moving north again, out of the Carolinas."

"All armies meet in Virginia," said Black Hawk.

"Evans is up in the hills, but he'll move out soon. At least, that's what Ian believes. If we can predict his movement, we can intercept him, and I'll make my way into his camp."

"It's a long distance yet," said Ethan. "We won't get there before June."

"The rivers swell, then fall back," said Black Hawk. "He is across the Potomac. Our way is his."

"Papa, you can't force me to marry Jeremiah." Nina stood in front of Iolo Evans, daring his wrath by her assertion.

"To hell and back!" Iolo turned on her, his fists clenched.

"You'll marry me. Or be facing hell instead!" Jeremiah appeared behind Nina, his face taut with anger. An innocent and boyish looking man stood at Jeremiah's side. If not for the situation, Nina was sure she would like him.

"What in the Name of God are you doing here, Watkins?" boomed Iolo. "And where's that fool chaplain?"

"The chaplain's taken ill, Colonel," said Jeremiah. "But Watkins here is a minister, too. Didn't you know?"

"How would I know that?"

"I am, sir," replied Watkins with pride. "Done my sister's wedding back in Hacketstown, I did. Right pretty it was, if I do say so myself."

This was a nightmare. This sweet-faced boy with big brown eyes was about to marry her to Jeremiah O'Grady while she bore Damian's child.

"I will not marry."

No one paid any attention to her.

"Watkins will marry us, Colonel, with your approval," said Jeremiah.

"Get it done with! We've got to start the move today."

Watkins appeared eager. "Yes, sir!"

Jeremiah seized Nina's arm and hauled her into the tent. Watkins brandished a Bible and began reading verses that seemed chosen at random. Few had any relationship to marriage.

" *'Have we not all one father? Did not one God create us? Why do we violate the covenant of our forefathers by being faithless to one another?'* "

Watkins seemed to like this passage, but Iolo sighed heavily. "Get on with it, Watkins."

" *'Why do you look at the speck of sawdust in your brother's eye, with never a thought for the great plank in your own?'* "

"How true!" exclaimed Watkins with blatant self-appreciation. Watkins skipped a bit, then continued.

" *'There is no such thing as a good tree producing worthless fruit, nor yet a worthless tree producing good fruit. For each tree is known by its own fruit: You do not gather figs from thistles, and you don't pick grapes from brambles.'* "

"Whatever," muttered Watkins. He read on with mounting enthusiasm. *"How blessed are you who weep now; you shall laugh!"* Watkins was clearly getting carried away with his sermon.

"The wedding, Watkins," Jeremiah reminded him.

Nina glanced up at her erstwhile friend, but she detected the faint hint of a smile around his lips.

"Oh, yes . . . Naturally. Just thought a piece or two of Good Advice might come in handy, here and there."

"Thank you. Now, if you please . . ."

"Well, then . . . I now pronounce you man and wife!"

Nina looked at Jeremiah doubtfully. "I didn't say, 'I do.' And I won't!"

Iolo's eyes wandered to the side. "This is legal, isn't it, Watkins? You've rambled on enough, for certain."

"Oh, yes, sir. As legal as I am a chaplain."

"Then they're married?"

"Married as they'll ever be."

"Very good. O'Grady, get your wife ready for the move. Watkins . . . go back to whatever it is you do."

Without a word to Nina, Iolo turned and exited the tent. Nina stood dumbfounded with Watkins and Jeremiah. Hot tears spilled from her eyes and she clutched her rounded stomach.

"How could you, Jeremiah? How could you?" She glared at Watkins. "You, you little pipsqueak! How dare you use your cloth to marry me against my will!" She stepped towards the slight man with the intention of doing him severe harm.

Watkins's round eyes grew rounder still, and he hopped back. Jeremiah caught Nina's arm and brought her around to face him. To her surging fury, he was fighting a smile.

"Watkins's *'cloth'* is suspect, I'm afraid. As is our wedding."

Nina's eyes narrowed. "What do you mean? He said we were man and wife."

Watkins looked proud. "So I did."

"And it had about as much value as if I'd said it myself," added Jeremiah.

Watkins appeared a little crestfallen. "Thought my

sermon went over well," he said rather sullenly. "A little pertinent advice here and abouts never hurt. Why, I might just be as suited to the pulpit as my ma always said!"

"Your words had no reference to anything." Watkins's face fell and his shoulders drooped.

"They were well spoken, though," offered Nina, though she couldn't imagine why she was moved to comfort Watkins's hurt feelings.

He brightened immediately. "Why, thank you, Miss Evans. I do believe you're right. Now, had I a bit more time to choose what I'd be speaking about . . ."

"We'd be still listening." Jeremiah was smiling pleasantly.

Nina looked between them. "What's going on here, Jeremiah? You haul me in here, force me to marry you, and now you're acting like nothing's happened at all."

"Nothing has. You, my dear, are no more my wife than you were before. For Watkins is no more a minister than I."

"What?" Nina's heart leapt. Jeremiah O'Grady hadn't betrayed her, after all. Jeremiah and Watkins both grinned. Nina jumped into Jeremiah's arms and kissed his face.

"We're not married? How did you arrange it, Jeremiah? Papa can't find out, can he? What if the real chaplain finds out?"

"Real chaplain knows," put in Watkins. "He won't be telling, though. Jeremy and I didn't have no trouble convincing him it was a greater sin to marry a pregnant girl against her will than to disobey a commander."

"So he's pleading sickness," added Jeremiah. "If need be, he'll verify our marriage to Colonel Evans, but I don't think your father will question anything. Everything's going the way he planned. He can't imagine anything could defy him now."

"I am so grateful to you two! Mr. Watkins, I'm sorry for threatening you."

"Don't worry your head about that," said Watkins. "I don't think much of being pushed into things. We've got a right to choose our own paths. That's what Jeremy says."

Jeremiah nodded. "Don't you be looking too happy, Nina. We don't want to raise your father's suspicions." He studied her appearance closely. "You look pale. I'd imagine the journey has been quite a strain on you. Whether I'm your husband or not, you can be sure I'll look after you."

"Thank you, Jeremiah. It's been hard. They kidnapped me, you know, and stuffed me in a trunk. I was so seasick and scared. Then the coach went on forever and I didn't know where I was."

Nina was running on a bit, she knew, but it felt so good to be safe at last, protected. She closed her eyes and told Damian across the miles that her danger had passed.

"You're in Virginia," said Watkins. "We've been here for months, but it looks like we're pushing east again, starting today. We're joining Lafayette!"

"Where are the British?"

"Cornwallis is headed north. They say he's outside of Petersburg now," said Jeremiah. "Lafayette will back this way, up the Rapidan River. General Wayne and our Penn line will meet him, then veer off south."

"War's heading to something, ain't it, Jeremy?"

"An end, I hope. The English generals are behaving strangely. Maybe they're tired of fighting, winning, and holding cities that don't make any difference at all. They win a battle, and it means nothing. We survive to fight again, and it's a great victory."

Nina thought of Damian. "Is there any way I can get a message to my mother in New York? I must tell her

I'm all right. I must warn Damian not to do anything rash."

Jeremiah considered this, but then he shook his head. "I don't see how we'd pull that off. We could get a letter out right enough, but if your father found it . . ."

"Wait a while," suggested Watkins. "We'll get something to her, don't you worry." He turned to Jeremiah. "What about the move? Should I muster up the men, Jeremy?"

"Do that," said Jeremiah. "We're moving under cover of darkness. Get them ready, and see that they rest up before dark. It's a long march."

Watkins groaned. "Damn! I hate night marches. Stubbing your toes on roots and tripping over each other." He bowed to Nina and smiled brightly. "It was good to make your acquaintance, ma'am. Wish we could've told you aforehand, though."

"I am in your debt, Mr. Watkins. For the first time since I was kidnapped, I think I can really sleep. And maybe have a bite to eat."

Jeremiah laughed. "I'll see that you're fed. You'll be staying in my tent, and that's fairly comfortable, actually. Sleep until nightfall. You'll be riding, but it's bound to be a long night."

"They've moved down from the hills, Damian," reported Ethan. "Looks like Wayne's division and Evans are planning to meet up with Lafayette."

"How long before they join?" asked Damian.

"A week? Maybe two. Why?"

"When two armies meet, even friendly ones, there is confusion," said Black Hawk. "A new face goes unnoticed."

Ethan looked at Damian. "You're sneaking in to Lafayette's army? Are you crazy? What if Evans sees you?"

"Have you a better plan?"

Ethan's face puckered in a tight frown, but he couldn't come up with anything. He eyed Damian. "Is that why you're growing a beard? Your hair is too long. You look awful."

Damian grinned. "Like a rebel."

Ethan considered Damian's plan. "I'll have to grow a beard, too."

Both Damian and Black Hawk looked at the smooth-faced boy doubtfully. Ethan's eyes widened indignantly. He ran his hand across his bare chin. "It might take a day or so . . ."

Ethan paused and cleared his throat while Black Hawk and Damian exchanged a grin at his expense. "I don't know, Damian. It sounds risky to me. You're just going to sneak in, find Nina in the midst of two armies, then take her out without anyone noticing? You'd have to be lucky to pull it off."

"I am lucky."

Black Hawk met Damian's gaze. "Even the best of luck runs dry."

"Why are we crossing this river again?" Nina stood with Jeremiah and Watkins while her father's army gathered for another crossing of the Rappahannock. It was nearly midnight, but the moon was shining bright on the river's shimmering surface. "I thought we were going south."

Jeremiah sighed. "We were. But the good earl, Cornwallis, is running along the Rapidan, twenty miles from Lafayette's army. Lafayette was ordered to harry the British, not engage them."

"The marquis is backing toward Maryland," added Watkins. "We're to join him, then head south again."

"It won't be easy," said Jeremiah. "With Banastre

Tarleton on our tail, there's bound to be bloody engagements."

Nina yawned, and Jeremiah studied her intently. "You're tired, I see. Are you feeling well enough to go on?"

"I'm all right, Jeremiah. Sleepy. It's just that I'm getting so big."

Watkins eyed her closely. "That you are. You look like a melon in a dress."

"Watkins!"

Nina laughed. "I feel like a melon."

"Get some rest, Nina. The crossing will take hours. I'll wake you when it's time to move on."

Nina wandered along the river, looking for a comfortable and safe spot to rest. She pushed her way through tall reeds to a giant willow and curled up as best she could at its base.

Iolo's soldiers made a great clamor despite strict orders for silence, but Nina was used to their racket. The earth welcomed her exhausted body, the river's hum lulled her into sleep.

Nina woke thinking she'd heard voices. She struggled against the blanket of sleep and listened.

"That's ridiculous, Watkins." It was Jeremiah speaking. Nina yawned, and started the laborious struggle to her feet. But Jeremiah's next words stopped her.

"It's you I love, and you know it."

Nina eased back into the reeds to avoid a very awkward moment.

"And I love you, Jeremy," said Watkins. Nina bit her lip in embarrassment. "But your Nina isn't what I expected. You could be happy with a girl like that. She's strong and beautiful . . ."

"And madly in love with another man. Have you forgotten that little detail?"

"No, but he's an Englishman." Watkins's voice lowered. "Don't think much of the English, Jeremy," he confided as if this might be a secret. "How do we know the fellow's intentions, anyway? Maybe he got the poor little thing with child, then ran off on her. After all, he didn't marry her in New York, did he? Maybe you're all she's got."

Nina frowned. Damian's intentions were honorable. When he learned about the baby, Damian would come for her. Nina could feel him drawing ever closer. Nina's frown tightened. Maybe she only wanted to feel him. Maybe he didn't really want her. She had been difficult about Ian Forbes.

"From what I saw of Damian Knox, that's not likely," said Jeremiah, reassuring both Watkins and Nina. "But I suppose something could happen to him, especially if he dares to come after her."

"Right enough. And what then?"

"Then I'll take care of her, naturally. But I will not give you up, Avery. We tried that, and it didn't work."

Nina smiled to herself. The earnest, sincere Watkins would be named "Avery."

"I can't picture myself married, that's for sure. I wish love was respected just for its own sake."

Nina peeked up out of the grass. The first light of morning struck the river, turning the leaves and grass from gray to green once more. She saw Jeremiah, tall and handsome, touch Watkins's face in an unexpectedly tender gesture.

To her surprise and confusion, Jeremiah kissed Watkins's mouth. It was gentle and sweet, the act of two who loved each other. Nina settled back into the grass, acutely embarrassed to have witnessed such an intimate moment.

The world turned upside down. Nina heard the English marching song in her brain. Nothing was as she had thought. She was in love with an Englishman. Jeremiah loved Watkins. Her father was Ian Forbes . . .

The world turned upside down! She did hear music! English music. "Jeremiah!" Nina struggled to her feet, and both Jeremiah and Watkins turned toward her in amazement. Neither had time for embarrassment, however. They, too, detected what Nina heard.

Jeremiah whirled toward the noise. "What is that?"

Watkins drew his gun. "Bloodybacks, Jeremy! And half our army's on the other side!"

"Where's the colonel?"

"Crossed over first, didn't he?"

Nina groaned. "What are we going to do? Someone's coming. Someone with the nerve to *sing!*"

Watkins groaned, too. "That can only be . . ."

"Banastre Tarleton," finished Jeremiah. "The most ruthless man in the British Army. The man who killed my brother." Jeremiah seized Nina's hand and pulled her along as they ran back to the crossing army. He shouted to his men. "Ambush! Come about!"

Weapons were loaded and readied, those in the midst of crossing the river turned back to fight. But more than half were already on the other side.

Iolo Evans shouted across the river at his scattered forces. "What in the bloody Name of God is going on over there?"

"Ambush, Colonel!"

"We're crossing back!"

"No, Colonel. We'll handle it. Stay safe over there. If we don't join you soon, pull out."

"Where's my girl?"

Iolo sounded frightened. With a strange, childlike thrill, Nina realized how much he cared for her. He would crush her happiness, but Iolo Evans still loved his daughter.

"I'm fine, Papa! Don't worry. I can shoot. You taught me yourself."

"You get yourself to the rear, girl!"

Nina loaded a musket and positioned herself to face the enemy.

"Are you sure? God's teeth, they don't have a chance!" Damian jerked Gambrinus's head up from the grass and leapt atop his back. "How far?"

"Half a mile, maybe," replied Ethan as he, too, mounted. "It's Tarleton, all right. Half of Evans' army has crossed the Rappahannock. Wayne's is too far ahead to be any good."

The two horses sprang into a gallop. "Where's Black Hawk?" shouted Damian as they raced toward the river.

"I left him by the river. He saw Nina with O'Grady, Damian. At least she's alive."

The horses bounded through the tall grass, flying like the wind toward the Rappahannock. But already Damian heard shots fired. And many more were fired than could respond.

"Ready! Hold your fire, men! Down, come around . . ."

Jeremiah shouted orders. His men responded with seasoned control. Nina aimed into the shadowy depths of the trees, too. She heard the approaching horsemen, her heart throbbed with terror. Watkins readied his weapon beside her, his boyish face hard and determined as he waited for Tarleton's Loyalists to draw closer.

Tarleton's cavalry charged into view. "Hold on! Wait . . . Fire!" ordered Jeremiah. Muskets fired. Tarleton's horsemen slowed, a few fell, horses stumbled, but the charge came on. Nina shot, too, firing her musket as the soldiers did. Her body jerked backwards with the musket. She steadied herself, then loaded again.

"Bayonets!" Jeremiah sounded calm. Watkins fixed his bayonet, but when Nina started to do the same, he seized her musket and shook his head.

"You get back, Miss Evans. You ain't no match for those black-hearted Tories, 'specially not in your condition. Get back."

Jeremiah motioned to Nina. "Take her across, Watkins."

"Ain't going nowhere. You go, Whitherweed," Watkins ordered another soldier.

"Yes, sir." Whitherweed took Nina's arm, but Nina was loath to leave her friends.

It was too late, anyway. Tarleton abandoned his head-on charge. Instead he circled around the small group. They were cut off from the river. There could be no retreat.

"Form!" ordered Jeremiah. Still his voice betrayed no fear. "In the center. Ready bayonets . . ."

Watkins pushed Nina behind him, then poised his bayonet for attack. The horsemen were ready for the fight. Tarleton delighted in hand-to-hand combat. Sabers were drawn as they moved in on the cornered Americans. Nina picked up her discarded musket and fixed her bayonet.

Watkins saw her, but he didn't try to stop her this time. "Aim high, jab low. Take 'em off guard."

Nina nodded, but she was too frightened to ask questions. The Americans backed in together, forming a tight circle to resist their attackers. Their remaining shots were fired, but Jeremiah's order surprised everyone.

"Charge!"

The American soldiers leapt toward their attackers.

Using their muskets as clubs, they engaged their enemy. Several horsemen were dislodged. Nina saw Banastre Tarleton wielding his saber against two Americans.

The Americans' unexpected attack took Tarleton's ambushers off-guard. They'd come in less than full strength; their intention had been to harry the rear of the rag-tag army. They hadn't expected any forceful resistance.

"Drive them in, curse you!" Tarleton drove his saber into his attacker's heart and the man fell lifeless. "Get them back, shove them into the river!"

The Loyalists regrouped and regained the advantage. Jeremiah's men began to fall back, though Jeremiah himself was at their fore. Tarleton swung his horse around, galloping toward Jeremiah with his saber readied to kill.

"Jeremy . . ." Watkins's voice was a whisper, but he raced toward Jeremiah, firing his musket as he ran. Tarleton's horse stumbled, then fell, but Tarleton leapt to the ground uninjured. He swung his weapon wildly, knocking Jeremiah to the earth.

Watkins hit Tarleton at a full run, knocking him off his feet. He grabbed Jeremiah's arm and hauled him up. Tarleton got up and aimed his pistol.

Nina screamed, but it was too late. Tarleton fired. Watkins jerked forward as the shot impacted in his back.

Jeremiah caught Watkins in his arms and carried him toward Nina. Men clashed all around, and now the Loyalists smelled victory. Jeremiah lowered Watkins to the ground beside Nina.

"Watch him." He turned back to the battle.

Nina knelt at Watkins's side, tears streaming down her face. The boy was bleeding heavily, Tarleton's shot had gone deep into his shoulder. But Watkins appeared calm.

"Jeremy . . ."

"He's all right." Nina tried to pack his wound, but her hand was soaked in blood. They were losing. Without help, Watkins would die.

"Surrender or die!" shouted a Loyalist, but to her revulsion, Nina heard Banastre Tarleton laugh.

"Surrender *and* die," he gloated. "Take no prisoners!"

Watkins tried to struggle to his feet, but Nina held him down. "You can't fight."

"I can, too. Grab a pistol and load it for me."

Nina looked around at the fallen. She saw a dead Loyalist lying nearby, his horse half on top of him. With shaking hands, she fumbled for his weapon. She found a pistol and powder, then scrambled back to Watkins.

Watkins rolled painstakingly on his side, then looked for a target. He fired, knocking an enemy soldier off his horse. "Reload."

Nina did so, and Watkins shot again. They repeated the procedure several times, with varying degrees of success. But the Loyalists were winning.

"What the . . . ?"

Watkins's eyes widened as three scraggly men leapt into the fray from the direction north of the river. One had long black hair and wielded a club with a jagged blade attached. Black Hawk knocked a Loyalist from the saddle, then turned and sent another to the ground.

Two bearded men fought beside the Indian . . . and they fought in Jeremiah O'Grady's defense. One was blond, and the other . . . It couldn't be. Nina swayed and clutched Watkins's hand. Damian . . .

His brown hair was unbound, long and flying behind his head as he fought. He fired his own musket, then seized a rebel musket, firing that, too. There was no time to reload. He used his musket like a club, slashing and driving against Tarleton's ambushers. They didn't fight like Englishmen—they fought with savage fury.

Metal crunched against bone, wood crushed against muskets. No longer did Banastre Tarleton fight a fleeting skirmish against surprised rebels. He was drawn into a battle such as a barbarian army would wage. And the Loyalists hadn't expected reinforcements.

"The rebels are coming back across!" shouted Banastre Tarleton.

"Retreat, sir?"

"Yes, curse you, retreat!"

The Loyalists abandoned their attack. They whirled their horses around and galloped from the fray.

Watkins lowered his weapon and closed his eyes. Nina shook him and he looked up at her. "It's bad. Remember me." Watkins uttered a faint gasp. "Tell Jeremy good-bye."

"I will not! Avery Watkins, you fight, and you fight hard." She pinched him fiercely. "You are not going to die."

Watkins looked a little surprised, but he set his face resolutely in an effort to survive. "As you say."

Jeremiah saw Tarleton race away and he clenched his fist. "If I had the men, I'd follow you to hell and back."

"That's just where you'd find him, too."

A slow smile crossed Jeremiah's face. "You're indomitable, aren't you, Knox?" Damian's brow rose, but Jeremiah shook his head. "Who else would come crashing to our defense with an Iroquois at his side? If you intend to pull it off, I'd send Black Hawk into hiding."

"Evans?"

"On the other side. But we'd better think fast, or you'll be hanging from the nearest tree."

Damian and Jeremiah picked their way through the fallen to Nina and Watkins. Black Hawk and Ethan joined them. Watkins nodded at her.

"Isn't this what you've been waiting for?"

Nina struggled to her feet. She felt suddenly aware of her bulging stomach, but Damian reached out his hand.

"Damian . . ." She placed her shaking fingers in his palm—his strong hand closed firmly around hers. He pulled her against him, holding her close while she cried.

"I'm here, love," he whispered against her hair. "You're safe."

Ethan groaned. "I can't believe we've done this. We've just driven off Englishmen." Nina peeked up at her brother. Despite his light beard, he still looked young. Her heart moved with affection.

Damian stroked Nina's hair. "Banastre Tarleton isn't English."

"He doesn't fight honorably, it's true." Ethan clasped his hand to his forehead. "But still . . . If Father knew I've taken up arms with the enemy . . ."

"Ian told us to do what was necessary. Banastre Tarleton doesn't take prisoners. Do you want me to tell you what he does to beautiful women he considers his rightful spoils?"

"No." Ethan patted Nina's shoulder. "We did the right thing."

Black Hawk appeared unmoved by their change of sides. He slung his Sauk club back at his waist, then studied the fallen. "What now?"

Iolo's booming voice prevented Damian from answering. "What in the Name of God is going on over there? Hell's bells, O'Grady, where are you?"

Nina's face drained of blood. "What do we do?"

Ethan started from the battlesite. "Let's get out of here."

Damian hesitated. Jeremiah looked between them. "If you take her now, he'll go after you."

"Tell him Tarleton took her," suggested Watkins from the ground. Ethan nodded, but Jeremiah shook his head.

"He'd send the whole army after her. You'd never get away in time."

"Ethan, you and Black Hawk get out of here," ordered Damian. "O'Grady, can you get me in without suspicions being raised?"

"No!" Nina grabbed Damian's hand. "Damian, if you're caught, he'll hang you. Please, you must leave, too. I'm all right. Papa hasn't hurt me. He thinks Jeremiah and I are married . . ."

"What?"

"Watkins married us." On the ground below, Watkins smiled and nodded.

"Lovely sermon it was. You should have been there, sir . . . What was the part about evil, Jeremy? And about the plank in the eye. I liked that."

Jeremiah knelt beside Watkins and patted his forehead. "I guess you'll live."

"O'Grady!"

Ethan clutched Damian's arm. "He's coming across. Damian . . ."

"I'm not going. You're joining Lafayette soon, yes, O'Grady?"

Jeremiah sighed. "That's the plan. Don't tell me how you know the Continental Army's plans."

"There'll be confusion when the armies meet. I'll take her then. It will give us time to plan."

"Black Hawk, you and Ethan get word to Ian. He'll be on *The Gladiator* in Chesapeake Bay. Tell him I'll bring Nina there."

"Major O'Grady!" Iolo had almost reached the southern shore of the river.

"Go!"

Ethan and Black Hawk hurried from the battle site,

taking Gambrinus with them. The big horse whinnied toward Damian, and Nina's heart chilled. It was as if the animal sensed a danger they couldn't foresee.

"What if Papa recognizes you?"

"Keep your head low," advised Jeremiah. "Iolo doesn't look close at anyone."

Nina looked up at Damian. If he hadn't been accompanied by Black Hawk, she doubted she'd recognize either Damian or Ethan.

"What do we call him?" asked Watkins. They all looked blank as Watkins pondered Damian's name change. "Nathan? No, Nathaniel! That's a good name. Nathaniel Hastings."

"Hastings?" asked Jeremiah. "Why 'Hastings,' Watkins?"

"Because he's English. Hastings, Jeremy. From the battle, of course. When William the Conqueror conquered England. The Norman invasion. In 1066 . . ."

"Never mind, Watkins."

Iolo's horse splashed up the bank and he cantered to his remaining soldiers. Damian left Nina's side and busied himself with the wounded.

"What went on here?" Iolo's ruddy face was pinker than usual, his wig was off center, and despite her fear, Nina smiled.

"We were ambushed by Banastre Tarleton, Papa."

"What? Name of God!"

"We drove him off, Colonel," said Jeremiah. "Don't think he expected much of a fight."

"We was all backed up ready to defend ourselves right good as he expected," began Watkins.

"What happened to you, Watkins?"

"Tarleton shot him when he saved Jeremiah," said Nina. Watkins beamed with pride.

"Very good, soldier. Go on."

"Well, as I was saying, sir . . . You should've seen us. We was something!"

Iolo growled in growing impatience. "Continue."

"Took 'em by surprise, we did. They came riding in as sure as anything."

"Watkins . . ."

"And Jeremy yelled 'Charge!' And we did."

"Good work, O'Grady." Iolo patted Nina's arm. "You're all right, girl. Glad to see it. And I'm pleased you saw fit to stay at your husband's side. Loyalty, woman. That's what sets a wife apart."

"She sure can shoot, sir, and that's a fact," put in Watkins. "Ain't no man ever going to get the best of her."

PART FOUR
Damian

TEN

Northern Virginia

May, 1781

Still posing as Nathaniel Hastings, Damian stood outside General Wayne's tent while the rebel conferred with his officers. He whittled a block of wood as he waited for Jeremiah O'Grady to return. Damian couldn't resist the opportunity to overhear the enemy's plans.

Nina grabbed Damian's arm and pulled him away from the commander's tent. "What are you doing here?"

"Waiting for O'Grady."

"What if Papa sees you?"

Iolo came out of the tent unexpectedly and bumped into Damian. Jeremiah followed him, and he cringed as Iolo scrutinized the scruffy soldier

"You need a shave. And a haircut."

Damian nodded, but Iolo studied him intently. "I don't remember you, soldier. Now then, what's your name?"

"This is Nathaniel," said Jeremiah. Both Nina and Damian were speechless. "You remember, Colonel. Nathaniel . . ."

Watkins appeared behind them, supporting himself dramatically with a cane. "Hastings."

Iolo's attention diverted to Watkins. "What are you doing out of the surgeon's tent?"

"All fixed up, sir. Took the shot out. It wasn't deep, and got myself stitched up."

Nina patted Watkins's good shoulder. "That must have been terribly painful."

"It did sting. And it'll be awhile afore I can shoot straight. Least with a musket. Could use a pistol, though," he added with a glance at Jeremiah.

"You're not fighting, Watkins."

Iolo nodded appreciatively at the young soldier's eagerness. "I'll see you're properly armed, Watkins. That reminds me, you've been promoted. Jumped a few spaces, too. How do you like the sound of 'Captain Watkins?'"

"Like it just fine!" Watkins seized Iolo's hand and shook it vigorously. He overdid it. "Ouch!" He grimaced before shaking Jeremiah's hand, too.

"Congratulations, Captain," said Nina. Damian watched the rebel's casual promotion doubtfully. This wasn't the way the English army handled promotions.

"We don't have a new uniform for you," said Jeremiah. "But I can find you a new hat."

"I'll stitch an epaulette on the shoulder of your jacket," offered Nina. Watkins beamed.

"Very good." Iolo eyed his daughter. "You be getting some rest, girl. Don't want you getting fatigued. We've got a long march tonight. There's a push to meet Lafayette within a day or two. Cornwallis has dropped back towards Williamsburg."

Damian listened with interest, but Jeremiah cringed as Iolo spouted delicate information. "Well, well, there's no telling what we'll do next. Now, then . . . Hastings, to my tent. And you, my sweet, will accompany us."

Nina looked up at Jeremiah in surprise, but she lowered her head deferentially. Iolo saw her wifely obedience and nodded.

"Do your husband's word, girl. Don't you be forgetting who's boss."

"Yes, Papa." Nina frowned as Iolo stomped away.

Damian grinned. "Good advice, woman."

Jeremiah led them to his tent and held open the flap. "In, both of you." They went inside and he turned to face Damian. His expression was solemn. "Now look here, Knox. It's well and good that you want your woman back. I'll do what I can to help you. But so help me God, you won't get away with spying."

"That wasn't my intention."

"I don't know what this war means to you, Knox, but to most of us here, it's everything. It's whether we're subjects of a far-off king or free men. I'd do most anything for Nina. But I tell you now, I won't risk losing one man because of you."

Damian didn't answer. Nina's eyes widened indignantly. "Damian!"

His silence was Jeremiah's answer. "I see. Then it's necessary to keep you from reporting back to them."

"Jeremiah, no. If you tell them, Damian will be hanged!"

"I'll say nothing. But Nathaniel Hastings had better stay in my sight at all times. Don't you even think of leaving, Knox. Not until Cornwallis learns our intentions first hand."

Damian frowned. "How long will that be? I don't particularly enjoy the thought of waiting around to be caught. Nor seeing the results of British engagements from the enemy side."

"Maybe you'll learn something. But you're staying. Or by God, I'll turn the whole army on you myself. Watkins, enter!"

Avery Watkins appeared at the door, looking innocent, as if he hadn't been eavesdropping, which Damian felt sure he had.

"I'm leaving my wife under Hastings' care. Watch this tent and see he doesn't leave. And make sure no one goes in without a good warning, too. Got that?"

"Yes, sir, Jeremy! Think he'll do a bit of spying, do you?"

"We won't give him the chance." Jeremiah looked back at Nina and Damian. "You stay here, Knox. I'll give you my wife, but not my army's secrets. Is that clear?"

Damian grinned. "It is. I'll take what is most precious and leave the rest to others."

Jeremiah left, but Nina peered suspiciously into Damian's eyes. "You wouldn't spy, would you, Damian?"

"Not at the moment. It seems O'Grady has removed that option."

"Damian!" Nina's brow puckered and her mouth tightened into a rounded pout. "You came for me!"

"I did, at that." Damian held out his hand, and she stepped forward and gave him her hand.

"I've missed you, so I will forgive your tendency toward spying."

"Thank you."

Damian cupped her face in his hands and gently kissed her mouth. She returned his kiss with a flare of pent-up passion. His body responded accordingly, he grew stiff and hard as her tongue slipped between his lips.

Morning was half over. If they were quick, they could make love and still find her well-rested by the evening's march. Damian started to lift Nina into his arms. She was unexpectedly heavy. He set her abruptly back to her feet.

"What's the matter?"

Damian groaned. "I'd almost forgotten!"

"What?"

"Our child! Why, I almost . . ."

Nina's face fell. "I am rather round, aren't I? I forgot about that, too. Of course, you wouldn't want me now."

"Want you?" Damian took her hand and kissed it tenderly. "I want you so much I can't make a fist, little rebel."

"You don't mind my shape?"

Damian studied her expanded waistline. "You're quite beautiful. Motherhood suits you."

"Well, if you want me, and you think I'm beautiful . . ."

"I don't want to hurt you."

"I don't think it would hurt."

"The baby is up here, see." Nina directed Damian's hand to the swelling beneath her rib cage. The baby kicked.

"There truly is someone in there, isn't there?"

"Someone very active. But since he or she plays up here, I see no reason why we shouldn't . . ."

"Do you suggest we lie as lovers while the rebel army mulls around outside? It's broad daylight. And you need sleep."

Nina seized his hand and directed him to her bedding. "I'll sleep better after."

"I hope Watkins watches that door well."

Nina lowered herself to the ground. "Maybe we shouldn't take everything off, just in case."

Damian pulled off his tattered jacket and lay down beside her. "A good idea. Though if I'm to be caught, it might as well be for this."

"You won't be caught." Nina unbuttoned his shirt. "Jeremiah won't let anything happen to you."

"You have great faith in him."

Nina pressed her lips against his throat. His pulse surged at her touch.

"I have greater faith in you. Only you could make me feel this way."

Damian undid the fat buttons of Nina's bodice, and slid the heavy material from her breasts. He untied her chemise and pushed it down to reveal the satiny mounds.

"No corset?" he teased as he brushed his lips across her creamy flesh.

"I outgrew it."

"I see that."

He ran his finger across the pink buds. Nina's breasts were full as they prepared for motherhood, her body ripe with desire. He circled the taut peaks with his palm, feeling their new size with the gentle play of his fingers.

"You are beautiful," he murmured as he bent to run his lips across the tempting summit.

Nina's body was sensitized by pregnancy. She quivered at his slightest touch. Damian reveled in her reactions. He laved a rosy nipple with his tongue until her breaths came in delicious gasps.

"Hush, love. We don't want Watkins bursting in here as your savior."

Nina bit her lip. "Don't stop, Damian. If you do, I will die."

"I've only begun." Damian forgot his concern for her condition and surrendered to the power of his desire. Nina's body was ripe with womanhood, she was filled with the product of their love. He turned her on her side and lay behind her and caressed her full breasts as she leaned back to kiss him.

Damian freed himself from his breeches, his staff seeking the softness between her legs. Her rounded bottom pressed against his groin. She arched to receive his length. He felt the velvet moisture urging him inward and he allowed his tip to enter her.

She was tight inside, her honey soaked him with desire. He moved inside her, his shallow thrusts caressing her inner fire as they rode the consuming waves of their passion. Her secret walls closed tight around his length, urging him to fulfill her need.

Damian moved with ever-increasing abandon. He buried his face in her thick hair to keep silent, but Nina moaned in pleasure. He clasped his hand over her mouth; she sucked hard on his finger as they writhed together in ecstasy.

The world outside was forgotten while they loved. When she at last lay still in his arms, the camp's hushed noises reached their ears, but the sound wasn't threatening.

Nina kissed his shoulder. "I can't believe you're here."

"Nor can I. This is one way I never expected to engage the enemy."

She pulled her bodice over her bare breasts and adjusted her soft chemise. "You must be careful to avoid Papa. If he recognizes you . . ."

"I know. He doesn't appear particularly observant, however."

"Papa thinks everything has gone his way. He doesn't consider anything else."

"At least he hasn't harmed you. I feared the extent of his anger."

"As long as I don't defy him. It's strange, Damian, but I think he cares for me. Even though he must know I'm not . . ."

She stopped. Her loyalty was instinctive, but Damian kissed her forehead.

"That you're not his daughter."

"You knew? Did my mother tell you?"

"Cora said nothing. I suspected that you were Ian's child from the day I learned who you really were. From the first, I noticed your resemblance to Ethan. Your startling likeness to Ian explains why Iolo told you that you resemble Cora."

"I know I was unfair to Ian Forbes. But whenever I think of him, my throat gets tight, I can't breathe. I feel like something awful is going to happen. I don't know why, Damian."

"Ian Forbes is a good man. I know he would never hurt you. He loves you, Nina, whether you believe it or not. Apparently you were with them for several months before Iolo stole you back."

"I don't remember. I remember his face, but maybe that's only from my dream." Nina paused. "When I was brought to Papa from New York, it seemed as if it happened before. I remembered being brought to him long ago. And I remembered Columbine O'Grady."

"She was probably in on your abduction. She was a nasty old crow, as I recall."

"That's true. But why do I remember Ian Forbes with fear, and recall nothing frightening about Iolo Evans?"

"I don't know. But if you talk to Ian, you might learn the truth."

"Moving out!"

Avery Watkins's cheerful call startled Nina and Damian from sleep. Damian groaned and extracted himself from Nina's arms. "Who is that little man, anyway?"

Nina smiled drowsily and stretched. "Captain Avery Watkins. He's a friend of Jeremiah's. He's quite unusual. But I like him. And he's very brave."

Watkins peeked into the tent. Seeing Damian and Nina dressed, he entered without trepidation. "Now then, Hastings, it's time to get going. Jeremy's put you in my company, for safe-keeping."

Damian towered over Watkins. "Captain, I am honored to serve you."

"And to have you, Hastings." Watkins paused. "What rank were you with the Brits?"

"Major."

Watkins's face fell. "Oh."

"But a British major is subordinate to an American captain," offered Damian. "When serving the American army."

"True enough!"

Jeremiah entered the tent.

"Just informing Hastings of the situation, Jeremy," said Watkins.

"What situation is that?"

"That I'm his superior officer."

"I see. Don't let it go to your head, Watkins. I put him with you so we could keep him out of trouble." Jeremiah glanced at Damian. "And to help him resist the temptation of spying."

"I wouldn't dream of dishonoring Watkins's command."

"See that you don't. By our complicity, our lives rest with yours."

Nina looked between them. Jeremiah and Watkins were risking everything for her, for Damian. "No matter what happens to us, we'll see you're not involved."

Damian nodded. "You have my word as well."

"Very good," said Watkins. "Jeremy, where's Owens?"

"Owens?" asked Nina. "The minister?"

An old man entered the tent, his pastoral calm much more obvious than Watkins's. He eyed Nina and Damian and sighed heavily.

"Is this the Brit, O'Grady?"

"It is."

"I don't know about this, O'Grady. If the Colonel knew . . ."

"He won't know," put in Watkins.

Jeremiah glanced pertinently at Nina's pregnant belly. "There isn't much time, as you can perhaps tell."

"What's going on?" asked Damian.

"This is Evan Owens," explained Jeremiah. "Since my marriage was . . . less than legal, I thought it wise to marry the girl off before it's too late. It's by way of an obligation of mine."

Damian grinned and took Nina's hand. "Proceed."

Nina stared up at him, her eyes glittering with tears. "You're going to marry me?"

"I didn't hunt you down for nothing. Whatever happens, that child is mine. He . . . or she, will carry my name."

"Knox," said Nina. "I will be Emmalina Knox, then. 'Nina' doesn't sound quite right."

In a few short minutes, Nina Evans became Emmalina Knox. The ceremony seemed perfunctory to Nina, but Damian's soft kiss proved to her just how much she'd gained. Watkins and Jeremiah signed as witnesses while Evan Owens glanced nervously out of their tent.

He pocketed the marriage certificate. "I'll keep this hidden." He glanced at Nina and Damian without sentiment. "Congratulations. And best of luck to you. You'll need it."

"You'd have been better off with me handling the service," remarked Watkins when Evan Owens left.

Nina sighed. "It wasn't particularly flowery, was it?" She looked up into Damian's face and her heart soared on wings of joy. He kissed her hand.

"We are one thing, Emmalina Knox. We didn't need anyone to pronounce it legal."

They kissed while Watkins looked on with a bright smile and Jeremiah waited impatiently.

"Well, well, it's finally done," said Watkins.

"And none too soon," added Jeremiah. "Come

along, Knox. You can celebrate your wedding later. For now, we've got a long night's march ahead of us."

Nina rode beside Jeremiah, but Damian marched with Watkins's company. He saw her riding just ahead, the light of a lantern flickering on her golden curls. *My wife. Soon our child will join us . . .*

The soldiers beside him seemed to fade away and an icy premonition flooded through Damian. Not for Nina nor their child did he sense danger. Damian's heart beat steadily, but he knew . . . One day, he would face his father's death. He had always known.

Unless someone he could not foresee entered to change his fate, that day would be his last.

"Halt!" Watkins's call disrupted Damian's thoughts and jolted him back to reality.

Damian waited with the rest as Jeremiah rode ahead to learn the reason for the sudden stop. Nina glanced back at him and guided her horse to his side as the soldiers mulled together.

"What do you see?" asked Watkins.

Nina stood in her stirrups, balancing her round self on the saddle as she peered into the darkness ahead.

"Not much. I think Papa's conferring with a messenger."

"From Lafayette?"

"How would I know that?" replied Nina with a doubtful glance toward Watkins. "Maybe."

"I hope so. The marquis is quite a fellow, they say. We're the same age."

"It will be interesting to serve under him," said Damian with a grin. Nina and Watkins glanced at him reproachfully.

"An *honor,*" she corrected.

"Alexander Hamilton is my age, too," declared Watkins. "I've been thinking there was something in the heavens around the year of our birth. Something that inspired, well . . . *greatness,* if you will." He looked thoughtfully into the distance while Damian eyed him with misgivings.

Jeremiah returned. Watkins practically bounced with enthusiasm. "Well? It's Lafayette, isn't it?"

"It is," replied Jeremiah. "His army's just ahead, and more . . ."

"What, Jeremy?"

"Cornwallis is just behind him, closing in on our flank. The bulk of his army is back a ways, unfortunately, but there should be one fine skirmish before we pull away."

"Wonderful." Damian's dry voice was a marked contrast to the rebels' enthusiasm for engagement.

"What's wrong, Hastings?" asked Watkins in surprise. "It's going to be a grand fight. You fought Tarleton well, as I recall."

"Banastre Tarleton was one thing. The earl is another. Those are my men."

Jeremiah nodded in understanding. "Well, then. I'll have to find a fit assignment. You guard my wife, Hastings. That should be something worth defending."

Nina chewed her lip. "Would Ethan be with them?"

"Possibly. Though I doubt it. He couldn't have reached Ian and returned to the army in this short time."

"It was so much simpler when I cared for no one on the enemy side."

Damian smiled. "It always is."

The two armies converged at dawn, merging together in a disorderly fashion. As her appointed guardian,

Damian stayed close to Nina while the rebel soldiers mingled.

Watkins seized one of Lafayette's New England captains and interrogated him with all the vigor of an enemy soldier. "How far back are the British?"

"Don't know for certain," replied the uncertain Yankee. "We done caught sight of the bloodybacks, then broke ahead a ways yonder."

Watkins studied the soldier. "Where are you from?" he asked suspiciously. "Massachusetts?"

The New Englander straightened indignantly. "Maine."

"Same state."

"We'll just see how long that lasts!"

Apparently, Watkins didn't care about New England politics, nor whether Maine remained part of Massachusetts or not. Soldiers from the North and South bitterly disliked each other, and those from the central states disliked both.

Damian listened to their deteriorating conversation with a heavy heart. The United States of America had a long way to go before it was truly a union.

Again, his strange foresight offered a glimpse of the future. Damian saw his own seed flowering: He saw two young men standing on opposite sides of a great war. Both carried his name, his blood and Nina's. A legacy that only love could conquer.

His vision passed and Damian sighed heavily. Nina watched him, a strange expression on her face. "Is something wrong?"

"It never ends. Wars are resolved, but always conflict rises again to take more toll in blood."

"That's not a very pleasant thought, Damian."

"No. But it is often true."

Watkins and the Mainer were engaging in an increasingly heated conversation. "Boston may have started the war," spouted Watkins angrily, "but Pennsylvanians will end it." Both had forgotten the South, but neither one cared.

"There'd be no revolution without New England," insisted the Mainer. "You're just along for the ride."

Watkins stepped angrily toward the Maine soldier, his fists clenched and ready for a fight. Nina looked anxiously to Damian, but he was at a loss to intervene.

The Mainer didn't back down. "You boys were the mutineers."

"One line in mutiny! And it got cleared up just fine."

"Don't want no weak-kneed, puppy-faced Quaker protecting my back!"

Nina fidgeted. "Damian, shouldn't we do something?"

"If you have a suggestion, I'd be happy to hear it."

"I'll show you 'puppy-faced!' " Watkins took a wild swing at the Mainer, who ducked and punched right back. Both missed, and Damian shook his head.

"When Englishmen take on our Hessian brothers, at least we connect with our blows."

"Damian! Do something."

Damian didn't take the squabble very seriously, but Nina urged her horse forward to stop the fight. The horse balked at the mad scramble of fists between Watkins and the Mainer.

"Stop that!" shouted Nina. Damian grabbed her horse's reins and directed her from the fight.

"I'm afraid," began Damian in a subdued voice, "that you boys had better save it for the enemy."

Damian's quiet voice startled both Watkins and the Mainer. They stopped fighting and looked at Damian.

"Cornwallis," said Damian calmly. As he spoke, the drums beat *To Arms,* and the rebels scurried into action.

Jeremiah came galloping along the disjointed line of soldiers, shouting orders to his men. They readied with surprising speed, and Watkins forgot his fistfight to face the larger enemy.

"Ready weapons!" ordered Jeremiah. "Skirmishers to the fore, hold them off while the army moves out of reach."

"Not going to engage them, Jeremy?" asked Watkins in disappointment. The Mainer waited beside him with the same expression of dismay.

"Hold them off, Watkins," repeated Jeremiah. "Cat and mouse, men. Let's not forget we're the mouse."

Damian watched the disorderly rhythm of the rebel army as it arranged itself in a perfect defense. Nina's horse stomped and quivered at the activity. Damian pulled her from the saddle.

"This is the strangest army I've ever seen," he muttered as he directed Nina toward the rear of the skirmish line. His voice betrayed admiration, and Nina glanced up at him.

"How would you confront a greater army? Would you line us up and throw us at Cornwallis?"

Damian hesitated, but then he smiled. "I would hide my men in the trees and scare the hell out of my opposition. Then back up and go at them again."

"I thought as much," said Nina with a nod of satisfaction. "As I said before, you're on the wrong side, Damian Knox."

Jeremiah overheard Damian's comment. "That's not a bad idea. Climb the trees, men!"

Without hesitation, both Pennsylvanians and New Englanders shimmied up the nearest branches. "You men are the first skirmish: The rest of you pull back and make ready to move in."

Damian sighed. "Perfect. I've advised the enemy."

"We'll see how well." Jeremiah laughed as he left the first line to await the British troops.

They backed away, leaving the hidden ambush in wait.

Intent on harrying Lafayette's army, the British took jabs at the rebel rear, but this time, it was they who were surprised. Shots rang out from above and the redcoats fell back in astonishment. The hidden rebels fired again, leapt down from the branches and raced back to Jeremiah's second line.

"Turn and fire!" commanded Jeremiah. "The rest of you, move out."

Damian hesitated. He watched his own command taken to success as the rebels shot and fell back, realigned and shot again. Jeremiah O'Grady had no qualms about changing his orders, nor taking unconventional advice. If only the English commanders had seen fit to employ this same wisdom, the long war might be already over.

The skirmish ended without rebel casualties. The British troops backed away and returned to their army disheartened. Lafayette directed his army north, and by midafternoon, they were safely twenty miles from Cornwallis's army.

"If you were on my side, I'd see you promoted." Jeremiah sat with Damian and Nina, but Damian wasn't overjoyed with the praise.

"Next time, I'll keep my mouth shut."

"When do we move next?" asked Nina. The ride and skirmish tired her, and the day's heat was especially difficult in her condition.

"Not until tomorrow," said Jeremiah. "We're a big enough force now to move safely during the day."

"I saw him!" Watkins pushed his way through a crowd of soldiers and sat down beside Jeremiah.

"Saw who, Watkins?" asked Jeremiah.

"The marquis, of course. Marie Joseph du Motier, the

Marquis de Lafayette! I don't know the rest of his names."

Nina's eyes widened excitedly. "Where is he? What's he like?"

"He's up a ways," replied Watkins, relishing his position of knowledge. "Spoke to me and my boys as friendly as anything. I think he recognized me as a contemporary. He's already met with Colonel Evans."

"He's coming this way?" Nina stood up and looked around for the Frenchman. A large group of Pennsylvanian soldiers were queuing up ahead, waiting to greet Lafayette. Cheers rang out and the soldiers formed a line as the marquis approached.

Damian stood beside her. "I don't relish saluting the enemy, however likable he might be."

"Hush, Damian! He's coming." Nina clasped her hands over her breast, standing on tiptoes to see the French commander's approach. Lafayette appeared among a tight group of soldiers, walking ahead as he bowed to the Pennsylvanians. He stopped often to speak as he passed by the admiring assortment of men.

Iolo Evans walked beside Lafayette, though he appeared less thrilled than the younger soldiers. "Maybe you should stand back a bit, Nathaniel," suggested Jeremiah. Damian stepped back from the crowd, but it was too late.

Lafayette noticed Damian, and Damian cringed. "Who is that?" he asked, his accent thick and rich. "One of your men, Colonel?"

Iolo squinted, then glanced at Jeremiah. "That would be Nathaniel Hastings," Jeremiah told the Marquis.

"Monsieur Hastings," said the Frenchman.

Damian forced himself to salute. It wasn't easy.

Iolo eyed him suspiciously. "Didn't I tell you to shave?"

"No time for it, Colonel," said Jeremiah. "Why, it was Hastings who suggested the ambush."

Damian drew a long breath and smiled without much feeling. Nina beamed with pride. "It is men such as yourself, Monsieur Hastings, that make me proud to serve your great nation."

Damian bowed, and the marquis bowed. His dark gaze went to Nina. "What lovely flower blossoms upon the bloody fields of war?"

"This is my wife," said Jeremiah. "And Colonel Evans' daughter. Nina O'Grady." The marquis looked doubtfully at the short, dark Welshman, but turned his attention back to Nina.

"Madame O'Grady. It is my great pleasure to make your acquaintance." He took Nina's hand and kissed it.

"Thank you," replied Nina happily. "As I am honored to make yours, General." Lafayette kissed her hand again, then released her to Jeremiah. Damian watched in irritation. The young man obviously didn't notice her pregnancy.

The marquis moved on, leaving Watkins and Nina breathless with excitement. "Damian!" A quick look from Jeremiah silenced her, and Nina bit her lip. "Nathaniel, I mean. Did you hear that? He was pleased to make my acquaintance!"

"I heard," said Damian dryly. "As he was proud to meet me."

"He took more pleasure from your lady, though," said Watkins.

"Isn't he handsome?" Nina was teasing him, too. Damian forced himself to remain impassive. "And so polite. Maybe Papa will invite us to dine with them tonight. You can be Jeremiah's aide."

Damian rolled his eyes. "I've drawn enough attention

to myself already. Dining with enemy generals wasn't part of my plan when I came for you."

May passed into June, and June ripened toward summer while Damian moved southward with Lafayette's rebel army. Cornwallis backed toward Chesapeake Bay. Washington sent troops by land and water in an attempt to surround the British army.

Damian and Nina were alone in Jeremiah's tent. Nina slept, but Damian had grown increasingly restless. Their baby would come within the next four weeks, if Cora was right. It would be hard enough to sneak a pregnant Nina from the rebel camp. Keeping a tiny infant silent while they fled would be impossible.

Damian left Nina sleeping and went in search of Jeremiah. He found Jeremiah playing chess with Watkins. By his expression, Watkins appeared to be losing.

"Be damned if you've got me again, Jeremy."

Damian glanced at the board as Watkins reached for a chess piece. "Don't move the queen, Watkins. The knight is your best choice."

Watkins seized the knight and cornered Jeremiah's king. "Got you now, Jeremy!"

Jeremiah glanced up at Damian. "Can't resist offering advice, can you, *Hastings?*"

Damian grinned. "As pleasurable as it's been, it's time I moved on, O'Grady. Nina will give birth soon. In a few weeks, it will be too late to take her anywhere. There's a ship waiting in the Chesapeake, but we're going to have to head north as it is, to get around the army."

"The colonel keeps a close eye on her. I can't imagine how you'll get her past the pickets, let alone all the way to the Chesapeake."

"Let's tell the colonel that Hastings fell for Nina and

ran off with her," suggested Watkins. "Then tell him they were spotted heading south."

Damian and Jeremiah considered Watkins's suggestion, but neither could find an obvious flaw in the plan. "It might work," said Jeremiah. "But you're right, Knox. If you're going to take her, it had best be soon."

Damian returned to Nina. Nina smiled sleepily and held out her arms to him. "Where have you been?"

He lay down beside her. "With O'Grady. We've been discussing our escape. It's time to go, love."

"I know. I've been so happy here with you. But it can't last. We have to leave before the baby comes."

"There's a push toward the Chesapeake. Another army is joining Lafayette's. We'll go as soon as it arrives. Watkins suggested that you be abducted by Hastings."

"Will Papa believe that, do you think? He's bound to figure it out, Damian. What if he blames Jeremiah?"

"There's no reason he should. If Evans realizes I am Hastings, they would be assumed innocent of knowledge. If O'Grady plays the deserted husband, Evans will believe it."

"I hope so," said Nina. "I'll leave a note to remove Papa's suspicions. But he'll follow us, Damian. Mama says he sent men after her when she ran away with Ian Forbes. He has men who seem to work for him, men I haven't seen in the army. Jeremiah didn't know them, either. From what I saw, they are ruthless."

"Then it will become a race to the Chesapeake. A race we'll have to win at any cost."

Night fell starless, and no moonlight pierced the heavy fog that eased westward from the Chesapeake. Nina huddled close to Damian behind a thicket as the army passed by. Iolo Evans rode past their hiding place. Damian held her hand and she squeezed her fingers tight around his, but no one noticed her absence in the long procession.

Jeremiah and Avery Watkins rode by with their soldiers and Nina's heart expanded with affection. "I'll miss them."

Damian nodded. "I'm not sure why, but I will, too."

They waited until the rear moved far from sight before they left their hiding place. Nina squeezed herself from the bush and looked around. "What now?"

Damian took her hand. "The race begins. We must reach Ian Forbes before Iolo Evans learns where you've gone."

He led Nina away from the army's well-trodden path, north toward Maryland while the war marched toward a climax in Virginia. Somehow, he had to get Nina to her real father. And he had one month to do it.

"Hastings."

Iolo's voice was cold and hard, but Jeremiah didn't flinch. "Yes, Colonel. A picket saw them heading south. My beloved wife left this note, as I told you. She resented being forced into marriage. Hastings was 'kind' to her. Ha! I've been made a fool again."

Iolo Evans said nothing, but his expression chilled Jeremiah to the bone.

"I've sent men after them," said Jeremiah. "They won't get far, I promise you."

"Where did you send them?"

Jeremiah hesitated. "South. That's where our pickets saw them."

Iolo's lip curled: "Get them back, O'Grady. Send no further couriers, tell no one she has gone. I'll take care of that son of a bitch this time. There'll be no mistake."

"Sir?"

"This isn't a job for your soldiers, O'Grady. I have

the men to find her. I promise you, Damian Knox won't
live to see his bastard child."

Jeremiah gulped. "Knox?"

"He dared sneak in here under my nose. He passed
himself off as a soldier well enough." Iolo's voice was
too calm, too even. "But he will never escape me now,
O'Grady. The war may end, but there's an old score to
settle. And Damian Knox will pay with his life."

Iolo returned to his horse and rode on ahead. Watkins appeared out of nowhere and seized Jeremiah's
arm. "What are we going to do? What did the old fellow
mean by 'his own men'? That don't sound too good to
me."

"I don't know, Avery. There's no way to warn them.
But when I saw the men Evans sent out after them . . .
Men who he got from prisons, probably. Who knows?
But there's not a one with scruples."

"All we can do is keep an eye on the old man. Find
out what he's up to. Maybe we can prevent disaster."

"Maybe. But he's closed off to me. It's as if he has
something planned that's too horrible to share."

"What?"

"I can't guess. But whatever it is, Damian Knox is in
greater danger than he knows. I've never seen the old
man like this, Avery. He's so controlled. It strikes me
that his restraint is sevenfold more deadly than his bluster."

"But we sent him south, didn't we?"

"He didn't fall for it. He knows there are British ships
in the Chesapeake. Where else would Damian Knox go?
Iolo's sent his men out, and they'll be hot on Damian's
trail by now. Pray, Avery, that Damian Knox moves
swiftly. His life, and maybe Nina's too, hangs on his
speed."

*   *   *

Nina slogged through the mud behind Damian, her head bowed, her body weary to the bone. "How much farther?"

Damian stopped and lifted her into his arms. "We'll stop soon, I promise. We've almost reached the river. It's only a little way yet."

"Put me down. You can't carry me all the way to the ship."

"This journey has already taken longer than I hoped."

"I know, but I'm all right. I can walk."

He set Nina back to her feet and they walked along the shore south of the Potomac river, heading towards the bay. "What ship is that?"

Light was fading, but Damian saw what he was looking for in the broad inlet. "*The Gladiator.*"

"Is that where Ian Forbes is waiting?"

"Nina, we'll be safe. Trust me."

"I know." She paused. "How will he see us, to send a skiff out, I mean?"

"He'll see us," said Damian. "But we must hurry. Come, love, just a little way further."

They started off again, but Nina lagged behind. "Hurry, Nina."

There was no reason to fear, he'd seen no one when he last scouted the area. But Damian's heart beat in dread as he led Nina towards safety. The ship rocked in the open river, lanterns glowed as evening settled.

Between the river and the shelter of trees lay a wide bank of trodden grass. They stopped beneath the eves of the wood, and Damian's breath caught. A group of men ambled across the field, neither British nor rebel soldiers.

Nina saw them, too, and she clutched Damian's arm. "Damian, those are Papa's men, the ones who kidnapped me!"

Damian stared at the ship, at the group of men. Too many to fight, too few to engage the attention of *The Gladiator.*

"What do we do?"

"We turn around. We'll go back along the shore, then cross farther north. The water is lower at that point. It's swift, but I'll help you. We can make it by the north shore before they see us. Come." He took her hand and they moved stealthily back into the woods.

"We'll have to keep going for a while, until we're out of sight. Can you make it, love?"

"I can."

"How will we cross?"

The bridge was miles further. Nina knew she couldn't walk that far in one night. Her belly hardened and she caught her breath. The tightening of her womb had happened this way for several weeks—it had become familiar. But today, her belly contracted with growing intensity.

Damian hesitated as he studied the river. "We swim."

Nina gulped. She tried to control her voice. "Swim? Damian . . . I would march with you, I might even crawl. But . . . *swim?* I'm not that good a swimmer!" Her voice grew shrill. Damian waited patiently for her to calm down before explaining.

"As it happens, I am an excellent swimmer. You'll have to take off your dress. I'll carry it, and help you. The water doesn't look as violent as usual tonight."

"Is that so? What a relief!"

"You might find swimming easier than walking." Damian eyed her round form. "You're probably quite . . . buoyant."

Nina closed her eyes. "You mean I'll float and you'll pull me along? Oh, *that* won't attract attention."

"We'll wait until it's fully dark, then cross. Rest a while."

Nina flopped to the ground. "Maybe we should just give ourselves up and die."

Damian sat down beside her and held her in his arms. "We won't die, love. We'll get to the other side, sleep through the night, then reach Ian's ship in the early hours. There's nothing to fear."

A half moon rose above the river as Nina stripped away her dress. She stood shivering in a chemise and petticoats while Damian tied their more cumbersome garments in a knot, then fixed it to his haversack. He secured the powder for his dragoon pistol where it would stay dry, then turned to Nina.

He held out his hand to her, a smile curving his lips. "Are you ready?"

Nina gave him her hand and followed him to the water's edge. "It looks cold."

"Refreshing."

"I can't see anything. It's so black."

"Look there, love. You can see the moon reflected on the surface."

"How terribly comforting!"

Damian led her into the river. She splashed in and looked back at him. "It's not as cold as I thought, Damian. And the bottom isn't squishy." Nina took a deep breath, then sank down into the water.

"Oh! Damian, you were right. I do float!" Nina kicked her legs and propelled herself into the darkness with such ease that Damian had to dive in after her. The current swept her downstream, but Damian caught her and pulled her back.

"What are you doing? I was going so fast!"

"In the wrong direction. The current is swift. Let me help you."

Her chin firmed. "I see no need . . ."

He loosened his hold on her and the water yanked her away. "Damian!"

Damian drew her back and smiled. "You have your brother's level of confidence."

Nina frowned. "Ethan has too much confidence."

"Exactly."

She issued a huff, but she didn't argue. Damian waded farther into the water, and pulled Nina along beside him. She floated like a buoy. He sank down to swim, and she bobbed along with the current. It was strong, but Damian kept himself steady.

"Where's the shore?" Nina sounded happy, and they stopped to rest when Damian found a rock.

"We're close." To his great surprise, Nina threw her arms around his neck and kissed him.

"I feel so light." She kissed him again and ran her hand along his muscles. Damian caught her wet hair in his hand and kissed her deeply in return. Every moment seemed precious, every joy should be seized and cherished. As if it couldn't last.

"The shore, my dear."

They started off again. Nina floated with a peaceful expression on her face. She stared up at the night sky as if contemplating the universe. The river's swift current spun her around, but she didn't seem to mind.

Damian untangled her chemise and spun her back. Her gaze shifted to him in suspicion. "Are you doing this on purpose?"

"What?"

"Spinning me."

Damian repressed a grin. "Not at all."

She turned her gaze back to the stars. "As it happens, I enjoy spinning."

She spread her arms wide and encouraged her rotation. Damian watched in amazement. "I love you so." She couldn't hear him, because her head was half-covered by water. He stared at her a moment longer, allowing the image of her floating body to permeate his memory, then started again toward the northern shore.

They climbed out of the water and squeezed out their clothes. Nina replaced her shoes and smiled to herself. "The night's getting warmer."

"How are you, love?"

"Much better, strangely. The swim did me good."

Damian shook his head in wonder, but then looked around for a place to spend the night. "You rest here. I'll see what's in the area."

Nina lay back in the grass and stared up at the stars and the half moon. The night seemed magical. All her fears eased and settled into peace. Her belly contracted again, and she laid her hand on her round stomach. The contraction didn't ease for a long moment, then abated only a short while before tightening again.

"We're lucky!" Damian came back and picked up their wet clothes. "There's an old watershed up ahead. Maybe it was used for duck hunting."

"A hunting blind? There's nowhere else?"

"It's good shelter. There's even a box of old blankets."

Damian held out his hand for her. Nina took his hand and struggled to her feet. "I hope so. This could be a long night."

"Why?"

"Our baby is coming."

Damian stopped, his face pale and shocked. "It can't."

"If I could convince it to wait, I would."

"You must be mistaken." Damian eyed her stomach suspiciously.

Nina grimaced as her womb grew hard. She bit her lip until it eased, then shook her head. "I don't think so."

"It's the swimming. If you rest awhile, you'll feel better."

Damian led her to the blind and put one of the duck hunter's blankets around her. He laid out the other as bedding, then put out their wet clothes to dry. Nina sat quietly with her legs crossed under her.

Damian lay back on the blanket. He looked over at Nina. She sat still as stone, her face blank, but he knew she concentrated intently on something. "Come, love, lie down with me," he offered drowsily. "You need sleep."

"I can't move." Nina spoke abruptly, then returned to her concentration. Damian sat up and stared at her.

"Why not?"

"I told you, Damian. The baby."

"The baby?"

Nina broke her concentration and cast a reproachful glance his way. "Yes."

"Now?"

Nina nodded. Her eyes widened in surprise and she looked down. Damian half expected to see a baby there.

"Oh! What was that?"

"What?"

"Water. From inside me."

"Nina, you really are giving birth."

Her brow rose. "I told you that."

Damian moved anxiously to her side, staring at her stomach as if he could will the baby back into place.

"What do I do?" asked Nina.

Damian put his arm around her shoulder and she rested her head against him. "I'm not sure, exactly."

"Don't you know anything about babies?"

"I know you keep them warm."

Nina drew a long, calming breath. Damian considered their situation, desperately trying to recall anything he'd ever heard about birth. "From what I've seen, the whole thing takes care of itself. Just stay calm."

"You've seen a birth?"

Damian hesitated. "Yes . . ."

"How lucky! Then you know what to do. Good."

He cleared his throat. "Of course, that was a sheep."

Nina drew a breath and nodded. "A sheep."

"Yes. But it was her first lambing."

She nodded again. "That should prove useful."

They stared at each other. A smile grew on Nina's face, mirrored on Damian's. A giggle erupted from her throat, and they both laughed.

Nina's mirth was cut off by another sharp pain. She clutched her stomach while Damian chewed his lip nervously. "How did the ewe handle this?"

With nothing else to go on, Damian searched his memory. "As I recall, she was breathing very deeply. She didn't exactly lie down . . . You might say she squatted . . . And then out came the first lamb."

"First?"

"I expect you'll have only one."

Damian held Nina tightly against him, she clung to him, digging her fingers into his arm when her womb tightened. No longer were there moments for rest between contractions. Her inner body had a will of its own. While Nina struggled to keep from panic, her womb pushed the baby toward its new life.

Nina gasped as she squeezed his arm. "Damian, something's happening."

"Yes."

"I think the baby wants to come out."

"Now?" Damian's voice sounded very small and weak.

"Now!"

Her whole body seized upon itself. The need to push was overwhelming. She rose up on her knees and leaned forward against Damian. She bit her lip hard and pushed. He held her through the long moment. She relaxed for a short while, then found herself pushing again.

"Damian . . . It's coming."

"It's all right, love. Lean against the wall and let me see what's going on."

Nina leaned back against the old wall of the duck blind and Damian looked at her bottom. "I see the head! Push again."

She had little choice. Her body bore down hard, she held her breath and pushed again. Something popped out from her body and Nina took several quick breaths. "The head is out, love!"

"Is it a boy or a girl?"

Damian peered up at her from between her legs. "I can't tell from this angle." He bent down and wiped the tiny face clean. "But he's very handsome."

"If you can't tell . . . Oh!" Nina paused as another contraction developed.

"His mouth is open. He's hungry already!" Damian looked up at Nina's strained face. "Like you."

Damian readied the old hunter's blanket as Nina's contraction seized upon itself. The baby slithered from its mother's body and Damian wrapped the little form in the blanket. Nina leaned back against the wall. "I'm hungry, too."

Damian held the baby close against his chest and brought him to Nina. She looked into his face and her heart soared in happiness. Damian's face glowed with pleasure as he looked at her and back to their baby.

"Well?" asked Nina.

"What?" replied Damian softly.

"Is it a boy or a girl?"

"I don't know. I'll check." He peeled away the blanket and examined the baby. A tender smile grew on his face as the little being asserted its first identity.

"We have a son."

Tears filled Nina's eyes as she looked at the tiny baby. Damian placed their child in Nina's arms and she cradled him. Her heart filled with overpowering love.

Damian studied his son's face. "What shall we name him?"

"We could name him Daniel, after your father."

"I wouldn't have my son haunted by my father's death. Let us name him something that recalls only joy."

"Well, then . . . How about Nathaniel? That makes me think of Avery Watkins, and that's surely a pleasant memory. He can be named for his father, and still have a name of his own."

"Very good. Nathaniel, he will be."

Damian touched the baby as it nestled at Nina's breast. "Tonight we are blessed, my love. What tomorrow brings means nothing."

ELEVEN

The sun was already high when Damian and Nina woke. The duck blind was sheltered from the heat, a cool breeze wafted from the Potomac's surface. Nina checked Nathaniel, but he was sleeping soundly at her side.

"He's such a good little baby."

Damian studied his son proudly. "And handsome. See how pink his cheeks are! He's not pinched like some babies."

"He looks like you. Just think, Damian. Nathaniel will grow up and marry, then have children, too. And our grandchildren will have babies . . ."

Damian nodded, but he didn't speak. A sense of urgency seemed to drive his actions. "Can you walk, love? We've got to get out of here. We've got to reach that ship."

"I can walk." Damian's anxiety spread from him into her as he helped her to her feet.

Nina's dress dried in the night air, and she tore the hunter's blanket into dousing strips to pack between her legs. She tied her petticoat snugly to hold the strips in place, but even that effort left her a little dizzy. She said nothing about it to Damian, however, as he was anxiously surveying the river bank.

"I'm ready."

Damian picked up Nathaniel, but the baby didn't wake. Nina's gaze met Damian's, and a silent communion between them said all that was needed. Their lives depended on the short distance to Ian Forbes's ship.

"It looks clear." Damian and Nina left the duck blind and walked along the marshy shore toward *The Gladiator*. The ship rocked in the harbor, but Nina closed her eyes in relief when she saw Ethan standing at the bow.

Nina waved. "Ethan!"

"Nina, hush!"

A group of men charged from the woods behind the duck blind. Their horses were still wet from the crossing. At the back, Nina saw Iolo astride a gray horse. "No. He must be mad."

Damian dragged her toward the ship. "He is mad."

Ethan shouted, and Nina saw him jump down into a skiff. Black Hawk followed him. But Solo's men were closer.

"What do we do?"

"Take Nathaniel." Damian placed the baby into her arms, then loaded his pistol.

"Damian, you can't fight those men alone!"

"I can hold them off. Go to your brother."

"I can't leave you! Please, let's run."

"You can't run."

"I can run." With Nathaniel in one arm, Nina held up her skirts and darted toward the shore. Ethan and Black Hawk were close, and two other skiffs with armed British soldiers were behind them.

Ethan and Black Hawk leapt from the skiff and raced to their aid. "Get in the boat, Nina," ordered Ethan. Nina carried Nathaniel into the skiff. But Damian hadn't followed.

She turned back to the riverbank and saw him firing his pistol. One of his attackers was struck, but the others came on relentlessly. Damian drew his saber, but he had no chance. The men would fight. Iolo Evans was behind them, shouting orders.

"Papa, no!"

Ethan fired into the group and Black Hawk leapt toward them with his Sauk club flying. Damian wielded his saber like a crusading knight, but he was surrounded.

"Get him, you fools!" yelled Iolo. "No shots! I want him alive!"

Damian turned toward Ethan. "Get her out of here! Ethan, get her to the ship!"

Black Hawk seized Ethan's arm and dragged him away. Damian was struck on the head and he fell to the ground. Nina screamed as Black Hawk and Ethan raced back to the skiff.

Iolo's men retreated, dragging Damian's body with them. Nina clutched the side of the boat as Damian was thrown on the back of a horse. Black Hawk and Ethan rowed her toward the ship, but she sobbed as she moved farther and farther from Damian's side. The English soldiers pursued Iolo's men, but Nina knew they'd never get Damian back.

Nina sobbed and held her baby close to her breast. "Damian, no . . ."

"They do not follow," said Black Hawk. Ethan stopped rowing and looked back, but his own face was streaked with tears.

"Why didn't they kill him? Will Evans use him to get Nina back?"

"The Welshman, he expected both," said Black Hawk. "He couldn't know only one will be his prisoner. Damian is kept alive for other reason."

"What reason?" asked Ethan, but Black Hawk had no answer.

Ethan helped Nina onto the British ship, and Black Hawk carried Nathaniel. Nina was weak, she leaned against her brother, but she stopped and looked back at the shore. She saw the British soldiers returning alone. Damian was gone.

Nina swayed and Ethan caught her in his arms. "Father!"

Ian Forbes came toward them from the bow of the ship, supporting himself on his cane, his face strained and pale.

"Take her to my cabin."

Nina heard Ian's voice, and she shuddered in a fear that seemed to rise from her very core. It was more intense now than ever. Why? What was she so afraid of facing? Why did it seem more real now that Damian was gone?

Nina couldn't look at Ian Forbes—she buried her head against her brother's chest. Her tears soaked into his coat.

Black Hawk followed with Nathaniel. The baby stopped crying and rested comfortably in his arms.

"Get this ship out of here!" ordered Ian.

The sails were hoisted and the cold morning wind eased them toward the open sea. Ethan took Nina to Ian's cabin and gently placed her on the soft mattress.

"My baby . . ."

Ethan pulled a quilt over her. "He's fine."

Black Hawk seated himself on a stool and placed the baby on his knees. Nina heard his soft, deep voice singing words she didn't understand. But Nathaniel seemed pleased.

Tears still flowed down Nina's pale face. Ethan stood beside the bed, patting her shoulder, saying nothing. Ian entered the room and Nina trembled with fear. She couldn't suppress it now. She had no idea why. *I can't look at you. I will see something too awful to endure.*

"Sleep now," he told her gently. "We are returning to New York, Emma, to your mother." Ian paused. "You are safe, now." Nina couldn't control her fear. She clung to Ethan's hand and hid her face from her father. Ian sighed. "I will send my servant to attend you."

Ian left, and Nina glanced up at Ethan. "There's no woman?"

"No. Just Caesar." Ethan touched Nina's brow and pushed back her tangled hair. "Sleep, Nina. We'll find a way to save Damian. You may not trust our father, but you don't know him the way I do. He has suffered for Daniel Knox for many years. He would give his life for Damian."

Ethan kissed her forehead, then left. She fell into a dark pit of sleep. But even as she descended, she was aware of Black Hawk's song. She didn't understand the Iroquoian tongue in which he chanted. Even so, pictures emerged in her head of woodland magic, of creatures that bore wisdom on their wings, and ancient figures whose knowledge lifted them far beyond mortal strife.

Nina woke to find Caesar bending over her. His face was furrowed as he laid his broad hand to her brow. Nina startled, but Caesar frowned.

"Hold still." Nina sank back into the pillows. "No fever," decided Caesar. "Just blood loss."

Nina's face twisted as the old man considered her feminine condition. "There's a stack of dousing strips," he informed her as he gestured toward a bureau. "Keep yourself clean."

Nina bit her lip, but Caesar's brow rose indignantly.

"Don't you be giving me them eyes, missy. I begetting thirteen young 'uns, and nine of those is girls!"

"Are they in Africa?"

Caesar looked at her doubtfully. "They be in Brooklyn."

"Oh." Nina paused. "I thought as a slave and all . . ."

Caesar's back straightened and his chin lifted. "I be no slave, missy. I be a free man."

"Ian Forbes doesn't own you?"

"Colonel Forbes pays me right well. I be the first of many."

Nina cringed. By the old man's expression, she was quite sure she'd offended him.

"It's time to be feeding your young fellow."

Nina looked around the room and saw Black Hawk asleep on a chair. Nathaniel was sleeping on his lap, but Caesar picked up the baby and brought him to Nina.

"You eat what I brung you, missy." He gestured toward a tray of food. "Else you'll be running out of milk."

A midwife couldn't have been pushier than Caesar, Nina decided as Nathaniel settled comfortably to her breast. She gazed down at his little, dark head and her heart expanded with love. The firm tugs at her breast reassured her—Nathaniel was part of Damian. The only part in her power to protect.

Ethan entered the room and stared at the nursing baby. "He's doing well, isn't he? Seems to be eating a lot."

Black Hawk woke and also checked on the baby's progress. "Damian's son is strong. He has a firm grip. Good round cheeks."

"Do you think he's getting enough milk?"

"Yes," replied Black Hawk.

Nina sat uncomfortably while the two young men assessed her fitness for motherhood. "Where are we?"

"We're sailing to New York." Ethan sat down on the edge of Nina's bed and adjusted Nathaniel's blanket.

"What then? How will we find Damian?"

Ethan glanced at Black Hawk. "We've been talking that over with Father. Don't worry, Nina. We'll come up with something."

"Rest." Black Hawk tapped Ethan's shoulder and the two left Nina alone with the baby.

Nathaniel filled himself to contentment, studied his mother's face for a few minutes, then drifted back to sleep. Nina watched him, then forced herself to eat the bread and cheese Caesar left. She utilized the dousing strips and washed her face in the basin, but she found it difficult to rest as her caretakers advised.

Nina knew what she had to do. The was only one route to save Damian Knox. And it led through Ian Forbes.

Nina stood outside Ian's cabin door. British sailors eyed her doubtfully, but it took a while to screw up her courage. Nina made a tight fist and knocked on Ian Forbes's door.

"Come."

He didn't expect her. He expected a sailor, or Ethan, perhaps. Nina pushed open the door and took a step inside.

He was seated at a small, captain's desk. An old map was laid out before him and he wore spectacles as he studied it. He glanced up, but his expression changed when he saw Nina watching him.

"Emma." Ian pulled off his spectacles, cleared his throat. *He is shy*, Nina realized with a strange chill. *He is afraid of me.*

Ian rose from his seat and went to her. He stopped

halfway across the room and waited. He wanted to go to her. Nina knew that. But he couldn't.

"Are you well enough to be out of bed?" His blue eyes were wide as he looked at her. "What is it, Emma?"

Nina stared at him. For a long, painful moment, she couldn't bring herself to speak. Wild washes of feeling from her childhood rose from the mists to cloud her thoughts. She wanted to ask Ian Forbes what to do about Damian. But no words would come.

"Why am I afraid of you?" Her voice came small and quavering, like a child's.

"Because I failed you. When you needed me most, I failed you."

Nina's head tilted to the side as she studied her father's face. She shook her head in denial. "No. You threw me away."

"It must have seemed that way." For a long while, he didn't speak further, but his eyes glimmered with tears.

"What happened?"

"We ran for almost a year. Iolo's men followed us from Pennsylvania into Canada. We were heading for Nova Scotia, where we would take a ship to England."

"Canada?" The land of forests and ice. Nina closed her eyes. She remembered the slap of tree branches in her face, she remembered the snow from her dream.

"You were carrying me."

"I was. We were near the port, I knew Iolo's men were close behind. But I couldn't run fast enough. We'd lost our horses, you had only me to carry you. Cora was pregnant with Ethan by then—she had fallen ill. I tried . . ." Ian faltered, his head lowered.

Nina stared at him, but she couldn't speak.

"We reached Halifax. We were almost safe when they caught us. Cora had a pistol, I had a rifle and a knife. We fought, escaped, and ran again. But not fast enough.

They caught us again, and we were surrounded. I was holding you when they came at me. I think Cora shot two of them before they reached us."

"They were howling."

"They had dogs. But the men Iolo hired were hardly less primitive. It must have seemed they were one and the same to you."

"You threw me," whispered Nina.

Ian smiled, though the tears in his eyes fell to his face. "I was struck on the head. Twice? Or three times, I don't remember. I tried to hold on. But I pitched forward into darkness and lost you."

Hot tears formed in Nina's eyes as she looked up at her young father. Even as she blamed him for her nightmares, he blamed himself for not being invincible.

"Why didn't they kill you and mother?"

"The French in Halifax came to our rescue. But too late. Iolo's men took you and fled. We tried to follow, but within two days, word came that you had been killed."

"They said they killed me?"

"They sent something of yours that you would never release in life. We believed you were dead. Iolo had no reason to keep you alive."

"What did he send?"

Ian went to the corner of the cabin and fumbled through his pack. He drew out a small, faded toy dog. Nina stared at the little object, but she began to tremble.

"Melody." Her voice was barely audible, but Ian smiled when she recognized her first toy.

"I wanted to give it to you at Christmas."

Nina caught her breath and her stomach twisted in remorse. "Oh!" A sob burst from her soul. She wrapped her arms tight around her waist. She forced herself to meet Ian Forbes's eyes, but she saw no recrimination, only grief.

A PATRIOT'S HEART

329

"I'm sorry."

"There is no need, Emma. I let you down. I failed you in Canada, and again in New York. I should have known Iolo would come for you."

"No."

At last Nina saw in Ian Forbes what sent terror through her soul: She saw herself.

She saw him as he had been—young and brave, a born leader. As she had been in Philadelphia. She saw a man transformed by forbidden love, she saw a man betrayed, a man who ultimately found himself powerless to save the ones he loved. As she had been unable to save Damian.

"My father . . . We are the same."

Nina stepped toward him—the only person who knew how it felt to have the world ripped away. Ian drew her into his arms and held her. He offered comfort where no one else could—he offered understanding.

"They took Damian. I couldn't help him." Nina had never cried so completely in her life. She never emptied her heart and known it was understood. Ian stroked her tumbled hair and let her weep like a child until her tears slowed.

"I will find him."

Nina dried her eyes and looked up at her father. His face was set and determined. In his assurance, her own confidence grew.

"He could be anywhere."

"No, Emma. Iolo Evans will take him to one place."

"Where?"

"To Onondaga."

Nina sat in her bed while Black Hawk sang to Nathaniel and Caesar busied himself around her room.

Ian sat beside her reading over a dispatch while Ethan waited impatiently.

"Well? Is it certain, Father?" Ethan leaned over Ian's shoulder to read the message for himself, but Ian rolled it up away from his son's eyes.

"For officers only." He grinned when Ethan's face tightened into a frown.

"What does it say?" asked Nina.

"As I suspected, the Continental Army can give no aid in the matter of Damian's abduction."

Ethan sighed. "Why not? They took him."

"Iolo Evans ordered non-commissioned soldiers in the attack. By this dispatch, we are informed Iolo has deserted his post. He is now wanted for court-martial by General Washington's army."

"He deserted?" Nina was stunned. Iolo had truly lost his mind. Independence meant everything to the old Welshman.

"Apparently his second-in-command, Major Jeremiah O'Grady, reported him missing and alerted his commanders."

"Jeremiah," murmured Nina. From a distance, her friend came to her aid once again. She could almost hear Watkins offering advice. *Report him missing, Jeremy. That'll stop him.*

"Why would he go to Onondaga?" asked Ethan. "What good will that do? The Iroquois are fighting with us, aren't they?"

"They are. If halfheartedly. Still, the war will end soon. Cornwallis will not withstand the siege at Yorktown much longer. Iolo Evans has sway with their chief, though I've never known their connection."

They all looked at Black Hawk, but he shook his head. "The sachem does not speak to me of Evans. He believes Daniel Knox destroyed the village. There my mother, leader of medicine women, was murdered—my brothers and baby sister as well."

Black Hawk betrayed no emotion as he spoke, but Nina looked at Nathaniel and her heart ached.

"What would they want with Damian?" asked Ethan. "They wouldn't risk English anger by killing him, too, would they?"

"Not while the war lasts," agreed Ian.

"It will not last long," said Black Hawk. "The Welshman will present Damian as a trophy of war."

Ian nodded. "He will undoubtedly remove all evidence of Damian's part in the British army. It will be easy to deny that Damian is an English officer."

"Why would this sachem kill Damian when he could sell him as a slave?" asked Ethan.

"Daniel Knox died, but his seed lives on," said Black Hawk. "My father does not forget the village, he does not forget his wife and his children. He is an old man . . ." Black Hawk paused. "He believes he is right. In twenty years, the sachem has not questioned that day."

Nina struggled to get out of bed. "Then we have to stop him ourselves!"

The men looked at her in surprise. Ian eased her back to her pillows. "We will stop him. But you will stay with Cora."

"I will not!"

"Emma, my dear child, you gave birth only a few weeks ago. Do you think you could make the trek to the Finger Lakes in your condition, with a baby in your arms?" When Nina didn't answer, Ian nodded. "I thought not. Leave your husband's rescue to me. Daniel Knox gave his life for mine. Whatever I must do, by life or by death, I will save his son."

* * *

New York was quiet, rattled by the siege at Yorktown, Virginia. Cornwallis, the brave and fiery second-in-command of the British army, was cornered. He'd wanted to fight, to push northward. But the cautious Clinton ordered him into a defensive position. It appeared to be his last.

Nina set aside the report. She didn't care anymore about the British army. She didn't even care about her own. Ian Forbes considered the war over. He'd considered it over from the beginning. All that mattered was finding Damian.

Cora leaned over her husband's desk and studied the map of her old homeland. "How long will it take to reach Onondaga?"

"Many days. We'll be riding, naturally, but the way is slow."

"But it will be just as slow for Evans," said Ethan. "Damian will find a way to disrupt his progress."

Nina listened to their discussion in growing anxiety. Nathaniel nursed quietly while Melody slept peacefully at her feet. Only Black Hawk seemed as ill at ease as was Nina.

"We must move with the wind," he told them. "The Onondaga sachem is not a man who hesitates."

Ian nodded. "The horses are being brought around now, with three others."

Cora looked at Ian and her face went white. Nina reached for her hand and squeezed it gently.

"They have Black Hawk. He is the chief's son. He won't let anything happen."

"Ian . . ." Cora breathed her husband's name as he donned his tricorn hat and went to the door. "Take me with you."

He turned back to her and smiled. "No, love. You

stay with our daughter, and watch over our grandson. I will always come for you, Cora Talmadge. You are mine."

Cora went to his arms and kissed his mouth, holding him desperately while the world once more threatened between them. Nina watched her parents, and for the first time she felt how much love created her life.

Ian released her and Cora stood away, clutching her sides as she fought her emotion. Nina stared at her father, then went to his side. She touched his hand.

"If anyone can save Damian and make things right again, it's you, Father. All my life, the world has been upside down. In your face, I see it as it should have been."

Cora's eyes flooded with tears as Nina stood on tiptoes to kiss Ian's cheek. Melody whined at Ian's feet, scratching at his boots. Ian hugged his daughter, but then he looked to Cora. Nina heard their silent words.

We are healed. Whatever comes, know that my heart is healed.

Ian, Ethan and Black Hawk rode away, but Cora and Nina sat silently in the parlor. Penelope had returned to England, but even her presence would have been welcomed as a distraction. Caesar brought around tea, but neither woman touched their cups.

Nathaniel slept in his basket with Melody guarding him, but the women were so lost in their thoughts that they jumped together when the door bell was pulled.

Nina heard Caesar greeting Anna Fairchild, and her mood softened. If she knew Black Hawk had come and gone, maybe her heart was breaking, too.

"Have you seen Black Hawk?"

"Mother saw him with Ethan. What happened?"

Nina took Anna into the parlor and explained the

whole story while Anna admired Nathaniel. "Black
Hawk isn't like his father. He was taken prisoner by the
Sauk when he was only two, and was raised by them.
He isn't representative of any one tribe. He takes what
is best from both, and directs his own life. He was at
odds with the sachem, I believe."

"Because of Damian's father," guessed Nina. "Black
Hawk believed that Daniel Knox was innocent, that
someone else massacred the Onondaga village."

"But that was so long ago," said Anna. "Damian's
father is dead. What does it matter what happened
then?"

Cora sighed. "It is a blood vengeance. Perhaps it's
understandable. So many children were slaughtered. I,
too, would find that impossible to forget."

Anna said nothing.

"Ian and Black Hawk will try to convince the sachem
that Daniel Knox was wrongly accused."

"Damian told me that Black Hawk has searched for
the one responsible," added Nina. "Maybe he has
learned something that will at least offer doubt."

"So many years have passed," said Anna. "Things that
should have been forgotten rise again."

"The Iroquois way is not ours," said Cora, but Anna
shook her head.

"Is there not a parallel in Christianity? The sins of
the father are passed to the child . . . And by that child,
are paid."

A loud rapping at the front door interrupted their
conversation. Caesar went to answer the call, but he
gasped when he opened the door.

"Get back!"

Nina, Cora and Anna peeked out from the parlor
and saw two American officers in full dress uniform.
They were holding the door open while Caesar struggled against them.

"What . . . ?"

"Jeremiah! Watkins!" Nina hurried to the door to greet them. Melody offered a menacing growl. "Melody, stop that! Caesar, let them in."

The old servant frowned, but he stepped back. "You boys come on in, now. But don't you be trying nothing."

Jeremiah walked past Caesar, but Watkins rolled his eyes. "Just what do you think we'd try, anyway?"

"With you rebels, anything's likely."

"Keep that in mind. And take care you don't anger us none."

"Watkins, we are guests here," said Jeremiah. "Under a flag of truce. This is Loyalist country, let us not forget."

"Not for long."

"Mother, this is Major O'Grady, whom I almost married, and Captain Watkins, who almost married us—in a particularly moving ceremony." She turned to Jeremiah. "Why are you here?"

"We were sent by Washington himself," said Watkins. "We're hunting for Colonel Evans. He's wanted for court-martial. He left us right during a battle. Good thing Jeremy was leading us, or we'd really have been thrown for a loop."

"He has taken Damian to the Iroquois tribe who killed Damian's father. To the Onondaga. My father, my real father, that is, has gone after him, with Black Hawk and my brother. They left three days ago."

"Three days . . . They'll need help, Jeremy. And we're under orders to bring back the old man."

Jeremiah O'Grady smiled. "Do you know your way into Onondaga territory, Watkins?"

"I do! Up the Delaware, then turn right to the Finger Lakes. Hacketstown is just a hop, skip, and a jump from New York."

"Of how many weeks? Well, no matter. As you said, we're under orders." He turned to Nina. "It's been good to see you, my dear. But Watkins and I must hurry if we're to intercept the colonel."

Nina's mouth dropped when the two young men departed.

"Who were they?" asked Anna in astonishment. "They seem awfully sure of themselves. They'll never find their way to Onondaga."

"Watkins can be surprising. But you're probably right."

"They'll send us right back." Nina considered Anna's suggestion, but it seemed impossible.

Anna's eyes gleamed bright. She appeared almost fey. "Not if we wait until they're far enough from the city."

Nina could convince Jeremiah and Watkins, of that, she was certain. "I'll have to leave Nathaniel." Her heart ached at the thought, but she knew what she had to do. "But Mother will care for him. She had offered to get me a wet nurse but I refused. Now I have no choice but to let another woman suckle my baby."

"I could go alone, Nina. I know the way better than Watkins."

"You were there years ago. You couldn't remember."

"I remember. I can get us there as fast as Black Hawk. Maybe faster, because I'm not so cautious. My father knew all the old trails. I learned from him."

"What about Lavinia?" Cora might let her go, but Lavinia was another matter.

"I'll leave her a note, naturally. But it's time Mother faced up to reality. We are all connected, aren't we? We all bear the responsibility of other's doings, and share in the results."

"We'll need horses," said Nina. "Ethan left Gambrinus here. I will ride him."

"Can you manage a horse like that?"

"Damian's horse is strong and gentle, like Damian. He will carry me, and Melody will come, too. She will protect us."

Melody glanced up at her mistress, and Nina patted her head. Melody would probably require more protection than she'd give, but her dog would be a comforting presence.

Anna left to ready her pack, but Nina sat alone with Nathaniel. "I have to do this. I love him so, Nathaniel. Do you understand?"

The baby turned his face to Nina's breast and suckled heartily while Nina cried. "Anna says we can save Damian, if we hurry."

Why she believed Anna Fairchild capable of influencing the Onondaga sachem, Nina wasn't certain, but it was with this conviction she began her letter to Cora.

Please take care of my baby, Mama. If I don't come back, let him be your son. I must go to Damian. As you once followed your heart, I must follow mine. I leave knowing Nathaniel is safe in your care. Your loving daughter, Emmalina Forbes Knox.

She knew that attaching Ian's name to hers would please Cora. Nina realized that just as she couldn't let Damian face death without her, neither would she allow her young father to die beyond her aid.

P.S. I won't let either your husband or mine die. You have my word. Ian Forbes will return to you alive.

Cora found Nina's letter in Nathaniel's crib. As she read the words, her hands shook and tears fell to her cheeks. She started to call for Caesar, but then she stopped herself. Nina made her choice, as had Anna

Fairchild. There was little her strong-willed daughter couldn't do.

Cora picked up Nathaniel and held him close. He didn't wake, and she kissed his forehead gently. They were already close. The baby gave her courage when her own heart quailed with fear. All she loved went to Onondaga. Only Nathaniel was in her power to protect.

"Missus Cora!" Caesar called in an agitated voice from the hall downstairs. "Missus Lavinia Fairchild is down here, and she's right adamant about seeing you."

Cora drew a long breath and gathered herself together. She carried the baby downstairs as if his tiny body could offer reinforcement. Lavinia was waiting in the parlor, fidgeting with her fan.

"Cora! Do you know what your daughter has done? She's hauled my Anna into the wilderness . . . into, heaven forbid, Indian territory!"

"Yes, I know."

"Naturally, I told Priscilla that Anna was with relatives in London. Dear Heaven, if anyone knew where she'd really gone . . ."

"Quite so."

"I'd be gone already if not for Anna, you understand. This country will soon fade into complete anarchy. Cornwallis is surrounded, the French are sailing with Washington . . . Imagine, the gall of living without a king!"

"It should prove interesting." Cora smiled down at Nathaniel. "I wonder if they'll let us stay? Perhaps if we swear an oath or something?"

Lavinia's mouth dropped. "You can't be thinking what you're saying, Cora. Of course, with your husband gone, and your son . . . Naturally, you'd be distracted."

Nathaniel wrinkled his small face. Cora felt certain he rolled his eyes in dismay.

"Emma and your daughter are reasonably safe, I assure you, Lavinia. They're accompanied by two very fine American officers."

"Rebel soldiers. Yes, that's what Anna wrote. It's so improper."

Cora's brow furrowed. A breach of etiquette, maybe, but it seemed a strange concern. "They appeared to be gentlemen."

Lavinia huffed. "There are no rebel gentlemen. But they're headed into Indian territory, Cora. Do you know what those savages do to young women? Dear God in heaven, they'll be taken as slaves, forced to marry . . . White women are desirable to the red man, you know."

"Black Hawk will be there, Lavinia. The chief's son. I don't think you need fear."

"Black Hawk? I've seen him eyeing my daughter. He's not to be trusted. He wants my Anna."

Cora studied a vase on the parlor mantelpiece. She moved it to the other side. "I thought it was the other way around. Don't worry, Lavinia. I'm sure they'll come to visit you. Black Hawk seems quite at home here."

"What?" Lavinia's face paled and her mouth dropped open. "What are you saying, Cora?"

She put the vase back where it had been. "Anna will stay with Black Hawk, I expect."

"No!"

Cora glanced her way before poking at the small fire. "As his wife, of course, not his concubine." Seeing Lavinia's stricken face, Cora frowned. "For Heaven's sake, Lavinia. Why else would she have gone? Your daughter was obviously in love with the young man. She'll be happy. No doubt she'll be adopted into his clan—I believe it's the Wolf. Anna is strong and quite practical. Native life will suit her."

Lavinia rose from her seat and aimed for the front door. "I'll tell Priscilla that Anna is dead. Yes, she came down with consumption in London . . . It's so cold and damp there. Anna's such a fragile little thing, as befits a lady. Naturally, in her delicate condition, she succumbed. Her grief over Philip Compton's death destroyed her will to live. Naturally."

Cora eyed Lavinia doubtfully, then shook her head. "You could visit her, Lavinia. Things will calm down when the war ends."

Caesar scurried to the door and held it open, his eyes gleaming in triumph. Lavinia fumbled with her shawl. "I will take the next ship to London. Yes. I must find my mourning wardrobe, naturally. I'll wait a few weeks, then invite Priscilla for tea. I'll tell her then."

"What a good idea."

"You won't mention this to anyone, of course. You must advise young Ethan of discretion. He can be indelicate. If he returns to England, I pray he will be discreet."

"Ethan will understand."

Lavinia left, and Cora picked up Nathaniel. "He'll understand that Lavinia Fairchild is made of more fluff than your bear."

Cora spun the baby around and they danced. "Your mama will come. As will your handsome father." She closed her eyes and held the baby close. "And Ian . . ."

Her heart tightened in fear. "We must face these days with courage," she told Nathaniel, but the baby batted his eyes shut and his mouth dropped open as sleep descended.

Cora set him gently in his basket. She paced around the room, drumming her fingers on the mantel. She moved the vase again.

"I must do something."

Caesar passed quietly by the parlor door, but Cora spotted him.

"Caesar! We must clean!"

"Clean, Ma'am?" The old man poked his head in the door, his face knotted in a doubtful expression.

"Clean. Emma's room must be arranged for a husband's needs. Ethan will need his winter clothes sorted. I want dried flowers arranged in every room. The war's end will wreak havoc at the markets. Go now, Caesar, and see that we have plenty of food for their return." Cora puttered around the parlor, straightening doilies, rearranging vases and statuettes.

Caesar sighed. "Very good, Ma'am. Cleaning, it is."

"Ready . . . Take aim . . ." Jeremiah held his dancing horse back while pointing his pistol into the forest. Watkins jumped from his own mount and knelt with his musket readied.

"Jeremiah! Don't shoot, it's us!"

Watkins sank to both knees and dropped his musket while Jeremiah stared open-mouthed as Nina and Anna came picking their way through the forest bracken. Melody followed close behind, peering uneasily around the forest.

"Nina?" Jeremiah stared at her in amazement. "What are you doing out here?"

"We followed you," replied Anna. "You make enough racket to be heard for miles—it wasn't difficult to track you."

"You can't mean to go with us."

"Where's the baby?" asked Watkins.

"He's with my mother," replied Nina. "And, yes, we mean to go with you. If you won't let us accompany you willingly, we'll follow you."

Jeremiah groaned, but Watkins stood up and put his musket back on his saddle. "Be good to have company."

"It will be good for you to have a guide," added Anna.

"You've already wasted the better part of a day taking this trail. From now on, you'll follow my direction."

Nina, Jeremiah, and Watkins stared at Anna in amazement, but she was already heading from the trail.

"She seems to know," said Watkins. "What do we do now, Jeremy?"

Jeremiah shrugged. "Follow her. What else?"

"I married your daughter because I love her, and for no other reason."

Iolo rolled his eyes. "You married her because it was the only way to exact revenge. You hunted her down, seduced her into your bed, filled her with your bastard child . . . But Jeremiah O'Grady is her rightful husband."

Damian frowned. "Their marriage was not binding. Apparently, O'Grady saw what you couldn't: Nina belongs to me."

Iolo slashed his leather gauntlet across Damian's face, but Damian wouldn't back down. His hands were tied behind the tree, he was already bruised and bloodied from Iolo's harsh treatment. But his spirit remained defiant.

"I'll never give my girl to the likes of you, Knox."

"Nina is Ian Forbes's daughter. Not yours." Damian dared Iolo's wrath by his assertion, but Iolo's reaction was contained.

"The child belongs to her rightful father, not the whoreson who put his seed in the mother."

"Why does it matter to you? Ian Forbes took a woman from you more than twenty years ago. Cora bore his child. Yet you've hunted Nina down like a madman. Why? Because my father died for Ian? You didn't even remember Daniel Knox."

Iolo's face was hard, his dark eyes burned like coals.

"I remember your father. He was an Englishman, like
Forbes. Gentle, gracious. He looked exactly like you.
The kind of man who would kiss a white lady's hand,
then turn around and cut a squaw's throat after he
raped her and killed her children."

"*What?* You know neither Ian nor my father massacred that village. Any fool would know you did it yourself."

Iolo's eyes glinted with deep hatred, but he laughed.
"Let's see if you can convince the Onondaga of that,
boy. These cursed rains may have held us up, but beyond
those hills, beyond that river lie the villages of Onondaga. I will drag you through each one and see you
beaten before I hand you over to the sachem. Then, boy,
you will learn how your father died. And by God, I'll eat
your heart myself."

Anna proved an accomplished and demanding guide.
They passed into the Catskill Mountains and left behind
them both the east and west branches of the Delaware
River.

"We will follow the Tioughnioga River into Onondaga Creek," Anna informed them when they settled
for the night. No one dared question her direction.

Jeremiah tied their horses and Nina lay exhausted
beneath the summer stars while Anna directed Watkins
in the proper making of a smokeless campfire. Jeremiah
sat down beside Nina and shook his head.

"We've made good time, I'll give her that." He paused.
"She's not related to the Prussians, is she?"

"I'm not sure," replied Nina. "At this point, it doesn't
seem impossible."

"At this rate, we'll make it to Onondaga before Iolo,"
said Jeremiah as he lay back beside Nina.

"O'Grady!" Jeremiah groaned at Anna's harsh command. "We could use more water. There's a stream yonder. Take the canteens and fill them."

"Yessum, Miz Annabelle." Jeremiah stood up and walked hunchbacked to the stream.

Nina giggled. The pressure of their journey kept her mind from her fear for Damian, but it was Jeremiah and Watkins's humor that made the long hours bearable. Anna seemed to know what she was doing, and Nina was content to leave their travels in her capable hands.

Nina started to get up, but Anna eyed her darkly. "You lie back down, Nina. You don't want to start bleeding again. Watkins will bring your supper there. Don't move."

Nina flopped back down onto her bedding and sighed. Watkins obediently brought her a roasted fillet of rabbit. "Looks mighty appetizing, doesn't it?" he observed as Nina greedily devoured her portion.

Jeremiah returned with the water and Anna seized the canteen. "Drink this. You need plenty of water to get through this heat."

Watkins poked at the remaining bits of rabbit that sizzled over the campfire. Anna turned toward him and placed her hands on her hips. "Watkins! You leave that be. Nina will eat that for breakfast. You can have the bread we brought and some dried meat. If you want hare for dinner, you'll have to shoot more than one. But don't eat too much bread, either. We've still got a long way to go."

Melody sniffed at the rabbit. Anna stomped her foot at the dog. "Drop!" Melody fell to the earth and whimpered, wagging her tail apologetically.

Jeremiah, Watkins and Nina watched as Anna doused the campfire and put away the remaining rabbit. Watkins sighed very heavily and chewed on a piece of stale bread.

"By the saints, she's a hard one," he muttered. Neither Jeremiah nor Nina disagreed.

* * *

"Does his spirit hover around you, Knox?" Iolo yanked the cord that bound Damian's hands and pulled him into the clearing. "Do you know this place?"

Damian looked around while Iolo's men walked around the ruins. "Get back!" shouted Iolo. The men looked at him in surprise, then moved back towards the trees. "This is sacred land. Don't any of you knaves touch a thing."

Damian glanced at his captor doubtfully. What interest had Iolo Evans in a ruined Indian village?

"Well, does he speak its name in your ear?"

Damian hesitated. "Who?"

"Your father. He knows this place because he brought about the destruction you see. The corpses no longer litter the earth, but their souls linger here, demanding retribution. How Daniel Knox must dread seeing his son walking in his own footsteps!"

"My father is dead."

"Is he? His body was torn apart and burned by the Iroquois. But a man is much more than flesh, Knox. The English have never understood that, have they? Since the bloody-handed Saxons first landed on British soil, they've pillaged native land. They went into Wales and drove my family into poverty, then claimed our farm as their own.

"I watched my sisters turn to prostitution to survive, selling themselves to the very bastards who destroyed us. I saw my father beaten to death when he dared defy them."

"You can't blame my father for what happened before his birth. It was you who sent him to his death in these primitive lands."

"Primitive? Aye, they're primitive, all right. Do you know nothing of history, Knox? Are these native peoples any more primitive than were the Celts when the Romans invaded Britain? Do the shamans order sacrifice any differently than did the druids?"

Damian sighed in exasperation. "You speak of the dawn of history."

"I speak of all history. How the 'civilized people' wreak havoc on those who listen to the older voices, how they deny the basic rights and use the word 'primitive' to justify brutal conquering."

"So you'll hold me responsible for all English evil? What good will that do?"

"I didn't see your father's death. I will witness yours, and know that he, too, watches."

"This is madness. My father did not order any massacre, nor did Ian Forbes."

"They did, boy. They carved the name of their regiment on a dead woman's forehead."

"No."

"All the while Forbes lay between Cora's legs, he had the blood of a squaw on his hands." Iolo's voice quaked with such hatred that Damian almost believed him. He closed his eyes and remembered his father.

"Ian Forbes killed no one."

"The whole company was there! Your father, Forbes . . . Filling their lust on the women before they slit their throats."

Damian grimaced. "It served your end to accuse Ian Forbes of these crimes. He took Cora, she was pregnant with his child. You slaughtered that village, Evans. You did it to rid yourself of the man who stole your woman. Why else would you seek vengeance for a society not your own?"

"I stand with the 'primitives,' Knox. Did you not know?"

TWELVE

"We'll never make it in time." Nina sat atop the weary Gambrinus and stared across the endless miles of rolling hills. Mist rose from two divergent rivers and spread through the valleys.

"Iolo was coming from the south," Jeremiah reminded her. "He has the longer route to travel. Ian Forbes and Black Hawk got a good jump on him leaving from the Hudson."

"They should reach Onondaga near the same time, if not before," added Anna. "The rivers will have swollen in the past week's rain. We take the high ground, and find it the swifter passage."

Watkins glanced at her doubtfully. "If this is swift, I'd hate to see slow. Have we got to cross all them hills?"

"We do," replied Anna. "Our path leads north now, away from the Delaware. The Finger Lakes lie beyond, but the village of Onondaga is close. Less talk, Watkins, and more speed. We'll ride until the last light if we have to. You'll see half as many hills come morning."

"What are we doing with the horses, Colonel?"

Iolo's men watched as several Onondaga braves led away their animals. Iolo called the village Toyadasso. It had been recently burned, but new bark huts had been erected and a few Onondaga worked to restore their land.

"They're needed more here," said Iolo.

"But, Colonel, how're we going get on back home?"

"On foot, of course. Hell's bells, can't you men walk?"

Iolo seemed in no hurry to reach the chief village of the Onondaga. Damian watched the horses tethered by the Indians, and he knew his own life had been prolonged by Iolo's goodwill gesture. It was small comfort. A few more days did him little good.

"What's this?" asked Damian when Iolo thrust a small pack at him.

"Shave," ordered the Welshman. "I'll not bring you to the sachem looking like that. I want him to see your face, the face of your father."

Damian took the pack and reluctantly complied. Iolo insisted he wash in a stream, and that he tie his hair back like an Englishman.

"I gather we're near the central village," said Damian as he buttoned the fresh shirt Iolo provided.

"We have a distance yet, boy. Onondaga is on the bank of Onondaga Creek. We will go northwest from here."

"What destroyed this village?"

"Toyadasso was burned by Colonel Van Schaick under Washington's orders last year. A necessity of war. The people will put our horses to good use."

"Washington's orders? Is your esteemed commander next on the Iroquois stakes?"

"The Onondaga were warned beforehand. They call Washington *Hanodaganear*—'Town Burner' now. Many Onondaga joined your army who wouldn't have otherwise. But it was a matter of war, Knox. Not murder."

Iolo was well known in the village, which surprised Damian. The Iroquois were English allies. How the old

Welshman maintained a friendship with American enemies, Damian couldn't guess.

"We will reach Lower Onondaga in the morning," Iolo informed Damian as they settled for the night. Damian was bound to a tree as always, but he was allowed to eat.

"Tomorrow, you will face the sachem just as your father once did. But you will not die so soon, Knox. Death in Iroquois lands is not a matter of a day."

Damian said nothing. Nothing in Iolo gentled toward him, yet Damian came to a new understanding of his captor. He still believed Iolo responsible for the massacre, but he also knew there was more to his hatred than jealousy over an escaped wife. Iolo rarely mentioned Cora; he seemed more disappointed in her character than injured by adultery.

"You make no sense," said Damian.

Iolo laughed. "Not to you, I'll warrant."

"Once I'm dead, will you hunt down my son and kill him, too?"

"My grandson is safe. By law, that is O'Grady's child. Just as Nina is mine."

Cora hadn't married Iolo, nor was Nina married to Jeremiah. But it didn't seem to matter to Iolo Evans. The only law that was real to him was his own.

"Curse you." He couldn't reach the old Welshman. The man long ago lost his mind. Men who committed vile acts in war often suffered from insanity, and Damian guessed this was true of Iolo.

"Look yonder, boy." Iolo pointed and Damian saw a fortified Iroquois village. "There flows Onondaga

Creek, and on the west bank lies Upper and Lower Onondaga."

Damian saw a town that stretched perhaps three miles along the bank of the creek. Cabins and long houses were scattered in groups amid lavish plantings of corn and squash.

"Do you see the fields, Knox? There grow the Three Sisters: Corn, beans, and squash. You are fortunate. The ceremony of the False Faces awaits you, for harvest is near. You will be the gift I present to the sachem, your death a great credit to his honor."

Iolo loaded his pistol and aimed at Damian's head. "From here, boy, you go with me. I wish your death to follow tradition. My men will stay here. If you try anything I'll blow you to Kingdom Come."

"You needn't worry, Evans. I wish an audience with my father's murderer."

Iolo's dark eyes flickered, but he said nothing.

"This sachem, Black Hawk's father," questioned Damian as they walked onward toward the village. "Is he the head chief of the Iroquois Confederacy?"

"Tiahogwando is the Onondaga chief of the Iroquois Confederacy. He has left the village with many followers. More still have left to battle. But there are perhaps fourteen sachems and many clans in Onondaga. I take you to the Clan of the Hawk.

"The sachem is called Thadodaho. For his quick temper, he was named for the Onondaga sorcerer who was reformed by Hiawatha and Deganawida to become Fire-Keeper of the Confederate Council."

Damian looked doubtfully at the Welshman. "How do you know these things?"

"Their tales recall the Welsh *Mabinogion*. The natives of America remind me of the Celts, as I told you."

"My ancestor, Duncan Knox, was Scottish."

Iolo scoffed. "An Anglo-Saxon invader who stole land from the Scots, no doubt."

He stopped just outside the village. "Onondaga is the League's center. You enter the very heart of Iroquois land, boy."

"The sachem awaits."

Iolo led Damian to a large council hall. Over the doorway, Damian noticed a carved hawk. If the sachem of the Hawk spoke English or French, he might stand a chance of making the man see reason. If not, his life rested in Iolo Evans's bitter hands.

The elm bark walls rustled faintly as Damian walked in the door of the long house. "You stand in the shadow of the People of the Long House. Tremble in their presence, boy, for they have lived here for years beyond count. And they will be your death."

Damian saw a very old Indian man seated beyond the cooking fire. Women busied themselves with corn and squash, and paid little attention to the two white men. The old chief didn't look up as they approached.

"Stay here," commanded Iolo. Had Damian any thought of escape, it evaporated when four young Onondaga braves surrounded him.

Damian watched Iolo kneel before the sachem. They spoke together in the Iroquoian tongue, and the sachem looked up at Damian. He waved his hand and the warriors shoved Damian toward him.

Damian met the old man's gaze without wavering. "You walk in your father's likeness," said the sachem in unbroken English.

"And I walk into darkness. Like my father, for folly and no more."

"Do you call the deaths of seven women and thirteen children 'folly'?"

"I do not. Twenty years ago, you killed my father for these crimes. You killed the wrong man."

The sachem nodded slowly. "As another would have me believe."

"Your son, Black Hawk."

The old man's eyes flickered. "Black Hawk, who wears the name of the Sauk and not his father. Black Hawk, who will not fight at my side and goes instead to the English."

"Black Hawk believes you killed the wrong man."

"Black Hawk was not in the village when his mother was murdered. He falls for the handsome face of your English father and does not see his black heart."

"Colonel Evans blackened my father's name. You took his word. This, I do not understand."

"Iolo Gray Beard is blood brother to the Onondaga," said the sachem. "His word is good." The old man looked away from Damian. "Take him. Tie him to the village pole and wait until dusk. Let him watch the people his father wronged before his own life ends. Tonight, Damian Knox, you will watch the ceremony of the False Faces. While the spirits of our dead dance around you, you will die."

The Onondaga youths dragged Damian from the hall and tied him in the center of the village. Iolo remained behind with the sachem. Damian steeled himself for the ritual acts of torture.

The Onondaga studied him suspiciously, but rather than violence, they simply touched him in ceremonial gestures. He noted that the women were somewhat rougher than the men or the children, but no blood was drawn.

Damian turned his mind from his captivity. He ignored the fire that was built on the hill beyond the village, he ignored the ceremonial hand-laying. It seemed to him that he truly felt the spirits of the dead, just as the sachem predicted.

But these bodiless souls weren't unfriendly, they

seemed kind and sympathetic. *See your life,* they whispered. Damian closed his eyes and recalled Nina's face when they first met. He saw her golden curls falling across her forehead, he saw her blow her wayward hair away from her cheek and watched it fall back again.

Damian remembered her first kiss, the look of surprise and subtle desire on her face afterwards. He remembered the thunderstorm when they first loved, he remembered the day he lost her. Then later, *I've come to tell you I'm not coming.*

I love you so.

Damian saw John André as if the young Englishman, too, had come to attend Damian's death. He saw André's laughing face as he danced at the Meschianza, he remembered his own strange reaction as a Knight of the Burning Mountain. His mind wandered onward, and he saw John André walk bravely to his hanging.

Last of all, Damian remembered the birth of his son. He felt the tiny body in his hands, the tight fists as he adjusted to his new world. The son he would never know. No, Damian didn't fear death. But he longed for life.

"What's that?" Watkins pointed to a hill on the horizon, and all saw a thick column of smoke rising above the trees. "It's hot for a fire like that, isn't it?"

"It is a ceremonial burning," replied Anna. "We must hurry."

Nina's face went white, but she said nothing as she urged Gambrinus down the steep ravine. He stumbled and slid, then regained his balance while Nina clung to the saddle. The others followed, but when they reached the path that headed for Onondaga, Nina pressed Damian's horse into a canter and they raced toward the hill of fire.

* * *

The sun was setting, the great fire burned. Thado-daho accompanied Iolo from the council house and stood among the gathering Onondagas in front of Damian.

"Twenty summers have passed since your father watched his last sun fade to night." The old chief pointed to the fire on the hill. "There, his life passed. There, he paid for the blackness of his heart."

"There, he paid for the blackness of another," countered Damian.

A slow rumbling of drum and rattle began, and from the council hall came a group of Onondaga warriors, each wearing elaborately carved face masks.

"Behold the False Faces." Iolo's dark eyes shone with wonder and admiration. "Tonight, they represent the spirits in unrest that fell to your father's murderous rage."

Five men danced to the ritual music, but one among them wore no mask though he wore an old blanket over his shoulders and shook a turtle shell rattle with the others. The unmasked warrior led the others, they circled and chanted until they came to the sachem. The figures of hawks were painted on their buckskin tunics, and they formed a semicircle around the sachem.

"The Maskless One speaks of your father's bloodlust," Iolo told Damian. "The False Faces are carved from a living tree. The masks hold the spirit of the tree, and the spirits bring order and healing."

"What has this to do with Daniel Knox?"

"The Hawk clan mask was kept by the medicine woman of Tiachton, the village your father destroyed. It was stolen."

"But not found on my father," said Damian. "Is that not evidence to support his innocence?"

Iolo shrugged. "No doubt it was buried or lost. But such items that are sacred to the Iroquois are valuable to English greed. Prized like scalps to the Iroquois."

The drums and rattle music increased and the False Faces danced with increasing vigor. "The souls of the fallen call for vengeance," announced Thadodaho. "My children, and the children of the village will now be joined by the child of their murderer."

A shout rang from Lower Onondaga, and all turned to see a group of warriors leading three prisoners. "Deiaquande," murmured the sachem. "Black Hawk."

Ian Forbes and Ethan were bound together by rope, but Black Hawk walked free before them. The False Faces fell silent as Black Hawk approached them. His black hair fell straight and unbound, he wore no ornaments other than his wampum belt and earring.

Without a word, Black Hawk went to his father and stood before him. He spoke first in Iroquoian, then again in English. "I have come to see the mistakes of the past repeated. But not too late to see the wrong made right."

"Damian!" Ethan waved through the crowd and Damian smiled despite the situation. They might have met this way on a bustling London street. At least, he would die in cheerful company. Ian met Damian's gaze, but he said nothing.

Thadodaho looked long at the Englishman, and the light of recognition kindled in his eyes. "Twice now you stare into the fire of death."

Iolo snarled and made a fist. "Look your last, Forbes. You're a fool for walking into Onondaga. You will never leave."

Ian turned to Iolo. To the old man's fury, Ian just smiled. "I have come to reclaim what was stolen. I have my daughter once again. I have my wife, and they are safe from your reach forever. I claim Daniel's honor, and I will restore his life by freeing his son."

"You will die in the fires with him!"

Ian ignored Iolo and faced the sachem, dropping his weapons to the earth before he spoke.

"I have returned, sachem," said Ian. "Twenty years ago an innocent man gave his life for mine. I watched him burn in your fires while the guilty man went free. Will you repeat your mistake twice?"

Iolo glared at Ian Forbes, but he let the sachem speak.

"What do you have now, English, that you had not twenty years ago?"

"What he had then is as strong," said Black Hawk. "He has truth."

"You have searched for this 'truth' many years," said the sachem. He did not look at his son. "What have you found?"

"A good man."

Ethan shoved himself to his father's side. "Let Damian go, or we'll bring the whole English army down on your miserable village!"

The sachem's brow rose, but he smiled faintly. "The English army sinks like a sandbar into an overwhelming sea. You and your father walk free, young English. The son of Daniel Knox will burn in the mountain's fire."

"Now what?" Watkins peered across the creek toward Onondaga. "They're all here, all right. Do we give ourselves up, too? I don't relish handing myself over to no Indian."

Anna turned her horse down the path. "It was the safest way for Black Hawk to bring Ian Forbes and Ethan into the village."

From the ridge above, they watched the Onondaga warriors seize Black Hawk's group. "We'll be spotted, too," said Jeremiah. "If they weren't so intent on Forbes, we'd be caught already."

Nina started after Anna. "You're an officer, Jeremiah. I'm by way of being your wife, and Anna might as well be Watkins's. Let's go in under a flag of truce. After all, you're under orders from our highest command."

They looked to Anna for approval. She nodded. "It will get us in. But it will do little good once we're there."

"We just need to get in. I have to find Damian. Whatever happens afterward . . . well, we'll take care of that when we come to it."

Gambrinus left the others behind as Nina galloped down the path into the village. No one was there, but she saw the townspeople headed toward the mountain. Nina stopped the horse and stared at the burning summit. In a flash of agonizing memory, she recalled her dream. The mountain was on fire. And Damian's life hung in the flames.

"Ahead," she shouted. Watkins, Jeremiah and Anna caught up with the English horse. Melody caught up with them and barked excitedly.

"We can fight 'em, Jeremy." Watkins started to load his musket, but Anna grabbed his arm.

"If you ride into their midst armed, Watkins, you can prepare to join Damian."

"She's right, Avery," agreed Jeremiah. "Keep your musket down. But ready. You never know . . ."

"We won't save Damian by fighting," Anna reminded them, but Nina, too, was readying a pistol.

"With Black Hawk, Father, and Ethan, we've got seven who can fight. That's better than nothing." Nina kicked her heels into Gambrinus's side, and he leapt away, surging up the mountainside like a deer.

She spotted a large procession heading up a steep hill toward the fire. Tall evergreens crowned the open summit, and giant rhododendrons filled in the brush along the walkway. The great fire burned hot amidst the clearing, and the villagers made a circle around it.

Gambrinus charged up the hill and the warriors whirled to meet the expected attack. Nina pulled him to a halt, and Iolo leapt in front of the Indians.

"No! Wait!" The warriors held their fire. Melody caught up with the horse and growled at the villagers.

Nina's heart stilled when she saw Damian bound to a stake by the great fire. His shirt was torn from his chest, his brown hair fell loose, lit with a golden glow by the fire behind him. He was surrounded by warriors in strange masks, but he was alive. Ian Forbes and Ethan stood near, but they, too, were held captive.

Damian struggled against his binding. "Nina, no!"

Nina didn't hesitate. She lifted a pistol in shaking hands and pointed it at the sachem. "Set my husband free."

Watkins, Jeremiah, and Anna rode up beside her. Watkins urged his horse forward. Ignoring the Onondaga, he faced Iolo. He unbound a dispatch and began reading.

"Colonel Evans, by the orders of His Excellency General George Washington of the Continental Army of the United States of America, I hereby place you under arrest for desertion of your post."

"Watkins," murmured Iolo. "What in the Name of God are you doing here?"

"They came with me," said Nina. "To save Damian."

The chief glanced at Nina's group doubtfully. "Who are these?"

"My daughter," replied Iolo. "And her husband."

"I am not your daughter!" Nina jumped from Gambrinus's back. "Ian Forbes is my father. And Damian is my husband, not Jeremiah." Nina stared Iolo in the eye. "Until this day, I believed there remained some good in you. Now I curse the days I spent as your child."

To her wonder, he looked hurt and said nothing. She shoved her way through the villagers, but they stopped her from reaching Damian. Ian broke free from his captor and went to her side.

The chief was unmoved by the display of loyalty. "Damian Knox will join the children of the massacre."

"Nina." Damian called to her, his voice gentle and calm. "It's all right."

Nina shook her head. "I won't let you die."

Ethan stomped forward to face the sachem. "You will burn an innocent man when the real murderer stands among you! Any fool could see that Iolo Evans himself slaughtered your village."

The sachem's brow rose. "Why?"

"His mind is poisoned with hatred and guilt. The old madman wanted to destroy my father."

The sachem looked at Iolo. "The young English knows little. Iolo Gray Beard was with me on the hunt when the village was attacked. Gray Beard was he who found the dead. The sight of his wife and his babies dead poisoned his heart, but not his mind."

Nina stared at the old chief, then looked doubtfully to Iolo. "Wife?"

Iolo met her stunned gaze and nodded. "My wife. Snow Feather and our three children. My wife, in whose forehead Daniel Knox carved his mark."

Damian's jaw set hard. "It was not my father."

"Daniel Knox had nothing to do with the massacre," said Ian. "Our company passed through the village on the way to Onondaga, yes. But no harm was done."

"You were there?" asked Ethan.

Ian hesitated. "I rejoined my company shortly afterwards."

"Aye," growled Iolo, "after Daniel Knox raped and killed my wife, after his soldiers slaughtered helpless women and children."

"This is ridiculous." Watkins dismounted and joined the others. "Obviously, none of you know who destroyed that village. I suggest you wait a bit there, sir." Watkins nodded respectfully to the sachem. "Let's sort this out afore you go roasting anyone."

"My wife, my sons." The sachem nodded to the False Faces, and they surrounded Damian. "Daniel Knox surrendered his life. It is not enough."

"Damian's death will not ease your loss, sachem," said Black Hawk. "His father's death did nothing. You see their faces in your dreams."

His son's words left Thadodaho unmoved. "The Faces call out for a greater sacrifice, they call for the son of Daniel Knox."

"If you kill him, you must kill me, too." Nina pulled away from Ian and ran to Damian. Melody followed Nina, winding her way through the Onondaga to sit obediently at Damian's feet.

"Nina, get back."

Nina wouldn't move. She touched his face, his mouth, then kissed his shoulder. "If you die, I die with you."

"I love you, but I won't let you die."

"Take them both," ordered the sachem.

Ethan seized a club from his captor, Watkins and Jeremiah aimed their muskets. Ian stepped forward and held up his hand.

"I offer myself, then. You believe a lie, you believe Daniel massacred the village. So be it. He was under my command. Take me instead. Spare his son."

"If I accept. Your seed dies with you." The sachem looked pointedly at Ethan, then to Nina.

"Nina is my daughter," injected Iolo. "She's all I have."

The sachem nodded. "Your claim is just."

"No," said Damian. "If my father did this deed, it is mine to repay."

Ethan stepped forward, too, his head high. "If you want death, then take me."

The abundance of offers confused the sachem and he looked doubtfully to Iolo. "Ian Forbes bears responsibility," decided Iolo. "Take his son, and the son of Daniel Knox."

Ethan closed his eyes, but he surrendered himself to his captors. They led him toward the fire.

Nina waved her fist at Iolo. "You would kill my husband and my brother! Is there no good in you?"

Ian bent to Nina. "Your gun . . ." Nina slipped her pistol into her father's hand. He raised it and pointed it at the sachem. "Release my son, or die."

Iolo lifted his own pistol. "Drop it, Forbes. I found my children dead. You will feel the same. He's a part of you, isn't he? You will feel every scream rent from his throat. And when he dies, the son of Daniel Knox will follow, while his own father looks on in despair."

"This is madness." Nina moved toward Ian, but Ian wouldn't back down.

"Wait," said the sachem.

Iolo leapt forward and fired . . .

Ian lurched backwards, struck in the shoulder. Nina screamed, Ethan struggled with his captors, but when Iolo moved to fire again, another shot rang out. Watkins had fired his musket. Iolo fell to the ground, the Onondaga leapt forward and surrounded the Americans.

"Take them all, burn them all!" The sachem's eyes were wild with anger.

A soft, low voice spoke behind Watkins and Jeremiah. Anna slid from her horse's back and faced the sachem. "No more blood."

Black Hawk stepped toward Anna, but she shook her head. "I told you we were parted 'til the world's end. I told you I couldn't follow you, nor be your wife as you asked."

Nina's brow furrowed. This wasn't the story she'd first heard from Anna.

"Across the ravine that parts us, there can be no bridge."

Black Hawk stood motionless while Anna reached into the heavy pack that was slung across her saddle. She drew out a wooden mask, painted green and rust, and held it up to the villagers. The Onondaga murmured in astonishment.

"What's that?" asked Nina in wonder.

Thadodaho stepped toward Anna and took the mask from her hands. "The Clan of Hawk face. How did it fall to your hands?"

Anna glanced at Nina, then at Black Hawk. "It was a gift. From my father."

"Your father?" Black Hawk stared at Anna in disbelief. "Charles Fairchild?"

Nina helped Ian to his feet. He seemed well, the shot merely grazed his shoulder. She looked to where Iolo lay, his injury far more grave, and her heart expanded in pity. Watkins's shot had torn through his back, he bled badly, but he listened to Anna's declaration with obvious shock.

"Charles Fairchild," murmured Iolo. "No."

"I remember him, I think," said Ian. "He served Sir William Johnson, the head of Indian affairs for the Crown. But what reason had he for the massacre of an Iroquois village? We were trying to win their loyalties, and to urge them against supporting France."

"My father cared nothing for the red man. They were pawns in a white man's war. He didn't care who won the war, only how it might profit him. When the Revolution came, he sided with the Loyalists, for they held our nation's wealth."

"A white man spoke to my people for the Français," said the sachem. "He was Yankee."

"My father inherited a large fortune during the French and Indian War." Anna looked toward the great fire, steeling herself toward her fate. "He is dead. By my life, I now fulfill his duty."

The sachem nodded. "You give yourself willingly. You will be remembered with honor."

Nina clapped her hand to her forehead. "This is madness! You can't kill Anna!"

The sachem glanced toward Damian and Ethan. "Set the English free. The girl will take their place."

"Can her blood erase the trickery of the past?" asked Damian as his bonds were loosened "Her death serves no more purpose than mine."

"It satisfies honor," replied the sachem. "It restores order."

Black Hawk stared into the fire. "You destroy the white man's seed. But that seed is entwined with your own, sachem. The fire will burn your own offspring."

Thadodaho turned slowly to his son. "Speak."

Anna glanced doubtfully at Black Hawk, but he didn't look at her. "I am your last child. I have no wife. But I have a woman—Anna. My child's heart beats within her."

Nina's eyes widened at this, but she said nothing. The sachem looked between his handsome, rebellious son and the white girl. "Your seed grows with your mother's murderer."

"This is the way of our people, sachem. The evil twin entwines with his noble brother, and from their union springs our people. My child is such."

"She's pregnant?" Watkins's stunned voice broke the Onondaga silence. "She drove us over mountains and across rivers like a Prussian general, all the while carrying a child?"

"Watkins!" Jeremiah elbowed Watkins in the ribs.

Watkins nodded. "Right."

Anna said nothing, but Black Hawk saw his father's doubt. "If she dies, I enter the fire with her, and the last of your seed dies forever."

The sachem relented. "She will be your wife instead. She will be adopted into the Clan of the Hawk. But she will not return to the white man again."

Anna didn't seem displeased with this. Nina detected the glimmer of a smile on her face, but the girl hid her pleasure beneath lowered lashes. Nina breathed a deep sigh of relief and sank into Damian's arms. He held her close and kissed her forehead tenderly. The sachem turned to Damian.

"I restore your life, English. But I cannot undo your father's end. His spirit is free now. His seed is free to grow."

Anna stood close beside Black Hawk. "I'm not pregnant," she whispered.

"You will be." Black Hawk took her hand and they walked together back to the village.

"Colonel, we will ignore our dispatch," offered Jeremiah. "You may stay with the Onondaga. Let us forget our hatred and leave this place untarnished by further strife."

Iolo looked toward the fire. "Do what you want, O'Grady." He coughed. "Charles Fairchild. I knew the bastard . . ."

Nina knelt beside him, her tears flowing despite her anger. "So many have died, Papa. The Tuscarora killed Anna's father long ago. Damian's father killed no one."

"Maybe not. But the English, they dishonored me nonetheless."

"I don't understand."

"Cora." Iolo coughed again and clutched his chest.

Ethan glared down at him. "But you already had a wife."

"Snow Feather, my wife. But Cora Talmadge was my due."

"Why?" asked Nina.

"Iolo Evans, blood brother to the Onondaga . . . When 'Gray Beard' asked, they destroyed the Talmadge's little farm. Robert Talmadge offered his daughter's hand in payment."

"You wanted her enough to destroy their farm?" asked Nina in wonder. "Why?"

"Cora is a beautiful woman." Ian sighed, a romantic expression on his face. "Her sweetness and dignity easily move a man's heart."

Iolo sneered in disgust. "Her grandfather was the English bastard who drove me from Wales and forced me into indentured service here. Cora's older brother, young Robert, took the Rhuthin manor that should have been mine."

"Uncle Robert's hall?" Ethan sighed wistfully. "It's a beautiful spot."

"Aye, and all would have been made right if this golden haired boy hadn't heaved himself between Cora's legs and spewed his filthy seed into her."

Ethan grimaced at the outright discussion of his parents' intimacy. "Why do Americans always have to go into such detail?"

Nina snatched her hand away from Iolo's. "I am that 'filthy seed!' You stole me from my rightful parents . . ."

"I am your rightful parent, girl." Iolo remained adamant despite his weakened condition.

"You meant to kill me, didn't you? What stopped you?"

"I intended to kill you, girl. No mistake. I intended

to take revenge for my lost children." Iolo's voice cracked, he fell silent.

"You did love your wife, then."

"That brief while with Snow Feather was like moving back in time. When all Britain was in Celtic hands. Oh, I took Cora in after Forbes's supposed death. She was my due. But I couldn't look at her as a woman, not with her constantly weeping over Forbes. Her poor choice in men destroyed my respect for her heritage."

Iolo glanced reluctantly up at Ian. "I believed those bastards murdered the villagers, just as those blond, blue-eyed Saxons murdered the Celts long ago. I couldn't leave Cora in his hands, you understand."

"Why did you keep me?"

"When Columbine brought you to me, I found I couldn't kill you. I decided to send you to the Onondaga, instead. I doubt they'd kill you. No, you'd have been adopted at your age. But Ian Forbes wouldn't walk away without loss."

"What stopped you?"

Iolo didn't answer at once. When he did, his voice was softer, quieter. "You called me 'Papa.' Oh, you were scared to death, but you remembered me. You remembered when I took Cora and you from New York. When the world believed she was my wife and you, my daughter. My little girl."

Iolo's voice trailed, and Nina took his hand. "You were a good father."

"Yes, I was. Of course. I had you set to marry O'Grady. O'Grady's the best husband for you, he's what a man should be."

Jeremiah's brow rose. Nina glanced back at him and they exchanged a smile. Jeremiah shrugged, still grinning. "It all depends on your point of view."

"I love Damian," said Nina. "As my mother loved my father. As you loved Snow Feather."

A faint smile touched Iolo's pale lips. "My Snow
Feather. And I will join her now, and our children. In
peace, at last."

Tears fell across Nina's cheek, but Iolo squeezed her
hand. "A child can have only one father. But you're a
woman now, girl." He eyed Ian Forbes. "Be damned if
he doesn't look like you. And the world turned upside
down . . ."

Iolo's eyes stared blankly at the Iroquoian sky. Nina
stared at him in shock. She was shaking when she rose,
but Damian drew her into his strong arms and held her
close.

"Gray Beard will rest in our burial ground," decided
the sachem. "Charles Fairchild will be forgotten. His
mind was twisted. It can only be made straight beyond
death."

Two warriors carried Iolo away. Thadodaho watched
them go, then sighed heavily.

"Gray Beard fought against an overwhelming tide,"
said the sachem. "He forgot the greatness of his ancestors. He saw only the invader. It is better to swim the
tide than to fight it. The people of Wales swim and
endure. The Iroquois do the same. The future will not
erase our past. One day, it will welcome our gift and be
content."

The old man walked away. "Got a gift for words,
doesn't he, Jeremy?" said Watkins. *Welcome our gift.
Swim and endure.* We'll do that, too."

"We will." Jeremiah touched Watkins's shoulder, and
they followed the sachem from the burning mountain.

"What have those two got to endure?" asked Ethan.

Nina shrugged innocently. "One never knows, does
one?"

"It appears both American and English are safe today
in Onondaga," said Ian. "Let us rest and watch the
ceremony of the False Faces. There was a time when all

our people lived this way, Celt and Saxon and Norman alike. Maybe the walk back through time will refresh our souls."

Ian looked into the fire, but then his gaze lifted to the endless sky. "Shall we go? Your mother is waiting."

Ethan nodded. "I suppose Mother will have Caesar cleaning the grates by now. And all my clothes will be pressed. I hope she doesn't shrink my breeches."

"They're already too tight for dancing, boy." Ian slapped his son's shoulder. "I was thinking . . . You might be interested in the priesthood . . ."

Nina laughed at Ethan's groan. Ian laughed, too. "Then again, you'd be caught stirring up trouble with the nuns, and I'd have hell to pay. Again."

Ethan blushed, but he supported his father as they headed down the mountain path. Damian and Nina stood together, hand in hand. "Papa wasn't evil. He just never doubted."

"Strange that he died with an English song on his lips."

"The world is in balance now. You are safe. We will go home and raise our son. That is, if Mama will let us take him back."

"Home . . . The war nears an end, my love. I have no home to offer you, except in England." He looked around the wide land, at the rolling hills that seemed to stretch forever outward. "I would spend my life in this country."

"We will spend our lives together," said Nina. "I will go to England with you, or stay among the Tories if that's what you want. But I will never lose you again."

From the village came the sound of drum and rattle. The ceremony of the Faces began.

"Well, love? Shall we dance with our ancestors tonight?"

"Do you think your father is here?"

"He is. The legacy he left to me is answered. We pass such things to our children. You learned to love your enemy, my dear wife. That, too, will pass on and be repeated by our descendants."

"A legacy of love. In a world turned upside down, only love can make it right."

The False Faces went from hut to hut performing the Traveling Rite that would purify their village. With the villagers, they proceeded to the long house for the ritual feast. Ian Forbes and Ethan stood among the villagers in the hall, but Damian saw Watkins sampling the food.

Black Hawk grabbed Watkins's wrist. "Hominy. Food of the spirits. Sacred."

"Oh," said Watkins. "Not to be eaten, eh?"

"Not yet. Watch."

Nina sat cross-legged beside Damian, and Melody watched the False Faces suspiciously as they began the ritual dance. The room was dark except for a small fire.

Nina leaned close to Damian. "Where will we sleep?"

"Together."

"They didn't hurt you?"

"I've been treated surprisingly well. One old woman pinched me rather severely, though."

"Repressed lust." Nina kissed his arm and leaned her head on his shoulder.

The sachem rose, and an old woman came to his side.

"Who's that?" Watkins's voice was the only sound in the room.

"Medicine woman," Black Hawk told him. "The sachem's sister."

Anna cast a reproachful glance at Watkins. "Hush!"

"English." The sachem nodded at Ian Forbes. "Stand before me."

"Not again," muttered Watkins.

Nina seized Damian's arm. "What's he doing?"

"I have no idea."

Ethan stepped forward, ready to fight. "Now, look here . . ."

Ian silenced him with a meaningful look.

"Young English learn patience." The sachem faced Ian. "Ian Forbes, you walk on one leg. The other was taken by the Iroquois." He nodded at the medicine woman. "Restore to the English what he lost."

The Faces chanted and encircled Ian Forbes. Nina seized Damian's arm when they began stirring the coals of the fire. The leader of the False Faces wore a strange mask with a twisted nose and mouth.

"Old Broken-Nose," said Black Hawk to Watkins. "It was this being who showed an Iroquois warrior how to carve a living tree into a face."

"What happened to its face? Did the fellow smash into a wall or something?"

"A mountain."

Watkins sighed. "That would do it."

Old Broken-Nose gathered hot ashes in bare hands, then took them to the medicine woman. She sprinkled a powder of herbs over the ashes, and a pungent odor filled the room. Then the Onondaga wearing the returned Clan of Wolf mask took the ashes and went to Ian Forbes.

"Lie flat," commanded the medicine woman in a mirthless voice.

Ian hesitated, but the medicine woman wasn't easily disobeyed. The False Faces moved around Ian while the medicine woman chanted. The Clan of Wolf Face drew out a scalping knife, and Nina gasped. Damian started to rise and Ethan stepped forward while Watkins fumbled with his musket. Melody growled.

In swift, skilled strokes, the Clan of Wolf Face cut away Ian's breeches and bared his injured leg. Nina,

Ethan and Watkins sighed a united relief. Melody relaxed.

"What was taken is now restored," chanted the medicine woman.

Through his mask, the Clan of Wolf Face blew the hot ashes first over Ian's head, and then on his crippled leg. Nina winced, but Ian remained immobile. The room fell dark while the Faces invoked their spirit ancestors.

"Rise," ordered the medicine woman. The Faces backed away, and Ian Forbes rose to his feet. Ethan went to his father's side, but there was no need

Ian stood square and tall on both legs for the first time in twenty years. He bowed to the medicine woman and the sachem, then in honor to the Faces who cured him.

"You are now a member of the Society of Faces," announced the medicine woman.

"Father . . ." Ian dropped his cane as Nina ran to hug him. "They fixed you! You can walk as if nothing happened."

"Better. The cured man is a mountain higher than one who has known no pain."

Damian said nothing, but his heart knew. Daniel Knox was near. He felt his father's pleasure, he knew with this ceremony, chaos eased into harmony once more. He saw Nina kiss her father's cheek. She looked across the room and smiled at him. He rose and held out his hand.

"Are you ready?"

Nina placed her hand in his. "I am."

"We'll eat later."

The feast began, and Watkins at last was allowed to sample the sacred meal. Damian laughed when Nina pointed at Watkins dipping into the corn soup and filling an overflowing bowl with hominy.

"Very tasty," he decided as he swirled the mush around in his mouth. "Have some, Jeremy."

Ethan took a bowl, also, but he was distracted by a pretty Iroquois girl. He smiled at her, but he was prevented from familiarity when her tall, powerful husband stepped to her side and glared at him. Ethan grinned sheepishly and returned to his hominy, casting a mournful glance Damian's way.

Damian laughed. "You'd be better off with the nuns, my friend."

Ethan's brow lifted and he grinned. "No time soon."

Ian was deep in conversation with the sachem. "I will do what I can to see the wampum treaty between our people honored, sachem. But the Americans will be distracted by their own government. I fear it will be long ere the red man is treated fairly."

Damian slid his arm around Nina's waist. "Many Onondagas have left this village. As such, there are huts that stand empty. Black Hawk has offered one to us."

Nina rose on tiptoes to kiss Damian's face. Her lips brushed close to his ear. "I've missed you, Damian Knox. Let me show you how much."

Damian's pulse quickened as his heart leapt against his ribcage. "The day ends in fire, after all." He bent and touched his lips softly to Nina's.

Damian led Nina from the longhouse. Melody watched them leave and fought between loyalty and hunger as she looked between her masters and the Onondaga feast. Ethan tossed a bone her way, and Melody remained with the food.

Nina and Damian walked through Upper Onondaga, then took a path to the Lower Village. He opened the door of a small hut. "We'll have privacy here."

The hut was dark inside, but Damian left the door

ajar to allow in the cool, night air. The light of the
moon was amplified by the fire that still burned on the
hill beyond.

His light brown hair fell to his shoulders, loose
around his beautiful face. Nina reached to touch a
strand, then ran her finger along his jaw.

"If you died . . ." Damian stopped her words with a
gentle finger upon her lips.

"I will come for you, Nina. Always. I'll hover around
you until the time came for you to join me."

Nina smiled and moved closer into his arms. His shirt
was torn open, and she traced her finger along the hard
muscles of his chest. She pressed her soft mouth against
his skin, teasing his flesh with tiny licks of her tongue.

Damian's breeches tightened as she ran her parted
lips along his collarbone and up to his throat. She ran
her hand down across his taut stomach until her fingers
brushed the hardened swell beneath his breeches. She
cupped his length in her hand as her lips found his.
She dipped her tongue between his lips. He groaned
when her tongue brushed against his.

"Will we do this in heaven?"

"Yes." Damian lifted her from her feet and held her
hard against his body. He lowered her to a deerskin
pallet and pulled away her clothes. He stared at her
naked body in astonishment.

"It's as if . . . You're so slender."

Nina glanced down at herself. "I am," she agreed in
surprise. "All the riding. Anna would have made a fine
drill sergeant."

Damian smiled. "I feared to injure you. I had forgotten what an indomitable woman you are."

He stripped away his breeches and boots as Nina
watched with a hot flare of desire. His erection was tur-
gid and dark with need. Nina ran her finger along the
smooth surface, across the swollen tip.

He caught her shoulders in his firm grip and pressed her back onto the pallet. "It's been weeks, woman," he growled hungrily. "Don't tease me now."

Nina's lips curved in a seductive, beckoning smile and she lifted her hips to brush against his staff. Damian groaned. "I want our union to last."

He pinned her arms over her head, baring her round breasts full to his sight and his mastery. He caught her wrists in one hand while he traced a light circle around one tender peak, then the other.

He circled her rosy nipples with the palm of his hand, and they turned hard and pebbly to his touch. He brushed his thumb back and forth across the erect buds until Nina squirmed and gasped with need.

Her head tossed back and forth as his tongue moved softly against her sensitized nipples. He caught the pink bud gently between his teeth and teased her until she cried out in the primal agony of pleasure.

A cord of fiery need seemed to reach from inside him into her. Damian poised himself between her legs, the hard, spongy tip just touching the swelling of her womanhood.

"Are you ready, love? Do you want me now?"

Nina's shuddering moan was his answer. Damian murmured his own pleasure when her hips rose to draw him inside her shallow entrance. He entered her gently, but his throat caught on a harsh groan when he felt the damp heat of her inner cavern closing tight around her.

"You're stronger . . . everywhere."

Nina felt his smooth, full shaft rubbing against her sensitive walls and she twisted against him, urging him deeper into her aching depths.

"I feel you more."

"Yes," groaned Damian as her inner flesh squeezed around him, letting go to squeeze again.

He kissed her neck and her face as he plunged inside her, thrusting deeper and harder as she answered his passion with her own. Nina clutched his hair, her gasps of rapture sweet in Damian's ear. They drove each other higher and higher, tightening circles that surged unbearably until they shattered into fiery branches of light.

Damian emptied the full force of his desire deep inside her while Nina writhed in ecstatic reception. Their bodies stilled and she drew him into her arms, feeling his shallow, quick breath against her hair and neck.

He moved from her, and they lay naked, letting the night air cool their bodies.

"It's a beautiful night," sighed Nina as the moonlight moved its shaft through the open door of the hut.

Damian rose and found a blanket in Nina's pack. "It's warm tonight. But I suppose we should close that door."

Nina got up, too, and stood behind him. She kissed his shoulder and wrapped her arms around his waist. She looked out the door of the little hut. To the left, she saw Onondaga Creek as it rushed passed the village in a never-ending song. Above, the stars glittered in the sky, and the moon cast a blue light over the endless forest.

Opposite the creek, the fire on the hill still glowed as it devoured the last of its fuel. Nina sighed. "It looks like a volcano."

"The burning mountain," said Damian. "The symbol John André designed for my knight's costume. As if he knew . . ."

Nina smiled and slipped her hand in his. "But this time, the mountain burns for love."

EPILOGUE

Maryland, 1840

"Did you see me, Gran'mama?"

"I didn't." Nina looked up from her knitting. "Try again, Jared."

The little flaxen-haired boy splashed out of the water, drew himself up and raced back toward the pond, hurtling himself into the water. A brown and white puppy barked and jumped in after him.

Nina clapped when Jared's golden head emerged. His face lit in a smile of great pride. He raced with the puppy up the bank and presented himself before Nina.

He shook the water out of his hair. "Do you swim, Gran'mama?"

Nina brushed the droplets from her face. "I did, when I was younger." A smile crossed her face at the memory. "I swam the Potomac with your great-grandfather."

Jared's blue eyes widened. "The Potomac?" He glanced back at his uncle's pond. "I've got a ways to go."

Nina smiled at his broad southern drawl. Her sons and grandsons had gone to school in England, but four-year-old Jared still spoke with a firm Virginian accent. He crawled onto Nina's lap and stared into her face.

"My papa says the Indians almost roasted you."

"Not exactly." Nina set aside her knitting. "We ate a very good meal with them, instead."

"Oh." Jared sounded disappointed. "Thought Indians liked roasting people." His cousin galloped by on a shaggy pony and Jared's attention wandered.

"I will ride like Garrett someday."

Nina saw her other great-grandson as he guided his pony around the field. The boy had been born with a love for horses. Like Damian.

Jared slid off Nina's lap and ran out into the field. Garrett halted the pony and called to him. Nina watched as he helped Jared into the saddle and directed him with a patience that belied his youth.

Nina and Damian moved to Maryland, purchasing the very land where she'd given birth to Nathaniel. The duck blind was still by the river. Nina went there sometimes, to remember. The fields were planted, but the real harvest was in horses. Horses who traced their line to Gambrinus. Nina saw the mares grazing while the foals played in the pasture beyond the great house.

Nathaniel married his childhood sweetheart and had two sons. William Knox now ran the farm, but his younger brother, David, moved to Virginia and lived on a vast plantation. Nina's grandsons were at odds, north and south. William Knox disapproved strongly of slavery, but Virginia's plantations couldn't be run successfully without it.

Their fathers' dispute hadn't touched Jared or Garrett. They were fast friends. Nina watched them, and her heart warmed with happiness. She saw Damian in Garrett Knox. Garrett, kind and strong, his natural empathy that drew him to those in need. But she saw herself in Jared.

You will love your enemy, Jared Knox. And one day, you will surrender.

Nina heard Damian's voice inside her head. It had

happened many times before, as if he was sharing his foresight with his living wife. *I miss you so.*

"Are you all right, Mama?" Nathaniel touched his mother's shoulder, but Nina took his hand and smiled up at him.

"I'm fine, dear." It was true. She was eighty years old, and no illness weakened her. Damian passed on seven years earlier; suddenly, without warning. Nina remembered his promise in Onondaga, and she waited.

"I think I'll have a nap."

Nathaniel took her arm and led into the house and up the long, open staircase to her bedroom. He kissed Nina's cheek and left her alone.

The windows in her room were open and the lace curtains danced in the summer breeze. Nina took off her shawl and looked out the window. Jared was clinging to the pony's mane while Garrett ran beside. She heard their laughter, she heard Nathaniel tell his grandsons to slow down.

Nina smiled and turned away from the window. Her gaze went to the broad canopied bed. Here she spent countless nights in Damian's arms. Age may have slowed them in some ways, but never here. Here, they celebrated love's fire a thousand times.

The smell of fresh cut flowers filled the room; a prize from Jared and Garrett's expedition through the gardens. Nina unbuttoned her bodice and undressed. She put on her nightshift and folded her undergarments. She hung up her dress in the wardrobe that still held Damian's clothes beside hers.

Nina ran her fingers along her bureau and opened the little chest that harbored her greatest treasures. She picked up the little, stuffed dog, Melody, that her father had given her. A book of poems had been passed to her as well, love sonnets by Cora for Ian Forbes. A small paint-

ing of Ethan and his family in Wales. Nina put them carefully back and went to her bed.

She lay down atop the covers. Her breaths came even and deep, filling her lungs with the happiness of her lifetime. The curls of her gold and silver hair brushed across her face. A warm ray of sunshine filled the room as Nina drifted toward sleep.

"You are beautiful in sunlight, little rebel."

Nina's eyes popped open and she looked around the room. Damian Knox stood by the open window, his soft brown hair loose about his face. He was smiling. Young, the way she most often remembered him. And handsomer than she ever saw him.

"Damian." She breathed his name in disbelief as he moved toward her. Only now did Nina notice the faint glow around him, the translucency of his magnificent body.

"I told you I would come for you."

Nina couldn't move. "You're so young. And I'm old. I have wrinkles."

"Do you know how I love your face? Every night while you sleep, I hold your little body close to me. I worship every line on your perfect face, my love."

Tears stung the rims of her eyes. "I've missed you so."

"We are one thing. We will never part again."

A compelling smile crossed Damian's face and he held out his hand to her. "Are you ready?"

Nina drew a deep, long breath, exhaling all the years of her life. The shell of her body sank into the soft mattress, but the shining essence of her spirit lifted.

Damian was waiting with his hand outstretched. Nina rose from the bed and placed her hand in his.

Dear Reader,

I hope you enjoyed *A Patriot's Heart*. I wanted to write a story about an Englishman during the American Revolution, who *wasn't* a spy for the winning side. Not everyone who backs the winning side is good, and not everyone who fights for the lost cause is evil.

When I researched this story, I found myself as opposed to John André's execution as Alexander Hamilton, and the other American officers who tried to change his fate. When Damian Knox stormed into George Washington's office to plead for André's life, I was right there with him. I fully intended to show a stubborn man bent on revenge because of Benedict Arnold's betrayal. Instead, I found a reasonable leader who made decisions not based on emotion.

For me, that is the magic of writing fiction. Characters take on lives of their own. I'm just following them along like a scribe, trying to be true to what I see. So I feel like I met Washington, and he explained himself, and now I can respect more fully the "father of our country."

I'd love to hear from my readers. You can write to me through my publisher, Kensington Books, at 850 Third Avenue, New York, NY, 10022, or E-mail stobie@ime.net.

Stobie Piel

FROM ROSANNE BITTNER:
ZEBRA SAVAGE DESTINY ROMANCE!

#1: SWEET PRAIRIE PASSION   (0-8217-5342-8, $5.99)

#2: RIDE THE FREE WIND   (0-8217-5343-6, $5.99)

#3: RIVER OF LOVE   (0-8217-5344-4, $5.99)

#4: EMBRACE THE
     WILD WIND   (0-8217-5413-0, $5.99)

#7: EAGLE'S SONG   (0-8217-5326-6, $5.99)

ROMANCE FROM ROSANNE BITTNER

CARESS   (0-8217-3791-0, $5.99)

FULL CIRCLE   (0-8217-4711-8, $5.99)

SHAMELESS   (0-8217-4056-3, $5.99)

SIOUX SPLENDOR   (0-8217-5157-3, $4.99)

UNFORGETTABLE   (0-8217-4423-2, $5.50)

TEXAS EMBRACE   (0-8217-5625-7, $5.99)

UNTIL TOMORROW   (0-8217-5064-X, $5.99)

SAVAGE ROMANCE
FROM CASSIE EDWARDS!